WHISPERS OF HEAVEN

CANDICE PROCTOR

TWO TALERS PUBLISHERS

For my daughters, Samantha and Danielle: may we always have the courage to reach for the cup of life.

1

Tasmania, September 1840

JESMOND CORBETT TIGHTENED her gloved hand around the strap, the starched skirts of her poplin traveling gown crackling as she leaned forward in anticipation, her gaze fixed on the familiar weeping gums and silver wattles flashing past the open carriage window. *Soon,* she thought, her heart humming with joy. Soon.

The snap of the driver's whip cut through the crisp spring air to mingle with the thud of hooves and the creak of harness as her brother's team of dapple grays plunged up the incline. The finely built carriage bumped and swayed around a bend; then a thick stand of native beech gave way to an outcropping of bare sandstone, and Jessie could see the lush, gently undulating valley spreading out below her.

Two years. It had been two long years since she'd been home. Perhaps because she'd never been away before, she hadn't expected to miss it so very badly. As she caught sight of her childhood home's sandstone tower and cluster of chimneys soaring above the feathery treetops, she knew a rush of emotion that caught at her chest and brought the tingling threat of tears to her face.

"Warrick—" She grasped the arm of the elegantly dressed young man who slouched on the leather seat beside her. "Stop here. Please. I want to get down."

Her brother shifted to stare at her. "Get down here? At the quarry?" He thumped the carriage roof to order the coachman to stop and cast a significant glance at the hillside above the road, where a dozen or so ragged, sullen convicts toiled with pickaxe, wedge, and sledgehammer to cut blocks of golden sandstone from the Corbett estate's yawning quarry. "Whatever for?"

"Because you get the best view of the house from here." Gathering her rose-colored skirts in one fist, she thrust open the carriage door.

"Did you miss it so much?" said Warrick with an odd smile. "I thought you wanted to go."

Without waiting for one of the men to let down the steps, she jumped to the road, her kid boots landing softly in the dirt, her skirts twirling about her ankles as she turned to watch her brother straighten languidly from the seat. "Just because I wanted to study in London doesn't mean I wanted to leave Tasmania." She tilted her head as she looked up at him. "Haven't you ever wanted two contradictory things at the same time?"

He paused, his hands braced against the sides of the carriage doorway, the smile fading from his features to be replaced by a sad, haunted look. "No. Never. In fact, I can't think of anything I've truly wanted for years."

Yes, you can, she almost said, but swallowed the words along with an unexpected lump in her throat.

He hesitated another moment, then hopped lightly to the road beside her. He'd grown taller while she was away. Taller and, at twenty-two, broader through the shoulders, although he was still slender and very fair. With his head of flaxen curls and smooth, almost too-beautiful face, he often reminded Jessie of one of Botticelli's angels. Except that there was nothing angelic about the brooding slant that could spoil the curve of his full, graceful lips or the dangerous, discontented fire that smoldered in the depths of his strange, crystal-gray eyes.

A sudden silence yawned between them, filled with unspoken thoughts oddly underlined by the *thwack* of metal hitting stone and the sharp crack of splintering rock from the quarry. The tang of dust and sweat mingled with the scent of eucalyptus riding on the September breeze, and Jessie shifted her gaze to the hillside above, where the swinging pickaxes and hunched backs of the convicts working the quarry rose and fell with monotonous predictability.

She had been born and raised here in the Colonies, so the sight of convicts didn't shock her the way it did settlers newly arrived from England. Gangs of convicts were as much a part of the Tasmanian landscape as the vast herds of sheep and fields of grain that brought so much wealth to the island's free landowners. Of course, most people called them "government men" rather than convicts—as if the term "convict" were somehow more demeaning than the chains that so often dragged from their wrists and ankles, or the cat-o'-nine-tails and triangle that brought fear and humiliation to the men's existence. Whatever term one used, nothing could alter the reality of what the men working the quarry really were.

As she watched, one of the men near the edge of the hillside straightened. He was of above average height, his bare, sweat-slicked torso thin but well formed, his even features set in angry lines. Irish, she thought, by the look of him, with that midnight-black hair and sharp-edged, aggressive bone structure. And young; he probably wasn't much older than Warrick. For one unexpected moment, his narrowed, hooded gaze met hers across the distance that separated them. Then the man beside him clapped him on the shoulder and said something that made the Irishman shake his head and swing away.

Jessie had grown up surrounded by convicts: convict house servants, convict grooms—she'd even had a convict dancing instructor. She didn't usually give them a second thought. But today, perhaps because of her long absence, the sight of this unknown man's shut-

tered face and the thought of his shattered, wasted life filled her with
a desperate kind of sadness.

Turning her back on the workers, she nodded toward the roughly
cut stone blocks stacked at the side of the road. "What are you
building?"

"Well, let's see . . ." Warrick blew out his breath in a long, exasper-
ated sigh. "I was expanding the stables. But Mother decided the old
picket fence around the cemetery needed to be replaced with a stone
wall, so of course the stables will just have to wait."

Jessie laughed softly. "She hasn't changed, I gather."

Warrick arched his eyebrows in surprise. "Did you think she
would?"

"I thought perhaps with Papa gone . . ." She swallowed hard, the
thought too painful to finish. Anselm Corbett had been a vigorous,
energetic man in his fifties when Jessie sailed for England. But he
died of a seizure just three short weeks later—although she hadn't
heard about it for months. Even now she found it difficult to believe
he wasn't waiting for her in the big stone house he had built in the
valley below.

"She's the same," said Warrick, his gaze drifting over the activity
in the quarry, his features impassive. "Only more so. She has
embraced the images and duties of widowhood with the same brutal
correctness as she shouldered the roles of wife and mother all these
years—although perhaps 'embraced' is too passionate a word to
apply to our mother."

"You're not very kind to her, Warrick."

He swung his head to look at Jessie, his eyes wide and a little wild.
"Am I not? And when was she ever kind to us, Sister?"

"Many times," said Jessie, warmed by gentle memories of bedtime
lullabies and veranda-shaded, white-linen tea parties attended only
by a little girl's collection of beloved and well-worn dolls. "You know
she loves us."

"Ah, yes." Warrick's smile was tight enough to make his mouth
pull white at the corners. "But it's a ruthless, unforgiving sort of love,
don't you think?"

"She only wants what's best for us," said Jessie softly. "It's what all mothers want for their children, isn't it?"

Warrick sucked in a quick, shallow breath, but before he could answer, a high pitched, nervous whinny jerked their attention to the road behind the carriage, where a magnificent, blood bay Irish Hunter stallion cavorted with impatience, its noble neck arching, its mane and tail flowing, its powerful haunches rippling muscle beneath sleek hide as it danced and pranced around the groom holding its lead. Its name was Finnegan's Luck, and Jessie had purchased the champion hunter at her brother's request and brought it back with her from England. Watching the stallion, now, Warrick visibly relaxed, a gleam of excitement banishing the sullen anger from his features.

"I've got to hand it to you, Jess; I don't think I've ever seen such a splendid animal." He flashed her one of his wide, angelic smiles. "I knew I could count on you to choose well. This lad's colts are going to make my herds the envy of the island."

Jessie looked into her brother's shining eyes and knew a craven impulse to keep her mouth shut. Instead she said, her voice coming out hollow, "Do you plan to hunt him?"

"He's a champion jumper, isn't he? Of course I'll hunt him. Why wouldn't I?"

Jessie loosened the strings of her bonnet, which suddenly felt as if they were strangling her. "It's just that he has this one bad habit—"

Warrick cut her off with a laugh. "Don't we all. I'm certain it's nothing I can't handle."

"Warrick, I need to tell you—"

"Tell me tonight." Taking her elbow, he steered her back toward the carriage. "We're late. Mother has probably been picturing you drowned this last half-hour or more."

Jessie held back, her hand twisting around to grab her brother's forearm. "Warrick, there are things you need to know about Finnegan's Luck before you ride him."

Warrick grinned. "What do you think he's going to do? Buck me off and break my precious neck?" The smile turned nasty. "My, my;

what would Mother do then? More importantly, dear sister: What would you do? All the weight of maintaining the family's honor and position would then fall to *you*. And you have a hard enough time trying to be what Mother wants you to be as it is."

A peculiar sensation gripped Jessie's chest, twisting and squeezing until she thought it might squeeze the life out of her. She pushed the feeling away with a shaky laugh. "I can still be myself around you, though. Can't I?"

His features relaxing, Warrick linked one of his fine, slender hands with hers. "Always."

Her fingers still laced through his, their joined hands swinging back and forth the way they used to do when they were children together, she turned to look out over the valley below. "It's good to be home," she said softly, drinking in the sight of wide, green fields cut by a deep-flowing river still brown with spring runoff from the rainforest-covered mountains in the distance. "It's so beautiful here."

He let out a soft huff that wasn't a laugh and shook his head. "Is it? I'm afraid you've always been far more attached to the place than I."

"It's beautiful." She drew the fresh, heady air of the island deep into her lungs and let it out slowly in a long, contented sigh. "I think Tasmania is the most beautiful place on earth. And I don't intend to leave here ever again."

2

L UCAS GALLAGHER LET THE PICKAXE FLY forward, felt the sharp point bite deep, felt the muscles in his arms flex and relax, flex and relax with each effortless series of movements.

There was a rhythm to the swing of a pickaxe, a flowing cadence of arc and rebound, arc and rebound. Once a man acquired the hang of it, once his hands callused over and ceased to bleed, once the appropriate muscles in his arms, legs, and back stopped screaming and hardened up, then each individual stroke required surprisingly little effort and no conscious thought.

Gallagher had acquired the hang of it long ago. Before being assigned here, to the Corbett estate, he'd spent a year on a chain gang. And on a chain gang, a man either learned to swing a pickaxe with thirty pounds of iron chained to his ankles, rain slashing at him out of a cold, dark sky, and hunger gnawing at his belly, or he died. It was as simple as that.

Now with decent sleep and good food starting to fill out his frame, Lucas let his arms rise and fall in an effortless blur of movement. The spring breeze cooled the sweat on his face, and he let his thoughts drift far away from the mindless work in the dusty quarry.

Compared to those on the chain gangs, men assigned to private estates such as the Corbetts' had it easy. But that didn't make it any less irksome for a man like Lucas Gallagher to have to acknowledge another man as his master. And it didn't mean Lucas no longer ran the risk of one day feeling the cat-o'-nine-tails rip again at the flesh and sinew of his back, didn't keep him safe from being sent back to the chain gangs or to someplace worse. Someplace like Port Arthur or Norfolk Island, where men were known to commit murder simply because a quick death via the hangman's noose was seen as infinitely preferable to continued existence in such a hell on earth.

Once, Gallagher had thought he could survive the seven or so years normally required for a transported convict to earn a ticket-of-leave and the relative freedom it brought. But then he'd realized that there would be no ticket-of-leave for a man who'd done what he'd done. And he'd realized something else: that no matter how strong he might be, a man cannot suffer degradation without being degraded, can't be treated like an animal without becoming brutish or broken. Already Lucas could feel himself changing. He didn't want to be the man he knew he would become after even another year of this. He refused to become that man. And so at some point during those long, hideous months on the chain gang, Lucas had made up his mind: as soon as he regained the relative freedom available to an assigned servant, he would escape. Or die trying.

"Sure if that isn't the handsomest horse this side of Ireland," said Daniel O'Leary, pausing beside Lucas and nodding toward the bay hunter cavorting in the road below. Like Gallagher, Daniel O'Leary was an Irishman, only Daniel was built big and brawny, with broad features and a shock of red hair and a thick scattering of freckles across skin so fair it still burned painfully in the hot Australian summer even after all these years. He'd been transported eighteen years ago, at the age of ten, for killing an English magistrate's dog. He should have been released by now, but Daniel had a quick temper and a passion for trying to run away—or "bolt," as they called it out here. He'd reoffended so many times that his sentence was now for life. Like Gallagher's.

Lucas straightened his back, a smile curling his lips as he watched the high-strung stallion. "Huh. If that's the horse I think it is, Warrick Corbett's going to be in for a wee surprise the first time he tries to mount his fine new hunter."

The sound of a young female voice, unusually low-pitched and rich, drew Gallagher's attention to where Warrick Corbett and the woman now stood looking out over the valley toward the big house. Lucas had been at Castle Corbett for less than two weeks, but he still knew who she was. Miss Jesmond Corbett, only daughter of the estate's late owner and sister to the present one. At the age of eighteen she had talked her father into letting her pursue her interest in geology of all things, and sailed off to attend some Ladies' Academy of Science in London. Now, two years later, she was back.

She intrigued him, this woman with her reputation for being unorthodox and adventurous, this woman who jumped unaided from her carriage and wasn't too self-conscious to throw back her head and laugh with honest abandon. She was not beautiful like her brother, Lucas thought, watching her walk up to the big stallion and laugh again when the hunter lipped her fingers. Her features were not so classically perfect and her hair was a warm, sunny gold rather than the striking, white-blond of Warrick Corbett. But there was something about her that drew Gallagher's attention and held it.

"Ah, laddie," said Daniel beside him with a low laugh. "You'd do better to keep your covetous eyes on yon horse. Fine English misses such as that one are not for the likes of us, mate."

Lucas grinned. "Neither is the blood stallion." He hefted the pick-axe, then paused again, his attention drawn back in spite of himself to the woman in rose poplin. "She's something, though; isn't she?"

A gruff shout floated across the quarry as the overseer cracked his whip warningly into the air. Daniel jerked away, while Gallagher let his body fall once more into the endless swing and heft of the pick-axe. He didn't look up again until the carriage and its occupants had long vanished from sight.

3
———

SPARKLING WHITE IN THE BRIGHT SPRING sunshine, the long drive of crushed shells wound through carefully tended, park-like grounds planted with sycamore and birch, English oak and black locust, Dutch elm and ash. As a child, Jessie had taken for granted the estate's broad lawns and stately, English trees; the formal walled garden and hedges of rose and lilac, camellia and clipped box. Now newly returned from the land all colonists still thought of as Home, she looked at the garden with fresh insight and realized just how hard her parents must have worked to recreate this miniature enclave of England in the midst of the Tasmanian wilderness.

Anselm Corbett had built his home along stately lines, a full two stories tall, of carefully crafted sandstone blocks. Although the sun shone less fiercely in Tasmania than in other parts of Australia, summers here could still be hot—especially to those accustomed to gentler English climes. And so as was the colonial custom he had wrapped his house in double verandas. Not wooden verandas, as was usual, but stone verandas shaped into wide gothic arches. The effect was something like a cross between a double-decker medieval cloister and a Levantine Crusader castle. Originally Anselm had named his new estate Ravenscroft. But when a spate of attacks by bushrangers led him to add a protruding front porch surmounted by a high, square tower, people took to calling the place Corbett's Castle. Not that Anselm Corbett minded. It was a fine thing, surely, for the son of a common Lancashire mill owner to live in a house grand enough to be called a castle.

Thinking again, sadly, of her father, Jessie listened to the shells crunch beneath the wheels with welcome familiarity as the carriage bowled up the avenue toward the house. All those long months away, she had dreamt of this moment. In her imagination her mother would hear the jingle of harness and the rattle of the wheels and be there on the tower-topped porch waiting for her when the carriage swept up before the house. Except of course that Beatrice Corbett would never do something so vulgarly impetuous as to rush from the house to welcome home her only surviving daughter, no matter how long she'd been gone. When the horses swung around the last bend, Jessie saw the porch standing shadowed and empty.

Hopping out first, Warrick turned to wrap his hands around Jessie's waist, then paused at something he must have seen in her face. "Don't tell me you expected to find Mother out here waiting for you?" He swung Jessie down to the drive.

"No." She let go of her brother's shoulders and turned to look up at the house's massive facade. "But I guess a part of me was still hoping."

Reaching out, he touched her elbow lightly, stopping her as she took a step toward the porch. An unexpected shadow of concern, perhaps even remorse, darkened his face. "She's probably been waiting for you in the morning room since breakfast, fretting and unable to do anything except pretend to embroider. She did miss you, you know. Terribly."

"I know," said Jessie, giving him a reassuring smile before running up the steps and letting herself in the wide double doors. In England, such a stately country home would have had a butler or at least a footman stationed ready to open the front door for the members of the household. But house servants had always been a problem in

Tasmania. London pickpockets and Irish Whiteboys didn't usually make good butlers.

Jessie's quick footsteps echoed down the wide, black and white marble hall. Despite the house's exterior medieval trappings, its floor plan was very much that of a Palladian villa, divided into a cross by two intersecting hallways: a main hall running through to the wide rear door and a smaller hall running east to west that contained the grand main staircase of polished blackwood at one end and the servants' stair at the other.

The morning room occupied the northeast corner of the house and had been placed to catch the morning sun, although Beatrice usually kept the shutters half closed at the room's twin sets of French doors so that only a pale light suffused the space. Decorated in delicate rosewood pieces and ivory damask, it was a feminine room, with a white marble mantelpiece surmounted by a massive, gilt-framed mirror. It was there that Jessie found her mother, gowned in the black silk of mourning and seated on a settee dating back to late in the last century. Her embroidery frame lay idle in her lap.

Beatrice Corbett's attire was always ruthlessly neat and correct, her hair never anything but impeccably coifed. In her youth, she had been considered quite a beauty, her features striking and regal. Affluence combined with repeated childbearing had thickened her figure, while the passing of the years had hardened her once soft, pretty mouth into a sour downward tilt. But she was still a striking woman.

She didn't rise when her daughter entered the room, although she did set aside her embroidery and stretch out her fine white hands, a suspicion of wetness adding a shine to her pale gray eyes. "Jesmond. Thank goodness. I was beginning to fear something had happened to your ship. The winds along the coast have been dangerous lately."

Tossing aside her bonnet, gloves, and reticule, Jessie stepped forward to take the tips of her mother's carefully manicured fingers, surprised almost to the point of speechlessness by her mother's words. It was the closest Jessie had ever heard her mother come to mentioning what must surely have been the most wrenching and unforgettable tragedy of her life, the tragedy that explained why Beatrice Corbett had not traveled to the small neighboring port of Blackhaven Bay to meet the coastal ketch bringing her daughter from Hobart Town, where all the London ships docked. The same tragedy lay behind Warrick's brooding restlessness and the aimless rebellion of his life, but no one in the family ever mentioned it.

"I'm fine, Mother. The voyage was blessedly uneventful. We're late because I asked Warrick to stop at the quarry on the way here. I've always so loved that view of the house. I am sorry."

Beatrice shook her head and smiled. "I should have known." Her grip on Jessie's hands tightened as if with a sudden spasm of emotion. "It's so good to have you home." And then, unexpectedly, she rose with the graceful elegance for which she had always been famous and enfolded Jessie in such a crushing embrace she could feel her mother's heart beating hard and fast. For one long, unforgettable moment, Jessie held her mother close, breathed in the familiar lilac-scented talc that brushed her mind with sweet whispers of gentle, half-forgotten childhood memories. Then Beatrice dropped her arms and stepped back, her gaze falling away from her daughter's as she self-consciously brought up one hand to touch the flawless French roll just above the nape of her long neck.

Jessie watched her mother resume her seat and reach for her embroidery frame, and knew that they would never speak of her mother's reaction to either her absence or her homecoming again. Emotional moments, like tragic ones, were never spoken of in the well bred colonial circles through which Jesmond Corbett moved. It was their way to go through life with a stiff upper lip no matter how unpleasant or even heartbreaking current circumstances or events might be. And afterward, one never mentioned such occurrences again. One certainly never hinted at or even acknowledged their private inner anger or pain. To do so would be not only improper but also ungenteel. When one lived on the edge of the world surrounded by English criminals, Irish rebels, and their free but tainted offspring, one had to be very careful of such things.

"I've arranged a homecoming party for you," Beatrice said, her hand flashing as she set a tiny row of neat stitches in her embroidery cloth. "A formal reintroduction to society to be held next month. And I'm going to insist that you rest until then. No riding about the countryside studying rock formations or investigating reports of some strange new variety of orchid, or any such thing. You'll need time to recover from the voyage."

"I'm not tired, Mother." Jessie sank onto a small stool near her mother's feet. "I certainly don't need a month to recover." And then she wondered why she had bothered to say it because she already knew what her mother's reaction would be.

"A lady should always rest after strenuous exertion. Your sisters understood that." She paused, but Jessie sat with her hands gripped tightly together and didn't say a word. Ever since she was a young girl, she'd heard herself compared unfavorably to her two dead sisters. No matter how hard she tried—and she did try very hard—she always fell short.

"I wouldn't even have invited Harrison and Philippa to join us for supper tonight," Beatrice continued, her attention fixed on her embroidery, "except that Harrison is so anxious to see you." She looked up and gave her daughter a warm smile. "He has missed you terribly. I couldn't make him wait any longer."

Harrison Tate was their closest neighbor and Jessie's dearest friend. He was also one of the wealthiest men in the colony since five years ago, when at the age of nineteen he had inherited his father's vast estates. They had all played together as children—Harrison, Warrick, Jessie, and Harrison's younger sister, Philippa. And two years ago on Jessie's eighteenth birthday, he had quietly taken her hand and asked her permission to announce their engagement.

That had been only a formality though, for it had all been settled long before between Anselm Corbett and Malcolm Tate, Harrison's father. Anselm's son and heir would marry Philippa Tate, while Harrison would marry Jesmond. Jessie had grown up knowing of the arrangement. It had never occurred to anyone that she might someday object to it, and she hadn't objected to it. Except she had wanted her time of study in London first, and Harrison had taken what her mother called "Jesmond's headstrong folly" in good part, even going so far as to promise to wade out to meet her ship with a bouquet of red roses clutched in one hand and her wedding ring in the other. Jessie had laughed when he said it, of course, because she had known it for the joke it was. Harrison was too punctiliously proper to ever seriously entertain doing something so emotional and demonstrative. Besides, public displays of affection always embarrassed Harrison.

"At one time he spoke of going with Warrick to meet you," Beatrice was saying, as if following the train of Jessie's thoughts. "But I discouraged him."

"You discouraged him?" Jessie linked her hands over her bent knees and leaned forward. "Whatever for?"

Beatrice glanced up again from her embroidery. "I thought it appropriate that your reunion with your betrothed take place in more formal surroundings."

Jessie rocked backward with a quick, startled burst of laughter. "My 'betrothed'? Goodness, you make him sound like some awe-inspiring stranger for whom I must be certain to display my most proper manners, rather than someone I've known since—since I was a babe in leading strings and he was a grubby little boy in shortcoats."

"I don't remember Harrison ever being grubby, even as a little boy. You're thinking of Warrick." Jessie laughed again, but Beatrice cast her a disapproving look. "You can laugh if you want, Jesmond. But you're far from being a babe in leading strings these days. And Harrison Tate knows what is due a young lady."

Jessie felt the laughter die on her lips as an indefinable sense of restlessness settled over her. Pushing up from her stool, she went to stand beside the partially shuttered French doors looking out over the formal gardens at the rear of the house.

All the house's windows were shuttered on the inside, so that they could be quickly barricaded against attacks by gangs of escaped convicts or angry Aboriginals. The island's native inhabitants were all gone now, and even the bushrangers weren't the threat they once were. But the shutters and their carefully placed musket loops remained, silent witnesses to those dangerous times and the loved ones who had fallen victim to their violence.

But that was another family tragedy one only remembered with quiet and private pain.

Jessie placed her hands on the edges of the frames and widened the gap between the shutters. From here she could look beyond the walled garden to the quadrangle of farm buildings and, to the right of that, the ornamental pond that marked the site of the old clay pit that had furnished the material for the estate's brick barns and sheds and huts. The family cemetery lay beside the pond. Jessie could see the placid waters and part of the new stone wall Warrick was building at their mother's request. But if a monument had been raised there to Anselm Corbett, it was hidden by the trees. Later, she told herself, she would walk down there to see where her father now lay beside his dead sons and daughters. But not yet.

"Do close the shutters, Jesmond. The sun will fade the carpet."

"Yes, Mother." She started to turn away, then paused, her attention caught by the estate's other burial ground, which lay beyond the pond near the convicts' barracks. Marked with simple wooden crosses instead of marble monuments, the second cemetery was the final resting place of some dozen or so of the estate's assigned servants, for the divisions separating convict from free were so vast and impenetrable that not even in death were those tainted with the stain of convictry allowed to mingle with the free.

"Jesmond. *The carpet.*"

Jessie closed the shutters and turned away.

THE WESTERING SUN was throwing long shadows across the carefully scythed grass when Jessie left her mother dressing for supper and made her way toward the pond. Most of the big landowning families in the district buried their dead in the churchyard at Blackhaven Bay, but not the Corbetts. The church at Blackhaven Bay had been built on a pretty, windswept hill overlooking the sea. And Beatrice Corbett avoided the sea.

There was no gate yet between the two new stone pillars that marked the entrance to the place where Anselm Corbett had buried his dead sons and daughters so that his wife could visit their graves without being reminded of how the first of them had died. Jessie hesitated at the opening, the bouquet of apple blossoms she'd picked now crushed in one fist, her throat swelling with grief at the sight of the newest grave in that line of loved ones.

Two years. After two years, freshly turned earth settles and grass grows thick and green. Her father had lain here dead for two years, yet she hadn't really believed it until now.

Swallowing hard, Jessie pushed away from the gateway and moved forward through a blur of tears to kneel in the grass beside Anselm Corbett's great marble headstone. The beech trees on the far side of the stone wall moved mournfully in a breeze sweet with the scent of newly cut grass and apple blossoms.

The apple trees had been blooming the day her father kissed her and told her goodbye. He hadn't wanted her to go to London, had thought the idea of a Ladies' Academy of Science preposterous, perhaps even a shade improper. Yet he had taken her part against her mother's objections, and because of that Jessie had been allowed to pursue her "unladylike" interests. Now she would never see her father again.

"Oh, Papa," she whispered, laying the apple blossoms against the white marble headstone. "I miss you." She felt the sting of threatening tears and brought up one splayed hand to hide her face as it crumpled.

She didn't know how long she knelt there lost in her grief. A pair of crescent honeyeaters rose screeching from the clump of white plumbago that grew near the cemetery entrance. Dropping her hand, Jessie twisted around on her knees to discover one of the assigned servants watching her from the open gateway, a rough-booted foot propped up on a loose stone, a wooden box filled with tools resting on his thigh. He'd put on a cotton shirt and tucked it into his rugged canvas trousers, but she still recognized him. He was the man from the quarry. The one with the Black Irish good looks and the disturbing, angry eyes.

"I thought work had finished for the day," she said pushing to her feet, both annoyed and embarrassed that someone had come to witness her temporary abandonment to grief.

He walked toward her, disconcerting her. She took a step back, and still he came at her. "There's only a wee bit of the coping left to be bedded in," he said, nodding toward the corner of the wall just beyond where she stood with her spine stiff and her hands fisted in her skirts. "I volunteered to come here after supper and finish it."

He paused some three feet from her. Jessie looked at the unfinished section of the wall, then back at him. "You *volunteered*?"

"Faith, but if she doesn't sound just like the lads in the barracks." His white teeth flashed in a smile that came nowhere near to warming the fierce glitter in his seafoam-colored eyes. "It's daft they think I am, as well."

She'd been right. He was Irish, the lilt of his brogue so thick and strong she suspected him of exaggerating it and using it to taunt her. "You were working in the quarry today," she said, then wondered why.

"Aye." He moved over to survey the unfinished section of wall, his hands resting on his slim hips, his back to her. "But it's helping to build the new extension on the stables I'll be, come morning."

She understood then. "Ah. Not so much daft, I think, as very clever. Building walls is surely a far easier task than breaking rocks in the quarry."

"That it is." He pivoted at the waist to regard her thoughtfully over one shoulder. He had a striking face, built wide at the cheekbones, with straight dark brows over deep-set, mysterious eyes. She found she could not look at those eyes. She looked instead at the wall.

"Do you even know how to lay masonry?"

Turning his back on her, he stooped gracefully to rummage

through the tools in his box. "After twelve months building roads and bridges for Her Britannic Majesty?" He paused. "I should think so."

"You were on a chain gang," she said, wondering why she found the thought so disturbing. Wondering why she was standing here chatting so familiarly with this rough-talking, oddly self-possessed convict.

The wind kicked up again, cool with the promise of approaching evening. She glanced toward the house where the flicker of the first candles shone golden and warm through the glass of the long French doors. It was time to leave, past time to be dressing for tonight's supper with Harrison and Philippa Tate. Still she hesitated, aware of a curious impulse to make some courteous comment in parting. But he had his back to her, as if he had forgotten her presence. He was, after all, simply an assigned servant going about his work. She couldn't understand what had led her to speak so familiarly with him in the first place, let alone tarry so long.

Turning without a word, she left him there to his labors while she cut across the lawn toward the glowing warmth of the big house. She didn't turn around to see if he watched her or not. But all the way across the park she was aware of him, behind her.

4

HARRISON WINTHROP TATE PACED up and down before the sweeping stone steps of Beaulieu Hall, the evening sun comfortably warm on the shoulders of his dark dress coat, the fine gravel of the drive crunching sharply beneath the soles of his boots. Up past the open carriage with its matched pair of snowy white mares. Down past the tan and black hound that wagged its tail in anticipation of an evening run and then drooped in mournful resignation as it realized the significance of Harrison's formally cut trousers and the elegant, silver-handled walking stick he carried only when making formal calls or traveling on business.

"Not tonight, old boy," Harrison said, then softened the rejection by stooping to scratch behind the dog's floppy ears. "Sorry." The hound sighed and laid down, its head resting on its paws, its big sorrowful eyes following Harrison as he straightened.

Swinging about, Harrison ran his gaze along the house's upper row of double hung windows. Ordinarily the sight of his home's magnificent, two story, white stucco Georgian facade—its symmetry and restraint embellished by nothing more than the fine iron veranda railings imported directly from Scotland—filled him with a quiet sense of satisfaction and pride. But today his mind was not on the niceties of architectural design. Today Harrison Tate was laboring under the strain of an emotion he did not often allow himself to experience: impatience.

Slipping one carefully manicured forefinger and thumb into the pocket below his sprigged burgundy satin waistcoat, he extracted the tastefully engraved gold watch his father had given him for his eighteenth birthday. Flicking it open, Harrison swallowed an ungenteel exclamation of annoyance. He had planned to be at the Castle by seven. It was seven-ten already.

He was seriously considering doing something totally out of character, such as storming into the house and demanding in raised voice that Philippa *Hurry up, please!* when his sister appeared trailing a gauze shawl, ruffled parasol, and fidgety maid who darted down the steps behind her still straightening flawlessly draped yellow taffeta skirts over wide starched petticoats.

Harrison let out his breath in a quiet sigh of relief. But he kept his watch in his hand a moment longer to let Philippa know he was displeased with her.

"Don't glower at me, Harrison," Philippa said, tucking her parasol under her arm so that she could draw on her fine kid gloves. "We're not late and you know it."

"I never glower."

"Of course not. You would never do anything so ill bred as to glower. You simply draw your eyebrows together and look down your long nose at the malefactor in question, like a bewigged judge on a high bench about to order another execution at dawn."

He opened the carriage door for her himself. "How do you know what a high court judge looks like?"

"I don't." She took his hand and smiled at him as he helped her into the carriage, although her lips remained reposed in a solemn, serene line. She had a way of smiling with only her eyes that most people missed. In fact, Harrison often suspected that there was a great deal about Philippa that most people missed. He was her only brother, yet even he sometimes had the uncomfortable suspicion that he didn't know her at all. That the calm, demure, and biddable face she showed the world was as carefully contrived as the facade of his house—elegant, artificial, and utterly for effect.

"How many times did you change your dress?" he asked climbing in beside her.

"Only twice." She opened her parasol and held it at just the right angle to protect her delicate complexion. Unlike Jesmond, Philippa knew better than to expose her pale, perfect skin to the Australian sun.

"Warrick might not even be there, you know."

The parasol dipped slightly as if the hand holding it went slack for a moment, then tightened. "Of course he'll be there," she said, her voice even, any possible emotion in her light brown eyes hidden by lowered lashes. "It's Jessie's first night home."

Harrison leaned back in his seat, the carriage jerking forward as the coachman gave the horses the office to start. "Well, if he's not, it'll be his loss, for he'll miss seeing how beautiful you look."

She rewarded him with a radiant smile that lit up her entire face. She did look unusually pretty tonight, Harrison thought, her full cheeks flushed with color, her light brown hair worn in clusters of curls falling fashionably from a center part with the back looped up.

She had been promised since birth to the heir of Castle Corbett, and although the specific identity of that heir had changed over the years as first one brother, then the next died, Philippa's general destiny had never altered. If the death of either Ethan or Reid Corbett had caused her any distress beyond the sorrow to be expected at the premature death of a friend, she'd never shown it. She had accepted Warrick as her future spouse with the same equanimity she had shown toward first Ethan, then Reid.

But Warrick, Harrison knew, was not so sanguine about receiving his late brothers' betrothed along with the rest of the family inheritance. He was to have formally asked for Philippa's hand in marriage when she turned eighteen. Yet Philippa's eighteenth birthday had come and gone several months ago and Warrick hadn't said a word.

It was an unfortunate thought, for it reminded Harrison that while Jesmond had accepted his own proposal more than two years ago, he had not yet succeeded in making her his wife. Instead she had insisted on sailing off to attend that ridiculous school of hers. Sometimes he found himself wondering uneasily what kind of an effect her studies and her time away might have had on her. He was sure of her, of course. He had always been sure of her. She wasn't deliberately, provocatively wild or rebellious like Warrick. But she did have a streak of unpredictability, of almost accidental nonconformity, that caused him no small amount of concern whenever he was honest enough with himself to admit it.

"You're gripping that walking stick as if you'd like to strangle it," Philippa said, the carriage bumping and swaying as it turned out of the drive and onto the main track. "You've been laboring under such a torment of anxiety and impatience these last few days, I'll never understand why you didn't simply go with Warrick to Blackhaven Bay and meet Jessie when she came in."

Harrison glanced at his sister, then swung his face away quickly, his gaze carefully fixed on the rolling green pastureland, his cheeks heating with a rare betrayal of discomfort. A part of him had wanted desperately to be there this morning, to catch that first longed-for glimpse of the woman he loved, to touch his fingertips to her soft cheeks and see her lips part in a welcome smile. Yet he'd been secretly relieved when Beatrice Corbett had gently suggested he come to supper this evening instead. Because the truth was, there existed a dangerously ungenteel, almost animalistic undercurrent to his feelings for Jesmond. On a windswept beach, with the sun hot on his skin and the pounding surge of the waves crashing around them, he might well have forgotten himself and allowed his passion for her to overwhelm him in a way that might frighten her and would certainly publicly embarrass him. Amongst the cold marble and stiff brocade of the Corbetts' punctiliously correct drawing room, he would be in no danger.

"Really, Philippa." He let his voice sharpen with a quick spurt of irritation. "Jesmond has just traveled half the way around the world. I would expect you of all people to understand her mother's desire to allow her some time to recover."

Philippa laughed softly. "I would likely need half a year at least to recover from such a journey. But not Jessie. When did you ever know Jessie to need to rest after anything?"

The carriage was already slowing for the turning into the tree-lined avenue leading to the Castle. They could easily have walked the distance between the two houses—had often done it in fact as children. But they were no longer the children they had once been. Besides, one did not arrive in response to a formal dinner invitation on foot.

Harrison gave his sister an indulgent smile. "Jesmond is a woman grown now, Philippa. You can hardly expect her to be the same rather unorthodox adolescent you remember, forever scrambling up cliff faces looking for fossils and risking her neck stumbling about in caves."

Philippa shook her head. "She'll never change."

"Of course she'll change." Harrison felt his breath quicken in anticipation as the carriage drew up before the Castle's tower-topped porch. "Those sorts of activities might be acceptable for a young girl, but they're hardly suited to the wife of a man in my position."

Philippa paused in the midst of gathering shawl, parasol, and reticule, and looked up at him, a frown drawing an unusual tiny line between her brows. "If Beatrice Corbett couldn't stop her all these years, what makes you think you can?"

He tightened his grip on his walking stick to step lightly from the carriage and laughed. "Don't worry; Jesmond might have unusual interests, but she's been well brought up. She knows what's expected of a woman of her station." He waited, correctly, while a servant assisted his sister to alight. Then he offered her his arm and turned, his eagerness carefully concealed as he prepared to be announced to the woman who would be his wife.

Jessie was half way through the side garden when she heard the jingle of harness and rattle of carriage wheels on the drive.

"Oh, Lord," she groaned beneath her breath.

Picking up her skirts, she ran across the rose-edged lawn. She reached the open archway in the creeper-clad stone wall that separated the garden from the drive just in time to see a tall, thin gentleman in a curly-brimmed top hat and elegant dress coat offer his arm to a smaller, less angular woman with light brown curls and a lace parasol. The carriage moved off toward the stable yard with a dignified *clip-clop* of hooves. Then Philippa looked up and said, "Jessie!"

The last rays of the setting sun cast a slanting golden light through the trees to shimmer over the taffeta of Philippa's gown and emphasize the expensive frill of Harrison's fine shirtfront. Jessie hadn't seen brother or sister for over two years. But they were her dear friends and the intimate familiarity of the scene, the rightness of it, filled her with a warm glow of contentment that helped dissipate the unsettling range of emotions of the past half hour or so. She was home where she had longed to be, with the people she had missed so much, and she was happy.

Quickly smoothing her grass-stained skirt over her full petticoats, she started forward with a laugh of sheer pleasure and held out her hands. "You've caught me late dressing for dinner. One might think I haven't changed a bit since I was a child."

It was Philippa who reached her first, laughing as she enfolded Jessie in a tight embrace. "Oh, I hope you haven't changed, Jessie. It's so good to have you home."

Leaning back, Jessie held her friend at arms' length and looked at her. Although she'd been only sixteen when Jessie left, the past two years seemed to have altered Philippa little. Of the four of them—Philippa, Jessie, Warrick, and Harrison—Philippa had always been the quiet one, her humor so low-key and unobtrusive her brother often missed it entirely. She had a kind of calm serenity, a strangely mature, unexpectedly wise acceptance of the vagaries of life that had always eluded Jessie and she suspected always would.

"It's good to be home," said Jessie. "I can't tell you how good."

"Welcome, Jesmond," said Harrison, stepping forward to take her hands in his and smile down at her with his fine, English gray eyes.

He was tall, taller even than Warrick, and thinner, with a lanky, loose-limbed, long-boned frame that he carried with the pride and self-assurance bred into him by generations of affluence and authority. She smiled up into his aristocratically handsome face with its high-bridged nose, neat mustache, and swooping side whiskers, and for one spinning moment, she felt as if she had never left.

He had always called her Jesmond, even when they were children. He was the only one besides her mother who did so. She'd asked him why once—why he never called her Jessie the way the others did. It had been years ago, on a gloriously warm, sun-filled summer day before Ethan died, when they were all down on the shingle beach of Blackhaven Bay. Harrison had waded through the surf to stand beside her and he'd looked down at her, for he'd already been tall then, thirteen years old to her nine.

"Jessie isn't a girl's name," he'd said in that serious, confident way he had. "It's a boy's name. And you act enough like a boy already without me encouraging you."

"I don't," she'd said, laying her palms flat against his chest and pushing hard enough to send him staggering backward through the foaming waves, despite his height and his extra years.

"Don't you?" he'd said, a triumphant smile curling his lips. "Girls don't push. And they don't argue."

That hadn't stopped her from arguing, of course. But she hadn't been able to change his mind. He still called her Jesmond and she knew he always would.

"Harrison," she said now, smiling at the memory. "How can it be two years when you haven't changed at all? When you still insist upon calling me Jesmond?"

He laughed, and she thought he might take her in his arms the way his sister had done. But he didn't. His grip on her fingers was tight, though; very tight. And his face when he looked down at her was unexpectedly strained and serious. She thought for one wild moment that he meant to kiss her and she knew a sudden, unexpected wave of shyness. Then he let her go and stepped back, as if he too felt the need to put some space between them, and she wondered at herself.

"You've been visiting your father's grave," he said, looking beyond her in the direction from which she had come. "I can't tell you how sorry I am."

"Thank you," she said quickly, her throat threatening to close with an upsurge of sorrow that was still raw. She knew he meant it, but she still wished he hadn't said it. She wasn't ready yet to speak of her father's death, at least not with Harrison. She always felt the need to be strong around him, to hide the vulnerable, needy parts of her soul. To be as calm and controlled as he was.

She went away soon after that, to dress quickly for dinner while Beatrice greeted their guests and led them into the large, ornately plastered drawing room with its marble fireplace and elegant settees and French consoles. By the time Jessie hurried back downstairs, Warrick had still not put in an appearance.

"He should be here," hissed Beatrice in a furious aside as dinner was announced.

"He will be," whispered Jessie. "Something must have come up to delay him."

Beatrice's thin nostrils flared angrily. "His brothers would never have behaved in such a fashion."

Jessie sucked in a deep breath that did little to ease the old, familiar ache her mother's words stirred within her. Ethan and Reid, like their dead sisters, Catherine and Jane, had been obedient, steady, and reliably conventional. It was a never ending source of chagrin to Beatrice that of the six children to whom she had given birth, only the two youngest and least satisfactory had survived. "Mother. He's only late for dinner."

Beatrice smoothed her skirts with a rustle of black bombazine and jet beads. "I fear there is far more to it than that."

Jessie stared at her mother's tense profile, but there was no time to say more for Harrison was politely holding out his arm to his hostess. Jessie could only follow them into dinner with Philippa.

It wasn't until halfway through the soup course, while Jessie was arguing with Harrison about the importance of providing girls as well as boys with a formal education, that Warrick finally put in an appearance.

"What would be the point?" Harrison was saying. "While I admit the existence of some unusually intelligent women, the fact remains that the vast majority of females are suited neither by temperament nor nature to the rigors of serious, prolonged study. It would be a waste of society's resources."

"Perhaps," said Jessie tartly, "if women were better educated, their temperaments would change."

Harrison shook his head. "You can't change nature, Jesmond. And in this instance, why would we want to?" He gave her a winsome, cajoling smile. "You ladies are so adorably lovely as you are."

She knew he meant it as a compliment, but she still felt her cheeks heat with annoyance.

"The trouble with you, dear sister," said a dry voice from the hall, "is that you keep forgetting the cardinal rule of our world." She looked up to find Warrick lounging in the doorway, one shoulder propped negligently against the jamb, a glass of what looked like brandy dangling from his fingers against his thigh. "The rule that says it's men who truly contribute to society. Whereas women—" He pushed away from the doorway and lifted his drink in a mock salute. "—women are intended merely to adorn it. Oh—and help reproduce it, of course."

"Warrick," said Beatrice, her voice like ice water. "Since you have condescended to grace us with your presence, perhaps you would be kind enough to take a seat so that the main course may be served?"

Warrick paused long enough to throw down the rest of his drink before saying, "My pleasure."

Stiff with embarrassment, Jessie watched her brother as he pushed off from the doorway and went to settle into his customary seat at the head of the table, his cravat askew, a lock of hair tumbling over his brow in romantic dishevel. He had made it deliberately, ostentatiously obvious to everyone that it was some wild impulse of contrariness rather than an unexpected hitch in the workings of the estate that had delayed him. She glanced quickly from her mother's angry face, to Harrison's hard jaw, to Philippa's typically unruffled, calm demeanor. And she understood suddenly why her brother was behaving so badly and what it was that he had done—and not done—to earn their mother's disapproval this time.

It was Philippa, predictably, who smoothly guided the conversation to gentler, less explosive topics, while the servants moved quietly around the table and removed the soup bowls. Yet as the meal progressed, Jessie became aware of a curious sensation burning within her, as if she were experiencing some strange, unfamiliar emotion that welled up within her, unnamed and disconcerting. It wasn't until the covers were removed and the ladies rose to leave the gentlemen alone with their port and cigars that Jessie realized the source of that strange, illusive melancholy.

She was intensely, inexplicably jealous of Warrick.

SHE WAS GETTING ready for bed that night when she saw her brother standing alone at the far end of the second story veranda, near his room. He stood with his back to her, his outthrust hands resting on the railing, his gaze fixed on the black obscurity that enveloped the park and the hills beyond. Quietly, she opened the doors and felt the cool wind that ruffled the fair curls at the nape of his neck and caused her to tighten her grip on the shawl she held over her night-dress. She hesitated a moment, then walked toward him down the length of the veranda, for their rooms were at opposite ends of the house.

"I rather disrupted your homecoming dinner tonight, didn't I?" Warrick said, not looking at her. "Do I owe you an apology?"

"No." She went to stand with her back against the veranda post beside him.

He slanted a grin at her over his shoulder. "Then what is it?"

She sucked in a deep breath. "You haven't offered for Philippa, have you?"

He shook his head.

"Are you going to?"

He looked away again. "No."

"But . . . it's expected of you."

She watched as a slow smile curled his lips. "And when have I ever done what is expected of me? According to our mother, I delight in doing the exact opposite."

She thrust the fingers of one hand through her loose, windblown hair, raking it away from her face. "I always thought you liked Philippa."

She saw Warrick's chest lift as if on a sad sigh. For it was true: if Harrison had been the companion of Jessie's childhood, then Warrick had been Philippa's special friend, always baiting her hook with worms so she wouldn't have to do it herself and taking her side in her quarrels with Harrison. But now he only shook his head again. "Unlike you, I prefer to find something warmer than mere liking in my marriage."

"You shouldn't say such things."

He let out a low, harsh laugh. "Why not? Why is it we're never allowed to speak of anything that might make us the least bit uncomfortable? What do you find most alarming? That I should openly admit that I don't actually love Philippa? Or that I should dare to wish to find passion in the arms of my wife? What do you think? That if something isn't spoken of, then it doesn't exist?"

"No, but—"

He pushed away from the rail and swung to face her, his hands hanging loosely at his sides. "Are you trying to tell me you love Harrison?"

She laughed lightly. "Of course I do. I always have."

"Nothing has changed?"

"No. Why would it?"

He leaned into her. "Because you've changed, Jessie. You're not a child anymore. None of us are. Doesn't it bother you to realize that you love your future husband with the same affection that you once felt for a ten-year-old boy?"

She stared at him, her breath coming oddly quick and shallow. "Harrison is what I want in a husband."

"Which is what?"

"What do you mean, which is what? You know what Harrison is like. He's everything a true gentleman should be, always calm and controlled and self-possessed. He has always been utterly sure of himself—of who he is and what he wants out of life."

"Whereas you never have been." Warrick's voice softened. "What do you think, Jessie? That marrying Harrison will make you the same way?"

She looked up into his beautiful, tortured face, and it seemed to her that in the pale light of the moon he looked oddly older and wiser than she'd ever thought of him as being. "Harrison loves me," she said.

"You're right. He does love you. Unfortunately, I don't think he still loves you in the same way he did when he was a lad of ten and you were a six-year-old in plats."

Jessie thought of the strange tension she'd seen in Harrison's face as he stood gazing down at her earlier in the evening. And she knew it again, that sense of shyness edging toward alarm. Disconcerted, she turned away quickly to look at the darkened garden below. "I came here to speak to you of Philippa."

"Did you? I'm not so sure." Reaching out, he took her hand in both of his and drew her around to face him. "Jessie . . . Marriage is forever. Don't commit yourself to it unless it's what you really want. Not what Harrison wants, not what Mother wants, but what you want."

"I'm already committed, remember? Besides, you're wrong. I do want to marry Harrison. I do." She said it forcefully.

As if she could make it so, simply by saying it.

~

SHE AWOKE EARLY the next morning, disconcerted at first to find herself lying in a bed that didn't pitch and rock with the endless movement of the sea. Then memory returned and she rolled over, listening to the chirping calls and trills of lorikeets and magpies as she let her gaze rove contentedly over the sprigged wallpaper and cedar furniture that had been hers since childhood. It was so good, so very good, to be home.

Reaching her hands high over her head, she stretched once and then slid out of bed to paddle barefoot across the carpeted hardwood floor to the long French windows that gave access to the upper veranda. Throwing open both shutters and doors, she looked out across a park drenched in the warm, buttery glow of the strengthening sun.

Like the morning room directly below her, Jessie's room occupied the northeast corner of the house. From here she had a clear view of the quadrangle of farm buildings that stretched beyond the garden wall: the barns and shearing shed, the blacksmith's and smokehouse, the convicts' barracks and stables where Warrick's men were already at work on the new addition. She wondered if that Irishman she'd seen yesterday was among them. And then she wondered at herself for the thought.

The morning chill had a bite to it. She wrapped her arms across her chest and then smiled as a kookaburra on the veranda's railing opened its big beak and the familiar cackling cadence of the bird's song erupted across the gardens.

She ventured out a few steps, the boards of the veranda feeling smooth and cold beneath her curling toes. From here she could look down on the garden itself, at the parterres of sweet-smelling lavender and thyme, of hyssop and sage, all carefully edged with box. At the tall, slim young man with curling blond hair and angelic features who strode purposefully down the brick walk, his riding crop swinging.

Jessie caught her breath. She hadn't expected to see him up and about yet, for they had been late talking last night. Talking of so many things but not, she now realized, about the eccentricities of a horse called Finnegan's Luck. She watched in horror as Warrick let himself out the gate in the back garden wall and began to cut across the quadrangle, heading toward the stables and his new stallion.

"Oh, Lord," she whispered on a quick exhalation of breath, her hands tightening in panic around the railing, then pushing away as she whirled with trembling urgency toward her clothespress.

5

T HE DEW-DAMPENED BRICKS of the walkway felt cold and slippery beneath Jessie's bare feet as she ran toward the stables, her hair streaming unbound behind her in the chill morning air. She hadn't even tried to struggle into her corset and she'd only tarried long enough to tie on one of the half-dozen or so petticoats she normally wore, so that she had to hold the long, limp skirt of her dress twisted up in her fists to keep from tripping.

The garden gate banged behind her as she let herself out into the broad quadrangle, almost deserted at this time of the morning except for the three or four men at work on the new stable walls. Just beyond them she could see Warrick standing with one foot braced against the mounting block, a restless hand tapping his riding crop against the gleaming leather of his top boot as he watched a skinny, brown-haired boy with a pug nose and a gap-toothed smile lead Finnegan's Luck toward him.

"Warrick," Jessie called. "Wait."

At the sound of her voice, the stallion tossed its head in exaggerated, nostril-flaring nervousness. Warrick dropped his foot and turned, his features going blank with mild astonishment at the sight of her bare feet and loose hair. "Jessie. What the devil's the matter with you?"

"Finnegan's Luck," she panted, skidding to a halt beside him, her bare heels digging into the loose surface dirt. "I told you not to try to ride him before I had a chance to tell you about him."

Warrick's brows drew together in wary puzzlement. "What about him?"

She sucked in air, one hand pressed to her side. "He always bucks and throws his rider the first time anyone tries to mount him after he's been saddled."

Her brother swung his head to stare at Finnegan's Luck. The beautiful bay stretched out its nose and shook its mane, its tail flicking too quickly from side to side. Warrick brought his incredulous gaze back to Jessie. "Do you mean to tell me you bought a horse that can't be ridden?"

"No. I told you: he's a champion jumper and a wonderful hunter. He doesn't buck *every* time he is mounted, only the first. He never tries to get rid of you after that. Never."

Warrick let out a snort. "That's ridiculous. Either a horse bucks or it doesn't. It doesn't only buck the first time it's mounted."

"This one does."

He tucked his riding crop beneath his left arm and leaned into her. "And you still bought him?"

Jessie shook her head. "I didn't know. I hunted him twice before I bought him. But both times, Mr. Finnegan rode Lucky to the meets himself, so I was never the first to mount."

Warrick spun about to study the big bay stallion now standing with deceptive docility, its soft lips investigating the lapels of the stableboy's pockets as if looking for a treat.

"It's why he's called Finnegan's Luck," Jessie said wryly. "It seems Mr. Finnegan was in the habit of selling him at least once or twice each year—then buying him back again for a fraction of the original price and hunting him himself the rest of the season. Evidently Mr. Finnegan doesn't mind hitting the dirt first thing in the morning."

Hot, angry color flushed Warrick's normally pale cheeks. "So why the hell did you keep him?"

"Because he truly is a marvelous animal." Jessie walked over to rub her fist between the horse's wide, intelligent eyes. "He sires fine colts. And I hoped perhaps we could find someone to break him of his habit."

Warrick came to stand beside her, his gaze on his sister rather than the horse. Suddenly he grinned. "And because you wanted to pay this Mr. Finnegan back for tricking you. Fess up."

Jessie laughed. "All right. It's true. In fact by the time I was ready to leave England, poor Mr. Finnegan was in tears, offering to buy Lucky back for half again what I'd paid for him."

Warrick grunted. "Wouldn't that have been lesson enough?"

Jessie shook her head and ran her hand down the stallion's high, arched neck. "I've never ridden a horse like him, Warrick. You'll see."

Warrick grunted again and twitched the reins from the stable-boy's slack grasp. "All right. Let's see."

Jessie felt all trace of her earlier amusement drain out of her. "What are you doing?"

"Riding him."

She grabbed her brother's arm. "But he'll throw you."

A wild, reckless joy shone in Warrick's handsome face. He shook her off and reached for the stirrup. "So?"

"So let one of the men mount him the first time. If you get hurt, Mother will--"

She broke off as Warrick spun to face her, his features tight. "Jessie? Shut up and stand back."

Jessie closed her mouth and took two steps back.

Finnegan's Luck stood faultlessly still with quiet, good-natured patience as Warrick slowly, cautiously, thrust his foot into the stirrup. With a triumphant smile to his sister, Warrick swung up into the saddle, his seat descending toward the leather just as Finnegan's Luck leapt forward. His four splayed feet hit the earth together with a jolt that brought Warrick down, cockeyed, on the wide expanse of red rump. Warrick's hat went flying as his feet scrambled frantically to regain their hold on the stirrups. The stallion's beautifully formed head went down, his hindquarters rose impressively skyward. Warrick's eyes widened in alarm as he soared up into the air and then came down again, this time near the tail. Once more Finnegan's Luck bucked, both rear legs flashing up in a dazzling kick that sent Warrick sailing through the air to land on his stomach with a whacking *hoooph* as the air rushed from his lungs.

Whinnying in triumph, the red stallion shook its head and kicked its heels in the air one last time before loping in a wide circle around the quadrangle, reins dangling, its magnificent tail streaming behind. Warrick lay where he had fallen, motionless, face down in the dirt.

"Warrick!" Her heart jamming up somewhere in the vicinity of her throat, Jessie rushed to fall to her knees beside him. "Are you all right?"

She touched her hand to his shoulder, her breath coming out in a soft moan of relief when he swatted her hand away and rolled swearing into a sitting position. Wiping the dust from his face with one crooked elbow, he lifted his head and stared after the retreating hunter. "Don't just stand there, Charlie," he shouted to the wide-eyed boy who had retrieved his hat and was now holding it out to him. "Get that bloody stallion before he bloody well decides to make a bolt for the bloody parklands."

"Yes, sir," stammered the boy, his awestruck gaze lifting to follow the action of the stallion's powerful hindquarters. "Only, how am I supposed to catch him?"

Warrick tweaked his hat from the boy's grasp. "You run after him."

A shout brought Jessie's head up. One of the convicts working on the new extension had leapt the wall and was already racing across the yard at an angle to cut the stallion off. A leanly built man with devil-dark hair and features she recognized, he ran like a panther, gracefully, powerfully, easily. She heard him purring soothingly to the wide-eyed horse. But then he was shouting something, something about the reins, just as one of the stallion's flashing hooves landed hard on the dangling leather. The bay's head jerked down, catapulting it forward. Squealing, the hunter somersaulted and came down heavily onto its side.

And lay there.

"Oh, good Lord," whispered Jessie. Pushing to her feet, she picked up her dragging skirts and ran.

6

GALLAGHER STOOD WELL BACK from the downed stallion's flailing hooves as the bay's head lunged up and Finnegan's Luck, no longer stunned, scrambled to its feet, its glossy sides heaving in nervous excitement.

"Easy, boy," he crooned, moving in closer. "Easy." Catching the reins, Lucas touched the horse's nose, its ears, its shining neck before bending to run a practiced hand down first the near front leg, then the rear. The horse quivered and snorted, but Lucas kept up that low, soothing purr.

"Is he hurt?"

A pair of dainty but decidedly dusty bare feet appeared in the dirt beside him. Lucas turned his head, one hand still on the stallion's rear hock, to find Miss Jesmond Corbett crouched beside him, her fists clenching in the heavy folds of her limp skirts, her brows drawing together in concern. The wind billowed her loose golden hair around her head, and when she sucked in a quick breath, her firm young breasts, unshielded by the stiff propriety of a corset, rose and strained noticeably against the fine cloth of her bodice. For one deceptive moment, she looked free and uninhibited and nothing at all like the prim and painfully proper young lady he knew she must be.

He straightened quickly. "Just winded, I think." Turning his back on her, he went around to check the horse's off legs. Then his gaze met hers over the hunter's broad, high withers and before he could stop himself, he said, "Why did you stand there and let your brother mount this horse in the open yard? You knew Finnegan's Luck was going to buck."

Even after more than three long, grinding, dehumanizing years in the British penal system, Lucas could still forget himself sometimes. Still forget the humiliating demand for a never-ending outward pretense of servility he hadn't been raised to show. Still forget that an unwary tongue or even a simple, belligerent stare could get him flogged raw for his "insolence."

He watched the hot color flood the woman's smooth cheeks, watched the startled widening of her eyes before they narrowed in indignation. Her chin went up in that haughty gesture he had come to know well from women of her type. He waited, his jaw set, for the inevitable degrading reprimand—or worse—to come.

"You seem to have temporarily misplaced the brogue you used to such ostentatious effect yesterday, Mr . . ." She paused, her carefully modulated, oh-so-English voice rising in a question.

It wasn't what he'd expected. "Gallagher," he said. "Lucas Gallagher."

"Mr. Gallagher."

She was staring at him. And even though he knew it was insolent, even though he knew he could be flogged for it, he stared back.

She might be only half-dressed, with her hair hanging loose and windblown, but no one seeing her now would ever mistake her for anything but the expensive, well-bred Englishwoman she was. Although not as tall as her brother, she was still tall for a woman, her body slim but exquisitely molded, her legs long and lean and obvious beneath the limp folds of her skirt. Her features were not as perfectly molded as her brother's, either, her nose too inclined to tilt upward at the end, her upper lip too short, her lower lip too full. But her eyes were a magnificent, deep, fiery blue. Their sparkle of lively intelligence and flashing pride didn't surprise him. But he hadn't expected the shadow of what looked like anxious vulnerability he thought he glimpsed when she turned her head at her brother's approach.

"Is he all right?" Warrick Corbett limped up to them, one sleeve of his finely cut riding jacket hanging torn and dirty, his neck cloth dangling askew.

"Aye," said Gallagher. "Although the tendon of that near front leg might bear watching."

Corbett nodded. "You, Charlie," he said, turning to the skinny stableboy of about eleven or twelve who stumbled to a halt beside him. "Go find Old Tom and tell him there's a horse I want him to take a look at. And you—" Corbett's gaze flicked assessingly over Gallagher. "Take this stallion to the stables and wait there while I get cleaned up."

His sister laid her hand on his arm. "Warrick—"

He shook her off with a curt, "Don't you say a word," and limped toward the house.

Miss Jesmond Corbett stayed where she was, the early morning sunlight falling clear and golden on smooth, fine skin as she watched him go, an anxious frown on her face. Then she drew a deep breath, her nostrils flaring wide as she swung back to Lucas. "I'll admit you were right," she said, her features hardening, her voice coming so icy and crisp he decided he must have imagined that earlier, brief hint of vulnerability. "It was a mistake to mount this horse in the open." She punched one finger into the air between them as if making a point with a child. "But don't you *ever* speak to me like that again."

He felt the anger rise within him, hot enough to scald his veins and burn the base of his tight throat. Sometimes he thought it might choke him, the anger he had to hold inside. But he could only stand there, hating her, hating the nation and system of which she was a part, hating himself as he kept his jaw clenched against the kind of scathing retort the man he used to be would have made. The kind of response no sane convict would ever allow himself to make.

She started to follow her brother, then paused. "How did you know?" she asked, her head tilting as she looked back at him.

Somehow he managed to keep everything he was feeling out of his voice. "How did I know what?"

The wind blew her long, unbound hair across her face, so that she had to put up one hand and hold it back, the loose strands shimmering golden in the morning sunshine as she nodded toward the stallion. "How did you know his name is Finnegan's Luck?"

Deliberately, Gallagher gave her a slow, easy smile. "I recognized him."

Surprise caused that haughty demeanor of hers to slip a bit, so that she suddenly seemed more human although no more likable. "You recognized him?"

"Aye." He let his smile broaden. "The Gallaghers and the Finnegans are cousins. Of a sort."

She stared at him, her gaze hard and intense and seething with quiet indignation. "So you knew he would buck and run. You knew it, yet you didn't think to suggest he should be mounted in a paddock?"

Lucas ran his hand slowly down the stallion's glossy neck and let his brogue turn as broad and thick as an Irish bog. "Sure then, but it wouldn't be keeping to my place, now would it, for me to be so forward?"

"You don't strike me as the sort of man who worries a great deal about keeping his place, Mr. Gallagher," she said. And then she did leave him, standing there holding her horse and watching her.

"So it's working in the stables you are now," said Daniel O'Leary, "and not just toiling away at the building of it." Shifting a wad of tobacco from one freckled cheek to the other, the big Irishman tipped the laddered back of his chair against the stone outer wall of the barracks and tossed the small leather tobacco pouch to Lucas. "You're a wonder to me, lad."

His left shoulder braced against a rough-hewn veranda post,

Lucas snagged the bag out of the air and smiled as he tucked the tobacco into the pocket of the rough jacket he wore against the chill of early evening. He didn't chew himself, but Warrick Corbett provided all of his men—even the assigned convicts—with a ration of tobacco. Most settlers considered the practice generous, maybe even a tad indulgent, but Lucas knew Corbett was only being prudent. Men had been known to kill for tobacco in places like Port Arthur and Macquarie Harbor, and on the chain gangs.

It'd been on a chain gang that Lucas and Daniel had met just over a year ago now. Without Daniel, Lucas knew he never would have made it through the grinding hopelessness and despair of those first weeks on the gang. Once when they were building a road through a gorge south of Hobart Town, Daniel fell into the river and would have drowned, weighed down as he was with chains, if Lucas hadn't ignored the overseer's threats and jumped in to pull the big Irishman out. Daniel always said he owed Lucas his life, but Lucas knew that if they were keeping score, he was still deeply in Daniel's debt. For while Daniel's death would have had the grace of fate, if it weren't for Daniel, Lucas would have killed himself.

The front legs of Daniel's old wooden chair hit the flagstones with a thump as he leaned forward, elbows on knees, his lips pursed, and let loose a stream of yellowish-brown juice that shot off the edge of the veranda to plop in the hard dirt of the yard. He cast a quick glance around, and even though the rest of the men were too far away to overhear, he kept his voice low. "All you've got to do now is take one of them horses out for a wee bit of exercise one day and never come back. If you choose that red stallion, they'll never catch you."

Lucas shifted so that his spine pressed against the post. "No, they wouldn't catch me the first day. And maybe not the second. But they would catch me in the end, make no mistake about that. And then they'd hang me for a horse thief." Lifting his head, he looked out across fields lit now with the golden light of a setting sun that threw long, bluish shadows across the rich green of the valley floor. From here he couldn't see the sea. But he knew it was there, swelling restless and eternal beyond that low rise of hills. If a man breathed deeply he could smell the hint of distant brine on the breeze. The hint of brine and the promise of freedom it brought.

"I'll be riding out of here one day, sure enough," he said softly, his attention still caught by the purpling hills. "But not before I know I've a way off this island already waiting for me." He brought his gaze back to the big, red-haired Irishman. "And I'll be taking you with me, boyo." He smiled and jerked his head toward the man approaching them from the yard. "You and yon Fox."

"Huh," grunted the Fox, walking up to them. The Fox's real name was Todd Doyle, from Tipperary. He was built small and skinny, with a sharp-boned face and big, pointed ears, so that with a name like Todd, everyone had called him the Fox for so long he sometimes forgot to answer to Todd. Once, before he'd managed to get himself transported for embezzlement, he had been head gardener to the Earl of Swarthmore. But the Fox had a taste for the finer things in life, things a gardener's salary didn't stretch to cover.

He had been at Castle Corbett for a good year before Lucas and Daniel's arrival. But the Fox and Lucas had known each other before, since that day over two years ago when they'd been thrown together as messmates in the dark, dank, foul-smelling hold of the transport ship that was to bring them both across the oceans to Her Britannic Majesty's southern colonies. If Lucas were the Fox's employer, he wouldn't dream of trusting him with a spare load of fence posts or the payment for the nurseryman's delivery boy. But the Fox would give his last crust of bread to a friend, and it hadn't taken Lucas long to realize that.

"I can tell you right now," said the Fox, curling down to perch on the edge of the veranda, his bony forearms resting on his drawn-up knees, "if I have to make my escape clinging to the back of some four-footed beast, then I fear I am destined to tend Mrs. Beatrice Corbett's prize roses until I'm too old to hold a watering can." His feral-looking, yellow eyes gleamed as he cast a contemptuous glance back at Daniel. "And if that great clumsy oaf has ever sat a horse in his life, then you're an English lord and I'm the archbishop of Canterbury."

"A body'd think you were an English vicar at the least," said

Daniel, his fists tightening around the worn wooden arms of his chair, "to hear the mouth on you."

Daniel didn't like the Fox's affected ways any more than the Fox liked Daniel's unpredictable temper and hot-headedness, and Lucas knew it. But he was getting used to these kinds of exchanges and only laughed softly. "It's a carriage we'll be needin' then, from the sounds of it."

"What we need is a boat," said Daniel.

"That we do." Lucas smiled. "But there's no point in worrying about getting our hands on one until we find someplace to hide it."

"Where in the name of the Virgin—" Daniel began, then broke off, his head jerking around at what sounded like a child's gasp of pain followed closely by men's rude laughter and a single, choked off sob.

His back still pressed against the veranda post, Lucas shifted toward the yard, his eyes narrowing at the sight of the stableboy, Charlie, held fast in the grip of a black-haired, bear-like Englishman from Newcastle called John Pike. Pike was the estate's blacksmith and he had one of his beefy fists clenched in the boy's shaggy hair. Yanking his head back at a painful angle, he twisted the boy's right arm awkwardly behind his back in a way that brought the boy to his knees in the dirt. Tear tracks streaked the boy's dusty cheeks as his wide, terrified gaze fastened on a green glass jar sitting in the dirt some two or three feet in front of his face. Through the wavy round glass Lucas could see something moving. Something big and brown and hairy that he realized after a moment was a spider. A huntsman spider.

Lucas straightened slowly. The Fox shot up. "It's not our affair, Lucas."

"No," agreed Lucas, a smile tightening his mouth. "It's not."

"You like spiders, lad?" Pike was saying. "Because I've one here, waitin' for you. And there's plenty more where this one come from." The big man's grip shifted, causing the boy to wince although he didn't cry out again. "The way I see it, you've two choices. You already know what the first one is. And the second?" Pike brought his face down until it was level with the boy's. "Well, your second choice is to eat this here big, hairy mother for breakfast tomorrow mornin'. And the next day? Why, there'll be another just like him, waitin' for you. And then another and another. Every day. Think about it, lad. I ain't never gonna run outta spiders. When do you think you're gonna run outta the guts to keep tellin' me no?"

Lucas stepped off the veranda, his rough boots thudding softly in the hard packed earth of the yard. "Let the boy go," he said, his voice low and lethal.

7

J OHN PIKE'S HEAD FELL BACK, his protuberant black eyes shifting sideways to meet Gallagher's cold stare across the ten or so feet of beaten earth that separated them. Slowly the big man straightened and swung around, dragging the boy with him. "Talkin' to me, are you?"

Gallagher took another step forward, his hands hanging loosely at his sides, his weight shifted significantly to his back leg. "I said let him go."

John Pike had a reputation as a mean son-of-a-bitch and outweighed Gallagher by a good four or five stone. But Lucas Gallagher had a reputation of his own. Pike gave the boy a rough shove that sent him sprawling face down in the dirt. "I'll let him go. For now."

"For good." Lucas watched the boy scrabble backwards in the dirt, out of the big man's way. "Find someone who's willing, Pike."

The evening breeze blew between them, cold and lonely and scented with dust. The sun was almost down now, the light leaching from the sky to leave it pale. Soon they would all be locked in together for the night. A slight movement drew Gallagher's attention to the two-story, sandstone barracks beside them, where Corbett's overseer, Dalton, had finally bestirred himself enough to appear in the open doorway. What bullies like John Pike did to vulnerable young boys in the dark recesses of the barracks at night was one thing. But open fighting between the men out in the yard where the master might see was something else entirely.

Pike had noticed the overseer, too. He jerked his head toward the barracks, his lips curling away from his teeth in an ugly caricature of a smile. "You know what I want the lad for, do you?" He leaned forward, his fingertips tucked in the waistband of his coarse canvas trousers. "Maybe you'd like to take his place. I hear you've experience."

Daniel's big hand shot out just in time to snag Gallagher's arm and haul him back. "Don't do it." Daniel cast a significant glance toward the overseer watching them through slitted eyes. Throwing a punch at Pike now would earn Gallagher a week in solitary confinement. Or a flogging.

Lucas sucked in a deep, steadying breath, and Daniel let him go.

Lucas shook himself. "There's only one thing you need to remember, Pike. Touch that boy again and I'll cut out your guts out and use them to make a nest for those spiders you're so fond of." Deliberately, he turned his back on the burly Englishman and walked over to reach out his hand to the stableboy and haul him to his feet.

"You all right, lad?"

"Yeah," said Charlie, dragging a dirty sleeve across his wet face. "But you shouldna done that. He won't forget it. He'll get you back for it one way or another. You ain't been here long enough to know what Pike's like."

"I know what he's like." Lucas stooped to scoop up the boy's hat and set it on his head. "Mr. Corbett has asked me to start working with Finnegan's Luck in the morning. You want to help?"

Charlie's gray eyes went wide in a way that reminded Lucas that the stableboy was still very much a child, even if he had been transported for theft, even if he did know more than any child should have to know about things like starvation and the kind of predatory evil men like Pike could sink to when they'd been deprived of women for too long. "Gor," whispered Charlie. "You mean it? That big red stallion?"

"Sure I mean it." Lucas lifted his head, his gaze drawn one last time toward the distant purpling hills and the rolling sea they hid. "It's getting dark." He smiled down at the boy again. "There's a space beside the Fox where you can sling your hammock from now on, if you like."

The boy nodded and darted ahead, but Lucas lingered until the last moment. He sucked the sweet, night-scented air into his lungs, his eyes so dry they hurt as he stared up at the first stars winking at him from out of the darkening sky. Then he went into the barracks with its iron-barred windows and heavily bolted door that closed behind him with a familiar, dreaded *clang*.

IT WAS HIM.

Jessie could see him standing alone in the quickly darkening expanse of the yard. Impossible at this distance to distinguish his features. Yet there was no mistaking the proud line of his head and shoulders as he stared up at the evening sky, no missing the artless grace of his movements as he swung slowly toward the barracks. For one barely perceptible moment he paused, and she could see all of his pain, all of his desperation, all of his fear in the taut line of his back. Then he passed beneath the veranda and out of her sight. She was too far away for the slam of the barracks door or the noise of the bolts being shoved home to reach her. But she could hear them in her mind.

Her hands clenched around the brass handles of her room's French doors, although she didn't open them. She had come upstairs to dress for dinner. Yet something had drawn her to the windows overlooking the rear garden and the yard beyond it. Something she didn't understand and didn't want.

"The teal silk, Miss?"

"Yes, please." Jerking the damask drapes across the windows,

Jessie turned her back on the night. She watched the girl who had come to help her dress dart with a furtive kind of shyness about the room. She looked no more than sixteen, if that. She had a thin, sallow face and short, nondescript dark hair that stuck out from beneath her cap at odd angles. They always hacked off the women's hair when they put them on board the transport ships in London. The girl must not have been in Tasmania very long.

"What's your name?" Jessie asked.

The girl clutched Jessie's dress to her in a spasm of alarm and dropped into a frightened curtsy. "Emma, Miss. Emma Pope."

Jessie watched the girl duck her head and scurry across the room. Unlike the men, the house servants slept in two rooms in the basement, near the kitchen. But once they had finished their duties they were locked in for the night, too, the same way the men were locked into the big stone barracks in the yard. Jessie wondered what they thought, what they felt, when they listened to the sound of the key grating in the lock, sealing them into the darkness.

With an awed kind of reverence, Emma spread Jessie's dress in shining glory across the plump white softness of the four poster bed with damask hangings. They slept on hammocks in the men's barracks. Jessie knew that because as a child she'd sometimes peeked through the open door of the big stone building when she passed it in the yard. She'd heard that the house servants slept on bunks when they were locked in their rooms at the end of their long day. But never in her life had she descended the narrow service stairs to the basement to see for herself.

"Is it comfortable?" she asked suddenly as Emma unfastened her day dress. "Where you sleep below stairs?"

Emma looked up, her pale blue eyes widening. "Yes, Miss."

Stepping out of her day dress, Jessie crossed the room to her dressing table and picked up her silver handled brush. Her eyes met the girl's in the mirror. "Is it really?"

"Oh, yes, Miss. I ain't never been so comfortable in me life. I've a bed all to meself, with two blankets and all the food I can eat, every day. I ain't never known nothin' like it."

Jessie drew her brush through her long hair, her gaze still following the girl in the mirror as she went about her duties. She was a Londoner, her accent broad cockney. She'd probably grown up in some back slum, in an airless, windowless room crowded with anywhere from ten to twenty half-starved, ragged, lice-ridden brothers and sisters. Life as an assigned servant at Castle Corbett would seem comfortable indeed in comparison to such an existence, Jessie thought. Perhaps it was only convicts like that Irishman, Gallagher, who found their situation in Tasmania so crushingly onerous. Perhaps convicts like Emma Pope didn't mind what had been taken from them. Their homes. Their families. Their freedom. And yet . . .

Jessie remembered something Old Tom had said to her earlier that afternoon when she'd gone to visit him. Old Tom had been Jessie's groom since she was old enough to straddle a pony. He'd been a convict once. But he'd gained his pardon and now lived in one of the huts that straggled out in a line beyond the yard to house the workers whose sentences had expired or who had at least earned their tickets of leave. There were even a few workers who'd come free, but not many. For all its natural beauty and gentle climate, Tasmania had a bad reputation in Britain. Those with a choice normally went elsewhere.

Old Tom had been perched on a stool on his front stoop when she found him, playing his worn old Irish bagpipes, his arm pumping, his fingers flying. He had his eyes closed, lost in the sad wail of the pipes. He looked smaller than she remembered him. Smaller and older, his white hair thinner, the features of his face sunken and blurred by the ravages of the years. She'd felt a wrenching wave of sadness sweep through her. Then he opened his eyes and saw her. The pipes stopped abruptly. "So. You've come to see me, have you?"

She paused at the base of the rickety wooden steps, her head falling back as she smiled up at him. "Did you think I wouldn't?"

"Sure then, I knew the Miss Jessie who left here two years ago would come. But people change."

She climbed the steps to balance on the porch railing, the light blue fine wool of her skirt flaring out around her. "I haven't."

He didn't say anything to that. Turning with a studied care that spoke of arthritic old bones, he laid the bagpipes on the rough, weather-warped table beside him and slanted a look of pure amusement up at her. "That's some horse you bought, that Finnegan's Luck."

"Huh." She wrapped both hands around the railing at her sides and leaned back, the way she'd done as a child. "Go ahead and say it. I was a green fool to let myself be tricked into buying a horse with that kind of vice."

"Could be vice. Could just be a bad habit." Tom shrugged. "That young Irishman your brother's taken into the stables, now, he thinks it's habit."

Jessie looked up sharply. She hadn't known about Warrick moving Lucas Gallagher to stables work. *Oh, not daft, Mr. Gallagher,* she thought wryly. *Not daft at all.* Aloud, she said, "And what does he know about it, anyway?"

She was aware of Tom's watery blue gaze on her. He might be old but he was very, very wise. "More than most, I'd say. He's even got an idea or two about how to fix it."

She looked away toward the paddocks where the estate's riding horses were put out to graze. She didn't want to talk about that man, that strange man with his angry eyes and lean, graceful body. "I took a look at Cimmeria this morning," Jessie said, deliberately shifting the subject. "You've taken good care of her."

"Aye. Yer mare's in fine fettle. I've had Charlie exercising her, gettin' her back in shape for you." Stretching out his hand, Tom picked up a small knife and a half-whittled block of wood from the edge of the table. "And will ye be ridin' her tomorrow?" he asked in studied casualness, all his attention seemingly focused on the wood turning slowly between his hand and the blade. "Out to Shipwreck Cove?"

"No. Mother insists I rest for a few weeks." She hopped off the railing and went to stand at the edge of the porch and look out over the broad, slow-moving River Daymond that curled around the estate's outbuildings. "How is she, Tom?" she asked quietly without turning around. They both understood that this time Jessie wasn't talking about her horse.

He knew all of her secrets, Old Tom. How could he not, when he'd ridden faithfully behind her wherever she went for as long as she could remember? And the woman Jessie visited out on the headlands beyond Shipwreck Cove was her deepest and most dangerous secret.

"She's missed you, sure enough," said Tom. "It gets lonely out there sometimes, with only the sound of the waves on the rocks and the ghosts of the cove's wrecks for company."

Jessie swallowed. "I couldn't even write to her. I was too afraid Mother would find out. No one minds their own business on this island."

"Aye. We've a saying in Ireland. *Chan sgeul ruin a chluinneas triuir.*"

"Which means?"

"What three people hear is no secret."

Jessie smiled. Looking down, she saw the old man's bagpipes on the table beside her and reached out her hand to touch the slender reeds. "Do you miss it still?" she asked, looking up at him. "Ireland, I mean."

"Aye." His face remained impassive, but she heard the rough catch in his voice, saw the over bright sheen of his eyes before he turned his head away.

"Why didn't you go back? You could have gone long ago. Your pardon isn't conditional."

He swung to face her again, his throat working. She thought he was going to say something. Then he shook his head and went back to his whittling. "You don't want to hear it, Miss Jessie."

"Yes, I do."

He drew the knife with deliberate slowness over the block of wood, a thin shaving curling up to fall to the porch floor. "All right," he said, not looking up. "I'll tell you. I'd rather they'd hanged me, you see, than send me away from Ireland like that. I begged them to hang me. But when those soldiers dragged me onto that ship . . . well, I swore then on me mother's grave that I'd never go back. Not until the day there's nary an English boot left on Irish soil."

Jessie sucked in her breath in a startled hiss. "But you live amongst the English here."

"Aye. But it's no' my country, now is it?"

She watched the thin curls of wood drop one after the other to the weathered plank floor. She'd never really given much thought to why Old Tom had been transported. If she'd considered it at all, she'd have assumed it must have been for poaching a rabbit or selling an illegal batch of poteen. Now she wasn't so sure.

"Do you hate us so much?" she said softly. "I never knew."

He shook his head. "Not you, Miss Jessie."

"Why not me? I'm English."

"You are and yet you're not. Besides, in your own way, lass, you're as hemmed in and controlled as any convict ever was."

"I don't understand."

"Don't you?" He looked at her shrewdly. "Why did you ask me about Ireland? Why now, after all these years?"

"I don't know."

They'd gone on to talk of other things then. About her mare Cimmeria and her brother's hounds and the homecoming party her mother was planning. But she hadn't forgotten his words. Oh, no. She hadn't forgotten.

"Miss Corbett? Miss Corbett?"

Jessie turned from the dressing table to see Emma Pope waiting in the center of the room, the silk evening gown held ready in her hands. Lifting her arms, Jessie let the girl drop the dress over her head. The teal silk shimmered sensuously in the candlelight, then settled in soft whispers about the stiff, carefully corseted confines of her body.

8

THE NEXT MORNING Jessie walked down to the stables to watch the Irishman try his hand at "fixing" Finnegan's Luck. She told herself she went because of her interest in the horse. When a niggling, honest inner voice tried to suggest a different reason, she ignored it.

It had rained during the night, leaving the ground dark and wet, the vegetation of the garden lushly green and dripping. Clouds still bunched low and thick over the valley, a mist turning the park's trees into murkily indistinct shapes that seemed almost to float in the opaque, flat light. The promise of more rain hung heavily in the crisp morning air, along with the scents of wet hay and warm horseflesh that intensified as Jessie neared the stables.

She could hear the drumming of hooves and a man's low, soothing voice even before she reached the small paddock to the left of the stables. From his perch atop the high, whitewashed fence, Warrick acknowledged her appearance with only a grunt, his attention fixed on the big Irish Hunter that trotted past, powerful muscles bunching and flexing, noble head held high, dark mane and tail streaming in the wind as it circled the paddock guided only by the sure hands and voice of Lucas Gallagher. She paused beside her brother, the fingers of her gloved hands coming up to curl in ladylike restraint over the top railing as she watched the magnificent, high-spirited horse and the man who worked it.

He stood in the center of the paddock, his long legs braced wide, his dark hair fluttered by the wind as he pivoted gracefully, the longeing rein held lightly in a series of loops across the palm of his left hand. Slowly he began to draw out the leather with his right hand, his dark, strong-boned face taut with concentration as he urged the big bay stallion from a fast trot into a rolling canter that took it in a steady circle around and around the man and the skinny, half-grown boy who stood beside him intently following the Irishman's every move.

She knew this man was brutal and lawless, a wild and dangerous rebel of the kind she had been raised both to fear and to despise. Yet the beautiful, evocatively powerful synergy of the man and the beast he controlled stole her breath. For one unguarded moment, she gave herself up to staring at him, at the artistry of his scarred, long-fingered hands, the curve of his leanly muscled back, the strength of his spread thighs. Then his gaze lifted and for one brief, flaring instant their eyes met and held, and the moment spun out of time. She knew an odd tightening in her throat, a squeezing of her chest that left her breathless and lightheaded. The relentless, rhythmic pounding of the stallion's hooves seemed to reverberate through her, thrumming her blood with a strange need only dimly understood.

She jerked her gaze away. "I fail to see how this is supposed to teach Finnegan's Luck to stop bucking," she said to Warrick, her voice coming out unnaturally tart and disapproving.

Her brother grunted, his gaze still following the stallion. "The man's simply getting to know the horse for now, Jess. He says these things can't be rushed if they're to be effective."

"Huh. Why didn't you have Old Tom work with Finnegan's Luck?"

Warrick glanced down at her, his delicately arched brows drawing together in a puzzled frown. "It was Old Tom who suggested Gallagher. Tom says the man knows what he's doing, and I believe him. Don't you?"

"Of course. It's just—"

The sound of a firm step behind them brought her head around. Turning, she saw Harrison's tall, thin figure striding across the yard toward them. He was wearing an expensive bottle-green riding coat, buckskin breeches, and shiny, knee-high leather boots, and he looked so familiar and safe, with his calm demeanor and proud, confident carriage, that she felt a sensation of relief flood through her at the sight of him. It was as if she'd momentarily found herself drifting into a strange, somehow frightening world, and he'd brought her firmly back to earth.

"Harrison," she said, stepping forward to hold out both of her hands as he came up to them. "This is a pleasant surprise."

"Your mother thought I would find you someplace around the stables." Harrison took her hands in his and squeezed them gently before letting her go. "She offered to send someone to fetch you, but I couldn't resist the opportunity to come and see for myself this Irish Hunter I've heard so much about."

"A faux pas, that one," said Warrick idly, his gaze once more following his horse. "I fear you have unwittingly deprived our dear mother of an opportunity to pry her daughter away from her outdoor pursuits and thrust her into the drawing room where all respectable ladies supposedly belong."

A gleam of amusement lit up Harrison's sober gray eyes. "Yes, I fear I did rather disappoint her. But I reinstated myself in her good graces by promising to bring Jesmond back up to the house with me in time for tea."

Jessie laughed softly, and Harrison's features relaxed into the slightly crooked smile she'd always found especially endearing. Then his gaze slid past her to the cantering stallion and he said, "So this is Finnegan's Luck." Stepping forward, he leaned his forearms along the top rail of the fence and watched as the Irishman brought the bay back down to a fast trot. "Marvelous. Have you ridden him yet, Warrick?"

Warrick caught Jessie's meaningful glare behind her betrothed's back and flashed her a wicked grin. But all he said was, "I thought I'd let the groom work him for a few days."

"Hmmm." Harrison's eyes narrowed as he watched Gallagher skillfully keeping the horse always between his two, outstretched hands. "New man, isn't it?"

Warrick nodded. "You don't often find a convict as good with horses as this one."

By now Gallagher had brought Finnegan's Luck to a stand. Harrison continued to watch, his face unreadable, as the Irishman walked forward to unsnap the longeing rein and then began to walk in a circle himself, the stableboy trotting behind him and the horse, no longer restrained by the rein, obedient at his side. "Perhaps he's a horse thief," said Harrison.

Warrick laughed out loud. "Perhaps. Although I suspect treason and rebellion are more likely crimes. He's Irish, after all. And he used to be a gentleman. You can hear it in his voice when he forgets to lay on the brogue."

As they spoke, Gallagher began to step back, moving gradually farther and farther away from the hunter until he stood again in the center of the paddock, the stallion still moving obediently in a wide circle around him.

Jessie glanced up at her brother. *Used to be a gentleman.* It was an expression she'd heard all of her life applied to those in degraded circumstances who had been born into better situations. But she'd never liked it, always thought it contradictory that the acquisition of fine clothes and wealth could never turn a base-born man into society's concept of a gentleman, yet the loss of those two requirements was nevertheless considered enough to send a gently-born man tumbling from the ranks of the godly. Rather like a fallen angel cast out of heaven.

"What a singularly ridiculous expression," she said, surprising herself by voicing her thoughts aloud. " 'Used to be a gentleman.' Really, Warrick; think about it. I can understand saying a man 'used to be a vicar' or 'used to be a doctor.' But how does a man stop being a gentleman when he was born and bred as one?"

Warrick made an impatient sound in his throat. "You know what I mean. Look at him, for heaven's sake."

Jessie looked. Despite the morning chill, the Irishman wore only a drab waistcoat and a rough cotton shirt, his uncut, dark hair hanging long and ragged over the shirt's open, collarless neck. The years he had spent working ten- and twelve-hour days in the hot Australian sun had browned his face and left clearly defined muscles in his forearms. He stood with his booted legs astraddle, his slim body turning in a slow, tight circle that matched the horse's wider ring as he now controlled the big stallion with nothing but his soothing voice and the inescapable power of his personality. He looked wild and dangerous and faintly menacing, but not like a gentleman. Not like a gentleman at all.

"Frankly," said Harrison, removing some infinitesimally small particle of lint from the sleeve of his fine wool jacket, "I've always thought such men even more contemptible than those convicts from the lower classes. After all, a man born to privilege could have made of life whatever he wished. Instead, he brings himself to *this.*" Harrison threw a speaking glance in the direction of the man in the paddock. "It truly is a sad comment on such an individual's character and moral state."

She had forgotten how pompous Harrison could sound sometimes, and the way his nose quivered when he contemplated something or someone he held in disdain. Looking at her betrothed, now, she thought how very much he was the embodiment of everything a gentleman was supposed to be, with his determinedly cool demeanor and inflexible, self-righteous attitudes. She couldn't imagine him ever doing anything that might set at risk the privilege and comfort to which he had been born. She had known him her entire life, yet it struck her in that moment that she really didn't know him at all, not in the ways a woman should know her husband. She had no notion of the dreams and passions that lived in the heart of him, in the soul of him.

"You're scowling at me, Jesmond." Harrison tilted his head in that way he had when he was teasing. "Quite fiercely. Do you think I judge your brother's new groom too harshly?"

"I think you're very quick to judge someone about whom you know almost nothing."

His eyes widened, then narrowed in concern. Reaching out, he took one of her hands in both of his, his grip cool and light. "You're right, of course, darling. How unchristian of me. But to demonstrate that my own character is not irredeemably lost, let me hasten to inform you that this Saturday, the Blackhaven Scientific Society is hosting a lecture on speleology to be delivered by one Professor Heinrich Luneberg. Knowing your interest in the subject, I have come to offer my services as your escort. And Philippa and I would like to request your presence at dinner tomorrow evening. There. I've offered to feed your hunger for knowledge as well as the less exalted requirements of your mortal self. Am I forgiven?"

It was the kind of frothy nonsense Harrison always threw up to disguise his deeper emotions. And so while Jessie dutifully laughed, she didn't miss the earnest, strained look in his eyes. "Thank you, Harrison." She twisted her hand to link her fingers with his. "I'd like that very much."

"Speleology?" Warrick slipped from the fence in one easy motion to cuff his friend on the shoulder. "Good God, Harrison; that is above and beyond the call of duty, even if you have committed yourself to marrying her."

"Listening to lectures about caves I don't mind," said Harrison, drawing Jessie's hand through the crook of his arm as they started toward the house. "As long as Jesmond doesn't try to drag me into actually exploring the wretched things."

Warrick and Harrison both laughed. Neither noticed when Jessie didn't join in.

Walking between them, she crossed the yard, her hand on her betrothed's arm, her thoughts wandering far from the others' conversation. She could not understand what had driven her to defend that man, that dark, hateful convict with his glittering, hostile stares and bitterly defiant attitudes. She quickened her step, barely suppressing the urge to pick up her skirts and run.

Run away from the thunder of the stallion's hooves and the caressing warmth of that Irishman's voice and a swirling onslaught of wild, dangerous impulses she didn't understand and didn't want.

COLD but sweet and blessedly cleansing, the water closed over Gallagher's head. He dove deep, swimming along the bottom of the riverbed, pushing himself to go farther, farther, before finally arching upward, his legs kicking hard as he shot to the surface.

From the hazelnut trees farther up the hill near the stables came the melodious call of a thrush. Lucas shook his head, clearing the tumbled hair from his eyes and smiling as he sucked the early evening air into his lungs and felt the dirt and sweat of the day leave him. It'd been one of the things he hated the most about the chain gang—the festering, stinking, dehumanizing filth. On the chain gang, a man could go for months at a time without being given a chance to get clean. Now he came here whenever he could, to swim in the broad, gently flowing waterway known as the River Daymond that curled around the base of the high ground on which Anselm Corbett had built his fortress-like stone house and outbuildings. Once or twice a week, Lucas tried to wash his clothes as well, if he could grab the time before the sun slipped too low on the horizon. It would be easier now with the coming of spring and the lengthening of the days.

Turning, he swam back against the current, back and forth, back and forth, letting the familiar rhythm cleanse his soul as the water cleansed his body. He'd been born in a low-slung, rambling old whitewashed house overlooking the wild and turbulent Irish Sea. As a child, he'd grown up darting through the dangerous currents that swept along that part of the coast. If he closed his eyes he could almost—*almost*—imagine that he was there, where he'd never be again.

No longer smiling, he opened his eyes and stood up to wade to the grassy riverbank. The air was heavy with the fragrance of lemon gums and wattles; evocative yet alien scents that he thought in a rush of homesickness he almost hated. Reaching his spare set of clothes, he hauled a clean pair of canvas trousers up over his still wet hips and let the warm evening breeze dry his naked torso as he hunkered down near the shallows, his work-stained clothes in his hands.

The problem with physical labor, he decided, pushing his old shirt beneath the free flowing water, was that it gave a man entirely too much time to think. Endless hours, day after day, in which the body labored but the mind was left floating free to wander down dangerous, tortuous paths. He suspected it accounted for the blank, staring expressions to be seen amongst the old incorrigibles, those men who had suffered under Britain's grinding, brutalizing penal system for twenty, thirty years or more. When a man finds his past too painfully sweet to be remembered and his future too barren and hopeless to be contemplated, the result is a tendency to think of nothing. Nothing at all.

Sitting back on his heels, Lucas watched the water ripple over the smooth pebbles of the riverbed. He'd thought once that he might be able to use this river to reach the sea, but it hadn't taken him long to discover that the River Daymond emptied into Blackhaven Bay. And Blackhaven Bay was home port to a Royal Naval vessel with little to do beyond apprehending absconding convicts.

He'd heard about another outlet to the sea, through a cove to the north of Blackhaven Bay. He hadn't been given an opportunity to visit it yet, but now that he was working in the stables he'd find some way to manage it. Already he had started collecting materials—hemp and tar, lumber and tools—in case they couldn't find a boat and had to build one. He spent a lot of time mentally designing that boat, deciding what they'd need. Planning his escape—that was how Lucas Gallagher kept from dwelling on the killing memories of the past, kept that blank, hopeless stare of the half-dead from creeping into his expression.

He lifted the shirt from the stream and twisted the coarse cloth in his hands, wringing the water from it before tossing it over a low bush beside him. He was reaching for his dirty trousers when the sound of gentle footfalls in the grass brought his head up.

A warm evening breeze skimmed across his bare torso, tantalizing his senses and stealing his breath. He'd been expecting a wallaby or some other native animal venturing down to the riverbank to drink. Not this elegantly gowned young woman in lilac and white stripes, her sleeves gathered into lace-trimmed bands at her small wrists, her golden hair falling in gentle curls from beneath a delicate straw hat with ties of lilac ribbon that fluttered free in the wind.

She paused, her full lips parting, one hand coming up to close over the ribbons beneath her chin. "Mr. Gallagher," said Miss Jesmond Corbett.

9

———

L UCAS WATCHED HER HESITATE at the top of the grassy bank, one hand crushing the fluttering lilac ribbons of her hat, the other fisting in her skirts as if she were about to run away. He held his breath, waiting for her to go. He wanted her to go.

Instead she said, "I saw you longeing Finnegan's Luck this morning." As if he hadn't seen her; as if he hadn't been vibrantly, unnaturally conscious of her watching him. "You're very good at it."

It came out sounding almost grudging, and he gave a low laugh. "To hear you, one would think you'd been hoping I didn't know squat-all about working with horses."

"Don't be ridiculous," she said, her haughtiness betrayed by the band of honest color on her cheekbones that told him he'd hit it right.

He didn't say anything, just stared back at her standing there so straight and slender and elegant. The wind gusted around them, sweet with the scent of the formal gardens beyond her. He was suddenly acutely conscious of his shabby convict trousers and bare feet and naked, sun-darkened chest. He wondered if she'd seen the crisscross of scars on his back, that degrading legacy of humiliation and debasement. And then he wondered at himself, for why should he care what this woman thought of him?

Deliberately, he turned his back on her. Catching up his trousers, he crouched down beside the river and thrust them beneath the cool running water. Yet even though he couldn't see her, he remained painfully aware of her behind him, remained aware of her watching him. She wasn't leaving. He realized he was still holding his breath and let it go in a long, shaky sigh into the awkward silence.

"What are you doing?" she asked.

He snorted but didn't look up. "I should think that would be fairly obvious."

"Isn't there a woman who washes the convicts' clothing? There always used to be."

"Aye, there is. She just doesn't do it often enough to my taste."

"So you come here in the evenings and wash them yourself?"

The surprise in her voice flicked him on the raw. He paused in the act of wringing out his trousers, his elbows resting on his spread thighs as he threw her a glance over his bare shoulder. "Faith, it's hard to credit it, isn't it? We're such a filthy lot, we Irish. As dirty as we are lawless and rebellious and savage."

They had a bad reputation, the Irish convicts in Australia. A reputation for defiance and intractability and bitter, resentful hostility. Most of the English colonists out here were afraid of them. She was afraid of him. He could see it in the way she stared at him, her eyes wide and turbulent, her nostrils flaring as she drew in a quick breath. She had the most beautiful eyes, a dark, velvety blue with flecks of some unearthly light, like a moon-tossed sea on a stormy night.

He thought she would go away now and he waited, tense with expectation and an odd twinge of regret. But she didn't go. Instead she came sliding down the bank in a rush that kicked up her skirts and petticoats in a froth of lacy ruffles to reveal a pair of slim ankles and dainty booted feet. He knew he should look away, but he didn't.

Tilting her head, she gazed at him from beneath the brim of her hat, the fancy patterned straw allowing through pinpoints of light to dance across her delicate features. "And you're excessively proud of

it, too, aren't you?" she said, smiling a little. "Not only of your Irish-
ness, but of your lawlessness and your wildness and your
notoriety."

He stood up in one easy motion and swung to face her. He was
wearing nothing but his old trousers and she skittered backward a
few steps, her throat working as she swallowed quickly. He hooked
his thumbs in the waistband of his trousers and cocked one hip in a
deliberately blatant, masculine pose. "That's what being Irish is all
about, isn't it?" he said. "Just like being English is about moderation
that's all too easily taken to the point of repression."

He meant to drive her away. He wanted her to go away and stay
away, far, far away from him. She did tremble a little, as if she were
fighting an urge to put more distance between them. But she held her
ground, her voice remaining cool and composed. "Don't you think
you're being rather simplistic?"

He gave her a slow smile that showed his teeth, although his eyes
narrowed. "So you don't like that, do you? It's all right to say an Irishman's nothing but a lazy larrikin who cares more about fun and
mischief than for things like work and wealth. But it's a different
matter entirely when someone dares to suggest that some of your
precious Englishmen are pompous sourpusses who worship
authority."

She sucked in a quick, indignant breath that lifted her chest and
drew his attention, dangerously, to her breasts. "There is a difference
between worshipping authority and having respect for the law." Her
head tilted upward in that haughty way he hated. "British law is the
envy of the world."

He gave a harsh, ringing laugh. "Oh it is, is it? That's why you're so
bloody generous about spreading your 'British law' around, I
suppose. Greed and selfishness have nothing to do with it, do they?"

She tied the loose ribbons of her hat with swift, angry motions.
"Greed and selfishness?"

"That's right. Greed and selfishness, all dressed up as moral supe-
riority and sanctimonious nonsense. What do you think? That God
created the whole world just for you lot? So you could bring *British*

law and *British* liberty and the bloody *British* empire to everyone, like the great, God-appointed civilizers of the world?"

She stood very still, still enough that he could see her heartbeat fluttering the pulse point at the base of her pale neck just above her white lace collar. "We have created the greatest empire the world has ever seen," she said, her voice so calm, so in control, so bloody *English*. "An empire that is shining and glorious and—"

He swiped one hand through the air in an angry gesture. "Glorious, is it? Glorious? Well, let me tell you, there will never be any glory —not true glory—attached to your mighty empire, not as long as you can maintain it only by oppressing those under your rule—be they African, or Indian, or Irish. And that's why you'll lose it someday. All of it."

Her breath was coming so ragged she was practically shaking with it, although her voice was still admirably even. "You're a madman."

He gave her his best devil-damn-the-world smile. "Not a bit of it. I'm just Irish, remember?"

For a moment, she looked startled. Then she surprised him by laughing out loud. Not a polite society titter with no heart or soul in it, but a husky, earthy laugh that lit up her face in a natural, spontaneous way that seemed oddly at variance with her lacy trims and lilac ribbons and precious lady's manners. He stared at her, at the unexpected fullness of her lower lip and the gentle curve of her cheek. A strange silence crackled between them, a silence filled with the moan of the evening wind and the gurgle of the free-flowing river and a firm, steadily approaching tread that brought her head snapping around and jerked him to instant, quivering attention.

"There you are, Lucas me lad," said Daniel O'Leary, his carrot-topped head and big shoulders appearing over the bank. "You were so long comin' back, it's worryin' about ye, I was startin' to be. The sun's going down fast and—" He broke off, his eyes widening at the sight of Miss Jesmond Corbett.

She had been well trained. If she felt the least discomfited to be found here on the riverbank in the company of a half-dressed Irish convict, with the sun sinking low in the sky, she didn't show it. "You shouldn't swim alone, Mr. Gallagher," she said in that precise English accent of hers. "You might run into difficulties." And then she walked calmly away from him up the river, her head held high, her back straight, her lilac ribbons floating out behind her.

Daniel stood open-mouthed, staring after her. "What was she doing here?" he asked low voiced when she had gone.

Lucas shrugged and bent to pick up his clean shirt. "Going for a walk, I suppose."

Daniel shook his head and rubbed one hand over the back of his neck in a distracted gesture. "I hope you know what you're doing, laddie."

Lucas pulled his shirt over his head and laughed. "What are you talking about?"

But Daniel only shook his head and thumped Lucas on the chest with one pointed finger. "You be careful, you hear?"

THE NEXT NIGHT, Jessie, her mother, and her brother went in the carriage to Beaulieu Hall for dinner with Harrison and Philippa.

A fat silver moon rode low in the purpling sky, spilling a breathtaking blue light across the hushed fields and slanting in through the carriage windows to dance over the faces of the silent occupants. Jessie glanced from her brother's classic profile to her mother's bland features and back again. She didn't like the strange, worrisome glitter she could see in Warrick's eyes tonight. He had spent the afternoon in a gully in the foothills above the house, exploding clay wafers with a set of new silver mounted pistols and tossing down glass after glass of expensive French brandy. He had asked her to come along and throw for him, and she'd gone willingly enough, for she'd been unable to settle at anything all day herself. She couldn't understand this odd humor that had her in its grip, leaving her feeling inexplicably restless and lethargic at the same time.

She was glad she was going to Beaulieu Hall tonight, she decided;

glad she would be seeing Harrison. She felt in urgent need of his phlegmatic, very British personality. It was a thought that brought with it an unexpected bubble of amusement, and she smiled into the night.

"Why are you smiling so strangely?" Beatrice asked, her sharp voice breaking the silence.

"I was simply remembering something someone said to me recently," said Jessie, aware of Warrick shifting his position to stare at her with interest. She was careful not to smile again.

The drawing room at Beaulieu Hall was much the same as the one at the Castle, an expensive display of French walnut with white marble and a tasteful array of silks and satins and brocades. The dining room, too, was vaguely reminiscent of the one at home, the Cuban mahogany table in its center grand enough to seat twenty-four and surrounded by a veritable phalanx of balloon-backed chairs upholstered in a burgundy Italian silk that coordinated precisely with the figured brocade hanging on the walls. The heavy silver candelabra on the table were of Sheffield plate. More silver in the form of massive cruets stood atop twin satinwood Hepplewhite sideboards tucked away beneath twin Italianate arches, their moldings picked out in gilt and shades of muted burgundy, hunter green, and a deep, rich blue. A swarm of servants, surprisingly well trained for convicts, delivered successive courses of duck and swan, kangaroo and lamb. But then, as magistrate for the district, Harrison always had his pick of the best convicts available for assignment.

She found herself watching him more and more as the meal progressed. At the moment he sat slightly off center, one wrist casually resting along the arm of his chair, his pose relaxed now that dinner was almost at an end. He wore a long-tailed evening coat with a low collar and long lapels, and a fancifully embroidered silk waistcoat that made him look handsome and elegant and faintly witty, in a very English sort of way. She watched him reach out one white, well-manicured hand to choose a sweetmeat from the silver tray at his elbow and decided she felt comforted by his familiarity and predictability, by his calm urbanity. This was her world.

He was talking to Beatrice about a new dining service he was ordering from Worcester to be done in burgundy and blue, with the family crest highlighted in gold. Unlike Anselm Corbett, whose father had come out of obscurity to make his own fortune in the mills of North Lancashire, the Tates were old gentry, descended from the squires of a small but ancient manor in Hampshire. Yet as good as Harrison's lineage was, it wasn't quite as impressive as Beatrice's. Beatrice's own father had been a simple half-pay officer who'd lost an arm on some obscure French battlefield, but the family was old, old and well known and better connected even than the Tates. Birth still mattered here in the Colonies. But money mattered too, even more than it did in England. And in fortune, at least, the Tates and the Corbetts were of a par. It would be a good match.

Jessie reached for her wine glass, her hand not quite steady as she gripped the faceted crystal stem. Money and birth. They were the foundations of her world, the criteria by which all were judged.

Money and birth and freedom from the shameful, indelible stain of convictry.

IT WAS AFTER DINNER, when Philippa and Beatrice were playing duets on the piano and Warrick sprawled in a shadowy corner chair to nurse his inevitable glass of brandy, that Harrison invited Jessie to walk outside with him and admire the full moon.

It rode higher in the sky now, smaller yet brighter than before against the darkness of the late-night heavens, its reflected light shining incredibly clear and crisp and vivid. "You're right," Jessie said, smiling a little. "It is very beautiful."

"Is it?" His breath stirred her hair as he took her hand and pulled her around to face him.

She laughed up at him. "Aren't you looking at it?" Then she saw his face and the laughter died on her lips.

"No." A strange smile curved his thin mouth. "I fear I lured you out of doors under false pretenses. What I really came out here to look at is you." His smile faded to be replaced by a taut, intense expression that sent a tremor of an emotion that was not quite fear through her.

He's going to kiss me, she thought. *He's going to kiss me the way a man kisses the woman he will marry. The woman he will someday take to his bed.* She felt painfully shy at the thought. And then she told herself she was being foolish, that she had known this man all her life, that she would soon be his *wife,* for heaven's sake. She must accustom herself to this new level of intimacy, of *physical* intimacy, with him.

"Jesmond," he whispered, his breath warm against her cheek as she held herself quite still. His hands were at her shoulders now, pulling her to him, sliding possessively down her back to ride low on her hips. Then he bent his head and kissed her.

His lips were soft and cool and moist, and she thought perhaps it was a pleasant thing after all, being kissed. Then his grip on her tightened, his mouth pressing down harder, forcing her lips open in a rough urgency that sent a jolt of panic and faint revulsion through her. She endured it for a moment, unable to breathe, her eyes wide and staring, her hands gripping his shoulders. Then she made a faint mew of protest in her throat, her palms flattening against his chest.

He let her go at once, swinging away from her to stand at the edge of the veranda, his head thrown back, one of his hands coming up to shade his eyes, his shoulders held stiff and straight. She stayed where she was, feeling foolish and embarrassed and terribly inadequate.

"I'm sorry," she said in a small voice, glad he had turned his back on her so that he would not see her when she quickly wiped away the wetness his mouth had left on hers. "I don't know what came over me."

"No. No, don't say that. The fault was mine." He came to stand in front of her again and took both her hands in his to hold them tightly against his chest. "Forgive me, darling. I was wrong to—" His breathing was harsh, ragged, so that he had to swallow before he could continue. "You see, a man's passions run stronger than a woman's. It's natural. It's . . . to be expected. When a man is dealing with a gently bred woman, it's his responsibility to handle her carefully, to go slowly. Instead I frightened you. Please forgive me."

Jessie shook her head. "You make me sound like some bizarre cross between a skittish horse and an expensive china cup."

He laughed, and she touched her fingertips to his cheek. "I gave you the right to kiss me when I agreed to marry you, Harrison. It will be better next time, when I know what to expect." She told herself it would be better next time.

They returned to the drawing room not long after that. Harrison went to turn the pages for his sister at the piano while Jessie took a seat near Warrick in the shadows thrown by a flickering wall sconce. Warrick was too absorbed by his own devils to pay her much heed. But she knew her mother's eyes were upon her and saw the hardening of Beatrice's expression as she took in Jessie's high color and agitated breathing. Jessie knew she would hear about this, if not that night then the next morning.

SHE WAS PASSING the morning room on her way back from a late breakfast the next day when her mother called to her.

"Come in for a moment and close the door," Beatrice said from where she sat working on her interminable embroidery. "There's something I wish to discuss with you."

Jessie walked into the room and closed the door behind her. She hadn't slept well, her rest troubled by thoughts she didn't want to face, didn't even want to admit to in the light of day. The last thing she needed now was to discuss last night with her mother.

"And the shutters," Beatrice hissed when Jessie would have come to sit beside her on the settee.

Jessie crossed the room to close the paneled cedar shutters against the twin dangers of morning light and potentially listening ears, then leaned back against them, her hands behind her waist, her head tilted to one side. "What is it, Mother?"

Beatrice's needle flashed in and out through the fabric of her embroidery. It was like a refuge, Jessie had decided, her mother's embroidery, rather like Warrick's brandy glass. A refuge or a shield; Jessie could never decide which. "You were out on the veranda with Harrison rather a long time last night," Beatrice said, her voice as crisp and precise as her stitches.

Jessie let her breath out in a long sigh. "Mother, we are betrothed."

Beatrice paused in her stitches and then went on. "I know. That's precisely what worries me, you see. Harrison is such a gentleman that under any other circumstances, I would have no hesitation in trusting him to behave precisely as he ought. However, now that you are to be wed, he may feel that entitles him to take certain . . ." The needle hovered, then dove fiercely through the fabric. "Liberties."

"Mother, exactly what are you trying to say?"

Jessie watched, bemused, as a rare tide of color suffused her mother's normally pale, composed face. She met Jessie's eyes for one awkward moment, then looked away. "There are some women who find it difficult to resist a man's advances. They allow themselves to be swept up by the . . . the intensity of the moment, so to speak, with the result that they do things they know they ought not to do." Beatrice lowered her voice and leaned forward. "Things that belong only in the sanctity of the marriage bed."

"*Mother.*" Jessie felt her own cheeks flame as she pushed away from the window to take an agitated turn about the room. "Really—" She swung to face the settee, her hands cupping her elbows against her sides. "All Harrison did last night was kiss me. Surely that is to be expected between a betrothed couple?"

"Kisses can lead rapidly to other things." By now Beatrice had abandoned all pretense of embroidery and simply sat with the frame gripped tightly in her lap. "If that happens, you must stop him, Jesmond. Do you understand? Even if you don't want to. You must wait until the marriage vows are safely said."

Jessie let out a startled huff of something like laughter and went to sit beside Beatrice on the settee. "Mother, please believe me when I say there is no need for you to distress yourself with these worries. I don't think I am in any danger of being swept away by the heat of passion with Harrison."

"Jesmond, it was obvious to anyone who saw your face that something occurred on that veranda last night."

Jessie gripped her hands together, tightly, in her lap and stared down at them. "Mother, I told you. He kissed me. I found it both alarming and unpleasant, and not at all anything I would like either to extend or repeat. So you need not be concerned."

There was a long, tense pause filled with the ticking of the ormolu clock on the mantel and the distant sounds of the servants clearing breakfast from the dining room. "Forgive me, my dear," said Beatrice in a strained voice. "You are like her in so many ways, I simply assumed you were like her in this respect as well."

Jessie looked up quickly. "Like whom? Mother, what are you talking about?"

"Never mind, dear." Beatrice reached out to close her hand over Jessie's. "I hope you took care not to say or do anything last night that might lead Harrison to think you hold him in aversion."

Jessie blinked at her mother and might even have laughed, had it not been for the strange burning in her chest that stole her breath and left her feeling empty and sad. "A moment ago you were warning me against allowing Harrison to 'take liberties' with me. Now you seem to be telling me that I must be careful not to discourage him."

"Jesmond . . . " Beatrice paused as if summoning the will to put her thoughts into words. "These things are so awkward to speak of, but now that you are to be wed . . . " She drew a deep breath and let it out in a shaky sigh, her gaze resolutely fixed on the large, ornate Sevres vase near the windows as she forced herself to go on. "Most women find the male—" She hesitated, searching for an acceptable term. "—*physique* both threatening and repulsive, and the intimacies of the marriage bed unpleasant. Nevertheless, it is something that we all must endure when our time comes. It is the price we pay for our children, our homes, and our positions in society." She brought her gaze back to her daughter's face. "Remember that."

It was Jessie's turn to look away. Her mother's words hung in the air, bleak and sad and whispering softly of things that had not been said. Things that would never be said. Jessie rose and went to stand before the white marble mantle to stare down at the empty grate. She had never had any illusions about her parents' marriage. How could she have, when she had never seen them kiss, never known them even to touch when they could avoid it? They had lived their lives in parallel rather than together, going through their days in the same house and yet not really sharing it. Their dislike for each other was always there, politely hidden but nonetheless palpable, stealing the joy from their offsprings' childhood and bringing that pinched, sour look to Beatrice's face. Or was it the things she forced herself to endure in her marriage bed that had hardened Beatrice's mouth, Jessie wondered; that had killed whatever spark might once have animated her mother's now bland, drooping features and left her bitter and sad?

"Is that all you wished to say to me?" Jessie asked quietly.

Her mother busied herself with her embroidery, the needle flying in and out, in and out with unerring correctness. "Yes, I believe so. I see no reason to speak of this again."

Jessie was at the door when her mother stopped her. "Do you go for a ride this morning?"

One hand curling around the edge of the door, Jessie turned in surprise. "You said you didn't want me to ride until after your garden party."

"Oh, well—" Beatrice waved one hand through the air in a vague gesture. "I think perhaps you've grown too restless of late. Go ahead and get changed. I'll ask Warrick to send a message to the stables."

Jessie walked slowly up the stairs, feeling guilty and confused and ashamed. She had not set out deliberately to deceive her mother. She had not lied when she said she hadn't enjoyed Harrison's kisses. And yet . . . And yet she knew, too, that she was not one of those females who found the male physique repulsive, and she shuddered to imagine Beatrice's reaction if she knew the real truth. If she knew her daughter had stood on the banks of the River Daymond at sunset and admired the way years of hard physical labor could sculpt a man's naked chest. Or that her dreams had been haunted ever since by memories of a man's naked back, strapped with muscle and criss-crossed with a pattern of scars that could only have come from hundreds and hundreds of lashes delivered at the triangle by the vicious claws of a cat-o'-nine-tails.

10

LUCAS PERCHED ATOP the whitewashed split-rail fence, his forearms resting lightly on his bent knees, the toes of his boots hooked behind a lower rail. His gaze followed the big bay stallion that cantered in an easy, endless circle, its silver hooves flashing, its red hide sleek and gleaming in the fitful morning sun.

The paddock was big. Big enough to give the horse the illusion of freedom—until it ran up against the far fence line and stopped, its neck arching, its ears twitched forward, its nostrils quivering. "That's right," whispered Gallagher. "You can run, but you can't really go anywhere, me lad. They've got you surrounded."

"You gonna try ridin' him today?" asked Charlie, his voice tight with excitement as he climbed up to stand on the bottom railing of the fence beside Gallagher.

Lucas smiled. "Not yet. I want to get to know him a wee bit better first." He cast a sideways look at the boy. "Like to try working him on a longeing rein yourself, then?"

"Wouldn't I just!" Charlie's face broke into such a wide smile that Lucas had to turn his head away, his eyes narrowing at the sight of Warrick Corbett strolling across the yard.

Lucas watched him walk toward them. He hadn't quite taken the measure of Warrick Corbett yet. In some ways he seemed a good man to be assigned to, seemed free of the sadistic tendencies that English public schools could sometimes breed into a man along with a taste for cricket and Cicero and Shakespearean poetry. But then, Corbett had never been to Eton or Winchester. He wasn't really an Englishman—although Gallagher doubted the man realized that yet. Corbett had been born and bred here in Australia, and whether he admitted it or not, that made him different.

But it didn't entirely account for that disconcerting wildness that could blaze in Warrick Corbett's eyes or that dangerous, wild smile that could come out of nowhere. There was a volatility, an immature recklessness about the man that Gallagher didn't trust.

"You, Charlie," Corbett called when he was still some six to eight feet away. "Go catch my sister's mare, Cimmeria, and saddle her up. And get the gray for Gallagher while you're at it," he added as the boy hopped off the fence and took off at a run for the far paddock. His head tilting back, Corbett swung to face Gallagher, that devilish grin of his firmly in place. "I've got a job for you."

Lucas twisted sideways and swung his legs over the top of the fence to balance there, his arms braced wide. "I thought you wanted me to continue working Finnegan's Luck today."

"I did. But it looks like that'll have to wait until later." Corbett paused beside the fence, his gaze following the restless stallion. "My sister needs a groom."

Lucas tightened his grip on the rough wood of the fence and pushed off to land lightly in the yard. Whether in Hyde Park or the hills of Hampshire, no young Englishwoman with any pretense of gentility would ever think of riding alone without a groom in atten-dance. To do so would outrage every rule of propriety her society enforced. Yet it seemed a curious custom to follow here, where the groom was more often than not a convict.

"I thought Old Tom was her groom," Gallagher said, his voice rough with a tension that stole his breath and twisted his gut. To be forced to ride at a respectful distance behind that beautiful but haughty young Englishwoman, to be at her beck and call as her groom, as her *servant*, struck him as more degrading and insufferable than anything he'd yet had to endure—more than the chains, more than the triangle and whip, more than all the grinding, day-by-day humiliations and indignities he'd endured through three long, soul-destroying years.

Corbett rested one elbow on the fence's high railing, his attention caught, once again, by the restless, high-spirited horse. "Old Tom can't take a ride of that distance any more. He was feeling badly enough this morning that I told him to go back to bed."

"Why not send Charlie with her?"

Corbett twisted to look at Gallagher over his shoulder. "Because Charlie's too young to be of much use if she should happen to run into a gang of bushrangers."

Lucas knew he was pushing the boundaries of his position, but that still didn't stop him from saying, "Surely one of the other men—"

Corbett pushed off from the fence and swung away, his face tight with annoyance. "None of the other men ride well enough to keep up with her. You're her new groom, Gallagher, and that's final."

JESSIE GLANCED up from latching the garden gate and saw a black-haired convict leading two horses from the stables. She faltered, the long, dark blue skirt of her riding habit slipping through her fingers as she stared at him. He had turned away from her to tighten the cinch of the saddle on an unfamiliar gray, but she recognized the leanly muscled length of his back, the sure, graceful way he moved as he pulled the strap tight and thrust it home.

Ignoring the peculiar pounding of her heart, she picked up the trailing skirt of her habit again and crossed the dusty, sunlit yard toward him. A magpie broke into song, its sweetly melancholy lament floating to them from the apple trees that edged the nearby pond. The man didn't look up. Deliberately, she stepped past him to the pretty little black mare with four white stockings that stretched out its soft velvety nose and nickered in greeting.

"Hello, beautiful," she murmured, rubbing her hand over Cimmeria's nose and down the shiny black neck. "Did you miss me? I missed you." Smiling gently, she pressed her cheek against the familiar dark, satiny hide. Yet even though she could no longer see him, that Irishman, she remained intensely aware of him behind her.

"Yourrr brrrotherrr says you'll be wanting to rrride out to the cove," said Gallagher, his brogue ostentatiously, provocatively in place. She turned her head and glanced toward him. He still had his back to her, his fingers busy adjusting the stirrup leather on the gray's saddle, but she could hear the laughter in his voice.

"That's right." She wished he would go away. She didn't understand this effect he had on her. He made her feel edgy and unsettled, not like herself at all. "Where is Old Tom?"

"He's not well. Your brother sent him back to his bed."

"His bed?" Never in her life had she known Tom to admit to being sick enough to take to his bed. "What's wrong with him?"

"Twinges of rheumatism, he says." Gallagher slid down the stirrup iron. "But his heart 'tis more likely. All the signs are there."

"His heart?" Jessie stared at that distant line of huts deserted now in the heat of the day. She knew the oddest sensation, as if her entire world had tipped slightly, so that she had to reach out her hand and steady herself by bracing her palm against the mare's saddle. The universe righted itself almost at once, of course, and yet . . . And yet she knew that nothing was quite the way it had been before. All her life, Tom had been there, strong and reliable, at her side. It had often occurred to her when she looked back on her childhood that she had far more memories of Old Tom than of her mother and father combined.

It had been Old Tom, not Anselm Corbett, who held Jessie on her first pony when she was barely old enough to walk. Tom who encouraged her wonder at the joys and mysteries of the world around her, who taught her to recognize and name the myriad of fascinating things, living and nonliving, that formed her world. It was Tom who explored with her the labyrinth of caves that honeycombed the nearby mountains and shared a thousand other adventures of her growing years. He had always been called "Old" Tom, although she'd never really thought of him as old. Not old enough to be so ill now, perhaps even dying. All that time she had spent with him the other day, she thought; all that time and he hadn't said a word to her about his failing health. But then, she'd told him she wouldn't be riding to the cove soon.

She lifted her head to find the Irishman watching her, his eyes narrowed. "Why are you here?" she asked.

"Your brother has assigned me to be your new groom."

"You?"

Something in her voice made him smile, bringing a softening to the edges of his lips, a lightening to the intense glare in those fierce green eyes. "Aye."

But I don't want you, she almost said, only just catching herself in time. She felt buffeted by an overwhelming tangle of emotions, concern for Tom's health oddly mixed up with dismay and an inexplicable breathlessness that might have been excitement, except that made no sense.

Giving the gray's withers a friendly pat, the Irishman came toward her, his face impassive, his cabbage palm hat tipped low to hide those brittle, angry eyes. He wasn't a big man, yet he seemed somehow threatening. It was all she could do not to take a step back. She tried to imagine this man as her groom, riding beside her as Old Tom had done, and knew it was impossible.

Summoning up a polite society smile of the kind that had been drilled into her since childhood, she said in her best drawing room voice, "Thank you, Mr. Gallagher, but I wouldn't want to take you away from your new responsibilities with the horses. If you would be so kind as tell that young stableboy, Charlie, that I—"

"No."

The abruptness of the word startled her into silence. He was unlike any servant she'd ever known. In fact, he wasn't like a servant at all. He was too self-possessed, too self-assured, too aggressively masculine in a way she did not like.

"I suggested Charlie myself," he said, gathering up her mare's reins, "but your brother seems to think bushrangers might not find a small, underfed boy much of a deterrent to mayhem and murder." He tipped back his head so that the sun fell full on the finely sculpted planes of his face. "If you're ready to mount then, Miss?"

Jessie knew all about the bushrangers that infested the island. Most were escaped convicts: desperate men, ill-clothed and ill-fed, for the Tasmanian wilderness was not kind to those unfamiliar with its ways. Not long before she left for England, three bushrangers had jumped a farmer's wife just outside Blackhaven Bay. They'd dashed her baby's head against a tree, then taken turns at the woman herself. The problem was, the longer the convicts remained at large, the more dangerous and ruthless they became, for they knew that their recapture could only mean death—or worse. Most convicts considered being sent to someplace like Norfolk Island or Port Arthur much worse than death. And from what Jessie had heard about those places, she figured they were probably right.

The Irishman's gaze was still on her, hard and challenging, as if he were hoping she'd change her mind and not go for a ride at all. "I'm ready," she said. With this man at her side in place of Old Tom, she wouldn't be able to visit the cottage on Last Chance Point. But she could still ride out to the cove.

Taking the reins, she let him boost her up, her right leg hooking automatically around the pommel. He backed away quickly, as if he couldn't wait to put some distance between them. But he could only go as far as his own horse.

She watched through lowered lids as he swung into the saddle, his movements fluid and practiced in a way that spoke of a childhood spent on horseback. So few of the convicts sent out to Tasmania knew anything about horses. Those who did had most often been grooms or stableboys, back Home. But not Gallagher. He might do his best to play it down, but he was inescapably the kind of man who had grown up as she had done, with a groom running beside his first pony. And she found herself wondering exactly what he had done to bring him so low. To bring him to this.

His head snapped around, his gaze tangling with hers, and for a moment she saw it all in his eyes, all of his rebellious pride, all of his angry, tortured self-loathing. He had such a striking face, the cheek-bones wide and flaring, the eyes beautiful and brilliant and frightening. So very frightening. Wordlessly, she kneed her horse forward, leaving him to follow or not. For one wild moment, she actually hoped he would not.

Except that he could no more disobey an order than she could ride alone and unattended beyond the Castle. In single file, they trotted out the yard toward the drive.

JESSIE SENT her horse at a canter down the sunlit, rutted road. A rich aroma of warm earth and sweet growing things rose up from the fields of wheat and pasturage beside her. The rushing wind battered her cheeks until they stung and whipped her hair loose from beneath the low crown of her beaver hat, but she didn't care. She felt the mare's strength surging beneath her, becoming a part of her, the great muscles bunching, hooves pounding in a joyous, primitive rhythm of speed and freedom.

But no matter how hard she rode, she found she couldn't forget the Irishman there behind her. He kept intruding on her thoughts, on her peace. Awareness of his nearness shadowed her, the persistent drumming of his gray's hoof beats chasing her, so that she urged the mare on faster and faster.

The track began to climb as they reached the hills that separated the fertile, cultivated valley from the sea. Here, fields of wheat and barley and hay gave way to open forest, the great beech and blue gums casting patterns of dusky shadow and golden spring sunlight across the narrow lane, the air smelling heavily of eucalyptus oil and damp earth. Reluctantly, she slowed the mare to a walk. Except that without the distractions of noise and speed, she found herself more and more aware of the man who rode silently behind her. Twice she barely stopped herself from glancing over her shoulder at him. She found it increasingly unsettling to think of him there watching her when she could not see him. Abruptly, she checked the mare and waited for him to ride up abreast of her.

He cast her a quizzical sideways glance, which she ignored. "So, Mr. Gallagher," she said, reaching down to pat the mare's sweat-stained withers. "Tell me: have you tried to ride Finnegan's Luck yet?"

She slanted a look up at him from beneath the brim of her beaver hat. He had his gaze fastened on the winding dirt track ahead, but she saw the creases beside his mouth deepen as if with an inner smile. "Not yet."

"Not yet? You astonish me, Mr. Gallagher. Perhaps unlike your cousin Mr. Finnegan, you have some aversion to hitting the dust first thing in the morning?"

"Aye, that's the way of it," he said, putting on the Irish for her so that she had to smile.

"I haven't heard precisely how you intend to cure Lucky of his famous habit. You did tell Old Tom you have an idea, didn't you?"

"I've a few notions." He tilted back his head, his gaze lifting to the rosellas that flitted, chirping and squawking, through the branches of the black wattle above them. "But I'll not be gettin' any closer to him than a longeing rein for a while yet."

She watched him, still watching the parrots. He had several days' worth of beard darkening his cheeks and his hair was too long and ragged, so that with his head tilted back like that it hung to his shoulders. He looked rough and dark and dangerous. Yet she knew that he was not entirely what he seemed. What he liked to appear. "Why do you do that?" she asked.

He brought his gaze back to her face. "Do what?"

"Put on the Irish the way you do. You're an educated man. I hear it in your speech when you forget to watch yourself. Yet you deliberately make yourself sound like . . . " She hesitated.

"Like a bog-trotting Irishman?" His voice grated harshly, his eyes narrowing to glittering green slits. "Isn't that what we all are, to you lot? Just so many ignorant, potato-grubbing Irish—good for nothing except being conquered and ruled by Britannia's fine sons?"

She sucked in a quick, startled breath. He swung his head away, his gaze focused once more on the road ahead. "Besides, it's not entirely put on," he added more quietly, the soft Irish lilt still there even if no longer exaggerated. "It's the way the men and women I grew up around speak—the fisherman and farmers, shopkeepers and day laborers. To them, your English is as foreign as your queen, something imposed on them by outsiders. In their own homes, amongst their own kind, they still speak their own language."

He drew the long length of the reins through his free hand, the leather straps twining over his bare fingers, for he had no riding gloves to protect his work-roughened hands, as she did. "My mother, she always spoke the Gaelic at home. She loves Ireland as fiercely as she loves each of her own children, you see, and she was determined to make sure we all learned its language. She wanted us to be able to teach it to our children and our children's children."

"And your father?"

An echo of a smile touched his lips. "My father? Oh, he's a patriot, but he's also a practical man. So while my mother worked on our Gaelic, he concentrated on our English. He always said keeping traditions alive is one thing, but a man's family needs to eat and a Dublin barrister can't afford to sound like one of your bog Irish."

She could no longer look at his face. Dropping her gaze, she found herself staring at his hands instead. They held the reins so lightly, so effortlessly. He had such beautiful, delicately shaped hands, even battered and scarred as they were by brutal, endless labor. He'd taken off his jacket in the midday sun and rolled up the sleeves of his rough shirt, exposing strong sun-browned forearms and fine-boned wrists marred by ugly rings of scars.

She'd seen scars like that all of her life. Irons did that to a man. Iron shackles worn month after month as a man toiled in the heat and rain. The flesh chafed and festered, sometimes wearing down to the very bone. Even after the chains were struck off, their marks remained, a shameful, telltale legacy of past servitude. He would have scars like that on his ankles, too, she thought. So many scars.

"Is that what you were, before?" she asked quietly. "A Dublin barrister?"

He shook his head, a smile that was more mean than amused tightening his lips. "'Tis what I was aiming for, brave-hearted, idealistic young lad that I was. I was going to fight for Ireland's freedom in the courts and in Parliament, using words and grand ideas, not guns and cudgels."

So what happened? she wanted to ask, but didn't. Her throat felt tight, her eyes stinging as if with unshed tears, although that was ridiculous, for why should she feel like crying? She wished she hadn't talked to him about his past at all. She didn't want to think about the life this man had lived before, back in Ireland. About the parents and brothers and sisters he'd been forced to leave behind. She didn't want to have to think of him as anything other than what he was now. A convict groom.

Her gaze fixed on the road through the dry forest ahead, she kneed the mare forward and left him to ride behind her, as was proper.

THE BREEZE HIT THEM, strong and laden with brine as they came out of the forest at a heath-covered bluff overlooking the distant sea. Sunshine sparkled off shifting waves of a deep, beautiful aquamarine dazzled with glimmers of silver by the brilliant light.

From here they could look down, to the right, on the broad sweep of the town of Blackhaven Bay, with its neat stone houses and shops, its weathered gray docks and warehouses, its military barracks and whaling tryworks strung out along a stretch of shingled beach. Just offshore, in the deep, calm waters of the bay itself, a small fleet of fishing boats and coastal ketches rode at anchor beside two great whalers, their bare, idle masts rocking back and forth against the clear blue sky.

Only the cradling arm of the wooded headland known as Last Chance Point separated this gentle bay from Shipwreck Cove, the deeply cut inlet to the north. If a ship anchored too far out in Blackhaven Bay and if the wind was blowing a gale and the rip tides running, the unwary could be swept out around the headland and onto the rocks at the base of the jagged, blackened cliffs that plunged into the waters on the far side of the cove. But on this bright spring morning, the cove lay peaceful and serene below them, the rocks hidden by the tide that rolled softly in to break on the sandy curve of the beach.

It was here at the top of the bluff that the road they followed divided into three, with the main road continuing to the right, to Blackhaven Bay. A smaller track took off to their left, winding down to the cove itself, while another path, little traveled and partially over-grown, continued on to a small, whitewashed, rose-covered cottage just visible at the tip of the rough headland that jutted out before them, separating the cove from the bay.

The black tossed its head impatiently as Jessie drew up at the crossroads, her heart pulling her toward that windswept headland even as her commonsense reminded her of the need to turn away, to the cove below. The thought of not visiting the cottage was insupport-able. And yet without Old Tom as her groom, she wondered how she would ever manage it.

"Sure then, but that looks like Shipwreck Cove down there on our left," said the Irishman, straightening his legs and standing in the stirrups in an lazy kind of stretch.

"Thank you, Mr. Gallagher. I am aware of that," she snapped and then regretted it as she felt his gaze upon her, considering and shrewd.

"I know about your visits to the cottage on the point, if that's what's worrying you."

She started so violently her hands tightened on the reins, jerking at the bit hard enough to cause the confused horse to begin to back. "Steady," she said, running a soothing hand over the mare's sweating withers. "Sorry, girl." Lifting her head, Jessie met Gallagher's enig-matic gaze, and somehow—somehow—managed to keep her voice calm and cool. "I beg your pardon, but I can't imagine what you're talking about."

"Genevieve Strzlecki," he said, not the least put off by Jessie's haughty demeanor. "The local Fallen Woman. She lives in splendid isolation in a cottage on that spit of land jutting out there. Every gently reared lad and lass in the area is forbidden to have anything to do with her, yet you've been visiting her regularly for years." He gave her that smile she didn't like, the one that flashed wide and handsome and did nothing to warm the penetrating cold of his eyes "It's where you were originally planning to go this morning, wasn't it?"

11

LUCAS WATCHED HER EYES widen in a start of disbelief and alarm that gave way, almost at once, to a hot rush of anger. He saw her consider, briefly, an attempt at dissemblance. Knew too the instant she rejected it.

"How?" she demanded. "How could you know?" The pretty little white-stockinged mare began to dance sideways, neck arching, tail high. Miss Jesmond Corbett controlled the horse easily, her measured stare still fixed on Lucas's face. "Never say Old Tom told you."

He gave her a tight smile. "We have a saying in Ireland. *Chan sgeul ruin a chluinneas triuir.* Which means—"

"A story that three people hear is no secret," she finished for him.

He let his smile broaden. "Sure then, but you got that right enough."

She regarded him steadily, her magnificent blue eyes hidden by half lowered lids. And then he decided perhaps he wasn't as good at reading her as he'd supposed, for he couldn't begin to imagine what she was thinking. Abruptly, she wheeled away from him and kneed the mare up the overgrown track to the cottage, leaving him to bring the gray into step behind her.

They rode in silence, the horses' hooves making soft thumps in the deep humus of the shadowy, little-traveled road, the stands of tall gums beside them under grown with sweet-smelling clematis and dogwood. He could hear the sea breaking in successive distant booms against the rocky cliffs of the headland before them and the soft cry of gulls drifting on the briny breeze. Tilting back his head, he scanned the sky, its deep blue contrasting vividly with the banks of clouds beginning to build on the horizon. Reluctantly, he brought his gaze back to the woman ahead of him.

She might be haughty and proud and typically, infuriatingly English, but a man would have to be half dead, Gallagher thought, not to admire the picture they made, the high-stepping, dainty black mare and the slim, gilt-haired woman on its back. She had an easy, natural seat in the saddle, her straight, relaxed body moving in effortless rhythm with the animal beneath. She wore a jaunty, low-crowned beaver hat with a black *coque* feather that curled beguilingly against the gleaming gold of her hair, while the jacket of her dark blue riding habit had been finished at the neck with an embroidered white collar that emphasized the translucent purity of her skin. He studied the strong line of her jaw and chin, watched the sweep of her dusky lashes against her pale cheekbones as she looked down, and knew a private coil of desire, unwanted and yet undeniable, deep within his being.

The absurdity of it, the impossible, wild longing of it, almost made him want to laugh. She was as inaccessible to him as the four winds of heaven, as the darkest unknown depths of the ocean. Warrick Corbett had to be some kind of a fool, Lucas thought, to have sent off this beautiful, very desirable young woman accompanied only by a hot-blooded young Irishman who hadn't known the tender touch of a woman's hand for three long years. But then, it was the usual practice. Sometimes Lucas wondered if the big landowners such as Warrick Corbett and Harrison Tate even realized their male servants were men and not some strange species of near-eunuch, created for their convenience and having no life, no existence, no reality beyond their master's needs.

He could see the cottage now, low-roofed and rambling. With its roughly rendered walls, black-painted casement windows, and thatched roof, it looked as if it might have been spirited here from the midlands of England itself. Abruptly, Miss Jesmond Corbett reigned in and wheeled to face him, the features beneath that cocky, low-crowned hat of hers set in proud, defiant lines. But the superb blue eyes were troubled. "Will you tell?"

He met her gaze squarely. "No."

Her chin came up, and he saw her slender white throat work as she swallowed. "Why not?"

Lucas rested his hand on his thigh, his head lifting as he turned to look out over the surging blue waves and small crescent of golden sand at the curve of the cove. In a high wind with the tide running swift and unseen, Shipwreck Cove was said to be deadly. But on a calm day, this was the only safe outlet to the sea for a good fifty miles to the north or south of Blackhaven Bay. Lucas might find the idea of serving as groom to this haughty, vibrant, and damnably desirable young Englishwoman both galling and unnerving, but the truth was he had his own reasons for wanting to get to know this area better.

He had heard about this cove just days after his arrival at the Castle, and ever since then he had applied himself to learning as much as he could about the place. Except for this one cottage high on the headland, the cove was said to be uninhabited, the only other house in the area being a burned-out shell tucked into the rolling hills near the beach. It was said the ruin had been the scene of some terrible tragedy so shocking that most people avoided it if they could. Which suited Gallagher just fine, since he figured the house must at one time have had its own dock. And a deserted dock was of considerable interest to a convict determined to escape his island prison.

But he wasn't about to tell her any of that. So instead of answering her, he asked another question. "Why didn't Old Tom tell?"

"He's not that kind."

He brought his gaze back to her face. And it occurred to him, looking at her, that even if he hadn't had his own reasons for wanting to visit Shipwreck Cove, he still wouldn't have betrayed her. "Neither am I," he said.

She stared at him, her eyes as dark and troubled as a stormy sea, those solemn, uncompromising brows of hers drawn together by worried thoughts in that way she had. She didn't trust him, of course. There was no reason she should. But she had little choice.

He already knew her secret.

Humming softly to herself, Genevieve Strzlecki snipped a half opened yellow bud from one of the climbing rose bushes that scrambled over the whitewashed walls of her cottage. They had to be hardy, those roses, to grow in the salt-laden, windy atmosphere of the point. Most of their energy went into simple survival, so that when they did somehow manage to produce a rose, she usually left it as a tribute to their hardiness and perseverance. But this one she would take into the house with her. Sometimes even an indomitable rose can provide company.

A faint, distant sound from below the garden brought her head up, one hand lifting to anchor her straw hat against the breeze that always blew up from the sea. She turned her wrist automatically, as most gardeners will do, so that she touched the hat with only the back of her knuckles, for her palms and fingers were often stained with soil and the green growing things of the earth. Once, years ago, on the Isle of Capri, she had held her bonnet just so, and a handsome, dark haired man with burning eyes had whispered in her ear how beautiful she looked. How beautiful and how desirable. She smiled at the memory. He'd been French, she thought; or was it Italian? She was no longer sure.

Once she had been beautiful, beautiful and young, with a flowing golden mane of hair and skin of the smoothest, most translucent eggshell sprinkled gently with cinnamon. Now she was old, with snow-white hair and deep laugh-lines beside her eyes. But her age was something she remembered only when she looked in the mirror or on the bad days in the deepest months of winter, when the wind howled up from the South Pole and her bones ached as she slipped from her bed in the cold, gray hours of morning. Deep inside, in the core of her being, she was still the same Genevieve who had shocked them all so many years ago.

Once she had run away from everything she knew in order to be with the man she loved. Once she had waltzed with kings and raced before the trade winds in the arms of her forbidden lover. Once she had dressed in silks and satins and diamonds, and traveled the world. Now her world was reduced to this small whitewashed cottage with its peculiar collection of beloved objects and dozen resident cats, to the wind-tossed eucalyptuses and soaring black rocks of the headland, to the endless sea that stretched out eternal yet ever changing, as elemental and necessary to her continued existence as the air. Not that she minded the change in her circumstances. For as much as Genevieve had delighted in the candlelit dinners graced with silver and crystal, as much as she had luxuriated in the sumptuous feel of silks and fur trimmed velvets against naked flesh, as much as she had enjoyed the hard-muscled, hard-driving men of her past, she loved this cottage and the sea and the life she had made for herself here. She had discovered early that what we want out of life can change; that the important thing is to learn to recognize or even simply admit what we really want, and then to have the courage to reach for it.

Now she heard it again, the unmistakable trample of horses' hooves. Setting the yellow rosebud in the straw basket she held looped by its handle over her arm, she felt her heart begin to thump in anticipation.

She might be cut off from "respectable society," but Genevieve still had friends amongst the small shopkeepers, fishermen, and nongentlemen farmers of the area. And so she knew all about the coastal ketch that had brought Jesmond Corbett home to Blackhaven Bay a few days ago. But Genevieve also knew that much can happen to change a young woman in two years, especially when that young woman has traveled far from family and home for the first time.

She held herself quite still, fearing the pain of disappointment.

Then she saw them, the slim, golden-haired girl and the dark, unknown groom who followed her. Genevieve watched them rein in, watched the groom swing from his saddle with rare grace and step forward after the barest hint of hesitation to help his mistress dismount. But he was too late, for the girl managed to slip out of the saddle before he quite reached her.

Setting aside her secateurs and flower basket, Genevieve allowed herself a wide smile. A smile that stretched out into a laugh of joy and welcome and gentle contentment as Jessie came running toward her.

JESSIE SAT CURLED up in a decidedly unladylike pose on the window seat in Genevieve's kitchen, a long-haired, chocolate-colored cat purring in her lap, her boots and stockings discarded in a careless heap on the uneven brick floor beside her.

She had always loved Genevieve's kitchen, with its big black stove and bunches of herbs dangling from the rafters and wide casement windows that could be thrown open to the sun and the sea air and the rain. Jessie might not have ever set foot in her own kitchen, but she had spent many happy hours here in Genevieve's.

"Enough now about caves and cadavers and electrical experiments," Genevieve said, pushing up from her rush-seated rocker as the kettle began to boil. "As fascinating as it all is, what I really want to know is . . . " She paused, steaming tea kettle in hand, her eyebrows raised in exaggerated arches as she glanced back at Jessie. "Did you take a lover while you were in London?"

"Genevieve!" Even after all these years, Genevieve could still shock her, although by now Jessie was wise enough to realize that her friend did it deliberately. She gave a shaky laugh. "You know I am promised to Harrison."

Genevieve looked up from pouring fresh cream into a blue and white glazed pitcher. "I know your father promised you to Harrison. But it's not your father who'll be marrying him."

The cat jumped off Jessie's lap, its ears pricking forward at the sight of the cream, and began to mew hopefully. Jessie laughed again. "I promised myself to Harrison, remember?" She stood up to get the cups and saucers from the old Welsh dresser near the door and carry them back to Genevieve. "Two years ago, before I left."

Genevieve reached for the earthenware crock where she always kept a supply of macadamia biscuits. "And how do you feel about that now?"

Swinging back to the dresser for another plate, Jessie let her gaze wander for one, unguarded moment through the open door toward the barn. Earlier, she had seen the Irishman there, watering and cooling the horses. He was no longer in sight. She turned abruptly away. "I want to marry Harrison," she said firmly and set the plate beside the tea pot on Genevieve's big tin tray.

Genevieve paused, the crock balanced in one hand, to give Jessie a slow smile. "Then I am happy for you." Reaching out, she plucked a small, perfectly smooth crystal ball of polished pink quartz from the windowsill over the sink. "Do you remember this?"

"Of course I do," Jessie said as Genevieve placed the smooth, cool sphere into her palm. "I was always so intrigued by it when I was little." She smiled and held it up to the light, her lips parting in pleasure as the stone seemed to glow from within. According to Genevieve, the crystal had come to her years ago from a gypsy. "I can remember peering into it for what seemed like hours. I was convinced that if I tried hard enough, I'd be able to see my future in it. But all I ever saw was my own reflection."

"I remember." Genevieve began to pile biscuits on the plate. "I also remember that I used to wonder why you were so fascinated by it, when you grew up expecting to marry Harrison."

The ball suddenly felt warm and heavy in her hands. Jessie set it aside, her palms coming up to clasp her elbows against her side.

"I always wished I could give it to you," Genevieve was saying, "but your mother would have wondered where it came from." The cat's mews became insistent and she stooped to pour some of the cream into a saucer near the stove. "How is she? Your mother, I mean. And your brother?"

It was a question Genevieve had never failed to ask through all
the years Jessie had been coming here to visit, although as far as she
knew, Genevieve had never met either of them. "They're the same."
Jessie grinned ruefully. "Only more so."

"I was sorry to hear about the death of your father."

Jessie nodded, her throat swelling with a quick spasm of grief.
"My mother seems to have taken it very well."

For a moment, she thought Genevieve was about to say something, but she busied herself instead with the teapot. "Come," she
said, picking up the gaily painted tin tray. "Let's have our tea in the
garden. No, leave them," she added, when Jessie would have reached
for her boots. "How long has it been since you walked barefoot in the
grass?"

"Two years."

Genevieve shook her head. "Far too long."

FROM WHERE LUCAS sat on the low stone wall beside Genevieve
Strzlecki's barn, he could see the wide, placid stream that emptied
into the gentler midsection of the cove, forming a wide estuary that
cut the sandy beach in two. Beside it, if he narrowed his eyes against
the sparkle of sunlight off the swelling waves, he could just make out
the blackened, overgrown walls of the house. But if there was a dock
there, he couldn't see it from here. Somehow, he thought, he was
going to have to get down to the cove itself.

The hills behind the crescent-shaped beach were rolling and
thick with trees and scrub. But on the other side of the cove from
where he sat, the land thrust up both higher and rockier than Last
Chance Point, the sea at the base of the cliffs beat to a frothing white
by the action of the waves breaking against the rocks. Leaning sideways, Lucas plucked a long blade of grass and began to twist it
through his fingers, his gaze still fixed on the cliff on the far side of
the cove and the rocks hidden beneath the waves at its base. In bad

weather, he thought, or on a moonless night, these waters would be dangerous.

"It is beautiful, isn't it?" said Miss Jesmond Corbett from behind him. "Beautiful and deadly."

She had paused some distance away from him, beneath the big old oak that grew at the side of the barn. He hadn't heard her come up and he had no idea how long she'd been standing there. He slid off the wall and swung to face her, and she jerked and looked away quickly, as if she had been watching him and didn't want to be caught doing it. And then he laughed at himself, because it was some kind of a joke, for sure, to be thinking a lady like her would be looking at an Irish convict groom such as himself.

"If you'd sent someone to warn me of your coming," he said gruffly, reaching for his hat. "I could have had your mare ready for you."

She shrugged and walked toward the open barn doors. "I can saddle my own horse."

"Can you now?" Drawing out his brogue, he followed her into the dim, musky-sweet interior of the old barn and brought her mare out of its stall. "What's the world comin' to then, a fine, gently-reared young lady such as yourself saddling her own horse?"

She smoothed the blanket over the mare's black hide. "Don't you think me capable?"

He handed her the sidesaddle and watched as she threw it up onto her horse's back. She did it effortlessly, with practiced ease. But then, that didn't surprise him. He'd known this about her, although he couldn't have said how. "Oh, I think you're capable, all right," he said and went to saddle the gray.

"There's a trail that leads directly from here to the beach," she said with what sounded like studied casualness. "We'll take that."

He looked up, his gaze meeting hers over the gray's back. "Why?"

She led the mare out of the barn, and Lucas followed. "I told my family I was going to the cove." She gathered the reins as he stepped forward to give her a leg up. "I don't like to lie."

He gave her a boost. Only, instead of looking away discreetly as she settled into the saddle, the way he was supposed to do, he kept his gaze on her face. "And if someone were to ask you, flat out, if you'd been to Last Chance Point? Then what would you say?"

"No one would ever ask me," she said, and kneed her horse forward.

12

J ESSIE URGED her mare down the steep, narrow path to the cove, the Irishman behind her. The track they followed emptied onto the southern end of the beach, where the sand was only a narrow band against which the waves hit and broke with wind-driven violence. At the edge of the water she reined in, waiting for the Irishman to splash his big gray up beside her.

"It's a thing of wonder, surely," he said as casually as if he were remarking on the weather, "the power of this wee snippet of sand. A minute ago your soul was tarnished with the sin of deceit; now your guilt is as if it never was."

The surf crashed against their horses' legs to send up a fine spray that felt damp against her face as she stared at him, her heart pounding uncomfortably in her chest. She couldn't have said why his opinion of her mattered, yet it did. "You despise me for keeping my visits to the cottage secret, do you?"

He shook his head. "'Tis not my habit to judge other people. I'm sure you've your reasons."

She kneed the mare into a walk, her gaze on the foam-flecked, turquoise-blue water beside them. Gulls wheeled screeching over-head. The brine-scented wind blustered up stronger than ever, loosening a wisp of her hair from beneath her hat. She lifted her head, one hand coming up to hold the stray lock out of her face, her gaze still on the beautiful, deadly surge of the sea.

He brought the gray into step beside her. After a moment he said, "Who do you know who died here?"

She stared at him. "How did you know?"

"It's there in your face every time you look out at this cove."

She swallowed and turned away. "My brother. My brother Ethan died here."

The beach had widened out by now as the land beyond the sand became more gentle, but the Irishman still kept his horse at the edge of the surf where the free rush and retreat of the ocean beat upon them. She could have moved away herself, but she did not.

"When did it happen?" he asked quietly.

"Ten years ago. We all spent a lot of time at the cove in those days, although none of us as much as Warrick. He could think of nothing except going to sea." The memory brought a smile to her lips that trembled and then was gone. "He had a small sloop he kept tied up at a wharf just there where the path comes down from the point." She paused, her voice going flat with an old pain. "It's gone now. A storm tore it away some four or five years ago, and no one ever bothered to rebuild it."

Her gaze drifted back to Last Chance Point, where Genevieve's cottage was just visible through the trees on the tip of the headland. "At the time, Rose Cottage belonged to my grandmother. Originally they used it as a summer home. But after my grandfather died, my grandmother gave up their house in Hobart and came to live here."

He slanted a glance at her from beneath the broad brim of his hat. "Ethan was your oldest brother, wasn't he?" She looked at him in surprise and he added, by way of explanation, "I saw the grave."

"Oh." She nodded. "He was to be my father's heir. Papa was so proud of him. We all thought Ethan didn't care about anything except the estate, but he must have secretly envied Warrick because one day he insisted on taking out Warrick's boat." She stared out over the cove, not knowing why she was telling him all this and yet needing to go on. "It was a beautifully clear summer day, but the wind was blowing hard and the rip tides were running. Warrick didn't want Ethan to go."

"Yet he did?"

"My mother . . . she accused Warrick of being selfish, of using the wind as an excuse. It was such a pretty day." She paused, her throat working as she swallowed. "Warrick was only twelve at the time, while Ethan was almost eighteen. But he couldn't handle the sloop, not under those conditions. He ran onto the rocks there at the base of the far cliff."

She watched as he studied the far side of the cove, his eyes narrowing against the sun. From here the submerged rocks looked like black, deadly shadows just visible beneath the blue-green swell of the waves. "He couldn't swim?"

"He could. But not well enough to fight that sea. He was thrown out of the boat and beaten to death against the rocks. My mother . . ." Pausing, Jessie drew in a deep, shuddering breath. "Ethan was always her favorite. She'd come down from the cottage especially to watch him sail that afternoon. And all she could do was stand on the beach and watch him die."

"Is that why she refuses to come near the sea? Because she blames it for her son's death?"

She studied the man beside her, oddly aware of the way the wind fluttered the rough cloth of his shirt around his torso. The sun had moved behind the thickening bank of clouds, casting long shadows over the golden sand of the beach and taking the warmth out of the blustery day. "My mother has always had a problem blaming herself for anything," Jessie said dryly.

"You blame her."

"Not for Ethan's death."

"For what, then?"

A sea eagle flew above them, casting a knife-like shadow over the shifting waves. Her head fell back watching it, her breath leaving her chest in a long sigh. "For the guilt Warrick has had to carry all these years, I suppose."

"It wasn't his fault."

She shrugged. "He's always felt it to be. He knew Ethan couldn't handle the sloop but he didn't stand up to her." She smiled sadly. "That's one mistake he has never repeated since."

"I'm surprised you come here," he said, reining in beside her as they reached the broad estuary of the stream that fed into the end of the cove, "feeling the way you do about this place and having to keep your visits such a secret."

"I come to see Genevieve." She looked away from him to where the ruins of the old Grimes homestead thrust up black and broken against the thickening clouds. Her friendship with Genevieve had always been a source of troubled confusion to her. All her life Jessie had struggled against her own nature in an effort to please her mother, to be the conformable young lady her mother wanted her to be. Yet for years Jessie had stubbornly persisted in this one, secret rebellion. She sucked in a deep breath of air scented with salt and wet sand, then let it out slowly. "I don't know why exactly," she said at last, although it wasn't quite the truth. She knew her friendship with Genevieve grew out of some deep, powerful need within her. Except that she had always been too afraid to ask herself exactly what that need was. "I come because I must."

He touched her cheek, his work-scarred fingers rough against her skin as he gently turned her to face him. "I won't tell," he said softly, his hand falling back to his side.

She should have resented his touch, yet she could not. It had seemed so natural, a spontaneous gesture of comfort that left her feeling warm and oddly shaken.

She let her gaze rove over his sun-darkened face, with its fiercely beautiful bone structure and deep-set eyes. And she felt something shift deep within her. She had thought of him as brutal and dangerous, a lawless rebel who defied authority and threatened everything she believed in. And he was all of that. He was. And yet . . .

"Why not?" she said, her voice a broken whisper. "Why wouldn't you tell?"

He had a boyishly rakish smile that brought a devilish twinkle to the depths of his Irish green eyes and caused a long, beguiling crease to appear in one cheek. "Because everyone is entitled to have some secrets." He turned his head then, his gaze shifting beyond her to the ruined house that sat back a short distance from the estuary in the rolling hills beyond the beach. "Does no one ever come here?" He nodded toward the shattered walls. "It looks deserted."

"Most people avoid it. It's a sad place." Jessie turned the mare's head back down the beach.

"I've heard said it's haunted."

"Yes. I've heard that."

He glanced at her, the corners of his eyes crinkling again as if in silent amusement. "Don't you believe in ghosts, Miss Corbett?"

The mare tossed its head and mouthed the bit in impatience as Jessie gathered the reins. "I neither believe nor disbelieve in them. But I do think that when something terrible happens in a place, that place can absorb the emotions of the people who suffered there."

"And something terrible happened here?"

"Oh, yes," she said and urged her horse forward into a gentle canter that carried her away from the house and its violent past in a soft spray of flying sand.

But he surprised her by lingering a moment longer, his narrowed gaze fixed on the abandoned house and the deserted dock beside it.

THE STORM BROKE JUST after supper.

Lucas stood at the edge of the barracks' veranda, the corner post rough against his back. Rain slashed down into the yard from out of a dark and threatening sky, partially obscuring the big house that rose up like a solid fortress of respectability and affluence, distant and forbidding, through the gloom. He stared at the warm glow from those upper floor windows and wondered which room was hers. And then he wondered at himself for such a ridiculous thought. What did it matter to him where she was, what she was doing at this moment? It was absurd, the feelings he was beginning to experience for this woman. It was ridiculous enough that he found her so damnably attractive without starting to actually *care* about her. The sooner he got away from here the better, he thought, letting the wind tear at his hair and throw a sea-scented mist in his face. He breathed in deeply, smelling salt and far away, beckoning places.

"Daniel tells me you've found someplace we can keep a boat," said the Fox, his voice low as he came to stand at Gallagher's side.

Lucas nodded, his gaze captured by the wild, lightning-split night descending rapidly over the valley. "A stream emptying into Ship-wreck Cove. There's an old dock that'll give us good access to the water, while the brush is thick enough to hide the boat until we're ready to use it. People seem to stay away from the ruined house beside it, so the chances of the boat being discovered before we're ready to use it are slim."

"A ruined house? At Shipwreck Cove?"

"Aye." Lucas shifted to look into the Fox's thin, sharp-boned face. "You've heard of it, have you?"

"Oh, that's just lovely," said the Fox as if talking to the damp, wind-tossed air. "He wants us to dance a cotillion with the ghosts of Grimes House on our way out the Colony."

Lucas grinned. "You don't believe in ghosts, do you, laddie?"

For a long moment, the Fox simply stared out into the driving rain, his nostrils flaring wide, his face white and set. "Yes, I do."

Lucas took his tobacco pouch out of his pocket and tossed it to his friend. "Here. Have a chew."

The Fox caught the pouch neatly in one hand and helped himself to a slice. "Now that you've got someplace to keep it, just where are you proposing to find this boat, anyway?"

Lucas pushed away from the post and stepped down into the muddy, rain-splattered yard. "We'll find one." He let his head fall back, the rain washing cool and sweet over his face. "One way or another."

"And if we don't?"

His boots squelching in the mud, Lucas swung to look back at the thick-walled building behind him. The barracks' iron-barred door yawned black and open, waiting to enclose them for the night. He breathed deeply, felt the wind plaster his wet shirt to his back, felt the storm-cleansed evening air fill his lungs and then leave. "If we don't?" He curled his lips up into a wry travesty of a smile. "Why, then we'll just have to build us one, won't we?"

13

GALLAGHER SPENT THE NEXT MORNING working the big bay stallion on the longeing rein. He thought she might come down to the stables again but she didn't. Not that morning or the next.

He didn't want her to come. He didn't want her watching him, distracting him while he worked the stallion, and he certainly didn't want to have to play the role of respectful, subservient groom again, following obediently behind her if she should fancy going for another ride. Oh, he needed to visit the cove again, needed a closer look at that ruined homestead and the abandoned dock beside it, needed to sit and watch the waves break on the sand and crash against the cliffs and eddy around the dangerous, half-submerged rocks he'd have to get to know before he tried to pilot a boat past them on his way to the open sea beyond. But he was beginning to realize that in her own way, Miss Jesmond Corbett could prove to be every bit as hazardous to him as the rocks of Shipwreck Cove.

No, he didn't want her to come. But he couldn't seem to stop himself from watching for her.

It wasn't until Saturday morning when he was in the stables getting ready to saddle Finnegan's Luck that he felt again that faint, indefinable hum in the atmosphere and looked up to find her standing in the wide open doorway to the yard. She wore a simple morning gown of some navy cloth with a white pleated tulle fichu, and she had her hair only half swept up into a soft French knot so that the rest fell in sunlit curls around her shoulders. The fresh morning air had brought a blush to her smooth cheeks, and for one, foolish moment he let the sight of her steal his breath.

"So," he said, swinging away to where he'd set his tack. "You've come to watch, have you?"

"A saddle, Mr. Gallagher?" She pushed away from the doorway and came toward him, her hands clasped behind her back, her full skirts swaying with each jaunty step, her lips pressed together in a tight smile belied by the hostile glitter in her eyes. "Don't tell me you've finally decided to try mounting the big, bad Irish stallion yourself?"

"Aye," he said, gently settling the saddle in place.

"And so soon. I am impressed."

Lucas eyed her over the bay's broad back. She was out for his blood today, no doubt about it. It was as if she'd come to regret the emotion she'd betrayed during that strange, unexpectedly intimate conversation on the beach and now he was going to pay for it. He stooped to reach for the cinch. "You think I should have done it sooner, do you?"

Beside him, the ruffled hem of her skirt swished back and forth, back and forth. "Warrick tells me you've been taking all this time because you think it's important to learn more about a horse you're working with." He glanced up to see that smile he didn't like still curling her lips. "But then, Warrick doesn't know how familiar you already were with this particular horse."

He straightened. "Not that familiar."

She tilted her head, her brow furrowing as if with thought. "Oh? So you've learned something new, have you, Mr. Gallagher?"

"Some things."

"Indeed. Such as?"

He watched as Finnegan's Luck, ever hopeful in search of sugar and other delectable treats, chose that moment to stretch out its neck and sniff interestedly at the white fichu on Miss Corbett's bodice. Disappointed, the stallion snorted, exhaling a blast of horsy breath against her face. She let out a startled laugh, her hands coming up to catch the bay's nose and turn its head away. "No, I don't have anything you can eat, you appallingly uncivil Irishman," she said to the horse, rubbing her palm over its cheek.

He liked what that laugh did to her face, the way it swept across her features, making her look both softer and more likeable. Abruptly, he turned to reach for the bridle. "Looks like you've discovered a thing or two yourself. He does love to eat, this here Irish lad. And he has a very sweet tooth."

She let her hands ease down the horse's satiny neck. "An interesting discovery, no doubt. But not exactly relevant to his bucking problem, surely?"

"That depends," said Lucas, easing the bridle over the stallion's big head.

"On what?"

"On whether or not he's had his breakfast."

"Has he?"

"No." Reaching for the reins, Lucas led the stallion out of the stables to the small paddock.

She followed him. "That's your brilliant plan, is it? To starve the poor brute into submission?"

In the paddock, Lucas paused to adjust the stirrups. "I'm not exactly starving him. I'm just upping his interest in my bribe."

"What bribe?"

Gathering the reins loosely in one hand, Lucas nodded toward the fresh, succulent bundle of green lucerne he had hung from the fence at about saddle height some four or five paces in front of the stallion's nose. "What do you think Finnegan's Luck is more interested in? Bucking me off or getting at that nice sweet bunch of alfalfa?"

"Bucking you off," she said with a broad smile as she backed out of the way.

Gallagher laughed and swung into the saddle.

The horse quivered a moment. But it didn't take its eyes off the succulent treat dangling just out of reach. And it didn't buck.

"That's me boy," whispered Lucas. Still holding the reins loosely, he walked the bay forward the few steps needed for it to reach out and pluck the alfalfa from the fence. The morning air suddenly seemed intensely still. He could hear the clatter of milk pails in the dairy across the yard, the happy chomping of the horse's jaws chewing the lucerne, the creak of the saddle leather as he stretched. He expected her to say something, but she didn't.

"So," he said at last, leaning forward to pat the bay's shiny withers. "Did you want to go for a ride, then? You're not exactly dressed the part."

"No. I'm attending a lecture in Blackhaven Bay this morning." She paused. "How did you know?"

He swung his head and looked at her over his shoulder. She stood with her back pressed flat against the far fence, her arms braced at her side, her lips parted as if in wonder. And she looked so damned pretty it took him a moment to find his voice. "How did I know what?"

"How did you know what to do?"

Turning the horse's head, Lucas nudged the stallion toward her. "A very wise man once told me that the best way to make a horse do what you want it to is to make obeying you more pleasant than disobeying."

She watched them come at her, her head falling back as he rode closer. "I didn't think you could do it," she admitted.

"I know." He drew rein before her and brought his hand up to push his broad-brimmed hat farther back on his head. "You came here hoping to see me go sailing arse over teakettle, didn't you?"

A startled leap of laughter sparkled in the impossibly blue depths of her eyes as a naughty kind of smile curled her lips. "Yes, I suppose I did. Why?"

He stared down at her upturned face. He was suddenly, intensely serious. "That's my question. Why? Why would you want me to fail?"

The teasing laughter died out of her eyes to be replaced by a curiously bleak, haunted look. She shook her head, and he saw her fine white throat work as she swallowed. "I don't know. Perhaps because you . . . You don't behave as one ought."

He rested his forearm along the saddle's high pommel and leaned into it, the big horse moving restlessly beneath him. " 'Behaving as one ought' is important to you, is it?"

"Yes." The breeze lifted the white satin ribbons of her hat, fluttering them and causing Finnegan's Luck to snort in alarm. Reaching out one hand she caught them, wrapping them over and over again around her fist. "Yes, it is. It's not always easy at times. But I do try to do what is expected of me. To be the daughter my mother and father always wanted."

"Why?"

She jerked, her breath coming quick enough to shudder the lace at her throat, her hands tightening on the ribbons in a curiously flustered gesture. "What do you mean, why? What kind of a question is that?"

He gave her a slow smile. "Obviously a pretty good one if you can't answer it."

Her chin came up, her nostrils flaring in that haughty way she had that never failed to rub him the wrong direction. "I should think the answer is obvious. After all, if you'd broken a few less rules in your life, Mr. Gallagher, you wouldn't be in the situation you are today."

He went quite still. "Perhaps." Straightening, he gathered the bay's reins. "Then again, maybe if you'd broken a few more rules yourself, you wouldn't be caught in the situation you're in, either."

"What's wrong with my situation?" she demanded, pushing away from the fence and going to open the gate for him.

"I don't know." He paused in the open gate and looked down at her. "You tell me."

The urge to linger was strong, the urge to stay and banter words with her, to watch the subtle play of emotions across her smooth young face. To notice so many things, things a man in his position had no business noticing, such as the regal curve of her long white neck when she held her head just so, or the way a stray shaft of sunlight peeking through the clouds brought out the fire in her golden hair.

Swallowing an oath, Lucas tightened his knees and sent the hunter past her through the open gate, toward the rolling expanse of pastureland beyond.

THE MONTHLY LECTURES of Blackhaven Bay's Scientific Society were held in the town's only church, a staunchly Anglican, convict-built, neo-gothic pile of roughly cut sandstone known as St. Anthony's, perched high on a grassy, windswept hill overlooking the sea.

Herr Professor Heinrich Luneberg proved to be a tall, gangly man with a craggy face dominated by a bold black moustache and startlingly thick eyebrows he had a habit of raising and lowering to punctuate each sentence. It was one of Jessie's favorite topics, speleology, and the professor's information valuable. And still she found her mind wandering.

There was something magical about the clear, vibrant quality of the light near the sea, she thought as she let her gaze rove over the church's soaring whitewashed walls and ceiling. No wonder Genevieve loved her cottage on the point. It would be nice to live by the sea someday, Jessie decided; to wake up every morning to a world bathed in this spectacular light. And then she remembered. She already knew where she would be living the rest of her days: at Beaulieu Hall, with Harrison.

He sat on the pew beside her, and she let herself look at him. He was a handsome man, Harrison Tate, his features even and regular without straying into the flamboyant beauty of Warrick or the darkly stirring ruggedness of a man like Lucas Gallagher. There was nothing extreme about Harrison. He was the epitome of a gentleman: balanced, moderate, and in control. Always.

As if sensing her attention, he glanced down to catch her looking at him and gave her a small smile. But the smile was tight around the edges, a gentle reminder to Jessie that she should at least appear to be listening to Herr Professor Heinrich Luneberg rather than admiring the effect of the light on the church's high vaulted ceiling, or wondering why the thought of living the rest of her life at Beaulieu Hall with Harrison brought a sad, hollow ache to her chest.

AFTER THE LECTURE, they walked side by side down the grassy hill, among the churchyard's jumbled granite tombstones toward where they had left the carriage. A fitful wind was blowing, chasing intermittent small, puffy white clouds across the sun so that the afternoon felt warm and cool by turns. In the bay below the sea surged dark and brooding, beating the shingled shoreline with a rhythmic rush and drag.

"Interesting lecture," said Harrison, crooking his arm so that she could place her hand on his elbow. "Although perhaps not quite as entertaining as the time that fellow used a jolt of electricity to briefly reanimate a dead frog."

Jessie laughed. "Poor Herr Professor Luneberg. He should have been allowed to present his lecture in the limestone caverns up in Fern Gully, surrounded by mysteriously glowing crystalline stalactites and stalagmites. Then I'm convinced you'd have found caves more interesting than dead frogs."

"Huh," said Harrison. "If the Professor had been lecturing up in Fern Gully, I for one would not have attended. I didn't enjoy the caves when you dragged me through them as a child and I certainly have no desire to revisit them now."

She swung her head to look at him. "You don't think it would be interesting to explore the caves again now that you understand them better?"

An odd silence lay heavy between them. He said, "You're not seriously considering it, are you? Exploring the caves again, I mean."

"Of course I am."

Harrison's nose quivered in that way he had, although he was still smiling. "Really, Jesmond. Attending fashionable lectures on speleology is one thing. But for a grown woman to go scrambling about in caves like some bizarre thrill seeker is something else entirely."

She turned to face him, her hand sliding off his arm as her step faltered. "Something else entirely? Exactly what else is it, Harrison?"

"It's just . . . not done." He was making an obvious effort to keep his voice light, although she could see the worry in his eyes. "Even you must see it wouldn't be proper."

A passing cloud threw a shadow across the hillside as the wind gusted up to send dried eucalyptus leaves rattling along the gravel path. "Is it really so important? To always do what the Polite World considers proper?"

"Of course it is," he exclaimed, genuinely shocked.

She looked at him, at his fine, handsome face, his faultlessly starched collar, his carefully knotted neckcloth. "Have you never done anything in your entire life, Harrison, that the Polite World might consider improper?"

An oddly boyish, endearing smile quirked up the edges of his lips. Reaching out, he recaptured her hand and held it in his. "I'd like to say no, but I must confess to one secret. At the age of fourteen, I fell madly, passionately, irrevocably in love with a beautiful, utterly fascinating if slightly unpredictable girl. And my obsession with her endures to this day."

"And is love improper, then?" she asked, her voice hushed. "Is it not the done thing?"

His grip on her hand tightened as his expression grew intent, earnest. "When taken to such an excess, I fear it must be. But this is one impropriety I have no intention of giving up."

The sun had come out from behind its cloud to pour warm and golden over the hillside and the sparkling sweep of the wind-whipped bay below. She told herself she should have felt both gratified and excited to know that he loved her with such uncharacteristically wild abandon. A woman should be relieved to know that the man to whom she had given her hand loved her with such passionate devotion.

Instead, Jessie found her breath clogging her tight throat, choking her. She had the oddest sensation, as if she were sliding helplessly into a deep, dark well of despair from which there was no escape.

JESSIE HAD ALMOST FINISHED SADDLING Cimmeria when Charlie wandered into the stable, his hands shoved casually into the waist-band of his trousers, his sharp, street-bred features contorting as he labored to whistle a tune she didn't recognize.

Coming after the bright afternoon sunshine, the gloom of the stable blinded him so that it was a moment before he saw her. He pulled up short, his boots digging into the dusty straw, his whistle cutting off mid-note. "*Miss.*" He started forward, his face going white beneath his freckles. "I didn't know you was wantin' to go for a ride. Here, let me do that for you."

She gave the boy a gentle smile as she slipped the bridle over her mare's ears. "You weren't here before I went away to London, were you?"

"No, ma'am." He hovered at her elbow and shifted anxiously from one foot to the other. "If you'll just let me—"

"I often saddle my own horse," she said, and led the mare out into the yard to the mounting block.

The boy followed her, his eyes widening. "But Miss—You can't mean to go riding without a groom."

She swung her head to look at him over her shoulder. "Heaven help me. You sound like Harrison."

"Miss?"

"Never mind." She gave the boy another smile so he'd know she wasn't irritated with him. "I looked in on Old Tom, but he's not well and I didn't want to trouble him." Gathering the reins, she reached for the pommel.

"I can get Gallagher," said Charlie, still dancing nervously about her. "He's just in the south paddock working with a chestnut gelding the master's been having trouble with."

Jessie settled into the saddle with practiced ease. "I don't need Mr. Gallagher, thank you. I'm not going any appreciable distance." And then, before he could say anything more, she touched her heel to the mare's side and cantered away.

She took the track toward the rainforest-clad mountains, although she wasn't intending to ride that far. The clouds had cleared, so that the sun shone warmly out of the clear blue sky and she was grateful for the forest of myrtle beech and gum, musk and blackwood that soon closed in around her, bathing her with cooling shade. She didn't understand the reckless moodiness that drove her, that squeezed at her chest and left her aching for things she couldn't name. She urged the mare into a trot, going farther than she'd meant to, not even knowing why she'd come this way or why she felt such a driving need to be alone, far away from everyone. It was one of burdens of being an unmarried gentlewoman. One was never allowed to be alone.

Once she was married to Harrison, she thought, at least some of the restraints under which she labored would ease. But the thought brought her no comfort, only a sick twisting of her stomach that both shocked and confused her. And then she wondered when it had happened, when she had stopped knowing her own thoughts and understanding her own feelings. When she had begun hiding her wants and needs and desires so deeply she could no longer recognize them herself.

She drew rein abruptly. It was only when she lifted her head and glanced around that she realized where she had come and why. She was in a small glade of open grass scattered with native blue orchids and fiery Christmas bells and delicate white butterfly iris. Surrounded by feathery ferns sheltered beneath tall stringybarks and silver wattles, the meadow seemed steeped in a timeless kind of peace. Yet it was here seven years ago that Jessie's brother Reid had been killed, the second of Beatrice Corbett's children to meet a violent death. He'd been only seventeen that day when a small band of Aboriginals had caught him on his way back from a hunting expedition and struck him with their spears and waddies so many times his casket had had to be kept discreetly closed. But the Aborigines were all gone now, the last ones rounded up like wild animals and herded off to a small, distant island where they were slowly dying of the white man's diseases and alcoholism and hopelessness. Here she could be utterly alone.

The weight pressing down on her chest seemed worse and she slid out of the saddle, her boots sinking into the soft green grass that grew high in the clearing. There was a log lying at the edge of the clearing and she went to it, her breath leaving her lungs in a soft sigh as she curled down to wrap her arms around her bent legs and press her forehead against her knees.

She didn't know how long she sat there, her eyes squeezed closed, her nose burning with unshed tears. She heard the wind rustling through the grass. The pink robin that had been singing fell still, and her heart began to thump wildly in her breast with an unidentified but very real fear. She knew quite certainly that she was no longer alone.

Twisting her head sideways, she opened her eyes to find herself staring at a man's thin, dirty leg, scarred and covered with the ragged remnant of a convict's coarse duck trousers. He wore no boots, only badly cured kangaroo skins wrapped around his feet and tied with thongs about the ankles.

Ankles that showed the dreadful, brutalizing legacy left by the deep bite of iron shackles.

14

A COLD, HELPLESS TERROR seized her, squeezing Jessie's lungs so that she couldn't even cry out. She let her head fall back, her gaze traveling upward.

The man was emaciated. His shoulders hunched forward in a stoop, and his skin where it showed through the jagged rents in his trousers was streaked with grime and covered in weeping sores. His dark brown hair and beard both hung long and matted with twigs and dirt, his eyes shining out at her from a curtain of reeking filth. But he wore a gentleman's fine linen shirt gaping open at the neck and barely soiled. He looked wild and crazy. Not human at all.

She surged to her feet and took a step back so quickly she stumbled. The man's lips pulled open into a smile revealing blackened teeth. "Well," he said. "Look what we got us here."

Another man laughed, drawing her attention. There were two others, she now realized. A younger, bearded man with dirty blond hair, tattered convict trousers, and what looked like a gentleman's jacket pulled over his bare chest. And another man, a black man. Not an Aboriginal black, but an African black by the looks of him, although he must have been in the bush for a very long time for his clothes were entirely made of animal skins. He wasn't as dirty as the other two, but for some reason he frightened her more.

"What do you want?" she asked, or tried to ask. Her throat was so tight with fear she barely pushed the words out.

The younger man, the blond man, wore a pair of fine boots and held a double-barreled flintlock pistol cradled in one hand. It was a gentleman's pistol, the handle inlaid with a design in mother of pearl. She wondered if the pistol had belonged to the same gentleman as the coat and boots and fine shirt, and what had happened to him.

She watched as the blond convict caressed the pistol handle, his gaze traveling over her in a way that made her stomach lurch. "What do you think we want, then?" He lifted his chin as he spoke, the words coming out soft and mocking.

"If you want my horse," she said, trying desperately to keep the quaver out of her voice, "you'd best take it and be on your way quickly, before someone catches you."

"Oh, we'll take your horse, all right," said the other white man, the one with the dirty brown hair and the sickening smile. "But we'll take a ride on you first."

Jessie had been raised with three brothers, and they hadn't always been as careful in their speech around her as they might have been. She recognized the expression and knew what it meant.

She ran.

The blond man stood between her and the downhill track so she ran the only direction she could, ducking beneath one of the low wattles that edged the clearing. She had to hold up the long, heavy train of her riding habit in one hand, which pulled the skirt tight against her knees, hobbling her. The frond of a tree fern slapped her in the eyes and she threw her free arm in front of her face, so that she missed seeing the rock half buried beneath a drift of old leaf litter until it caught her foot and sent her crashing down, her hands and knees sinking into the damp, spongy humus of the forest floor.

Desperately sucking air into her heaving lungs, she tried to scramble to her feet and felt a man's bony hand clamp around her ankle. "You wasn't tryin' to run away, now was you?" said the soft voice of the blond man.

"*Let me go.*" Rolling sideways, she kicked out at his face with her free foot, but he only jerked his head sideways and laughed at her.

"You fools," she heard the black man say. "Let her go so we can get out of here. You do this and her people will never rest until they've hunted us down."

"You don't want a turn, you don't gotta take one." The dark haired man loomed over her, his fine linen shirt glowing white in the gloom. "But I'll be damned if I'll pass up a chance like this."

"You'd be better off listening to your friend," said Jessie. The fear rose hot and thick in her throat, but she swallowed it down, trying to make herself sound confident. Credible. "My groom is right behind me."

The blond man grinned. "Now why don't I believe you?"

"*Quiet.* Someone's coming."

The black man's hissed warning cut through the trees, wiping the smile from the blond man's face. Grasping her arm in a painful grip, he hauled her up with him. She tried to jerk away, yanking at his hold on her, and felt the muzzle of his gun pressing cold against the side of her head. She sucked in the cloying scent of decaying vegetation and burnt powder and her own sick fear. Before she could stop it, a sound like a low whimper escaped from between her lips.

"Shut up," he whispered, dragging her with him back to the clearing. "Make another sound and I'll kill you. You and whoever's coming, both."

His fingers tightened on her arm, digging into her flesh and wrenching her to a halt so that they stood facing the spot where the track emptied out of the forest gloom into the meadow. It felt almost hot in the open, the sun pouring down bright and sickening through the yawning gap in the trees. She realized her hat was gone, lost somewhere in the wood. A bead of sweat formed on her forehead to trickle down the side of her face. She heard a fly buzzing past and the steady drumming of a horse ridden up the hill fast. Held tightly in a savage grip, she stared across the clearing and saw a gleaming chestnut appear from between the trees. The man on its back reined in sharply.

"Make any sudden moves," said the blond man, pushing the gun muzzle into Jessie's cheek hard enough for her to feel it against her teeth, "and her brains are gonna be decorating this pretty little glade."

The chestnut gelding was notoriously bad tempered. It sidled nervously, its head jerking up, its ears lying flat against the poll, its hooves prancing on the ground as if it could smell the fear hanging heavy and rank in the air. For one fleeting instant, Lucas Gallagher's gaze met hers across the hot, tense clearing, his face set in impassive lines. She could read nothing in his dark, hooded eyes—not sympathy, not alarm, not comfort. He was after all a convict, just like the three half-crazy, desperate bushrangers who held her. He had no reason to try to help her and every reason like them to hate her. Jessie sank her teeth into her lower lip and bit deep to keep it from trembling.

Controlling the restless horse with ease, Gallagher settled back in his saddle, his free hand lying relaxed and idle on his thigh. "Now why the hell should I care what you do with her brains?" he said calmly.

The blond man laughed and shifted the gun so that it now pointed at Gallagher instead of her. "No reason I can think of." The smile on his face faded. "Just make sure you get down nice and easy. All we want from you is the horse. And the clothes."

Gallagher hesitated in the act of throwing his leg over the pommel. Bushrangers often stole a man's clothes along with his money and his horse. The bush was hard on clothes, and most escaped convicts weren't very good at making do with kangaroo skins. "I don't particularly mind giving up the horse. It's not mine." He slid to his feet in one graceful motion. "But the clothes are a different matter entirely."

"Why? They'll give you new ones," said the dark-haired man, scratching his chest as he walked over to lay a hand on the chestnut's reins. The big gelding jerked up its head and whinnied sharply in a way that had the bushranger stepping back nervously.

"Once I get back to the estate," said Gallagher, his gaze shifting between the three men. "But I'm thinking the trip downhill won't be too comfortable, me on foot and exposed to the elements in every sense of the word. Besides . . ." He nodded to where Jessie stood, her fists knotted in the skirt of her riding habit. "There's a lady present."

"That there is." The blond man's gaze shifted to her, his face going oddly, frighteningly taut as he let go of Jessie's arm to run his hot, spread hand up her shoulder and down over her breast in a way that made her stomach heave. "And a mighty fine one she is, too."

"Keep your filthy hands off me," she said in a tight voice, wrenching sideways and brushing his hand away as if it were some giant insect.

Looking up, she found herself staring into the twin black holes of the pistol's muzzle. "Do that again," said the blond man, "and I'll kill you."

"You've got her horse," said Gallagher, beginning to strip off his rugged gray coat. He tossed it inside out toward the dark-haired man. His waistcoat followed. "Why don't you let her go?"

The blond man laughed, swaggering slightly as he swung to face Gallagher again. "You, my friend, don't have much of an imagination." Reaching sideways, he caught Jessie behind the neck in a killing grip and shook her, hard. This time, she didn't move. "But I'm willin' to let you have a turn on her anyway." His lips curled as he nodded toward the black man standing motionless at the edge of the clearing as if to disassociate himself from the events taking place before him. "Maybe we'll even let you have her before Parker there."

"Not me," said the man called Parker, folding his arms over his massive black chest. "I don't hold with forcing women."

Still struggling to turn Gallagher's coat right side out, the third man looked up, his dark hair falling in front of his face. "Why the hell not? They're going to hang you anyway. And the Lord knows you're already on your way to hell."

Parker only shook his head, while the blond man waggled the

muzzle of his gun at Gallagher again. "What about you? You got some moral objection to rape?"

Gallagher stood with his hands on his hips, his eyes narrowed. "Nope." Watching him, Jessie had to gulp down deep breaths to keep from sobbing out loud.

"Good." The blond man's smile dissolved into a cold, frightening stare as he leveled the gun once again at Gallagher's chest. "Now keep strippin'."

For one burning instant, their gazes locked, Gallagher's and the blond man's. Then Gallagher shrugged and turned half away. "All right," he said, and Jessie felt some secret hope she hadn't even dared to acknowledge drain out of her, leaving her weak and numb. She watched him loosen the ties at his neck and pull off his coarse shirt in one, easy motion. "Here." Bunching the shirt into a wad, he sent it sailing through the air toward the blond man, who had to let go of Jessie's neck and lunge forward to reach it. "Catch."

Crouching down, Gallagher fumbled with the laces of his boots. "Think these are going to fit those big feet of yours, Parker?" He cast a sideways glance at the black man who still stood impassively, watching.

"I don't need 'em," said Parker, his wide nostrils flaring with a quickly indrawn breath.

"Might as well try them, if you're going to hang for them." Tugging off his boot, Gallagher tossed it into the thick grass a short distance in front of the black man.

The black man was still bending over to pick up the boot when Jessie caught a glimpse of the knife that had appeared in Gallagher's hand. With a quick flick of his wrist, he sent the blade flying through the air with a lethal whistle that ended in a startled cry as the knife imbedded itself in the blond man's bare chest.

Jessie felt a scream rise in her throat and bit it back. The man stumbled, his stolen coat tails swinging, his gentleman's boots crunching in the grass. He dropped his chin to his neck, his eyes widening as he stared at the knife sticking out of the naked white flesh of his chest as if he couldn't understand how the thing came to be there. For the space of a heartbeat he wavered in the warm sun, the light slowing fading from his eyes. Her hands covering her mouth, Jessie watched him die.

He was dead before he hit the ground.

But Gallagher was already moving, curling forward into a roll that carried him across the meadow toward the chestnut. He came up clutching a thick branch in both hands that he swung like a shillelagh into the side of the other white man's filthy head, hard enough to spin the man around and send him careening into the horse's gleaming flanks. The gelding reared up, its hooves flailing the air. The dark-haired man disappeared.

Sobbing out loud now, Jessie fell to her knees, crawling on all fours through the high grass toward the dead bushranger and the pistol he still held loosely gripped in his outflung, motionless hand.

"It's been a while, Gallagher," she heard the black man, Parker, say.

She looked to where Gallagher stood, his half-naked body in a low fighter's crouch as he faced the remaining bushranger across some ten feet of sunlit meadow. "I have no quarrel with you, Parker."

"No," said Parker as Jessie's hand closed around the handle of the pistol. "But I reckon she does."

Jessie surged to her feet, the gun clutched in both hands and leveled on the black man's bare chest. Her breath came so hard and fast her entire body was shuddering, but she held the gun steady. "That's right," she said, her voice cold and tight with rage. "And I intend to see you hang."

The black man froze, hands splaying out at his sides.

Gallagher swung to stare at her. For a moment all was silent except for the rustle of the wind in the grass and the click of one of the horse's teeth on its bit. "You know how to use that thing?" he asked.

She nodded, not looking at him. "I could outshoot my father by the time I was twelve."

"Ever shoot a man?"

"No. But I could, if I had to."

He took a step toward her, and then another and another, until he was close enough that she could see the faint gleam of amusement lightening his shadowed eyes. "I do believe you could." Reaching out, he laid his hand over hers on the ornate handle of the gun. He was suddenly serious. "But I 'm asking you not to."

"*What?*"

His hold on her was light and nonthreatening, although he didn't remove his hand. She could feel the scars on his palm through the thin leather of her glove. He was close enough that she could see his naked, sun-darkened chest lift as he breathed, see the corded muscles of his throat work as he swallowed. "I'm asking you to let him go. I know him. He's not a dangerous man. And he did you no real harm."

Her hair had fallen into her face and she shook her head, trying unsuccessfully to clear her eyes. "No real harm? If you hadn't come when you did, those men would have *raped* me."

"I wasn't no part of that," said Parker, his wide-eyed gaze fixed on the pistol in Jessie's hand as if he expected it to go off accidentally at any moment. "You know I wasn't."

She stared at him coldly. "You were with them."

"A man doesn't last too long in this bush on his own," Gallagher said, his voice quiet. "You know that."

She glanced at him, although she was careful not to look at him too long. He was too close to her, too naked, too . . . male. "I heard a saying once, something to the effect that when a man lays down with dogs he must expect to rise up with fleas."

"*An te a luidheas leis na madraidh, eireochaidh se leis na dearnadaidh.*" He gave her a slow grin. "You've spent too much time with Old Tom." She watched the smile fade slowly from his lips to be replaced with an almost frighteningly intense expression. "Give me the gun, Miss Corbett. If you turn him over to the authorities, they'll send him to Port Arthur or Norfolk Island. Or hang him."

It occurred to her then that she ought to be afraid of him, of Gallagher; that he could simply take the gun away from her without asking. And she wondered if that's what he would do if she said no.

She searched his dark, closed face, her breath coming quick and tight. "You would do this for him?"

"Yes."

From deep within the forest came the harsh cry of a cockatoo. She realized there'd been a subtle shift in the light as afternoon stretched out toward evening. Torn apart by indecision and uncertainty and a deep sense of confusion, she let her gaze travel from Gallagher to the black man and back again. What he was asking of her was wrong by everything she had been taught. Yet he had saved her life at the risk of his own. Now he was asking her for this and she didn't see how she could in all justice deny him. "I won't lie about his presence here," she said. "When Warrick finds out what happened, he'll hunt your friend down and kill him."

"Yes."

She gave him the gun and walked away.

She went to sit on the log at the edge of the clearing. She sank slowly, her body trembling, her arms wrapping around her waist, hugging herself. "If you want anything from these dead men," she heard Gallagher say, "you'd best take it and get out of here fast." The other man's response was a murmur too low for her to hear.

She stared across the clearing to where the gelding now grazed peacefully, the sun shiny on its well-groomed hide. The body of the second bushranger lay sprawled nearby in an ungainly heap. She wondered if he, too, was dead. Then she saw his head and decided he must be. A fly buzzed and for a moment she thought she might be sick. She put her head on her knees and squeezed her eyes shut. She could hear the two men moving around the glade, but she didn't look up.

After a time she heard Gallagher say, "You stay on this island and they're going to catch you. Maybe sooner, maybe later, but it'll happen."

Raising her head, she stared across the glade to where the two men now stood near the uphill track. "Yeah?" said Parker, his chest rumbling with a mirthless laugh. "What you reckon I oughta do?

Swim back to Africa? Man, even if that was possible, I was born in *Georgia*."

She watched as Gallagher rested his hands on his hips, his pelvis tipping forward in that intensely masculine stance he had. He was facing away from her and he hadn't put on his shirt yet, so that she could see the lean, muscled line of his naked back, the beautiful, taut brown flesh crisscrossed with that patchwork of old scars that only could have been left by a cat-o'-nine-tails. Someone at some time had whipped this man long and savagely. Jessie drew in a sharp, oddly painful breath at the thought. She had seen men flogged. Seen them stripped and tied to the triangle, seen their backs ripped open and bloody, their bodies quivering with shock and agony. She thought of those things being done to this man and felt her chest swell with a confusing upsurge of dangerous, impossible emotions.

"You could make your way to the northwest," he was saying, "where the sealers' ships sometimes put in. They're always looking to take on new men and they aren't particular about any prior claims Her Britannic Majesty might have to their hides."

Parker shook his head. "I've heard about those sealers. They might take on men, but they don't treat 'em good. I already been a slave twice, first in Georgia and then here. I'd rather be dead."

"A slave can always run away again," Gallagher said after a moment. "A dead man can't."

Parker shrugged and showed his teeth in a wide smile. "At least when you die you're free." He held out his hand and Gallagher took it in a strong, two-handed clasp. "Thanks, mate."

She felt ill at ease, as if she were intruding on something private, something she had no business observing. Swinging her head away, she stared across the meadow to where a small brown quoll had ventured out, nose twitching and ears alert.

A shadow fell across her and she looked up to find Gallagher standing beside her, the pistol held loosely in one hand. She glanced beyond him. The black man was gone. They were alone in the wind-ruffled meadow.

Reversing the pistol, he held it out to her butt first. "Take it."

She stared at the gun, then raised her gaze slowly to the man who held it.

"Take it," he said again. "If I get caught with it, it'll be my death."

She took the pistol, the weight of it dragging her arm down to her side. She let it lie in the grass. "What you did was crazy."

"Was it?" He propped his foot up on the log beside her and leaned his elbow into his knee. "Parker is a good man. He doesn't deserve to hang."

"A good man?" she repeated incredulously. "He's an escaped criminal and a thief. And heaven knows what he was originally transported for."

"Murder, I think." He slanted a look at her, as if daring her to be shocked. His mouth was smiling, but his eyes remained hard and haunted. "A man doesn't always plan the direction his life takes, Miss Corbett. Sometimes things just . . . happen."

They stared at each other and the moment dragged out, became something more. She felt her breathing slow, making her acutely aware of the parting of her lips, the lifting of her chest, the flush of warmth in her cheeks. And all the while he watched her—watched her until the burning intensity of those dark, haunted eyes became too much for her to bear.

Lowering her gaze, she found herself staring at his leg, where the cuff of his convict trousers had pulled up, showing the old shackle scar ringing his ankle. She pushed up from the log and took a quick step away from him, away from what was happening. She meant to cross the clearing to where her mare, Cimmeria, grazed quietly. But then she saw the two dead bushrangers tied face down across her saddle and she paused, her hands coming up to cup her elbows and draw them in close against her sides. Tipping back her head, she stared at the clear blue sky above her. "I haven't thanked you for saving my life," she said, her back to him, her voice sounding strangled.

She was aware of him coming up behind her. She thought for one absurd moment that he might touch her, but of course he did not.

"Yes, you have. By letting Parker go. Besides, we don't know that they would have killed you."

"What they were going to do to me . . ." She swallowed painfully as the horror of it reared up inside her, churning her stomach and stealing her breath. "It's said to be worse than death."

"It's not."

She looked at him over her shoulder. "It's not what?"

"Worse than death. It's painful and humiliating and degrading, and you might feel like you want to die afterward. But if you're strong, you can rise above it and survive."

She studied his hard profile, the elegant flare of his cheek, the unexpectedly sensitive line of his mouth. He was so beautiful, so beautiful and fierce and frighteningly attractive that she sometimes thought she might burn up from the inside, just looking at him. "Why did you ride after me?" she asked. "Did Warrick send you?"

"No." Turning away, he went to pick up his shirt where it lay forgotten in the grass. "Charlie told me you'd taken Cimmeria out by yourself, and I knew there were bushrangers in the neighborhood."

"How could you have known?"

"I knew," he said simply, thrusting his arms through the sleeves of his shirt. And even though she knew she should look away, she couldn't help it: she watched him.

He was a fine figure of a man, his body browned by the sun and hardened by years of physical labor. She let her gaze rove over the carefully defined sinew and muscle of broad chest and taut stomach, of strong arms and powerful shoulders. She watched him pull the shirt over his head and ease it down over his torso, and she wondered what such a man's body would feel like beneath a woman's hands. And then her breath caught in her throat because she realized it was what she wanted—to touch him, to put her hands on him. It was a wicked impulse, an indecent thought. A forbidden yearning. She could not understand where it had come from, but she couldn't pretend it hadn't been there.

Still tying the laces at his neck, he walked to where he had thrown his waistcoat. She stood, her elbows clutched to her sides, her pulse racing as she watched the muscles flex beneath his shirt as he reached to pick it up. She noticed the way the sun struck his face as he straightened, the harsh light emphasizing the shadows beneath his brows and his high cheekbones. And then she realized she was doing it again, watching him, and she swung her head away and did not watch anymore.

The sun sank behind the treetops, throwing the glade into shadow. The breeze that stirred the grass and rustled the leaves was cooler now and scented with the approach of evening. She should be home safe in her own room dressing for dinner. Not here in this violence-haunted glade with two dead bushrangers lashed to her mare and an incomprehensible welling of impossible, reprehensible thoughts and desires stealing her breath and leaving her trembling and confused.

He swung into the saddle and kneed the chestnut toward her, leading the mare. "Give me your hand," he said, his saddle leather creaking as he reached down to her.

She held out her hand in its soft lady's riding glove and watched his strong, scarred fingers close around her wrist. She swung up behind him, acutely aware of the pressure of her inner thighs against him as she settled on the gelding's broad back. She remembered reading about how long ago, in the Middle Ages, noble ladies embarking on long journeys would often ride like this, pillion, behind their grooms. She thought about those ladies and their grooms as Gallagher kneed the stallion out of the sun-dappled glade and into the quiet gloom of the forest track.

It seemed such a familiar, intimate thing to do, to sit so close to a man, her legs spread wide by the horse, her body touching his so intimately, her hands resting low on his hips. She could feel the heat of him through the coarse cloth of his shirt, feel the supple leanness and strength of his body moving gracefully with the rhythm of the chestnut's gait. She was intensely, achingly aware of him, not as a simple convict but as a man. A man who had risked his own life to save hers, and then risked it again to save a friend. A man whose half-naked body fascinated her and intrigued her and left her wondering what he would look like without any clothes on at all.

A man whose very nearness made her heart race with an exhilarating, treacherous rush of forbidden excitement and unbidden, impossible desire.

15

THAT NIGHT THE WIND blew wild and fierce. Jessie stood for a long time at the French doors of her room, watching it and listening. Then she threw a cloak over her nightdress and went out into the storm-wracked darkness.

As she left of the shelter of the lower veranda, the wind slammed into her, stealing her breath and snatching at the billowing folds of her wrap until her knuckles ached from the strain of clutching it to her. The air was full of dust and the roar of the wind crashing through the trees in the park and the smell of coming rain, although the moon still shone fitfully through breaks in the jumbling, turbulent clouds. She had no particular destination in mind; she was simply surrendering to the need to throw open her soul to the wildness of the wind and the restlessness of the night.

She cut across the grass, the earth cool and damp beneath her bare feet. When she reached the rippling, moon-glimmered expanse of the pond, she stopped, one arm looping around a low branch of the old apple tree she had climbed so often as a child. At some point since she'd come home, the apple blossoms had all shriveled up and blown away. She hadn't noticed their passing, but she felt now a great aching sadness at their loss.

She looked back at the house rising so big and strong out of the darkness. She knew and loved each arched recess, each soaring chimney. Yet it all looked somehow different from the way she remembered. Or perhaps it wasn't different, she thought, sucking the storm-charged air deep into her lungs. Perhaps she was the one who had changed, or at least her situation had changed. Because in a subtle but very real sense, the house was no longer hers. Or at least it soon wouldn't be, not in the way it had been through all her growing-up years. If she married Harrison, she would come here only for brief visits as a guest before going away again.

And then she wondered at herself for the thought, because of course she would marry Harrison. She had always known she would marry Harrison. He had been her closest friend since childhood and he would make an ideal husband for her future. Everyone said so. He was gentle, handsome, well bred, and wealthy. Their lives together would be a familiar and therefore comfortable round of all that she had ever known. And if a dangerous, unwanted voice dared to whisper that such a future might not be what she really wanted, that didn't mean she had to listen. She didn't need to let herself—*shouldn't* let herself—remember the way a certain pair of Irish green eyes could light up with laughter, or the forbidden, unexpected way her heart beat faster and her breath caught whenever those eyes met hers.

She watched as a long shadow moved from beneath the stone arcade of the veranda and passed out into the moonlight; a familiar shadow that wound its way purposefully through the parklands toward her, not stopping until he was close enough that the moon cast his silhouette across the wind-tossed water.

He was still dressed as if for riding, in knee-high boots and doeskin breeches, for they'd been out until long past dark, the men, visiting the glade where she'd been attacked and arranging to have an Aboriginal tracker brought in to study the site in the morning. He'd come in too late for dinner, so that he'd simply ordered a tray and retreated to the library with a bottle of brandy. She hadn't seen him since.

"Care to tell me why you've developed this disturbing predilection for wandering off by yourself?" Warrick asked, his gaze on the shifting surface of the pond.

The wind blew her loose hair into her face and she brought up one hand to catch it. "How did you know I was out here?"

"I saw you." He dropped his chin to his chest, but not before she caught the slow smile that curled his lips. "I was on the veranda."

"Perhaps it's that kind of night," she said, trying to keep her voice light. "It calls to the restlessness within us."

He swung his head to look at her. "Are you restless, Jess?"

She tightened her arm around the branch, feeling the bark rough and cold through the thin cloth of her nightgown. "This afternoon was . . . unsettling."

"Near rape generally is."

"Please." She put out her hand as if to hold him off. "Don't you scold me, too. I've already had enough of that from Mother."

He let out a short huff of laughter. "I'm not enough of a sanctimonious ass to tell you off for anything you've done. You know that. Just like I know you're not here, now, because of what happened with those bushrangers. My guess is that whatever drove you out here tonight is the same thing that made you ride off alone toward the mountains this afternoon." His expression became serious, his gaze probing. "What is it, Jess? What's wrong?"

She let go of the tree and went to stand beside him, her arms crossed at her chest, her hands anchoring her cloak closer to her body. She found she couldn't look at him and ask what she wanted to ask, so she stared instead at the choppy waters of the pond. "Do you know what you want out of life, Warrick?"

She looked at him then and saw the bitter twisting of his lips that might have been a smile. "Hell." He let out his breath in a sound that was supposed to be a laugh but wasn't. "I'm lucky if I know at any given moment whether I want a shot of brandy or a pint of bitters, let alone what I want out of life."

"You did know, once."

He turned to stare off into the darkened, wind-thrashed parkland, his shoulders in the flawlessly tailored riding jacket held painfully taut, his head thrown back, the fingers of one hand tapping restlessly against his thigh. "Did I? I thought I did, all right. I was going to sail every sea known to man and then a few more no one had even discovered yet. I was going to be an officer by the time I was sixteen and captain of my own ship before I was twenty-five." He paused, holding himself very still. "All boys have dreams. Not many of us get to live them."

"Some do."

He spun to face her, his eyes a little wild, his breath coming so hard and fast she could see it lifting the fine cloth of his shirt. "Do they? Ethan dreamed of growing up to make this estate bigger and more prosperous than our father ever imagined."

"Ethan died," she said quietly.

"That's right. Ethan died. And my dreams of going to sea died along with him. With him and with Reid."

The wind gusted between them, colder than before and heavy with the promise of the coming rain. "What do you think Reid dreamed of?" she asked, her throat tight.

"I don't know. He never said." Warrick took a step that brought him beside her again, his eyes narrowing. "Is that why you went to the clearing this afternoon? Because of Reid?"

"I'm not sure."

The wind blew her hair across her face again and he brought up both hands to gently rake back the tangled strands. "I thought you always knew what you wanted, Jess. Marriage. Children. This valley. And don't try to tell me you've developed a hankering to run off and study the geology of Outer Mongolia because I won't believe you. You love this island."

"I do. It's not that. It's . . ." She wrapped her fingers around his wrists, gripping him tightly, straining to put her thoughts into words. "All my life, it's as if I've had this struggle going on inside of me. Between the Jessie who wanted to learn about things like botany and astronomy and gallop her horse faster than was considered proper for a gentlewoman, and the Jesmond who wanted to make Mother and Father happy by being the kind of daughter they could be proud of."

"You mean, by turning yourself into Catherine and Jane."

"No. Yes. I don't know. That's the problem. I don't know who I am anymore. Who I even want to be."

"Don't you?"

She found she couldn't answer him, could no longer even bear the intensity of his gaze, and bowed her head. It had begun to rain. She could hear the splattering of big drops hitting the leaves of the trees and pocketing the surface of the pond. She felt the wetness on her cheeks but didn't realize she was crying until Warrick's arms came around her, pulling her tight against him so that she felt the rumble in his chest when he said, "I'm sorry, Jess. Oh, God, I'm sorry."

EARLY THE NEXT MORNING, Warrick and Harrison assembled in the yard with the dogs and an Aboriginal tracker and the constable and his men from Blackhaven Bay. From the upper veranda, Jessie watched them milling about, the dogs barking in the crisp morning air, the men arguing, the horses tossing their heads and feeling their bits. She watched them ride off toward the cloud-covered mountains, then she went inside.

She spent the morning in genteel pursuits, embroidering a spray of rosebuds on the yoke of one of her nightgowns and then reading *The Pickwick Papers* to her mother, who was suffering from nervous prostration brought on by the previous day's incident. In the afternoon Jessie walked over to spend some time with Philippa Tate at Beaulieu Hall. She cut through the park the way she had done so often as a child, enjoying the freshness of the rain-cleansed air and the sting of the cool wind against her cheeks.

She did not go near the stables.

The men came back late that evening, hot and tired and frustrated with their lack of success, for the night's rain had washed away the escaped convict's scent and much of his sign. Jessie stood in the hall listening to their grumbling and felt her heart lighten with a relief that both surprised and disturbed her.

But of course they went out again the very next day. The morning dawned sunny and dry and the constable was confident that the dogs would run across the "bolter's" scent before noon.

This time she didn't watch them ride out but went instead to the top floor of the house. There were eight bedrooms in the house that Anselm Corbett had built, for his family had once been large. She walked first to Catherine's room, then to Jane's. Neither room had changed much; the heavy mahogany four-poster beds, dressers, washstands, and hipbaths were all still there. Only the personal touches, the straw hats and seashells, the posy holders and silver-handled hair brushes were gone, swept ruthlessly away by Beatrice Corbett, who could talk endlessly about the virtues of her dead children but could not bear to look upon anything that had once been theirs.

Standing in the middle of Jane's shadowed room, Jessie turned a small circle and tried to remember what the room had looked like when her sister was alive. Except she couldn't.

They'd all caught the scarlet fever that summer—Catherine and Jane and Jessie. Catherine had been twenty-one and preparing to wed a wealthy merchant from Launceston, while Jane was seventeen. Jessie remembered them both as quiet, composed young women, gracious and demure and properly subdued. But lately she'd begun to wonder if she really remembered them as they were or if she remembered Catherine and Jane only as her mother liked to remember them, as her mother's words had painted them over the years. Once when Jessie had done something particularly disgraceful, her mother had flown into a cold rage and said she wished Jessie had died that summer instead of her sisters. Beatrice never said such a thing again, of course, for rages were bad form and Beatrice seldom succumbed to them. But Jessie had never forgotten her mother's words. And she never would.

Her chest tight with a tumult of emotions, Jessie walked to the window and folded back the long cedar shutters to let in the light.

But even the sun couldn't warm the room; it remained cold and empty and dead.

For a long time Jessie stood with her hands on the shutters, her forehead pressed against the glass of the French doors. Then she quietly closed the shutters and went back to her own room. And then, quickly, before she could change her mind, she put on her riding dress and went down to the stables.

"ANXIOUS FOR A RUN, ARE YOU, BOY?" Lucas stroked the young gray's cheek and laughed softly when the gelding shoved its nose against his chest and snorted as if in agreement.

Something made him look up then toward the young woman who worked beside him saddling her mare in the warm, diffuse light of the stables. She wore a different riding dress today, this one made of a dark cloth of hunter green with a frothy jabot of lace at her throat and a nipped-in waist that emphasized the sensual flare of her hips. He supposed the other one must have been ruined by the rough handling the bushrangers gave her up in that glen. He tried not to remember what she'd looked like, with her hair coming down and her dress torn and her face trembling with fear.

She didn't look the least bit trembly today. There was a kind of coiled defiance about her, an almost determined recklessness that worried him. But then she tended to worry him a lot because he didn't quite understand her and couldn't predict her. She didn't always behave the way he expected her to, didn't say the things he would have expected a woman such as her to say. For she was not, he was beginning to realize, the woman he'd thought her to be. And that worried him more than anything else.

He'd learned that she wasn't simply capable of saddling her own horse; she actually preferred it. Whereas most women of her kind exaggerated their weakness and incompetence as a way of under-scoring their femininity and gentility, she seemed to like the idea of being strong and capable. Strong and capable and smart. It was one of the things he liked about her, one of the things he admired about her. And he did admire her even though he didn't want to. He'd thought her haughty and spoiled at first, and he knew that in some ways she was. But there was so much more to her than that, so much more he'd like to come to know and understand—if he weren't a convict and she weren't . . . who she was.

He watched mildly puzzled as she buckled a leather satchel to the back of her saddle. "Where are we going, then?" he asked, fitting the bridle over the gray's head.

She glanced over her shoulder at him, her lips curling up into a saucy smile. "That's not exactly the sort of question a humble groom is supposed to ask, Mr. Gallagher."

"Yeah? Well I've always had a difficult time with humility."

She turned away abruptly to gather her mare's reins. "There's a series of limestone caves to the south of here at a place called Fern Gully. I want to explore them."

"Caves?" he repeated.

"You don't like caves, Mr. Gallagher?"

"Well now," he said as they led their horses together out into the yard. "That depends. They're all right I suppose, as long as you don't have to live in one." He had lived in one in the Comeragh Mountains when there was a price on his head and he was on the run from the British army. But he wasn't about to tell her that.

She laughed softly. "I don't intend to live at Fern Gully." She adjusted her reins and prepared to mount. "Unless of course we get lost."

He gave her a leg up. "Shouldn't you tell someone where we're going? Just in case we do get lost."

"I've told Old Tom." She focused on arranging her skirts, her face half-averted.

"Old Tom?"

"That's right."

He took a step back, his head tilted as he watched her. "None of them know you very well, do they?" he said quietly. "Your family, I mean."

Her head snapped up, her lips parting on a quickly indrawn breath as she sent the white-socked mare dancing sideways in a caper that was both deliberate and damnably attractive. "You, sir, are impertinent."

He held himself quite still, his gaze never leaving her face. "Yeah, I suppose I am. But at least I'm honest."

He watched, calmly, as her fist tightened around her riding crop. He thought she might bring it down across his face, but he made no effort to move out of her way, simply stared up at her. And he realized with an odd sense of detachment that he wanted her to strike him. He wanted her to make him hate her.

Without a word, she turned the mare's head and touched her heel to the horse's side, sending Cimmeria cantering out of the yard so that he had to vault into the saddle and hurry to catch up with her.

16

W ARRICK LIFTED HIS BROAD-BRIMMED HAT and swore softly as he swiped one well-tailored arm across his damp forehead. The day had turned warm. Too bloody warm to be out beating the bush for some bloody bolter who was obviously bloody good at not getting caught. He turned his horse off the main road onto a half-hidden track that snaked down a hillside covered with blackwood and stringybark thickly under grown with dogwood and sassafras. He swore again.

After thundering about the district in a show of force that was as useless as it was supposed to be impressive, they'd finally agreed to split up, the constable and his men taking the Aboriginal tracker up into the mountains while Harrison and his hounds crisscrossed the north end of the valley with the kind of systematic thoroughness for which Harrison was known. Warrick himself had offered to check out the hills that sheltered the valley from the storm-battered coast. Not that he was expecting to find anything. He was beginning to think it'd just be sheer, dumb luck if any of them stumbled upon the man they were after.

He'd heard about this particular absconder before, this Parker

Jones, for big black men with American drawls weren't that common in Tasmania. They said he was a runaway slave who had escaped from some Georgia plantation by stowing onboard a ship going to England. Except that he hadn't enjoyed his freedom for very long. He'd made the mistake of killing a sailor in a brawl on a Portsmouth dock, which landed him free passage on another ship, a convict ship, this one bound for penal servitude in Australia. They weren't called slaves, of course, the men who labored in chains and under the lash on the government roads, or down in the mines, or on the private estates with their big, fancy houses and vast fields. It wasn't exactly slavery. But Warrick wondered if a man like Parker saw much of a difference.

Warrick thought about the senselessness of the man's life, the bloody, soul-destroying irony of it, as he let his horse pick its way across an open slope of daisy-sprinkled grass waving lazily beneath a gloriously clear sky. Then he crested a small rise and there unexpectedly stretched the ocean, swelling blue and breathtaking into the distance. He reined in hard, his chest aching with bittersweet joy the way it did each time he caught sight of the sea.

It had always been his passion, the sea, since before he could even remember. His father had laughed at him for it and teased him and wondered aloud how the grandson of a Lancashire miller and a Hampshire half-pay army officer could have come up with such a notion, of going to sea and captaining his own ship. But Anselm hadn't discouraged him. Not until that dreadful summer when the grinding waves and jagged, deadly rocks of Shipwreck Cove took Ethan. After that the mere mention of the sea was enough to make Beatrice go white and tight-lipped. Warrick had hoped that in time she'd get over it. But then just a few years later, his second brother, Reid, had died, too, beneath the Aboriginals' spears. And then there had been no question of Warrick going to sea, since of Beatrice and Anselm Corbett's three sons Warrick was the only one left alive. Which meant that the Castle and its vast estates would some day be his. Whether he wanted them or not.

He sucked in a deep breath, filling his head with the scent of warm grass and sweet dogwood and the faint briny tang of the sea. Then he turned his back on that shining vista and nudged his horse forward.

A pair of Cape Barren geese took flight, beating the air clumsily with their great wings. He let his reins go slack, his hat brim tipping up as he watched them gain altitude and grace as they rose to the sky. And then he became aware of a strange stillness, an indefinable tingling of awareness, and he knew he was being watched himself.

He swung about sharply, his gaze sweeping the nearby line of mountain lilac, his hand going to the pistol he'd stuck in the waist-band of his doeskin riding breeches. The breeze blew through the treetops, shifting the leaves and swaying the branches. There was no one in sight. But the feeling of being watched remained. He slipped his gun from his belt.

A girl's laughter rang out, soft and gurgling like the rush of a clear mountain stream. "Are you going to shoot me then? Should I be afraid?"

His head fell back. She sat perched in the lowest branch of the tree right above him, a slim sprite of a girl with long, dangling brown legs and hair the color of a fiery sunrise that tumbled in wild, sinful disorder about her shoulders and down her back.

"What are you doing out here all alone?" he asked, easing his gun back beneath his waistband.

She pushed off the branch to land with a lithe, feline grace close enough to startle his horse into a head-tossing snort. "I live here."

She was built long and thin, with a small head and exquisitely fine bones, like some kind of exotic, well-bred cat. She had eyes like a cat, too: big and golden and gleaming with some inner knowledge that beckoned him and intrigued him and scared him all at once. "No one lives here," he said.

She laughed again.

She wore nothing but an old-fashioned gown of blue cotton with a pointed bodice and a ragged skirt that was too short, so that he could see the long length of her bare calves and her feet. He didn't think she could be wearing anything beneath it. The material stretched tightly across her firm young breasts, showing the clear outline of her dark nipples. As she walked up to him, the skirt shifted sensuously against her lean flanks and hugged the long stretch of her thighs. She was all legs and hair and eyes, and he thought he had never seen anyone so captivating. Reaching up, she put her hand on his booted calf. "We do."

He saw it then, beyond her. A crude cottage of freestone with a thatched roof and plank door built so that it faced the sea. It looked like something out of the wilds of the Scottish highlands or the poorest dell in Ireland. Yet this exquisite creature lived there.

"You look hot," she said, smiling up at him.

She had a wide mouth for such a dainty face, the teeth even and white, her lips full and beckoning. Warrick felt his breath catch in his throat so that he could barely force the words out. "I am."

She turned, her hand brushing across his knee, brushing him with raw fire. "Follow me."

She didn't say where she was going, but he followed her. She led him not toward the hut but down the slope into a ravine that plunged toward the sea. The ravine was deeper than he'd expected it to be, the vegetation lush and dense with great reaching branches of myrtle beech and celery-top pine that met overhead to create a leafy green canopy of deep shade and sweet coolness. A strange hush closed around him and it was as if he moved through an enchanted world, the only sound the dull thump of his horse's hooves in the thickness of the path. And still he followed her, descending into a shadowy realm of ferns and lichens and moisture-laden air. He heard the rush of nearby water and knew that she had led him to a stream.

He could see it now, a swiftly flowing brook of clear water and tumbled, moss-covered boulders shaded by tree ferns and native laurels. Where the path ended, the stream widened out into a small pool backed up behind a crude stone cairn. He reined in, nodding toward the dam. "Did you make that?"

"No. It was here when we came. I think the black men made it."
She waded out ahead of him into the pool until the water lapped
almost to her knees, then swung around to face him. "Come in," she
said, and began to unfasten her dress. The cloth of her dress slid up,
slowly revealing naked hips and waist and breasts. Her body was slim
and lithe and achingly desirable, and Warrick wanted to laugh—not
at her but at himself, because he was so bloody shocked he almost
fell off his horse. He'd always thought of himself as wild and reckless
and daring, as a man who flouted the rules and did exactly as he
pleased. But he realized now he wasn't really that way. Not compared
to this girl.

She pulled the dress off over her head and draped it across a
nearby overhanging branch. He'd been right; she wore nothing
beneath it, nothing except a sheathed knife strapped to her naked
thigh. He watched as she untied the thongs that held it in place and
set the knife on top of her dress. She tilted her head, smiling up at
him. "Aren't you going to get off that horse and come in?"

He stretched back in the saddle, straightening out his legs in the
stirrups and ducking his head so that his hat brim hid his face. "I
don't think so."

"You're shy."

He gave her a slow smile. "I think I've just discovered that I am."

She had a beautiful body, long and lean, with high small
breasts and an unbelievably tiny waist. Her woman's hair was the
same fiery hue as the curls that tumbled about her shoulders, the
flesh of her breasts and hips the same golden color as her arms and
legs. She obviously spent a fair amount of time out in the sun
without her clothes. It was a thought that both excited and worried
him.

"Aren't you afraid?" he asked.

She took a step back to where the water was deep enough to come
up to her waist. "Of what?"

He rested the palms of his hands on the pommel of his saddle
and leaned into it. "Of me."

She took another step. The water must have been over her head now, for she was forced to make wide sweeping motions with her hands to keep afloat. "You wouldn't hurt me."

He watched the graceful movements of her long arms, watched the way her breasts showed firm and luminous through the clear water. The urge was strong in him, the urge to get down off his horse and wade into the water and pull her up against his hard body. He wanted to take her with swift savage lust, to bear her down into a bed of ferns and wrap her long naked legs around his waist and bury himself inside her here beneath the wide blue sky. Not since he'd lost his dreams of the sea had he wanted anything the way he wanted this woman with the wild hair and wild ways. This woman who was everything he'd always wanted to be and more.

"You can't know I wouldn't hurt you," he said, his voice rough. "You have no idea who I am."

"Yes, I do. You're Mr. Warrick Corbett of Castle Corbett." She arched her neck, shaking her hair back from her face. Dark and wet and clinging, it slid over her shoulders to float dreamily about her naked breasts. "I've seen you before." Her smile broadened. "Seen you and wanted you."

She was utterly guileless and direct, a bewitching contradiction of simplicity and wisdom, innocence and experience. "Do you always do what you want?" he asked.

"Yes." She studied him, her brows drawing together, her cat's eyes glimmering. "But you don't."

He started to argue, to say he always did as he damned well pleased. Then he remembered he was still sitting on his horse.

She rolled forward, giving him a glimpse of small, tight buttocks beckoning pale and gently rounded beneath the shimmering water. "Why are you out here anyway, Mr. Corbett of Castle Corbett?"

He lifted his gaze to the sea just visible as a vivid band of blue up ahead and realized that he had utterly forgotten the reason he was here. "I'm looking for a bushranger. A big black man with a bad reputation. An American black, not an Aboriginal. You might want to be a bit more careful until he's caught."

"I've seen your bushranger."

He swung his head to look at her again. She waded into the shallows, her naked body glistening wet and beckoning in the shadowy light. Looking at her, he felt the breath leave his chest in a painful rush, felt his entire body tightening up with desire, tighter and tighter, so that he was barely aware of the sense of her words and had to swallow before he could even speak. "When?"

"This morning." She stepped from the pool, her head tilted at a pensive angle as she looked up at him. "He's dead."

Warrick's hands tightened on his reins. "Where?"

"I'll show you." She snagged her dress off the branch and put it on again as she moved downstream, the worn cloth clinging to her wet skin, revealing and enhancing rather than hiding the lean line of her flanks, the incredible length of her legs. There was a small path there that he hadn't noticed before, almost lost amid the leafy sassafras and dogwood and fern. He followed her toward the sea, his gaze fascinated by the swing of her skirt, the flash of her bare calves. He found himself forgetting again about bushrangers and runaway slaves for whole minutes at a time until he saw a man's body lying face up in the bracken some fifteen to twenty feet from the edge of the cliff. The thunder of the falls made by the stream shooting over the cliff face rumbled loud in the air.

"How did he die?" Warrick asked, sliding carefully out of the saddle, his gun in his hand.

She shrugged. "Dicken found him like this."

Warrick crouched down beside the body. "Dicken?"

"My brother."

Warrick slipped his gun back into his waistband. He didn't need to be a doctor to know that Parker Jones had been dead for hours, although he could see nothing on the man's kangaroo-skin-clad body to suggest how he might have died. Gingerly, Warrick turned the dead man over and saw the knife wound high up and to one side in the man's back.

He glanced at the girl. "Do you have a horse I can put him on?"

"No. We've only a donkey name of McBain."

He stood up. "I'll see it's returned to you."

"No." She shook her head, an enigmatic smile curling that impossibly wide mouth. "You've got to bring it back yourself."

He met her strange, golden-brown gaze. He knew what she was suggesting. Knew too that he was accepting when he said, "All right. I will."

It wasn't until he rode away that he realized he'd never even asked her name.

17

JESSIE REINED IN to let Gallagher catch up with her, her undignified, unladylike burst of fury as short-lived as it was inexplicable and troubling. She waited until he was abreast of her before kneeing her horse forward again into a trot. They rode through the fields side by side, the atmosphere between them heavily charged and uncomfortable.

"I would like to beg your pardon," she said after a moment. "My actions were inexcusable." She waited through a tense, seemingly interminable silence, then prodded gently, "Now it's your turn to apologize for deliberately goading me."

He swung his head to look at her, his face dark and unreadable. "What I said wouldn't have touched you on the raw like that if you hadn't been thinking the same thing yourself."

It was true, of course, although ungentlemanly of him to say it. But then he didn't play by her society's rules of polite falsity. It was one of the things about him that both fascinated and attracted her.

She studied him from beneath her lashes, aware in spite of herself of the graceful way his lithe body moved to the rhythm of the animal beneath him. He had his hat pushed negligently back on his head as he stared up at the rainforest-covered mountains rising misty and lushly green ahead of them. The day had turned surprisingly warm for this early in spring, the bright sunlight catching the highlights in his ragged dark hair and causing him to squint in a way that brought creases to the corners of his eyes and made it look as if he were smiling, although she knew he was not. He looked wild and rough and breathtakingly, dangerously attractive, and she knew she'd been wrong to risk this ride with him. To risk herself with him.

The track was growing steeper, the beech and celery-top pine denser, shutting out the light and the heat and the wide-open spaces. She reined the mare in to a walk, her gaze on his face as he pulled the gray in beside her. "Why did you save my life the other day?" she asked abruptly.

He stared back at her in that proud, defiant way he had. "You think I should have let them have you, do you?"

She leaned forward to pat Cimmeria's hot, sweat-darkened withers. "It's what most men in your position would have done, isn't it? Why risk your life to save someone you despise?"

There was a pause filled with the gentle plodding of their horses' hooves and the almost audible hush of the moist, heavy air of the rainforest closing in around them. He said, "What makes you think I despise you?"

She swung her head away to fix her gaze on the thickly towering, moss-covered trunks ahead. "Because I am English and you are intensely, fiercely Irish. Because I try to play by society's rules even when I think they're wrong. Because I hide the things I do, the person I really am from those closest to me. Because I visit my dearest friend in secret as if I were ashamed of her, when I'm not. I'm not."

Even though she wasn't looking at him, she was aware of his gaze upon her. She could feel him looking at her—it was that intense, whatever this thing was between them, this thing neither of them wanted. "What'd she do, then," he asked unexpectedly, "this Genevieve Strzlecki, that makes her such an unacceptable person for you to know?"

"She fell in love with a Polish count," Jessie said simply, for Genevieve's past was no secret on this small island.

"Och, 'tis a terrible social solecism, sure enough," he said, his brogue thickly exaggerated. "Especially for an Englishwoman."

His words surprised her into a laugh that faded into a soft sigh. "Under the circumstances, I'm afraid it was. Her parents had already arranged a match for her with a gently bred and very wealthy merchant from Hobart."

"Was he poor then, this count?"

She shook her head, her gaze coming back, inevitably, to the fierce profile of the man beside her. "Quite the reverse."

He slanted a glance at her from beneath the broad brim of his hat. "So why would her parents favor some Hobart merchant over a well-heeled count? Surely his title more than made up for the deficiencies in his nationality and religion?"

"It would have, no doubt, if he hadn't already had a wife."

"Ah," he said in a way that made her smile again.

"He was the victim of an arranged marriage himself, you see, and the resulting union was not a happy one. He and his wife lived completely apart."

"So this count, he fell in love with your Genevieve, did he?"

"Oh, yes," she said, a little shocked at herself for the frankness of the things she was saying. She tried to imagine herself discussing lovers and unhappy marriages with Harrison and couldn't. It should have seemed strange to be having this conversation with this rough Irishman, this servant, this *convict*. It should have seemed strange but it didn't. And that was the strangest thing of all.

"Genevieve knew he would never be able to marry her," Jessie said. "She knew it, but she loved him so desperately she couldn't conceive of life without him. So she ran away with him." It had always struck her as such an intolerable choice to be faced with having to make. She drew in a deep, soul-shaking sigh just at the thought of it, her gaze falling to the reins woven loosely between her gloved fingers. "I can't imagine doing such a thing. Leaving my home, my family, my friends. Turning myself into a social outcast cut off from everything I'd always held most dear. It must have been like a kind of death."

"She evidently thought it was worth it."

Jessie glanced up to find him staring at her through narrowed, unreadable eyes. "How can anything be worth that?"

An odd smile touched his lips, a smile so sad and sweet it tugged at her heart. "You've obviously never been in love."

Have you? she wanted to ask, although of course she did not. However strange this conversation might be, she couldn't bring herself to be that bold.

The rainforest grew thicker around them, the leafy crowns of the spreading trees meeting overhead to throw the path into dense shadow. The air here was cooler and damp, the smooth brown of the tree trunks contrasting with the dark green of the ferns and mosses and splashed with color from the native laurels and the fragrant, star-shaped white flowers of the sassafras.

"So how long have you been visiting her?" he asked quietly.

"Since I was twelve." She tilted back her head to a watch a honeyeater take flight from a nearby branch. "My friend Philippa Tate has always thought my study of science a daring sort of rebellion, but it's not. Not really. My mother might try to discourage me from my interests, but she has never actually forbidden me to do any of the things I do. Yet with Genevieve ... "

"Your mother forbade you to have anything to do with her, I've no doubt."

Jessie huffed a soft laugh. "Quite specifically. As a child of course I had no idea what Genevieve had done. I didn't even know her real name. She was simply the Fallen Woman of Last Chance Point. I didn't know what a fallen woman was in those days, so I decided she must have suffered a fall from the cove's cliffs that had left her hideously deformed and shocking to look at. I thought that's why my mother warned me away from her."

"Is that why you went to see her? Because it was forbidden?"

"I'm not the type to do something simply because it's forbidden, remember? I leave that sort of blind rebellion to Warrick."

"So what happened?"

"I was hunting for fossils in the limestone beds near her cottage one day when we met quite by chance. We got to talking about rocks and . . ." Jessie shrugged. "She became my friend."

"And if you were to sit down one day and calmly announce to your mother and your betrothed that Genevieve Strzlecki is your dearest friend? What would happen?"

"They would be shocked. Mortified. Hysterical. They would forbid me to have anything to do with her ever again."

"And would you? Would you stop going to see her?"

"No." She let out a long, painful breath. "No, of course not. But my life would be . . . hideous."

"So you visit her in secret. You try hard to be the woman your family wants you to be and when you decide you simply can't, you avoid flinging your choices in their faces. The way I see it, if anyone is at fault it's them for not accepting you the way you are. For forcing you to choose between the woman you were meant to be and their love."

He paused, and she swung her head to find him watching her, his eyes shadowed by his hat brim.

"I don't despise you," he said softly. "Who am I to despise you or even presume to judge you for the choices you've felt you had to make in your life? And as for the other . . ." He gave her a crooked smile that deepened the dimple in his cheek in a way that clutched treacherously at her heart. "Well, it's not your fault you're English."

She laughed out loud, then knew a swift rush of sadness as the sounds of her laughter faded away into the hushed silence of the rainforest around them. She didn't want to see him in this way; didn't want to see him as wise or admirable or any of the other things she now knew him to be. She wanted to go on thinking of him as rough and uncivilized and savage. What could have possessed her, she wondered, to forget for so many minutes at a time both who and what he was?

To speak so freely of love and risks and impossible choices to an Irish convict with a disreputable past and a blighted future and shackle scars on his wrists.

"I'M NOT sure this is such a good idea," said Lucas, raising his candle so that the flame leapt up to cast flickering light and darkly shifting shadows across the low ceiling and smooth, close gray walls of the cave entrance. The gurgling rush of the water flowing beside them filled the frigid air, echoing and re-echoing with a beckoning promise of mystery he found both seductive and dangerous.

They had left the horses tethered a short scramble down the hill, beside the stream that flowed swift and clean and unbelievably cold from the bowels of the mountain. Since the unexpected intimacy of that strangely frank conversation on the track, they had both withdrawn largely into silence. Yet the memory of the words they'd spoken seemed to hang between them.

The words they'd spoken and the ones they hadn't.

"Afraid, Mr. Gallagher?"

He met the challenging sparkle in her eyes and grinned. "I prefer to think of it as being sensible."

"Huh. I've been here before, remember?" She tilted back her head to study the rock ceiling arching above them. "It's a maze of passageways and interlocking chambers, but as long as we follow the stream we'll be in no danger of getting lost."

He watched, quietly, hopelessly mesmerized as the golden light of the candle she held played over the fine features of her face, emphasized the curve of her cheek, the sweep of her lashes, the delicate length of her slim white neck. She looked so utterly feminine and yet so strong and brave and vibrantly, energetically alive, that he smiled. Then something caught within him, something jagged and wrenchingly painful, and he found he had to turn away.

"We've caves like this in the Comeragh Mountains," he said walking ahead of her up the gentle slope of slippery smooth rock that edged the stream, his candle held before him. "In county Waterford not far from where I was born. People go missing in them all the time."

"You mean the cattle thieves and highwaymen who hide in them?" she said, falling into step behind him.

He laughed softly. "Aye. A few of those, too. Although mainly your bespectacled, pipe-smoking Englishman-types who fancy themselves scientists." He heard her huff of expelled breath and smiled into the candlelit gloom. "Are we just going for a stroll here or is there actually something to see?"

"Be patient, Mr. Gallagher."

"For what?" he said, or started to say when the low, darkly walled gallery they followed opened up spectacularly into a great soaring chamber of glittering crystalline beauty, its walls draped in gleaming flows of delicately fluted and undulating calcite. From the ceiling dripped stone icicles that reached down to the counterparts thrusting up from the cavern floor to create great thick pillars that sparkled wetlike in the candle's glow.

"Jesus, Mary, Joseph, and all the Saints," he whispered, holding out his candle. The light flickered over a gleaming frozen waterfall rendered in brilliant, translucent stone that ranged in color from clear to white streaked with yellow and orange and brown.

She came to stand beside him. The beauty of this place, of this moment, became something they shared, something intimate and memorable. "So?" she said quietly. "Is this something to see, Mr. Gallagher, or what?"

He stared down at her. She stood hugging herself with one arm thrown across her breast, her hand clutching her opposite shoulder. She turned in a slow pirouette, her candle held high. She'd managed to get a smudge of dirt on one pale cheek and her hair was coming down in little stray wisps. No one seeing her now, he thought, would ever mistake her for being haughty or unapproachable. He watched her lips part on a sigh of pleasure, watched her eyes widen in awe, and he knew it again, that swift rush of dangerous emotions that caught at his chest and stole his breath. "It's something to see, all right," he said, his voice coming out rough.

She glanced up at him, and a sudden shiver quivered through her body, hard enough to make her shudder.

"You're cold," he said, turning away to carefully nest his candle in a crevice beside them.

She shook her head. "No. I'm all right."

"Take my coat," he said, stripping it off.

"But you'll get cold yourself."

"I'm used to the cold." He held it out to her. "Here."

Her mouth trembled into a smile as she reached for it. "Thank you."

Her hand closed over his, and the shock of it, the burning ignition of that simple unexpected touch flared between them. He felt it in his flesh, in his blood, in his being. And God help him, she must have felt it too because he saw her eyes widen, her chest rising as she sucked in a gasp of air and stepped back quickly—too quickly, for the stone floor of the cavern was smooth and damp and slippery. She gave a startled mew of alarm and lurched sideways as her feet shot out from beneath her.

Lucas lunged forward, his fingers digging into the soft flesh of her arms as he caught her just above her elbows. She fell against him, her candle tumbling into darkness as her hands clutched wildly at his shirtfront. He tried to steady her, but her momentum was too great. She simply pulled him over with her.

"Bloody hell," he yelped, twisting as they fell so that his hip struck the cold stone first, then his shoulder, then his back. "Bloody hell," he swore again and heard her start to laugh.

They rolled together in a tangle of arms and legs and mingling laughter that echoed about the ancient chamber. Rolled until she came to rest flat on her back with him on top of her. He was laughing still when he raised himself up on his elbows and gazed down at her in the flickering light cast by their remaining candle. Then the laughter died on his lips.

She had her head tipped back, her neck arching white and tempting, her eyes almost squeezed shut as her body convulsed with her own laughter. He was achingly aware of her soft body beneath his, of the delicate strength of her lady's hands clenching his shoulders, of the hot rush of unbidden desire that swelled within him.

And then she wasn't laughing anymore, the smile on her face fading slowly as her gaze caught and held his. The strained hush of their breathing hung heavy in the air. It was as if his world had narrowed until it consisted of nothing but the golden flair of candlelight and the pungent scent of cold wet stone and this woman.

He saw her lips part, felt her hands quiver on his shoulders in a movement that was almost but not quite a caress. A breathless silence opened up between them, a silence filled with the dangerous lure of the forbidden. She had the most beautiful eyes, he thought. Eyes set deep and wide and dark now with unmistakable desire. And for one, unguarded moment, he lost himself in them.

His lips hovered no more than a breath from hers. It would have been the most natural thing in the world for him to simply lower his head and kiss her. If he had been anyone else he would have done it. But he was a convict groom, *her* convict groom, doomed to a life of servitude and disgrace or an early death, while she was . . . who she was.

He rolled away from her and sat up, his back to her, his head bowed as he sought to bring his ragged breathing and raging desires under control.

"You were right," she said, her voice echoing queerly in the vast, primeval chamber around them.

He swung his head to look at her over his shoulder. She sat with her knees bent to one side, her hands folded together and pressed beneath her chin. In the faint light of the remaining candle, her face looked pale, her eyes dark and huge. He felt the memory of what had happened between them—what had almost happened—pound through him. "What was I right about, then?" he asked hoarsely.

He watched, surprised and entranced, as a strange smile curled her lips. "This wasn't such a good idea."

18

"I THINK WE NEED to be talking about this."

Jessie turned her head to look at him across the jumble of wet-dark rocks and sun-dappled white water that separated them. He stood on the near bank of the fast-flowing stream, his legs braced wide, his hands resting on his hips. There was a small waterfall here, a white veil of roaring water that threw up a fine, cooling mist to drift through the tangled temperate rainforest of smooth-barked trees and leafy ferns and lush creepers.

After leaving the cave she had climbed out here to the middle of the stream, to sit on one of the big boulders that had tumbled down from the mountain and bathe her face in the clear water. To bathe her face and tidy her hair and put some distance between them while she tried to come to terms with what had just happened—or rather almost happened in the dark, secret depths of that cave.

She had thought she could control the impossible, unbidden, unwanted attraction she had developed for this man, for this rough, rebellious Irishman, for this *convict,* God help her. She had thought she could control *herself.* But nothing she had experienced thus far in life had prepared her for the wondrous shock of finding herself pinned beneath his body, or for the sweet temptation that shimmered in the air as his lips hovered so close to hers. She had known such a swift rush of want, such an aching need, that she hadn't been able to hide it.

And neither had he.

She had seen the look of arousal sharpening his features, the hunger in his eyes; felt the quivering need in his body as he gazed down at her. He had wanted her with a fierceness that both frightened and excited her. And she wondered now if there had ever been a time when he hadn't been aware of her in that way a man is aware of a woman. For the awareness had been there, surely, in the heart-stopping intensity of his smile, in the smoldering fire of his eyes whenever he looked at her—a fire that warmed her belly and stole her breath and robbed her of any reflection except forbidden, sinful thoughts of him. He might have come close to dipping his head and tasting what he surely knew she was willing to give. But he hadn't done it because no man in his situation would. Not even such a wild, mad Irishman as he.

She curled her fingers around the damp stone at her sides, the sharp edge biting into her flesh. She had thought— hoped—that they might be able to go on as they had before, simply pretending that dangerous moment in the cave had never occurred, pretending that this—this thing between them, whatever it was, wasn't really there. She had forgotten that he wasn't like her, that he believed in brutal honesty whatever the cost. He didn't play by her society's rules.

"In my world, we don't speak of such things," she said, her voice so hushed that it was almost drowned out by the roar of the water and the incessant *creek-creek* of unseen frogs. "Anything awkward or even slightly untoward, we simply behave as if it never happened."

"Is that what you want?"

She looked at his compelling, high-boned face with its dark, powerful eyes and hard mouth, and she felt something crack within her. She sucked in a deep breath as if that might somehow ease the pain, although she was beginning to fear this was one pain that was only going to keep getting worse and worse. "Nothing did happen. I fell and you caught me. That's all." And then she said it again, as if saying it could make it so. "Nothing happened."

"You're right." He crossed the stream toward her, his gray convict coat flaring open, his gaze never leaving her face as he leaped nimbly from one rock to the next. "You're right," he said again, pausing on one of the huge boulders that loomed over her so that she had to tilt back her head to look up at him. "Nothing happened. Nothing's been happening since that first day when you saw me splitting rocks in your brother's quarry. Nothing happened when you watched me work that crazy Irish stallion you bought or when we rode along the beach of Shipwreck Cove. But if we're not bloody careful, something is going to happen one day soon. And then there will be the devil to pay. For me and for you."

She dropped her gaze to her hands, clasped fast now in her lap. "Warrick is petitioning the governor to grant you a full pardon for saving me from the bushrangers. Once that's granted, you'll be able to go away from here." It was what she wanted, for him to go away, far, far away. It was what she wanted and yet the mere thought of it shifted the pain within her, made it strike deeper, sharper. "You'll be able to leave then. We need never see each other again."

"It won't be granted."

"The petition?" She watched him step down to a lower rock, his back held straight and taut, his face turned half away from her. "You can't know that."

"Can't I?"

A fearful suspicion seized her and wouldn't let her go. "Why were you transported?"

One corner of his mouth crooked up in a smile that deepened that sinfully attractive crease in his cheek without quite warming his eyes. "For belonging to an illegal society."

"Did you?"

He kept his gaze fixed on the opposite bank. "Among other things."

"I can't see them denying you a pardon," she said quietly, "simply because of that."

"No."

She gazed at him, at his rigid profile, at the gentle rise of his chest as he drew in air, and felt a desperate need to know more about him, to understand him better. "Is it because of why you were flogged?"

She expected him to resent the question, but he only shrugged. "Which time? A man can get fifty lashes for insubordination and twenty-five simply for swearing."

"The bad one."

There was a brief, perceptible pause filled with the roar of the water and the harsh screech of a black cockatoo from deep in the forest. "Oh, that one." He brought up one hand to settle his hat lower on his forehead. "That was when I took it into my head to kill this particular overseer."

"Why?"

He let out a harsh laugh. "Because I'm a bloody-minded brute of an Irishman, of course."

"No you're not."

"No? Well when I first arrived, I was assigned to the regimental stables in Hobart. The men there, they don't have a very flattering opinion of those of us from the Emerald Isle."

Jessie swallowed, trying to clear the sudden lump that had risen in her throat. She'd heard about the way the men in the regiment could treat convicts, particularly the Irish ones.

"They had this rule," he said, "that convicts were only allowed to receive one letter every two months."

"That's so cruel."

He glanced at her over his shoulder, his expression closed, almost hostile. "We're here to be punished, remember? Not coddled. The overseer there, he said that so many times I can't see an egg to this day without thinking of him."

She watched, surprised and oddly touched, as a brief flare of humor lightened his features. "He was a big, ugly brute of an Englishman named Lamb. Leo Lamb." His gaze met hers for an instant of shared irony, then the smile faded into a look so bleak and haunted it was all she could do to keep from reaching out to him in comfort. "That Leo Lamb, he had this thing about what they call 'special convicts,' the ones who know how to read and write and who make the mistake of talking like their betters. He thought men like that needed to be humbled. He sure enough set about trying to humble me."

She curled her hands into fists, her fingernails digging into her palms. She knew something about the ways an overseer could make a man's life hell. Such as seeing a man get twenty-five lashes for an inappropriate smile...

"He was at me day and night, giving me the worst jobs, taunting me, trying to make me crack. But I was determined he wasn't going to get to me."

"So what happened?" she asked, her voice coming out torn.

"A letter came for me one day. A letter in a black-edged envelope."

Oh, God, Jessie thought, her heart aching for him. A black-edged envelope meant a death notice.

"Only thing was," he continued, "it hadn't been the required two months since my last letter had arrived. So he burned it. Right in front of me."

He paused, his head tipping back, the cords of his throat working as he swallowed. "I knew that someone I loved had died, but I didn't know whom. I went...a little crazy. I didn't kill him, although I probably would have if they hadn't pulled me off him in time. They sentenced me to a year in the chain gangs. And three hundred lashes."

"Whose was it?"

He looked at her, his eyes wide and a little wild. "What?"

"The death notice. Whose was it?"

For a moment, she didn't think he was going to answer. Then he said, "Her name was Caroline. Caroline Reardon. She was to have been my wife. She died in childbirth."

The roar from the falls suddenly seemed too loud, the air so thick and damp it hurt to breathe. "I'm sorry."

He shook his head. "Don't get me wrong. It wasn't my child she was carrying."

"She wouldn't wait for you?"

He was silent a moment, his head bowed, watching the white, frothy water swirl through the tumbled rocks at his feet. "I told her not to. After I was convicted and sentenced to be transported, I told her that she had to think of me as dead." He moved his foot, pushing at one of the smaller loose stones with the toe of his rough work boot until the stone rolled over to hit the water with a splash. "She wouldn't listen to me—was furious with me for even suggesting it. She said she'd wait. Wait forever if she had to."

"But she didn't."

He lifted his gaze to follow the length of the moss-covered trunk of a giant eucalyptus that thrust up from the far bank of the stream. "She came to see me not long before they were to load us on the transport that was to take us first to England, then here. She said she'd met a man who loved her, a man she thought she could be happy with, and she wanted to tell me about him to my face. She said she owed me that, although God knows it wasn't an easy thing for her to do."

"Harder for you, I should think."

He leaned his back against the boulder beside her, his arms crossed at his chest, his face flat and unreadable and still turned half away from her. "I'd meant it when I told her to think of me as dead. She had her own life to live. I didn't see any reason to destroy her life along with mine."

He was so close now, she could have reached out and touched him. She ached with the need to touch him, to comfort him. She watched as a slow, sad smile curled his lips. "She said she still loved me, that she would always love me. But she also said she'd come to realize that I'd never really loved her as much as she needed to be loved. She said if I'd loved her—if I'd truly loved her, loved her more than honor, more than life itself—then I wouldn't have done the things I did."

"That wasn't fair."

"Wasn't it?" He swung his head to look at her. "She was right. I did love her, but not enough for it to stop me from doing what I felt needed to be done."

She knew then that whatever it was he had done that he thought would block the petition for his pardon, it had little to do with illegal societies or even the overseer Leo Lamb. And she knew too that she wasn't ready to hear what it was.

"The man Caroline married," he said, still looking at her, "he was a giant of man and his babe was big, too. Too big for her. She was such a wee, dainty thing. She looked a fair bit like yourself, only with hair the color of rose hips and autumn leaves rather than the liquid gold of the morning sun."

She was aware of his gaze lingering on her hair, and she thought for one wild moment that he might touch her there, where a stray lock tumbled against her neck. Except of course he could never touch her hair, just as he could never kiss her lips, no matter how much she wanted him to. And she did want him to, God help her. She wanted to feel his touch, to know his kiss, more than she'd ever wanted anything in her life.

"It wasn't your fault," she said softly.

He closed his eyes and sucked in a deep breath of air that shuddered his chest. "Wasn't it then? If I hadn't done those things, if I hadn't got myself transported, if that'd been my babe she'd been having, she wouldn't have died."

"You can't know."

He looked at her again, and this time, all of the pain, all of the anguished guilt he'd kept hidden before broke through. "Can't I?"

She reached out to him then, the need to touch him, to somehow try to ease his pain too great to be resisted. Her fingertips brushed his cheek. And it happened again, that hum of sensation that stole her breath and filled her with fire. She felt the roughness of the several days' growth of beard on his face and the smoothness of his skin and the warmth of his being. He went utterly still beneath her touch.

"Miss Corbett—" he began.

"No." She brought her hand to his lips. "Don't call me that. Don't say anything. Don't—" She sucked in a sharp, quick breath, her gaze tangling with his, her fingertips sliding over his mouth to curl around the back of his neck. "Don't stop me."

And then, because he couldn't kiss her, because she knew he would never kiss her, she tipped her head and kissed him.

19

I T WAS AN AWKWARD KISS, a naive brushing of her lips against his. But his mouth was so warm and sweet, and it moved gently beneath hers. She heard him let out a throaty groan, felt his hands grip her arms, slide up to her shoulders, clench in her hair to hold her tight. Then his mouth opened against hers and turned the kiss into something she'd never known a kiss could be.

She hadn't known . . . that a man's mouth could look so hard and yet be so soft, or that it could feel so exquisite sliding across her own. She hadn't known that a man put his tongue in a woman's mouth when he kissed her or that it felt so wonderful, beyond wonderful to sinful. She hadn't known that a kiss could steal her breath and set her blood on fire and awaken this yawning, aching need so deep within her.

She clenched her fists in the cloth of his coat, felt the tension of the muscles in his shoulders as she drew closer to him. The rush of the waterfall roared in her ears and threw up a fine spray that felt damp against her face, but she was barely aware of it. Her world had narrowed to the heat of his body and the magic of his mouth moving against hers. Then he tore his lips from hers and her world shattered.

He looked down at her, his breath ragged, his face dark and tortured with need.

"Don't," she said, her grip on his shoulders tightening, her own breath coming so shaky she could barely push out the words. "Don't tell me you're sorry. And don't you dare say this was a mistake."

She saw the crease flash in his cheek with a smile that was there and then gone. "Sure then, but you're very free with your *don'ts* this afternoon, Miss Corbett."

"Don't call me that," she said, then smiled wryly when she saw his eyebrows shoot up. "Please. Call me Jessie."

He brought up his hands to smooth the tangled hair from her face, his work-scarred fingers gentle and a little shaky against her skin. "It seems a dangerously familiar line to cross, that one."

"Not such a great step, surely, after you've had your tongue in my mouth."

He laughed then, a laugh that was low and throaty and somehow intensely, evocatively erotic. She saw the flicker of fire in his emerald green eyes, the flare of his nostrils as he sucked in a quick breath of air. For one heady moment she thought he would kiss her again. Instead he swung away from her, his head tipping back as he stared up at the white cascade of the falls. "Whether you want me to say it or not lass, it's true. It was a terrible mistake what we did here today."

She wanted to argue with him, but she couldn't because she knew he was right. How could she have known? she thought in despair. How could she have known that one kiss would never be enough? That it would only make her want more? That it would leave her body trembling and on fire with an aching, burning need?

"You know what they would do to me, don't you," he said, "your brother and Mr. Harrison Bloody District Magistrate Tate between them, if they found out I'd even thought about touching you, let alone actually kissed you?"

"They wouldn't—Harrison wouldn't—"

He turned to meet her gaze, his face set, his eyes brittle and a little frightening. "Yes he would and you know it."

Her fist came up to press against her chest as if she could

somehow hold back this terrible inner welling of despair and fear. "Perhaps you're wrong. Perhaps my brother's petition will be accepted."

"Perhaps," he said although she knew he didn't believe it. "In the meantime, Miss Corbett, it might be best if you didn't go riding too often."

She heard the rush of the wind moving through the canopy of leaves high overhead, stirring the branches and shifting the pattern of light that filtered down through the breaks in the trees. She could stay away from him, she thought.

For a day. Or perhaps two.

~

THEY WERE REINING in before the stable door when the braying of a donkey brought her head around.

"Warrick," Jessie said, slipping from the saddle with an unexpected laugh as her brother trotted swearing into the yard, an unhappy dun-colored donkey balking at the end of a lead behind him. "Whatever are you doing with that donkey?" Then she saw the dark, still form tied across the animal's back and the laughter died on her lips.

She threw a quick, silent glance at Gallagher's face, but he was wearing that flat look, the one that always disturbed her because it hinted at all the things that had been done to him, all the things he'd had to endure.

"Don't look at him, Jess," said Warrick, swinging out of the saddle to throw both his reins and the donkey's lead to Gallagher. It took her a moment to realize her brother was talking about the dead man.

"Did you kill him?" she asked, staring anyway at the black man's dark head. He had frightened her, this man. Frightened her and threatened her. Yet he had done her no real harm. It didn't seem right that he should have had to die for it. That he should end up like this, tied facedown across a donkey.

"He was dead when I found him," said Warrick as he turned to

Gallagher. "Put the body in the chapel for the night. I'll get someone to dig a grave in the morning."

"I'll bury him," she heard Gallagher say in a flat voice that matched the look she'd seen in his eyes. This time she was careful not to glance toward him.

"Good," said Warrick. He turned toward the house, doubtless, she thought, dismissing the dead man from his mind.

And then she did glance at Gallagher again, because she couldn't leave without looking at him one more time. Their gazes met. But she could see nothing in his eyes. Nothing at all.

She hurried after her brother, the long skirts of her riding habit held high. "Warrick, wait," she called, catching up with him as he paused to unlatch the garden gate. "I was wondering if you'd remembered to petition the governor? About Gallagher?"

He glanced back at her, a lock of his fair hair falling carelessly across his forehead. "Didn't I tell you?"

She shook her head. "Tell me what?"

"I asked Harrison to look into it for me. I don't know what the hell that Irishman did, but Harrison says the man could save the life of the Queen herself and he'd still end his days in chains."

Jessie stood quite still, the breath leaving her body in a painful rush. "But . . . how could Harrison know?"

Warrick shrugged. "It's in the man's papers. Harrison looked them up the other day."

He would have turned away, but her hand shot out to grasp his sleeve, stopping him. "Why would Harrison do that?"

She was aware of Warrick looking at her queerly, but at that moment she didn't care. "He was curious, I suppose. He is the local magistrate, remember? The convicts in the district are all ultimately his responsibility."

She unclenched her hand and let her brother go.

So Lucas Gallagher had been right after all, she thought; there would be no pardon coming from the governor. She had to hold herself stiff to keep from looking back over her shoulder toward the stables and the man she knew was still there. The clouds had begun to turn a faint pink as the sun slipped lower in the horizon; it would be dark soon. She thought about that iron barred door clanging shut on him, locking him into the barracks tonight and tomorrow night and the night after that. She thought about all the nights of all the years that stretched ahead of him, and she felt such a crush of despair she wondered how he bore it.

And then she thought about tomorrow and the day after that, about all the days to come when she would see him in the stables and ride beside him. All the coming days filled with temptation and danger. And she knew a terrible fear that welled up inside her, closing her throat and stealing her breath. Fear not only for him, but for herself.

20

LUCAS BURIED PARKER JONES early the next morning

He thrust the shovel into the dark earth at his feet and then swung it up, the dirt flying in a fan-shaped spray to land with a soft hiss on the large mound beside him. Thrust and swing, thrust and swing, a familiar, endless pattern. He'd dug a lot of ditches in the past three years. A lot of ditches and a lot of graves.

He paused to glance up at the thick, heaving storm clouds building overhead, then sent the shovel biting deep into the ground again, the muscles of his bare arms and back flexing as he swung the full shovel high. The hole was deep, but not quite deep enough yet and he wasn't sure how much longer this rain was going to hold off. A gust of wind swept down the hill to cool the sweat on his bare back and thrash the branches of the nearby grove of oaks. He kicked the shovel deeper with his boot . . . and knew she was there.

He straightened slowly to find her standing some three or four feet from the edge of the grave. She wore a gown made from some shiny burgundy and white-striped material, with a V-shaped waist and wide lace collar that emphasized the fullness of her breasts. He felt a swift, unwanted rush of desire followed closely by a helpless welling of frustration and anger. "I thought we'd agreed it would be best if you stayed away from me," he said, and turned back to his digging.

"You were right about your pardon."

The easy flow of his rhythm broke, then resumed, that betraying instant of disappointment surprising him, for he'd known, he'd known . . . Hadn't he known? "All the more reason for you to stay away then," he said, his voice coming out rough.

"I need to ride out to Last Chance Point. Once you've finished here." She walked a distance away to where an old cedar grew amongst the simple wooden crosses of the convict cemetery, then swung back to face him again, her hands clasped together in front of her skirt, the color riding high in her cheeks.

"The point?" He propped one elbow on the handle of his shovel and tossed the loose hair out of his eyes. "Have you looked at the weather lately?"

She wasn't looking at the weather; she was looking at him. "I'm sorry about your friend."

He went back to his digging. "Parker wasn't that close of a friend. Just someone I knew and respected." He glanced up at her. "Does that surprise you? That someone could respect a runaway ex-slave dressed in kangaroo skins?"

"No." She shook her head, her eyes wide and dark with some emotion he could not name. "I heard what you said to him, up in that glade. About absconding convicts needing to get off the island. You've obviously given the subject considerable thought."

"Huh." He kept his voice casual, the shovel striking deeper. "Show me a convict who hasn't."

"Perhaps. But with you, it's different, isn't it? You're actually going to try it."

He straightened slowly, the head of his shovel coming to rest on the grass as he stared up at her.

"I was thinking last night," she said, "about what it would be like to be a convict, to know that I would never be free." She half turned away from him to run her hand along the top of one of the nearby crosses, her head bowed, her attention seemingly focused on the movement of her hand. "In the past, I could never understand why men like Parker Jones would take such risks to try to escape. But now . . ." She brought her gaze back to his face. "Now I think I understand."

"Miss Corbett, exactly where is this conversation leading?"

She dropped her arm to her side. "I asked you not to call me that. Not when we're alone."

He flattened his palms on the grass and leaned into them, levering up out of the grave to stand before her, his hands at his sides. "What do you think? That giving me permission to use your first name in private somehow makes my position of servitude less humiliating? Or does it just make it easier for you to pretend it's not a barrier?"

He watched the color drain from her cheeks. "It was not my intention to humiliate you."

"Ah, hell," he swore and swung away.

"Don't you understand," she said, coming to stand behind him. "When I look at you, I don't see a convict. I see a man. I quit seeing a convict long ago."

He spun to face her, his sweat-slicked, naked chest heaving with his agitated breathing. "But I am a convict. Nothing is going to change that. Not even death." He swung his arm in an angry arc over the isolated rows of plain crosses. "Just look around you."

She stood before him slim and straight, the wind plastering her fine skirts against her long legs and fluttering the loose strands of hair around her pale face. "And I am an Englishwoman. What do you see when you look at me?"

His anger collapsed within him. Reaching out a hand that was not quite steady, he brushed the loose hair away from her face and tucked it behind one ear. "I see you," he said softly. "Just you."

His knuckles brushed down her throat, and he saw a shiver ripple through her, saw her breath catch. And he wanted . . . ah, how he wanted to take her in his arms and hold her warm and close. He wanted to bury his face in her hair and breathe in the sweet fragrance of her. He wanted to taste her lips and feel the softness of her skin beneath his hands. He wanted her in every way a man can want a woman and he was never, ever going to have any more of her than what he had now.

"For the love of God." Somehow he forced himself to take a step back and then another. "Ask your brother to assign you a different groom."

She shook her head. "I can't. You know why."

He let out a harsh laugh and swung away from her, his hands on his hips. "If you think your family and acquaintances would disapprove of your friendship with Genevieve Strzlecki, how do you think they'd be reacting if they knew you'd stooped so low as to kiss your Irish convict groom?"

"That won't happen again."

He looked at her over his shoulder. "And if it does?"

"It won't," she said quickly.

Too quickly.

21

The girl sat curled on the window seat in Genevieve's kitchen, a cup of hot cider cradled in both hands, her gaze fixed on the heaving dark waters of Blackhaven Bay far below. It was only early afternoon, but the coming storm had darkened the day to the gloom of near twilight. A wild wind whipped the sea to a dangerous churning froth and battered the gnarled trees of the point with a fury that whined through the eaves of the cottage.

Genevieve brought her own cup to her lips and took a thoughtful sip, her attention caught not by the storm but by the girl who watched it. There was something different about Jessie today, some uncharacteristic emotion that brought a faint flush to her cheeks and a sparkle to her eyes and a kind of quick restlessness to her movements. "What is it, Jessie?" Genevieve asked, letting her rocking chair creak gently back and forth. "What's happened?"

Jessie swung her head to look at Genevieve and smiled. "Am I so obvious?"

She shook her head. "It's not exactly the type of weather one normally chooses for an afternoon ride."

The girl turned to stare again at the ships riding at anchor in the bay, their bare masts thrashing back and forth against the gray sky.

The rain had held off so far, but the threat of it was there, heavy in the lightning-charged air. "I like watching a storm over the sea. It makes me feel so . . . alive."

"But that's not why you came, is it?"

Jessie let her breath out in a short sigh. "No." She pressed one splayed hand against her thigh and smoothed the fine cloth of her riding habit. "Harrison kissed me the other night."

"Ah," said Genevieve, smiling softly to herself. "So that's it. I should have thought he'd have kissed you long before now."

"He has." Jessie bowed her head, her gaze fixed on the agitated movement of her hand. "But not . . . Not like that. I . . ." Her throat worked visibly as she swallowed. "I didn't enjoy it."

"Oh, Jessie."

"Mother says that men's passions are stronger than women's, that with women it's a matter of simply enduring the physical side of love. But it's not that. I know it's not that."

The wind threw a scattering of rain against the window, big drops that hit as sharply as pellets. And Genevieve understood, suddenly, that air of suppressed excitement she'd sensed. That glow of inner awakening. "There's someone else, isn't there?"

Jessie nodded her head slowly.

"Is he unsuitable?"

A sad, soft smile touched her lips. "Very."

"Do you love him?"

The girl's head came up, her eyes widening. "No. How could I? I barely know him." She sucked in a quick breath that lifted her breasts. "I mean . . ."

Outside, the wind shrieked, the bay and its storm-threatened ships disappearing in a swirl of lowering clouds and wind-tossed rain. "But you kissed him?"

She didn't say anything, but a smile broke across the girl's face, a smile so dazzling in its brilliance and just a bit naughty that Genevieve thought, *Oh, Jessie.* Then the smile faded and Jessie swung her head away to stare out at the storm, and Genevieve knew a swift stab of uneasiness. "He has a wife already?"

"No. It's worse than that. By far." A quiver of pain crossed the girl's face, quickly smoothed out by years of training. "There can be no question of anything between us, not even friendship."

The gloom in the kitchen deepened as the rain poured down, streaming across the windowpanes in wind-driven sheets of water. "Then what . . ." Genevieve's hand tightened around the mug and set it aside. "Ah, Harrison. That's your problem, is it?"

The girl nodded, her eyes wide and confused, her lips pressed into a tense line. "I feel so terrible. He doesn't deserve this. But it isn't anything I've willed. It simply . . . happened."

"The heart has a will of its own, Jessie. No woman can decide whom she will love and whom she won't." The wind screamed around the house, almost drowning out the distant boom of the surf against the rocks and the faint but unmistakable peal of church bells. Genevieve half rose from her seat. "What can that be?" she began, just as the kitchen door flew open to slam against the wall with a crash.

Michael, the old emancipist who did odd jobs for Genevieve, stood on the threshold, his oilskin streaming water, his face white with horror. "There's a ship in the cove!" he said with a gasp, trying to catch his breath. "It must've snapped its cables and now the wind's carried it around the point and onto the rocks."

DOWN AT THE COVE, half the beach had disappeared beneath the heavy dark waves that swept into shore to break against the sand with a booming, wind-whipped roar.

With the sea running so high they'd had to take the long way around, doubling back toward the track to Blackhaven Bay before striking down to the cove itself. Gallagher drove a small cart of Genevieve's, loaded with flasks of hot cider and warm soup and blankets wrapped in oilcloth.

There were others already on the beach ahead of them, dark, cloak-wrapped shapes huddled against a violent sea and a low, pewter-gray sky. "Oh, Lord," whispered Jessie, one hand tightening on the side of the cart as the terrified, wide-eyed horse lurched to a stop in the deep, rain-drenched sand. "Look!"

The ship was a sleek-hulled ketch, its sails struck, its deck tilted at a crazy angle, for it had plowed bow-first into the rocks on the far side of the cove. The momentum of the impact had carried the front of the ship up until the prow thrust into the air and the stem disappeared into the surging sea, the rear decks awash with the swirling, white-tipped waves that crashed against its sides.

"Perhaps she won't sink after all," said Genevieve.

"Her hull's been stove in," said Gallagher, hopping out to help Genevieve alight from the cart, his shout barely audible above the howl of the wind and the pounding of the rain and the booming crash of waves breaking against sand and rock. "Right now, the rocks themselves are keeping her afloat. But she won't hang there much longer. Eventually the tides are going to suck her off, and when that happens, she'll go down."

Jessie watched him turn toward her, the rain streaming over his face as he reached up to catch her by the waist and swing her to the ground. Her gaze locked with his, her hands clutching at his shoulders, and for one impossible instant it seemed as if something leapt between them, an invisible skein of charged energy that might have come from the storm itself. Then Jessie took a step back, her arms falling away, her face turning toward the stricken ship. "How long?" she asked. "How long before it slides off?"

The Irishman shrugged. "Fifteen minutes. Maybe twenty."

Genevieve had spotted a man she recognized: Jack Carpenter, the publican of the Black Horse. Jessie sloughed across the sand toward them, one hand clutching her hood tight around her throat. "How many people on that ship?" Genevieve was asking, her voice a shout against the wind. "Does anyone know?"

He swung toward them, a broad-faced, middle-aged man with rain-washed skin and gray whiskers and narrowed, worried gray eyes. "Just four. A seaman and three children."

"Children?" repeated Jessie, coming up beside them.

"Aye. The parents are on their way to take over a run up the coast. They came ashore with the rest of the crew this morning for supplies, but the bay was so choppy they decided it'd be safer to leave the children on board the ketch. That's the father, there," said Carpenter, nodding toward the cove, "with the captain in the ship's boat."

Jessie turned to look out to sea where a small boat could be seen heaving and lurching with the ugly swell sweeping around the point. Its six oarsman fought hard to wrest control of the craft from the pull of the tide. The two men in the prow were bailing frantically, but Jessie thought the boat must still be taking on too much water, for it rode dangerously low, the waves breaking over the gunwales in a violent crash of white spray.

"They're veering too close to the shore," she said watching the small boat lifted up and flung forward by the surge of the sea. "They're going to miss the ketch."

"Miss it?" said Gallagher coming to stand behind her. "Sweet Mary, they're going to *join* it."

She wondered afterward how he knew the rocks were there, submerged beneath the high tide when she who had spent so much of her life in this cove did not. At that instant the small boat struck with a violence that sent the stem shooting up toward the roiling, lightning-split sky. The men within spilled into the sea to become dark, thrashing specks in a swirl of rain-beaten white foam.

"Ben!" screamed a woman. Jessie turned to see the children's mother hunched over, her arms gripping her sides, the breath leaving her body in a low keening moan as she staggered to where the breakers smashed against the shore. Angry waves soaked her dark skirts and threw up a wild, wind-whipped frenzy of spume that plastered her dark blond hair to her white, wet face. "*Oh, God, no.* Ben."

Someone grabbed the woman's arm to pull her back, while farther down the beach men were already splashing into the surf to catch the small boat's gasping, choking survivors as they rolled in on the giant, curling waves.

"You can see the children," said Genevieve in a tight voice. "There, on the deck."

Jessie looked again toward the ketch. A great flash of lightning lit up the dark, angry afternoon with a flood of jagged white light. She could just make out a huddle of small figures beside the starboard rail. The seaman was nowhere in sight.

"They'll need to bring another boat from around the point," said Carpenter as a heavy wall of water slammed into the side of the stricken ketch with a hissing boom, dashing the great wave into a fan of white spray. Impaled on the rocks, the small ship lurched and tottered, its timbers squealing, its lower decks boiling with foam. Carpenter shook his head. "Problem is, it's going to take time."

"There is no time," said Gallagher, shrugging out of his coat and waistcoat. The rain drenched his shirt to plaster the coarse cloth to his body. "Listen to that. The ship's breaking up."

"What are you doing?" Jessie demanded, her fingers closing around the tensed muscle of his arm as he bent to pull off first one boot, then the next.

He straightened, his gaze stark and fiercely fixed on her face. Her hand fluttered back to her side and he went to work on the wet ties of his shirt, his gaze still locked with hers. "I'm going to swim out to it."

"You can't," she said, her voice coming out high and panicky. Rain ran in her eyes and she drew a quick breath heavily scented with brine and fear. "You can't. You'll be swept against the rocks just like that boat."

He pulled the coarse convict shirt over his head and dropped it in a sodden heap by his boots and socks. "I doubt it."

"Even if you do make it," said Genevieve, rain dripping from her white face as she stared up at him, "what can you do? One man with three children and no boat?"

Jessie watched him turn to look at the older woman. Rain plastered his dark hair to his head, streamed down his angular cheeks and chin. "I can put at least one child on my back and swim to shore."

"You'll never make it," said Jessie, panic gripping her stomach so hard it hurt.

He swung to face her, his naked chest lifting on a deep breath. "I can try."

"But—"

He reached out as if he would stop her words with his rough fingers, although he didn't touch her. His eyes were wide and dark, his face gaunt with a fierceness that caught at her chest. The wind howled around them; the rain poured. Breakers piled one on another, crashing against the shore with a deafening roar as thunder rumbled low and threatening across the thick gray sky. For one, suspended moment, they might have been the only people on the beach.

"I can die like Parker," he said quietly, so quietly she almost didn't hear him, "or I can die trying to save those children." His fingers curled to fall back to his side, and for an instant she thought she saw him smile. "Which do you think is the better end?"

And then he was gone, running into the boiling surf, his naked torso gleaming wetly, his body arching as he dove into the surging wall of water.

THE SEA WAS COLD, Lucas thought with calm detachment as he turned his head and sucked a quick gasp of life-giving air into his lungs. But not as cold as the northern seas that wrapped the green and rocky shores of Ireland.

After the first shock of submersion, he struck out quickly, legs kicking, arms slicing with precision through the surging waves. The wind and the tide were both against him, driving him back toward shore. But he had expected that, had known that each wave would become a rolling black wall to be crested, beaten. Rain pounded his shoulders, pockmarked the raging sea around him. He could see the rocks looming up dark and jagged on his left, hear the violent explosion of the waves striking stone with a force that sent spume soaring into the sky. The fierce currents of the cove sucked at his body, tugged him closer to the towering cliffs than he wanted to be yet. He could see the hull of the ketch ahead of him, but the pull of the rocks was powerful and deadly and dangerously seductive. It would be so easy, so very easy to end it all here, now . . .

Except that if he gave up now three children would die alone and frightened. Lucas knew what it felt like to be alone and afraid. And so he fought, fought both the sea and the temptation simply to cease struggling and let the storm take him. The ketch was very near now, its sleek brown hull rolling with each kick of wind and wave. He lifted his head, shaking hair and water from his eyes as he focused his salt-blurred vision on the companion ladder. He would be given no second chance. If he missed the ladder he would be swept into the rocks whether he willed it or not.

He kicked hard, arms cutting through the curling white tops of the ugly swelling waves, every muscle straining for strength and control. The noise was deafening, the creaking of the dying ship's timbers added to the howling roar of wind and rain and breaking surf. The sea eddied treacherously around him, sucked him toward the rocks. He fought with all his strength and still the sea took him, an unexpected splash of cold, salty water filling his eyes and his mouth and his lungs. For one wild, terrible moment he thought he'd misjudged. Then the cold swirling current gave one last tug and released him.

His flailing hand sought the nearest rung; caught it. He hauled himself upward hand over hand, the cold wind shuddering his wet body, his muscles unexpectedly weak and quivering so that he found it hard to pull himself up and over the low rail. He slithered to the wet, lurching deck, his breath coming in painful gasps, his hands braced against his thighs, his head bowed as he coughed up water.

"Sir," said a small voice.

Lucas flung up his head, his chest still heaving with the effort of drawing air into his strained lungs, and found himself staring into the anxious gray eyes of a sharp-faced boy of perhaps eleven or twelve years of age. Behind him stood a second child, a girl of something like eight, clutching against her side another little girl of four or five who was sobbing. Like her brother, the older girl was wide-eyed and stiff with awe-inspiring control.

"Sir," said the boy again, his wet body shuddering with cold and shock even as he somehow managed to keep most of what he was feeling off his face. "Have you come to help us?"

Genevieve Strzlecki stood at the rain-pounded shoreline and watched Jessie watching her groom.

She waited at the edge of the raging surf, a tall girl with a wet tangle of golden hair clinging to her shoulders, her skirts dark and limp with sea and rainwater, her back held painfully stiff as she stared out over the heaving, deadly waves. A giant, white-curled breaker smashed against the beach, drenching her with frigid salt water and she barely flinched. Every fiber of her was focused on the man who swam toward near-certain death.

Oh, Jessie, thought Genevieve, wading into the swirling water to stand beside her. *Not that man. Not that wild Irishman with his dark good looks and doomed future. Not him.*

Jessie's hand reached out to clasp Genevieve's. "There. See? He's made it," she said with a gasp that brought Genevieve's arm about her waist to hold her up as she sagged with relief. "He made it."

"He's made it to the ship." Genevieve hugged her young friend close as they watched the Irishman disappear over the ship's rail. "Now he's going to need to swim back."

22

A MASSIVE WAVE RAMMED into the side of the ketch, sending up a plume of spray and causing the wet deck beneath Gallagher's feet to lurch ominously. Overhead the remaining masts swayed against the gray, lightning-charged sky with a creaking groan that caught the boy's attention. He looked up, a quick, scared breath shuddering his chest as he watched some of the mainmast's rigging snap and come down with a rending crash that could have killed them had they been standing beneath it.

"The ship's breaking up, isn't it?" the boy asked stiffly.

"Yes," said Lucas, reaching out one hand to grip the boy's thin, cold shoulder. "What's your name, son?"

"Taylor, sir. Taylor Chantry."

Gallagher let his gaze drift around the ruined, rain-washed deck with its scattered rigging and shattered mizzenmast and broken planks. The impact with the rock had loosed the livestock from their pens, so that the air filled with the squeal of pigs and the bawling of frightened cattle. "I thought there was a seaman with you."

"There was, sir," said Taylor. "He jumped overboard and tried to swim to shore when the cables snapped. I don't think he made it."

"Excuse me, sir," said the older girl, looking up at Lucas and blinking as the rain ran in her eyes. "But how are you going to get us to shore without a boat?"

"What's your name?" Lucas asked, turning to the girl and giving her what he hoped came out as a smile. She had dark blond hair like her mother and little sister, and her brother's pointed chin. She was thin and wet and cold, and in another half hour she might be dead.

"Mary."

"How old are you, Mary?"

"I'm eight."

Lucas hunkered down to bring himself to the child's eye level. The wind shrieked, fluttering the girls' straggly hair and torturing Lucas's wet, tired body. "You're a very brave young woman, Mary. How old is your sister here?"

Mary tightened her grip on the little girl's shaking shoulders. "She's four. Her name is Harriet."

"I'll tell you what I'm going to do, Mary. I'm going to try to swim to shore with you."

"Swim, sir? But . . ." Mary's chin quivered, then held firm. "I can't swim."

"You won't need to. I'm going to swim with you and your sister tied to my back." *Which means that if I go down, I'll drag you to the bottom with me,* he thought, although he didn't tell her that. Without him the little girls wouldn't stand a chance in these seas anyway.

"All you'll need to do," he told the rigid little girl, "is hold your head out of the water and keep Harriet here from wrapping her arms around my neck and strangling me." He captured Mary's frightened gray gaze and held it. "Do you think you can do that?"

She hesitated, considering what he was asking her to do, and he admired her all the more for it. He threw a quick glance toward the beach. A faint light glimmered through the gloom and he realized the people there must somehow have managed to get a fire going. Feeble as it was, it would help.

Mary blew out her breath in a slow, oddly adult sigh. "I can try, sir. But what about Taylor?"

Gallagher looked up at the boy beside them. "Can you swim?"

Taylor swallowed. "Yes, sir." A wave exploded against the hull with a crash that drenched them all and set the ketch to rocking dangerously. The boy flinched. "But not in a sea like this."

Straightening, Lucas unsheathed the knife he kept strapped to his calf and went to work cutting a length of the scattered wet rope. "Listen to me, Taylor. The only thing holding this ketch up right now is the rock that punched a hole in her bottom. Any minute, some wave is going to knock us off that rock into deep water and she's going to sink like she's got lead shot for ballast. One way or another, you're going to end up in the sea." He turned, two strips of rope in his hands. "Believe me, you don't want to be on this ship when it goes down."

Taylor blinked up at him. "I don't think I can do it, sir."

Lucas tied one of the ropes around Harriet's waist with quick, practiced movements. "All right. I'll take your sisters and then come back for you."

Wordlessly, Taylor stared out over the surging, wind-whipped, rain-battered sea toward that faint beacon of light on the beach. A violent gust of wind slammed against the ship, thundering a loose sail and bringing down more rigging. Beneath their feet, the deck pitched and groaned. It was obvious that even if Lucas had the strength and endurance to make such a trip twice, the ketch probably wouldn't hold together long enough for him to swim out a second time, and the boy seemed to know it. He gritted his teeth and gulped hard enough to send his small Adam's apple bobbing up and down. "I'll do it, sir."

"Good on ya, lad." Lucas bent to allow Mary to scramble onto him, piggyback fashion. "You go first," he said quickly. "We'll be right behind you."

The boy made it over the pitching railing and down the slippery ladder. But at the bottom he stopped, the waves licking his ankles, his eyes wide and dark.

"Take a deep breath and let go," Lucas said calmly.

The boy dangled there, his fingers white with the strain of clutching the rope. "I can't!"

Beside them the ketch heaved up and then slipped sideways with a great tearing of timbers that almost threw Lucas, off-balanced as he was by the girls' weight, into the water. "You can do it, Taylor. I'll be right beside you. I'll try to help you as much as I can. Now go."

The ship lurched again and Lucas knew they were off the rock and floating free. They could hear the sound of water rushing into the smashed hull, fast and deadly. "Listen to me, Taylor. You have to do this. Now. Let go."

The boy sucked in a deep, desperate breath of air, squeezed his eyes shut, and let go.

JESMOND CORBETT STOOD on the beach of Shipwreck Cove and watched the ketch slip from the jagged rocks that had killed it. The ship swung about sharply, shuddering and sucking as the viciously cold water rushed in to fill its bowels. With a suddenness that was both awe-inspiring and frightening, it plummeted down, the strain of the descent tearing it asunder with a groaning scream that mingled with the rumble of thunder and the smash of the surf. Then all that could be seen was a frothy expanse of debris-clogged, seething sea churned by the frantic thrashing of squealing pigs and lowing cattle and two dark forms that might or might not have been human.

Her body wet and chilled, her heart pounding painfully in her chest, Jessie watched him come at her through the powerfully breaking waves, a familiar, dark-headed, lithe body with strongly reaching arms who stopped every now and then to urge on his smaller, frailer shadow. Sometimes they would disappear from her vision for endless agonizing seconds at a time when they sank into a deep trough between waves. She would wait, the wind lifting her sodden hair and the rain wet on her face, for them to reappear, borne up on the crest of the next sweeping wall of gray water.

It would be easier for him now, she reasoned; easier to swim with the tide and the wind—except, of course, for the double burden he carried on his back and his care for the child who flailed gamely in his wake. The nobility of what he had done, of what he was doing—

the sheer, bloody-minded majesty and guts of it—stole her breath, leaving her feeling both proud and oddly humbled. The wind howled around her, driving the next wave to strike the beach with a thunderous spray. Water ran down her cheeks; she tasted salt on her lips and knew it was not all from the sea.

"I don't see them," said Genevieve beside her, staring out over the incoming sweep of white-tipped waves.

"There," said Jessie, the breath leaving her body in a joyous rush when she saw the dark, heavily burdened figure emerging from the foam-flecked gray water that broke against the shore. "Oh, thank God. He made it. He's all right. He's all right."

A strange emotion welled within her, a powerful, unfamiliar surge only dimly understood. Behind her, farther up the beach where someone had rigged up a shelter, the bonfire crackled and hissed, filling the salty air with the tang of wood smoke. People were shouting, running, dark drenched forms moving across dark wet sand, yet she might have been alone. Alone with the low bunching clouds and the soaring cliffs of the cove and the man emerging, exhausted, his face drawn, his naked chest heaving, his back bent beneath his burden as he rose from the storm-racked sea. Rain ran down her face and soaked through her clothes. The sea roared in her ears. She took one hesitant step forward. Then she was flinging herself into the surf, her heart soaring with a wildly intense joy, her legs splashing through the spent waves swirling over the sand. The long green velvet train of her riding habit floated out behind her on the brine, hampering each step, slowing her down. So exultant was her heart, so intent was she on reaching this man, that she was only dimly aware of a voice calling her from behind. Then a hand closed above her elbow, checking her forward momentum and drawing her half around.

She found herself staring into Genevieve's wise blue eyes. "Have a care, Jessie. There are too many here on this beach who would see, and remember, and talk."

A wave broke against them, deluging Jessie with a cold shock. A man pushed past her, a small, officious man in a naval officer's uniform who was barking orders. Other men and women crowded around them, enlarging her world with awful suddenness to remind her of who she was and where she was and what she must not do. She drew the cold, damp air into her lungs and nodded, her gaze still locked with Genevieve's. There was no time now to ask how Genevieve had known.

"The boy's right behind me," she heard Gallagher say, his voice shaky and spent. "Help him. Quickly."

Turning, Jessie watched the captain work at untying the ropes that still held one coughing, half-drowned girl to Lucas Gallagher's back. The wail of a frightened child cut through the air as a younger child, a smaller girl, was passed from one man to the next until she reached the arms of her sobbing mother and father.

From over the water came a hoarse shout, drawing the attention of those still clustered near the surf. Another boat had finally appeared around the headland, a pinnace from the British frigate anchored in Blackhaven Bay. Then a wave broke against the beach hard enough to knock Gallagher, still bent beneath the weight of the older girl, off his feet. Hands reached out, supporting him, helping him rise from the swirl of water as the second child was lifted from his back.

At the edge of the sand he collapsed again, sagging to one knee, a hand braced on his thigh, his head bowed, his chest shuddering as he sucked in air. The muscles of his bare back flexed tight, the flesh wet and cold and drained of color, the old flogging scars standing out white on white.

Torn apart by conflicting needs and compulsions, Jessie stared at him. She trembled with the urge to go to him and wrap her warm arms around his cold, shuddering body. She wanted to hold him close, to cradle his exhausted face between her hands and kiss his lips.

She wanted him to be hers.

Instead, she walked stiffly to where they had left the blankets and warm drinks. Someone had already thrown a blanket around his shoulders, but she poured him a tin pannier of hot cider and took it to him. "Here," she said, touching his bent shoulder, for she was allowed to do that, surely? It was such a natural human gesture of comfort. "Drink this."

He flung up his head, his eyes wide and dark, his face gaunt, his mouth open as he continued to gulp in air. Blood trickled down the side of his face from a cut near his eye and he had a bruise purpling on his ribs where he must have struck a rock or debris from the ship. "The boy," he said hoarsely, his hand closing around the mug, "is the boy all right?"

And then Jessie became aware of the sound of a woman sobbing up near the fire, her voice breaking as she cried, "Taylor! But where is Taylor?"

Hot cider spilled steaming into the sand as Gallagher surged to his feet, the blanket slipping from his wet shoulders, his narrowed, bloodshot gaze scanning the heaving, wind-whipped waves where a score of men splashed back and forth, searching, shouting to the sailors in the pinnace. "Aw, Jesus," he said on a harsh expulsion of breath and started back to the sea.

Jessie's hand lashed out, snagging Gallagher's arm. "No! You can't go back out there again. You can't."

He swung his head to look at her, his gaze locking with hers, and in his eyes she saw such a fierce agony it stole her breath. "You don't understand. I told him . . . I told that boy I'd watch out for him. He was right behind me. I thought they had him. I thought—"

"No." She shook her head, wanting desperately to comfort him, to fold him in her arms and draw his head down to press his pain-ravaged face to her breast. But she could do nothing because he wasn't hers. He was a convict, an *Irish* convict, and her whole world was watching. All she could do was say lamely, "You tried. The men in the pinnace are looking for him. They'll find him."

His head jerked, nostrils flaring as he sucked in air. "I'll find him."

~

IT TOOK him what felt like forever to find Taylor.

Too many minutes of fighting the thunderous surf, of willing the muscles of his increasingly cold, exhausted arms and legs to obey him. Too many minutes swimming from pigs' carcasses to dark bobbing casks to broken spars. From the fringes of his consciousness came awareness of the splash of oars from the pinnace, crisscrossing the cove, bent upon the same hopeless task. Then his seeking hand touched matted brown hair and smooth young flesh, soft and cold. So very cold. Lucas gathered the boy to him and struck out for shore.

Jesmond Corbett was waiting for him there in the surf when he staggered to his feet, the boy's thin body cradled against his chest like a babe. "Is he . . ." she began, her face pale and drawn, her voice faltering as she reached out her shaky hand to touch the child's cheek.

Lucas collapsed to the sand, his body heaving, his mind oddly, blessedly numb. "He's dead."

23

J ESSIE STOOD BESIDE the open graves, the soothing tones of the vicar's voice washing gently over her as she stared out at the waters of the bay. The once fierce wind was now only a cool spring breeze that whispered through the leaves of the oak trees on the hillside and nudged the gentle sea into small waves that threw back the sun in a random pattern of sparkling diamonds. Then all at once the terrible beauty of the sea below overwhelmed her and she had to turn her gaze away, to where Lucas Gallagher stood with his head bowed and his hat in his hands.

He had driven her here in the shay, this man who had risked his life to save three small children he didn't even know. But he was only her groom, a convict groom, and so he stood a proper distance from her, near Genevieve. Watching them, it struck Jessie that she now had not one but two forbidden friendships. Except that it wasn't friendship she felt for this man, but something far more dangerous and frightening.

She wondered how it could have happened, how that strange awareness and reluctant fascination had shifted subtly, inevitably, into something different. Something deeper and more powerful. Something her woman's heart could no longer deny.

She watched the breeze ruffle a dark curl of hair that fell forward onto his sun-browned forehead, watched the strong sinews of his throat work as he swallowed, watched the muscles of his lean cheeks bunch as he set his jaw. And the reality of her love for this man, the pain of it, the awful soul-destroying impossibility of it slammed into her with a force that took her breath and brought the sting of tears to her eyes.

He could never be hers, not in the way she wanted, and she wanted him in every way a woman can want a man. She wanted him in her life and at her side not just now, but forever. She wanted to share his dreams and his joys and his sorrows, and to share hers with him. She wanted to know the wonder of taking his body into hers and the joy of bearing his children. She wanted to spend a lifetime coming to know the mystery that was him, to grow old watching the play of emotions across his beloved face. She wanted, wanted, wanted . . . and none of it could ever be, for it was forbidden, what she wanted. Forbidden, impossible, and dangerous.

She wished she could speak of these things with Genevieve, but there had been no time yesterday. And Jessie knew she would need to be particularly careful now with her visits to Last Chance Point, for there was no knowing how many people on that storm-racked beach yesterday had seen the two women arrive together in Genevieve's cart, had seen them gripping each other in support through that interminable wait at the surf's edge, had seen and wondered and whispered. Jessie wished she did not care. She wished she could follow the promptings of her own will with no thought to the confining expectations of her family and their society. But she did care and there was no sense in simply pretending she did not.

" . . . in the midst of life, we are in death," droned the vicar's deep voice, drawing Jessie's gaze again to the open graves. They were burying not one but three victims today, for the seaman who had tried to swim to shore when the ketch's cables first snapped had never made it, and the body of one of the oarsmen from the ketch's smashed boat had been recovered only this morning.

Death came quickly and often here in Tasmania.

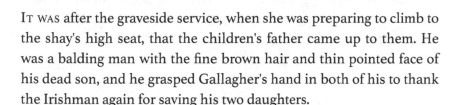

I𝚃 𝚆𝙰𝚂 after the graveside service, when she was preparing to climb to the shay's high seat, that the children's father came up to them. He was a balding man with the fine brown hair and thin pointed face of his dead son, and he grasped Gallagher's hand in both of his to thank the Irishman again for saving his two daughters.

"I've written to the governor," he told Jessie, turning to her, "asking that your man be granted a full pardon for what he did. Such heroism and self-sacrifice should not go unrewarded."

She saw the sardonic gleam that flickered in Gallagher's eyes even as he mouthed the appropriate words in response. For there would be no pardon, she knew; not for Lucas Gallagher. And she found herself wondering again what he could have done that had earned him such implacable enmity from the unforgiving nation that had conquered his island homeland.

T𝙷𝙴 𝚂𝙷𝙰𝚈 𝙻𝚄𝚁𝙲𝙷𝙴𝙳 and swayed up the muddy road that led to the top of the hill, where the road from Blackhaven Bay came together with the tracks from the point and Shipwreck Cove. Lucas held the reins loosely in his hands, his boots braced wide against the unpredictable sliding jolts that came whenever the big iron-rimmed wheels hit another wet patch. Except for the boggy condition of the road and the fresh green exuberance of the gums and acacias, the storm was already a memory. The sun bathed his face with a gentle warmth, but inside he felt cold, so cold, as if he were still in the grip of the deadly currents of the cove.

Was it unbearably cold at the end? he wondered, staring out over the now deceptively calm waters below. *Were you afraid? Or did you find some measure of peace?*

He didn't even realize he'd pulled up at the junction with the track that led down to the beach until Miss Jesmond Corbett said gently, "Don't blame yourself."

He turned his head to meet her troubled gaze. "How can I not? That boy trusted me and I let him down." The words surprised him. He hadn't meant to speak them aloud to anyone. But then he hadn't expected her to read his thoughts so accurately. Hadn't expected her to care.

"That boy trusted you to help him try. That's all you could do."

He looked hard at the dark, sea-splashed rocks in the cove below. She was right, of course. He knew she was right. But that didn't make it any easier to bear.

"If you'd like to drive down there," she said, "we've time. It might help."

He glanced again at the woman beside him. She sat a respectable distance away, her back ramrod straight, her expensively gloved hands resting on the voluminous folds of a somber black gown relieved only by a simple round gold locket she wore pinned at the neck. They might have been any young lady and her servant out for a drive ...

Except for the high color that touched her cheeks whenever their gazes met, and the powerful energy that seemed to hum in the air between them.

For one stolen moment, he let his gaze linger on the exquisite line of her cheek, the finely etched arch of her lips. But it was an unwary thing to do, for there could no longer be any denying the dangerous strength of the physical pull between them, and he was too emotionally battered at the moment to trust himself to resist that other force —that rare yearning of heart and mind and indefinable being that scared him even more, for it was infinitely harder to withstand. "Would that be wise?" he said, his voice rough.

She swallowed, fluttering the wide black ribbons that tied her somber satin capote beneath her chin. She kept her gaze fixed straight ahead. "No one would think anything of it even if we were seen."

"That wasn't what I meant."

She swung her head to look at him, her eyes wide and still. "I'm tired of always trying to do what other people think is wise."

He held her gaze for one meaningful moment, while the breeze loosed a lock of golden hair to flutter against her cheek and the gulls wheeled, calling, high above the sparkling blue sea. Then he spanked the reins against the horse's rump to send the carriage bouncing down the narrow, rutted track to the cove.

~

THEY LEFT the carriage not far from the brooding ruin of the Grimes House and walked over the dunes to the beach.

Refuse from the storm and the wrecked ketch littered the golden sand at the head of the cove and had wedged high between the rocks near the base of the cliffs. Sun-bleached driftwood and giant whale-bones lay jumbled together with the ketch's freshly torn planks, broken spars, and shredded canvas sails, all draped with long tangles of brown seaweed that steamed sharp and salty in the warm sun. The scavengers had already been at work, carrying away most of what was of value, although the sea would continue to give up bits of its grim harvest for months to come.

Jessie sat on the smooth trunk of a long-dead gum and watched as Gallagher walked to where the waves lapped gently against the shore. He stood turned half away from her, his hands on his hips, his hat brim tipped low as he stared out over the cove. She ached with the need to go to him, to slip her arms around his waist and press her cheek in comfort and understanding against the tense muscles of his back. But all she could do was wait, one hand closed around the gold locket that had been hers since childhood, and give him the gift of her silent companionship.

They stayed that way a long time. Seagulls soared overhead, the sun bright on their outspread white wings, their calls mingling bleak and a bit sad with the rhythmic rush of the sea. The tide drifted in slowly, and after a while she noticed he wasn't looking out over the cove anymore. He was staring at the sand beneath the sole of one restlessly moving boot.

"There was a cove below our house," he said, his words coming out soft and lilting in the tones of his lost homeland, "not too different from this one. It claimed its fair share of wrecks as well."

"Is that how you knew the ketch was breaking up?" she asked, her hands gripping her knees.

He raised his head, his hat brim lifting so that she could see his face, the sun showing her the strong line of cheek and chin that never failed to catch at her breath. "There's a certain sound ships' timbers make when they're under too much strain. If you spend enough time around them you get to know their music."

"And you spent a lot of time around ships?"

He shrugged. "My father owns a shipyard back in Ireland. I grew up with the music made by ships and the sea."

She put up a hand to catch a stray lock of hair that drifted across her face. He was looking out to sea again, although now, she suspected, his thoughts were not of the tragedy of this cove but of home. "Why won't the governor grant your pardon?" she asked abruptly.

He went very still, although she could see his chest jerk as he sucked in a quick, painful breath. "Because I killed a man," he said, his voice coming out so cold and flat that it frightened her. "A man named Nathan Fitzherbert. He was a major in the British army and cousin to your young Queen, even if his father's marriage was never recognized by old King George."

All the warmth went out of the day, leaving her cold and shaken. *Because I killed a man,* he'd said; he hadn't said, *Because I was convicted of killing a man . . .* "You were transported for murder?" she asked in a broken voice.

"*Och,* no." He shook his head, that sardonic smile curling his lips. She wondered if the smile mocked himself or the British legal system, and decided it was probably both. "I was transported for being a member of an illegal society, like I said before. They couldn't make the murder charge stick, you see, so they had to find something else to convict me on."

"Why did you kill him?"

That brief, humorless smile faded. "I had reasons," he said, his face as hard and emotionless as his voice. "I don't regret what I did." The breeze rose off the cove, cool and salty, to catch at his coat so that it billowed open as he came at her, his boots crunching the hard sand. She rose, troubled and tense, to meet him. "I don't regret it and I'd do it again, if I had to." He planted himself in front of her and leaned into her, a strange, frightening glitter lighting his eyes. "So you see, Miss Jesmond Corbett of Corbett Castle, you'd do well to keep your distance from me. For more than one reason."

Her breath left her body in a painful rush. "I don't believe you'd harm me."

He opened his eyes wide at her, something that was not a smile curling his lips as he exaggerated his brogue. "Sure then, and what would you be basing that comfortable assumption on?"

She lifted her chin until she was meeting his hard, challenging gaze. "Empirical observation."

He laughed, the sudden flash of genuine amusement chasing the shifting shadows from his eyes and deepening the crease in his cheek. They turned together and began to walk along the beach. After a moment he said, not looking at her, "And have you given much thought then to what we talked about the other day, about having your brother find you a new groom?"

She shook her head. "I keep telling myself I'm twenty years old now, that I should simply tell my mother about my friendship with Genevieve. But every time I think about how she'll react . . ." She swallowed hard, not able to look at him. "I am such a despicable coward."

They had reached the edge of the estuary now and swung away from the beach to follow the sluggish water through the grassy dunes toward where they had left the shay. "Not so despicable," he said, his hat brim lifting as he squinted at the blackened walls of the house before them. "You love your mother and you want her to love you, to be proud of you. Honesty can be expensive. You're the only one who can decide if it's worth it."

They had reached the edge of what had once been a garden, the now stark, blackened branches of its trees choked by ivy and other creepers running rank and rampant in the damp air. It felt oddly colder here by the house. But then it always did. It was as if the place were permanently impregnated with an unnatural chill that brought with it a profound sense of uneasiness and despair.

"Who's the ghost that haunts this place?" he asked, pausing at the edge of the ruined garden, his gaze fixed on the broken stone walls of the house that rose three stories tall to a blackened, collapsed roofline.

"Do you feel it?" she asked, looking not at the house but at the man beside her. "The chill?"

He nodded, his face oddly tight. She still wasn't convinced herself of the existence of such things as ghosts. But this place had always disturbed her. And she thought, studying the way his eyes narrowed, that it affected him too. "So what happened here?" he asked.

There was an elm near the broken fountain at the edge of the garden that had escaped the fire. She went to stand with one gloved hand resting on the cool bark, her gaze on the blackened stones before them. Sometimes when she breathed deeply she thought she could still smell the smoke, still hear the crackle of the flames. "The house was built by a man named Grimes. Mathew Grimes. He was a widower who came here from Sydney with his only daughter, Claire." At the mention of the name, Jessie felt the chill in the air deepen, so that she shivered. "She was sixteen and very lovely. Her father was supposedly devoted to her."

"You say that as if you don't believe it."

She shrugged. "He was a very hard and ambitious man. He wanted this house to be known as the grandest on the whole island. That's why he built it here, so it could be seen from the sea. He even imported a massive staircase made of ancient oak taken from some Elizabethan manor in England. It was quite spectacular. I remember seeing it when I was younger and my father brought me here on a visit."

She thought he might say something but he didn't, so she went on. "One morning, the household servants awoke to discover Claire lying at the foot of the stairs. Her neck was broken. Her father claimed she must have arisen during the night and fallen."

He came to stand beside her, close enough that she could have touched him, although she didn't. "Was there a reason to doubt him?"

She nodded. "The servants had heard them having a terrible argument the night before. It seems Grimes had discovered Claire was in love with one of the convict servants and he was threatening to send the convict away." Jessie found she couldn't look at the man beside her, although she was powerfully aware of him, of the energy that seemed to emanate from him like a conflagration in the air between them, searing her flesh. She sucked in a quick breath that fluttered the black satin ribbons of her hat. "That's when Claire told her father she was carrying the convict's child."

"So her father killed her?"

She shifted until her back was against the tree and looked at him. "No one knows. Perhaps he struck her and knocked her down the stairs accidentally. Or perhaps he pushed her. It would have been a terrible disgrace, if the truth had become known."

He tilted his head. "Yet it did become known."

"There were whispers. But Grimes was a brutal, ruthless man and his servants were too afraid to speak out openly."

He went to stand with one booted foot braced against the broken foundation of the old fountain, his elbow resting on his bent knee as he stared again at the house before them, his face intent. "And the girl's lover?"

"A few days later, Grimes accused the convict of stealing some of the silver."

He swung his head to look at her over his shoulder, his gaze sharp. "And?"

"He was hanged."

A strained silence settled over the clearing. She could hear the cry of the gulls above the cove, the rush of the nearby sea sweeping in and out over the sand. Then he said, "So how did the house burn?"

She swallowed, a useless attempt to ease the ache in her throat. "A year later, exactly to the date of the convict's death, the house caught fire. No one knows why. The household servants were locked in the basement, but someone opened the door so they were able to escape. It wasn't until they were outside that they heard Grimes pounding on his bedroom door upstairs. He was locked in."

"No one let him out?"

She stared at the blackened, empty windows, then looked away, shaking her head. "That grand old oaken staircase went up like a torch. There was nothing anyone could do." Overhead, a lorikeet flitted from branch to branch, chattering noisily. She watched it in silence for a moment, her fingers curling against the trunk's bark. "The servants said that at the end they could hear him screaming his daughter's name over and over again, begging her not to let her lover kill him."

Gallagher let out a huff that wasn't anything like a laugh. "I can't say I feel sorry for him. Who haunts the house then? Claire?"

Jessie felt the breath leave her chest in a painful sigh. "Some say it's all three. The sadness that seems to hang over the place comes from Claire, while the unnatural coldness is Mathew Grimes. But the anger..."

"The anger is the convict," he finished for her, his foot slipping off the foundation stones as he turned to face her.

"Yes," she said meeting his gaze.

They stared at each other forever. The sun filtered down through the leaves of the elm overhead, stirring fitfully in the afternoon breeze. He stood silhouetted against the golden brightness of the clearing behind him, a lean, dark man, beautiful and frightening. She stared at his face, at the strong jaw held defiantly high and proud. Too proud, she thought, for one in his position, and she felt a great fear for him, a fear that caught at her chest with an unexpected pain. She drew a deep breath trying to ease it and smelled again that elusive hint of smoke and charred wood. Startled, she sucked her lower lip between her teeth... And saw his gaze fasten on her mouth.

Something shifted deep in his eyes, something that seemed to echo the turmoil of emotions that welled up hot and wild within her. The sea breeze caught at her skirts, fluttering them out before her as she took a step toward him, then another. He thrust out one hand as if to stop her, but she simply put her hand in his. After a moment, his fingers tightened around hers and he pulled her to him, his hips resting against the fountain behind him so that she settled naturally into the widespread vee of his thighs.

"This is a mistake," he said, his hands riding low on her hips as she wrapped her arms around his neck.

"I know," she said, or started to say, except that his palms were already sliding up her back to draw her closer to him. Her head tilted as his mouth sought hers. Found it.

It was like coming home, to be kissing him. She knew again that warm liquid glow that spread through her body to steal her breath and her will and her conscious awareness of anything beyond the wonder of him. Her fingers dug into the muscles of his shoulders, holding him to her. She heard him make a breathy sound in his throat, felt his grip on her hips tighten, knew the heat of him pressing against her. And still it wasn't enough. And she knew with awful clarity that touching him or even kissing him would never be enough. She wanted him to take her the way a man takes a woman he is hungry for, with no thought of the consequences or tomorrow.

"God, how I've wanted this," he murmured against her open mouth. "How I've wanted you." His fingers tangled in her hair, pulling her head back and knocking her bonnet off so that it dangled from its ribbons as he kissed her eyes, her ears, the sinews of her throat, his breath warm against her flesh. His hands swept her body with a fierce desperation, then suddenly stilled.

He raised his head and looked at her, his eyes dark with desire and what might have been a hint of anger. "This is a mistake," he said, his breathing harsh, rapid.

She stared into his face. "Don't keep saying that."

She bit back a gasp as his hand closed over her breast, the sensation so sharp it might have been pain, only it wasn't. "Don't you understand?" he said, his voice coming out rough, tight. "Do you have any idea what it means when a man says he wants a woman? Do you know what I want to do to you?"

"I know."

His hand moved over her breast in a desperate caress, sun browned, scarred fingers against black satin that they watched together. "Do you?" he said, his face taut. "Do you understand that when I say I want to touch you, I mean I want to touch *all* of you—all those secret places where you've never been touched before, where you've probably never even dreamt of being touched? It means I want to lay you down in this grass with your skirts rucked up about your waist and your flesh bare beneath my hands. And when I say I want you, Miss Jesmond Corbett of Castle Corbett, it means that I want to bury myself inside of you. Here. Now. Because I am a hard man and my life is rough and you have no idea of the hunger that burns inside me."

He was being deliberately raw, deliberately trying to push her away from him with his words. He didn't understand this was a part of what attracted her to him, this dark side of him, this side that was dangerous.

"You think to frighten me with what you're saying," she said, holding herself very still. "But I'm not afraid."

"You should be. Believe me, Miss Corbett, you should be."

She shook her head, her hand coming up to close over his and press his palm against her aching, wanting breast. "I am. But not of you. I'm afraid of a life half lived, of losing myself in other people's expectations of me. The only time I feel like myself anymore is when I'm with you."

The crease beside his mouth deepened. "That's not you, is it, sitting there at your mahogany dinner table every night, drinking champagne and watching the candlelight sparkle on all your fine crystal and silver?"

The edge of acridity in his voice surprised her. "I'm there," she said, "but I'm hidden. And I'm afraid that someday I won't be there at all."

His face gentled unexpectedly. "You don't have to be marrying your Mr. Harrison Tate."

She swung abruptly away from him, a wave of consternation

sweeping her as she realized that she herself had not given one thought to Harrison—to her *betrothed,* God help her. She knew she should be feeling guilty for finding such pleasure in another man's kiss and another man's touch, for *loving* another man. But when she thought of Harrison all she felt was helpless despair.

"How can I not?" she whispered, hugging her arms close to her body. "I have been promised to him since I was born. I pledged *myself to* him over two years ago. He loves me."

"Do you love him?"

She kept her face turned away, for fear he might see the truth of her love betrayed in her eyes. "I don't want to hurt him."

He pushed away from the edge of the fountain and straightened, coming to stand behind her. "Even if marrying him hurts you?"

"You see," she said, smiling sadly, "that's why I need you in my life. To remind me that there's another way to look at things."

He laid his palm against her cheek, urging her around until she was looking up into his dark, intent face. "And this thing between us, this wanting? Where does that fit into your life?"

A terrible pain gripped her heart and stole her breath. "I don't know."

"Yes you do. Whether you marry your Mr. Harrison Tate or not, there can never be anything between us." He nodded his head toward the blackened, tragedy-haunted ruin beside them. "You know it, and I know it."

THEY DIDN'T SEE the boat until they left the ruins of the formal garden and took an overgrown path that wound along the water's edge.

Its staves smashed, its upended white-painted hull smeared with mud and brown seaweed, the ketch's small boat lay amid the reeds that lined the upper part of the estuary. "Look," she said pausing on the path, her hand coming up unthinkingly to touch his sleeve. "Who'd have thought the force of the storm would drive it all the way up here?"

A faint ripple disturbed the surface of the water, rustling the reeds and setting the boat to rocking gently on its ends, the movement slow and sluggish and a bit sad. Then something about his stillness drew her attention to the man beside her, and what she saw in his face stole her breath and turned her sadness to fear.

24

BEATRICE WAS IN HER ROSE GARDEN snipping spent blossoms, a pair of secateurs in hand and a basket looped over her arm, when Jessie let herself in the gate from the yard.

"Jesmond," Beatrice called, lifting her head to peer out from beneath the wide-brimmed straw hat she always wore in the garden. "If I might have a word with you, dear?"

Jessie hesitated only a moment, then made her way through the concentric rings of Bourbons and damasks, rugosas and ramblers that were her mother's greatest joy. Unlike her children, Beatrice's roses grew in strict conformity to her wishes. And they seldom died. "Your garden's looking lovely this spring," Jessie said, kissing the air beside her mother's pale cheek.

"Do you think so?" A slight frown puckered the bridge of Beatrice's thin, aristocratic nose as she stooped to snip off a spent bloom. Beatrice might allow her gardeners to water her roses and tend the rest of the park, but she always insisted on pruning and deadheading the roses herself. "I must confess I am rather worried about black spot. We've had so much rain."

Jessie laughed softly. "I'm convinced your roses wouldn't think of succumbing to something as ordinary as black spot."

"Hmm," Beatrice said, stepping back to critically assess the symmetry of a white Bourbon. "You were a long time coming back from the funerals."

Jessie kept her gaze carefully fixed on the bloom before her. "I decided to go for a walk along the beach afterward."

"While you were gone, I had a visit from Captain Boyd."

Jessie looked up. "Captain Boyd?"

An unusual touch of color tinged Beatrice's cheeks, making her look both younger and prettier. "The captain of the frigate, the *Recluse*. He mentioned that he saw you at the cove the night of the storm. With That Woman."

"You mean Genevieve Strzlecki?" Somehow, Jessie managed to keep her voice light and casual although her heart was thumping wildly. *I'm not a child anymore,* she reminded herself. *I can't be beaten or locked in the tower room and kept on bread and water for days.* And still all she could find the courage to say was, "I took shelter at the cottage when the storm struck."

"Really, Jesmond." Beatrice shook her head and *tssked* in that way she had. "She is not at all a proper person for you to know. You never seem to give a thought to what people will say."

The ribbons of Jessie's hat suddenly felt too tight. She untied them with swift, angry jerks and pulled the hat off. "On the contrary. Mother, I seem to do nothing but worry about what people will say, with the result that I live my life in accordance with everyone else's thoughts and wishes instead of my own."

Beatrice stared at her daughter with that puzzled, faintly appre-hensive expression Jessie knew so well, for she'd seen it often enough all the years of her growing up. "I'll never understand you," Beatrice said, cinching her lips down into a thin, sour line that was also famil-iar. "Perhaps Harrison will be able to manage you better than I have."

At the thought of being "managed" by her future husband, Jessie felt a wave of panic surge through her. She told herself that Harrison loved her, which surely meant he liked her as she was. Once she had believed that. Only she was beginning to worry that it wasn't true and that in marrying Harrison she would be exchanging the critical, disapproving frowns of her mother for those of a husband.

Jessie swung away, her gaze sweeping the upper verandas of the house. "Where is Warrick? Do you know?"

"Really, Jesmond. We were discussing something of importance here. Warrick rode off shortly after midday to return that ridiculous donkey to its owners. I told him I saw no reason why he shouldn't send one of the men, but he insisted on doing it himself. He seems to have no notion of the degree of dignity to be expected from a landowner of his station. And look at this," she continued in the same tone of voice, her secateurs snipping viciously at the offending bush before her. "Black spot. I knew it. I've always had trouble with this particular rose. I'm seriously considering having it removed."

Jessie stood, the sun warm on the black satin of her dress, and watched silently as her mother attacked the rosebush, her problems with her unsatisfactory children temporarily forgotten. She became aware of a strange heaviness in her chest, an ache that was like a sadness for things lost, or perhaps for things she'd never had but wanted desperately.

It was a feeling that was to stay with her the rest of the day, although she never came any closer to understanding it.

THE BOY SAT on the rough drystone wall that encircled a small, muddy croft beside the hut, a knife and what looked like a thin wooden pipe in his hands. He watched Warrick rein in his showy chestnut gelding before the hut's crude door, the donkey braying foul-temperedly and lagging on its lead. An uncut thatch of fiery gold hair framed a delicate, elfin face and a pair of wide, changeling eyes that stared up at Warrick. In age, the boy could have been anywhere between thirteen and seventeen, his thin, almost feminine face at odds with his height. He didn't smile and he didn't move.

"You must be Dicken," said Warrick.

"Aye." The boy shifted his attention back to the wood in his hands, the knife moving with a swift, sure efficiency that had Warrick wondering if it was this knife and this boy who had ended Parker Jones's life.

Warrick raised himself in his stirrups, stretching his back, the saddle leather creaking. In the distance a dog barked, although he could see no one, the sun shining warm and bright on an empty hillside of wind-ruffled grass. "Is your sister around?"

"Aye."

Warrick kneed his gelding up to the wall and held out the donkey's lead. "Thank you for the use of your animal."

For one, blazing instant, the boy met his gaze. Then he shrugged and returned his attention to the pipe. "Take the rope off her halter and let her go. She won't stray."

"Now that I believe," said Warrick, unsnapping the lead. "The beast definitely possesses a decided aversion to movement."

The boy started to smile, then checked it, as if he knew why Warrick was here, what Warrick wanted with his sister. But then he probably did know.

Warrick collected his reins. He was about to turn the gelding's head toward the stream where he'd first met her on the off chance she might be there, when he saw her.

She was coming down the slope of the daisy-strewn hill behind the stone hut, a tall slip of a girl with impossibly long legs and a regal neck and hair the color of a sunrise-gilded sea. He cantered the gelding up the hill toward her and drew rein. She reached up to him and smiled.

The fragile bones of her wrist stood out stark against her fine, golden skin as he closed his hand around it. With her other hand, she lifted her skirts high, the worn blue cotton falling away from her thin legs as she put her bare foot on the toe of his boot and hauled herself up behind him with a sinewy strength unexpected in one of her delicate frame. The movement rucked up her skirts but she made no attempt to straighten them, simply hugged his hips with her thighs in a way that pressed her bare knees and calves against his taut, hungry body.

"Where do we go?" he asked.

"That way." She pointed toward the sea, then slid her hands up under his coat and around his waist in a slow caress that had his breath hitching in his chest.

She guided him to a high, grass-covered cliff that thrust out into the sea, the land falling away steeply on three sides in a sheer rock face high enough to make him dizzy if he looked down at the wave-washed rocks far below. "Here?" he said.

She slipped from behind him and spun around in a circle, her arms held wide, her hair flying, her faded blue skirts twirling about her. "Yes."

"Why here?" he asked as he swung out of the saddle, his gaze never leaving her face as he stooped to tether the gelding to a stunted eucalyptus.

She twirled toward him, a quicksilver spirit of sun-warmed female flesh and cascading silken hair and eyes that flashed provocatively as she drew up a tantalizing arm's span away from him. "Because when I'm here, I feel like I'm on top of the world." She raised her arms, a mysterious smile curling her lips, her elbows pointing to the sky as she began to unfasten her dress. "I come here whenever I can. I like to take off my clothes and just lie here in the sun."

She eased her dress down slowly as she spoke, making of her body an offering. Small high breasts kissed with a sprinkle of cinnamon. Narrow stomach tapering to boyish hips. Sunlight gleamed, soft feminine curls. The long length of her thighs. The dress sank to the grass with a whisper. She stood naked before him and smiled.

He looked at her and felt his breath leave his body in a hot rush of desire. She stood slim and straight, a golden reed of a girl grounded in green and framed by the blue of the sky and the sun-sparkled infinity of the sea. She was so beautiful it made his throat ache just looking at her. To touch her ... to touch her would be an ecstasy, and his hand trembled as he reached for her.

"You're golden and glowing everywhere," he said as he spread his hand over her breast and felt her nipple harden against his palm. "You look as if your body has been kissed all over by the sun."

"You kiss me." Her eyes dark and compelling, she let her head fall back, her fingers entwining at the base of his neck to draw him down to her. "I want you to kiss me everywhere the sun has touched."

He bent his head and rubbed his open mouth against the delicate curve of her throat, breathed in the scent of her, warm, musky, feminine.

So vibrantly alive.

He'd never known a woman who would even think of climbing a sea cliff to slip off her dress and revel in the warmth of the sun on her naked flesh. He'd never known anyone, man or woman, who was this uninhibited and natural, this careless of common expectations of proper behavior. She partook of life with a wild kind of joy—drank of life with her eyes wide open and a laugh on her lips. When he was with her, he felt alive himself. More than alive; he felt revived, reborn, as if he'd been dead for years and hadn't even noticed it.

Groaning, he tangled his fingers in the silken warmth of her hair, his thumbs brushing back and forth beneath her chin as he kissed her neck. She arched her back, her breasts pressing against his chest, one of her legs lifting to entwine erotically with his. Then her mouth found his and he lost himself in the wild magic of her kiss.

Her mouth was hot and wet and delicious, a seductive swirl of teeth and tongue and carnal promise. He felt reason and self-control begin to slip away as his world narrowed to a whirling vortex of sensation and lust and driving, urgent need. He knew nothing but the soft moist heat of her mouth and the firm ripeness of her naked body beneath his seeking hands and the tingling fire spread by her touch.

She jerked loose his neckcloth, opened his waistcoat and shirt, tore them with his coat from his body. He felt the sun warm on his flesh, felt the sea breeze lift the hair from his damp forehead. With gentle urgency, he bore her down onto her dress in the grass, her legs spreading wide beneath him, her fingers impatient with the flap of his breeches. Then she took his hardness in her hands and he hissed with the agonizing pleasure of it.

He was mindless now, a lust-driven animal stripped of all pretense of civilization or chivalry. He wanted to bury himself inside her, hard and deep, to pound into her, to fill her with himself, to make himself a part of her, to feel her legs wrap around his hips and her teeth nip at his shoulders. He was gasping, shaking with the need to be inside her.

He fumbled with the French letter he'd brought and heard her laugh breathlessly when he put it on. "And who is that to protect? Me or you?" But she didn't seem to expect an answer because she took him in her hands again and put him inside her.

Moist heat clenched around him, consumed him, and he lost his ability to speak. He buried his face in her hair, breathed in the scent of her, kissed her eyelids, her mouth, as his body quivered, wanted. Her hips moved beneath him, met him stroke for stroke until he was pounding into her. He could feel her fingers digging into his shoulders, her nails raking his back; see her eyes glazed, unfocused, glittering.

She was making breathy, erotic noises deep in her throat like a wild thing. He was a wild thing, an animal, taking his mate with brutal lust on the ground, the sun hot on his naked, thrusting flanks, the sea breeze skimming his sweat-slicked back. He felt her inner heat begin to throb around him, saw her head fall back, her neck arching on a gasp of ecstasy, heard her joyous scream of pleasure and fulfillment, and was lost himself.

Teeth clenching, his eyes squeezing shut, his fingers digging into the earth, he exploded into her long and hard and wondrously.

THE SHATTERED PIECES OF HIMSELF, of his world came back together slowly, glowing with joy and a sweet firmament of fulfillment. The brightness of the sun, the vivid blue of the sky hurt his eyes. He became aware of the harsh rasp of his breathing, the sweat that trickled down his cheeks and pooled in the small of his spine. He heard again the rhythmic swell of the sea beating against the base of the cliffs, the harsh cry of the gulls, the whisper of the wind in the grass.

He raised up onto his forearms to ease some of his weight from her slim frame. But he couldn't bring himself to separate from her yet. He wanted to stay in her, to stay a part of her, forever. "I love you," he said, resting his forehead against hers, their breath-ravaged chests shuddering together. "I love you and I don't even know your name."

She reached up, her slim arms twining about his neck, her mouth taking his in a long, hot, sucking kiss that ended too soon. "How can you love me?" she said, easing back down, a smile curling her impossibly wide mouth. "You know nothing about me."

Her words disturbed him. It worried him to think that she might not be feeling what he was feeling, for she knew little more of him than he did of her. He kissed the tip of her nose. "I know you live in a stone hut overlooking the sea with a brother named Dicken and a donkey that would have been happier being born as a very sedentary rock." She laughed, her golden brown eyes sparkling, and he thought she was the most beautiful thing he'd ever seen. A fierce rush of emotion gripped at his heart, stole his breath and left his voice shaky. "I know that you like the feel of the sun on your skin and that you're the most beautiful, free-spirited person I've ever met."

Her smile faded, her brows drawing together in thought. "You think that's all there is to me?"

He eased himself sideways so he could settle her in the crook of his arm and look down at her. "No. I want you to tell me."

"Tell you what?"

"More about you." He smoothed the damp tendrils of fiery hair back from her forehead. "Tell me where you come from. How you came to be here in Tasmania, in that hut in the middle of nowhere."

She put her hand on the bare flesh of his chest, her gaze fixed on the caressing motion of her fingers rather than his face. "Well, let's see. I was born in a wee, mean croft in the Highlands, near a place called Strathspey. One afternoon when I was thirteen, the laird's son and two of his friends caught me in the glen and took turns at me with the other two holding me down."

He closed his arm protectively about her thin shoulders. "Jesus . . . I'm sorry."

She shrugged, although it didn't deceive him, for he saw the quickly suppressed sigh that quivered her breast. "Bein' untouched is no' as important to a girl raised in a croft as it might be to some grand lady living in one of your big, fancy houses. Me father though, he took it hard, what they did to me. He went after the laird's son with his fists, and there was . . . a spot of trouble. We had to leave."

He traced the curve of her shoulder, ran his fingertips along the line of her clavicle and down between her breasts. She was so beautiful, so beautiful and joyous and free, and these terrible things had been done to her.

"I used to have two wee sisters," she said softly, "but they died on the ship coming out here. Me sisters and me mother, too. The da, he lived long enough to get this bit of land and help us build the house. But he was never well after the laird finished with him and he died near two years ago. So now it's just Dicken and me."

For the first time in his life, Warrick felt the comfort of his own existence as something vaguely shameful—the grand, fourteen-room house with its gleaming mahogany and polished silver, its feather beds and silken curtains pooling ostentatiously on the floor, its four-course dinners washed down with vintage brandy. "It can't be easy for you," he said quietly.

She put her hand over his, holding his palm pressed against her skin. "We get by just fine. We've a few chickens and sheep, and I grow enough potatoes and carrots and things to feed us and still have some left to sell to the shopkeeper in Blackhaven Bay. And Dicken, he fishes, and hunts for wallabies and birds with his sling. It's a good life. I like it here. I'm happy."

Watching the guileless smile that touched her lips, he wondered if he had ever heard anyone in his world say that. *I am happy.* If he had, he couldn't remember it.

He dipped his head and nuzzled her neck. "Now I know you," he said, his breath blowing warm and moist against her flesh. "So now you can believe I love you."

She rolled onto her side to face him, her eyes unexpectedly solemn as she gazed up at him. "You canna know a person by the things they tell you."

"No," he agreed, his hand riding low on her naked hip, his thumb moving in small, restless circles. "Then again, you can live around a person your entire life and never really know them."

"Know this," she said and took his hand to put it on her breast, her head tilting as she leaned forward to touch her lips to his.

The love they made this time was slow and sweet and wondrous, a gentle exploration of flesh and sinew and muscle. A giving of pleasures that led inevitably to a hot rush of overwhelming desire and the coming together of their bodies in an urgent culmination of wet blinding heat.

"Your name," he said with a gasp, his body thrusting into hers. "You never told me your name."

She dug her fingers into the clenched muscles of his naked hips, pulling him to her harder, faster. "Faine. My name is Faine."

"I love you, Faine!" cried, his body convulsing in the ecstasy of release, his shout of triumph ringing out over the rush of the waves and the restless moaning of the wind.

25

"M R. WARRICK, SIR," called Charlie, hurrying from the stables. "I didn't hear you ride in."

Warrick swung out of the saddle, his gaze drifting about the nearly deserted yard where the shadows of the outbuildings stretched long and cool. It would be dark soon. "Where's Gallagher?" he asked, holding the gelding's reins out to the boy as he skidded to a halt, his boots sliding in the mud.

Charlie straightened slowly, pale-lashed gray eyes going wide in a blank face. "Out working Finnegan's Luck."

"This late?"

"Yes, sir.

"Huh," said Warrick and started off toward where he could see Jess perched on the top rail of the paddock fence, one arm thrown around her mare's neck, the other hand stroking the horse's white nose. As he drew nearer, he heard the gentle murmur of her voice, saw the mare's ears twitch back and forth as if the dainty little black were listening.

"When you were a little girl," he said, propping one elbow on the railing beside her, his gaze on the sky that was turning aquamarine and pink as the sun sank toward the hills, "whenever you had a problem you needed to sort out in your head, you used to come down here and sit on this fence and talk to your horse."

She smiled sadly, her hand rubbing softly over the mare's satiny cheek. "The way I remember, it used to help more."

Grunting, he swung about to lean his shoulders against the rail, his arms crossing at his chest. "I was here when Captain Boyd paid our dear mother a morning visit."

Her hand stilled, her fingers splaying against the mare's glossy hide. "Ah. So you've heard about my latest attempt to bring shame upon the family and hasten our mother's sad decline."

He raised one eyebrow. "Surely you know that being caught in a storm—even if it should lead to death from pneumonia—is infinitely preferable to announcing to the world that one has come into contact with the local Fallen Woman?"

A cool breeze rustled the leaves of the trees in the park and brought them the scent of lilacs and lemon gums and the warm, earthy smell of horses. She met his gaze, her eyes dark and serious. "I like her, Warrick."

"Well I should think so, when one considers you've been visiting her for so long—*hey, careful there,*" he added, grabbing her arm when she tottered dangerously on the high rail.

She closed her hand on his shoulder, her gaze bright and earnest on his face. "You knew?"

"For years."

She turned away to look out over the paddock where some half a dozen horses grazed, muted shades of charcoal and amber shifting in the fading light. "Have you told Harrison?"

He gave her a long, steady look. "Right. That's exactly the sort of thing I'd do."

A hint of color touched her cheeks. She shook her head. "Sorry."

He watched her, a faint, barely acknowledged uneasiness shifting within him. "I can tell you one thing, though: Harrison wouldn't approve. He can be devilishly strait-laced about that sort of thing."

She stared into the darkening distance. "If I were the kind of person I like to think I am, I'd tell him. I'd tell them both."

"There's nothing wrong with the person you are."

"Isn't there?" She swung her head to look at him again. "Why would this Captain Boyd come running out here, carrying tales of me to Mother?"

"He's Mother's suitor. Didn't you know?"

She wobbled precariously on her perch. *"What?"*

He flung an arm around her waist, steadying her. "Jesus, Jess! Get down off that fence before you fall off."

She rested her hands on his shoulders and let him swing her to the ground. "But surely Mother is not encouraging him?" she said, her head bowed as she adjusted her skirts. She looked up sharply, her eyebrows drawing together in a frown. "That I cannot believe."

He linked his arm with hers and began to stroll with her toward the house. "Oh, Mother will never marry again, no need to fear that. Her first experience was too miserable for her to be inspired to repeat it. But I think she does enjoy Boyd's company. He has the most depressing views imaginable on the wretched state of society and the decline of modem morality. They can sit and tut-tut together happily for hours."

She choked on a quickly swallowed spurt of laughter. "You shouldn't say such things, Warrick."

"Why ever not? It's true. Watch them together at Mother's garden party next week." He glanced down at his sister's drawn features and noticed for the first time the shadows that lay beneath her eyes, the tightness around her mouth. Whatever was troubling her, it was more than the small furor over the incident in Shipwreck Cove. Poor Jess, he thought, always trying so hard to be what their mother and their society decreed a gentlewoman should be. Always trying but never succeeding because it wasn't precisely what she was meant to be. Yet she kept trying, and one of these days she was probably going to succeed—at least to a point. Then there would be nothing left of her but a pale reflection of other people's expectations and a haunting echo of all she could have been.

He thought of Faine, twirling through the grass, her head thrown back in laughter, her arms reaching for the sun. She might be poor and ignorant, she might go barefoot and live in a crude stone hut, but Faine knew something—*had* something that he and Jess had looked for their entire lives and never found.

"Next week?" Jess was saying, looking at him in surprise. "I thought Mother wasn't having the party for a while yet, until the weather improves."

"She wasn't." He flashed her a grin and reached to unlatch the garden gate. "But since your unwise behavior on the night of the storm, she's decided she ought to move the date up. Display you at your most sedate and conformable to all our curious, speculative friends and neighbors, and all that." He held open the gate for her, then paused to throw a last glance across the yard and frown. "I was hoping to speak to Gallagher tonight about putting up a marquee."

"Gallagher? But . . . he's a groom."

Something in her voice brought his gaze around to her again. "He's also a very handy man with a hammer. I think he used to be a shipbuilder or some such thing."

She turned her face away from him to stare up at the house. "Some such thing."

He studied her pale, half-averted face and felt it again, that indefinable sense of uneasiness. He wanted to ask her what was wrong. He wanted to ask if there was anything he could do to help. But how could he help her, he thought wryly, when he didn't even know how to help himself?

THE THICK BLACK muck of the marsh held the smashed bow of the boat in a tight grip, the water of the estuary lapping at Lucas's bare thighs as he heaved and swore, then heaved again.

He could hear the steady rush and retreat of the tide coming in, rolling up over the nearby beach with a foaming swish. In another half hour he'd probably be able to float the damn thing free. But he didn't have half an hour; he was going to be lucky to make it back to the barracks before sunset as it was.

Gritting his teeth, he heaved again, hard, and felt the mud release its captive with a loud sucking pop that filled the air with the fetid stench of dampness and decay. Lucas flipped the boat over onto its hull, then paused to swipe his bare arm across his sweaty forehead, his chest heaving as he drew in air.

The boat was big, bigger than he'd have preferred. True, its size would make it safer in the open sea. But it also meant they'd need to take more men with them when they made their escape. And more men meant more mouths, more chances of secrets leaking out, more chances of getting caught.

Stooping, he leaned his shoulder against the stern and pushed, grunting with the strain. He'd been so long getting back here to the cove that he'd been afraid he was going to find the boat gone already, carried off by the scavengers who picked over the debris on the beach. But it had been washed surprisingly far up the estuary. And people tended to avoid the Grimes House if they could.

Even as he worked dragging the boat deep into a thicket and covering it with bracken, he was aware of the darkly silent walls of the house, brooding over him. It was like a tangible thing, the evil in this place. The evil and the anger and the despair. Even the birds and small animals seemed to avoid it, the ruined garden remaining oddly empty and quiet as the evening air around it filled with the chirrup of crickets and the noisy chatter of birds coming in to roost for the night.

He shivered, the night breeze cold on his naked flesh, but he took the time to do what he could to smooth out the path of broken reeds and crushed grass left by the dragging boat. Thank God the growth was green and resilient; most of the evidence would be gone in a few days. He straightened, his eyes narrowing as he gazed at the sinking sun. It was getting late.

He had tethered Finnegan's Luck to the elm beside the broken fountain, and the Irish hunter nickered when Lucas cut across the overgrown garden toward him. "What's the matter, big boy? Don't you like this place, either?" Lucas murmured, rubbing the bay's velvety nose before he turned away to scramble into his clothes.

He'd expected to feel elation or at least satisfaction at finding the boat and securing it. The damage to the boat's hull wasn't as bad as he'd feared; he'd be able to repair it easily given the right tools and materials, and the Fox would doubtless be able to scrounge up some oars. He should be buzzing with expectation and hope. The freedom he'd wanted for so long now seemed within his grasp. Yet all he could think about was the taste of heaven he'd found in Jesmond Corbett's arms and the look in her eyes when he'd come at her out of the storm-driven surf that night.

Lucas's hands stilled at their task and he found himself wondering what it might have been like, what might have happened if he'd walked into some Dublin lecture hall one day and seen her there, her features intense with concentration and interest. If they had strolled along the Irish Sea and talked of her dreams and his. If he had met her in the days when he still had dreams rather than one wild, dangerous ambition—to escape.

Swearing softly under his breath, Lucas thrust his arms through the sleeves of his coat and jerked the bay's reins free from the elm. The sooner he got away from here, the better it would be, he thought.

For both of them.

"You cut it a wee bit close there, laddie," said Daniel, his voice almost drowned out by the harsh clang of the barracks' door locking them behind thick stone walls and iron bars for the night.

Lucas grinned into the darkness. "Aye. A wee bit. But I got it, Daniel. We now have a boat."

26

JESSIE STOOD ON THE SECOND-STORY veranda and looked out over the sun-gilded garden below. The warm afternoon air was filled with the clatter of lumber and the steady banging hammers and shouts from the workmen busy knocking together the wooden frames that would be used to support the canvas awnings for Beatrice Corbett's garden party.

As if he sensed her gaze on him, one of the convicts straightened, a lean man with midnight-dark hair and the graceful, controlled movements of a born athlete. He turned slowly, the sun glazing the striking features of his face as his head fell back and his gaze lifted to the veranda. He had stripped off his coat and waistcoat, his rough shirt hanging open at the neck, his forearms showing sun-browned and strong where he'd rolled up his sleeves. As she watched, he swiped an arm across his sweat-glistened face, his chest rising and falling with the exertion of his labors. She stood well back from the railing in the shadow of one of the stone arches, but there was no doubt he knew she was there, knew she watched him. It was that powerful, the connection between them. Powerful and dangerous.

She had never meant for this to happen, this painful wanting, this impossible love. She'd never meant for it to happen, but that didn't

make the danger to Gallagher any less deadly, didn't make her disloy-
alty to Harrison any less wrong, didn't make her weight of guilt any
easier to bear.

She'd thought she could ride beside this man she loved, talk to
him, be with him, and still control her feelings for him, still control
herself. But that sunlit afternoon in the ruined garden beside the
beach, when they had talked of doomed love and kissed with such
wild abandon, had forced her to admit to herself what she had always
known: that Gallagher was right, that it was a mistake for her not to
stay away from him. A mistake for her to tempt fate by following the
siren call of this forbidden longing.

And so for three days now she had kept away from him. She
hadn't been riding, had avoided the stables, had stayed away from
anywhere she thought she might encounter him. But she couldn't
seem to stop herself from searching for him in the distance, couldn't
keep herself from watching him as she was now. Watching and
wanting him. The desire was still there, along with the temptation to
give in to it. She was going to have to get away from here, she thought
in desperation, backing farther into the shadows. She was going to
have to get away from the Castle, away from temptation, away from
him. For weeks Harrison had been gently hinting that it was past time
they set a date for their wedding. She realized now that she'd been
deliberately delaying her commitment. But no longer, she decided.
Once she married Harrison, once she was living at Beaulieu Hall
instead of the Castle, she would seldom see Gallagher. She wouldn't
be able to watch for him, wouldn't be tempted to seek him out,
wouldn't be tempted to touch him, to kiss him, to give herself to him .
. .

A whisper of sound brought her head snapping around, her body
tensing as if she'd been caught doing what she was only thinking
about. She saw Warrick, brandy glass in hand, lounging against the
open French door behind her, and she relaxed.

He wore buckskin breeches and high boots and looked as if he'd
only just come in, his hair still ruffled by the wind, his warm body
giving off the pleasant scent of the sun and the road. He had devel-

oped the habit of riding off first thing in the morning and not returning until late in the evening. She didn't know where he went or what he was doing; she knew only that *something* was different in his life. And she wasn't sure she liked the effect it was having on him.

"Home so soon, Warrick?" she said. "It won't be dark for . . . oh, at least another three hours or so."

He gave her a twisted grin and lifted his glass in a half-salute. "Mother commands my presence. Something to do with the smoking room and chairs and I don't remember what else." He threw down the contents of his glass with a quick flick of his wrist. "I'll be glad when this damned party of hers is over."

"I hope the weather holds."

He sauntered forward to stand at the railing, his brooding gaze only half-focused on the activity below. "Do you really? I'm rather inclined to wish for rain, myself. An afternoon spent in the company of an assemblage of people selected entirely on the basis of their wealth, genteel birth, or positions of authority is enough to drive a man to drink."

"You drink too much already, Warrick," she said softly.

He pivoted to face her, an errant blond curl falling across his suddenly narrowed eyes. "So I do." He lifted his glass between them, the fine crystal balanced precariously on the tips of his fingers. "And I seem to be empty. Excuse me."

He brushed past her. She wanted to call him back, to tell him she was sorry, to tell him she was only worried about him. Except that she wasn't sure she knew how to say it. So much of the easy camaraderie they'd once shared seemed to have disappeared, a victim of her secrets and his.

She felt a burning weight of melancholy press upon her chest, stealing her breath and leaving her aching and confused. Wrapping her hands around the railing, she looked out over the garden again, but Lucas Gallagher had disappeared. She didn't know whether she was relieved or disappointed.

She should have been relieved. Only, she decided she was disappointed.

SHE'D MADE up her mind to tell Harrison the next time she saw him that she was ready to set the date for their wedding. Except Harrison was busy with estate business and she didn't see him again until the afternoon of Beatrice's garden party.

The day dawned blue and clear, with only a balmy breeze to sway the trees in the park. "You see," said Warrick, pausing beside her, "not even God would dare to disrupt Mother's plans."

Caught in the act of drinking a glass of punch, Jessie choked and shook her head at him. But she didn't tell him he shouldn't say such things. She was learning.

For hours now the garden had been steadily filling with their neighbors—or at least those of their neighbors considered socially acceptable enough to attend one of Beatrice Corbett's functions: men in swallow-tail coats and top hats, ladies in fine gowns with wide swishing hems and old family pearls and veiled hats that shielded their complexions from the ravages of the southern sun. The gentle strains of a sonata, played by the Blackhaven Bay String Quartet, floated away through the trees.

This was her world, Jessie thought with a bittersweet ache as she looked out over the swirl of rainbow-hued silks and carefully smiling faces; this world of champagne and smoked salmon and cucumber sandwiches, of carefully modulated voices underscored by the clink of crystal and the gentle whack of a croquet mallet striking a ball. This world of refinement and luxury sustained by the brutal labor of doomed men broken by chains and whips and the cold dark terror of the isolation cell. She and Lucas Gallagher were both a part of this world, but the roles they played in it were quite different. Their lives might brush one against the other's, but only in certain carefully prescribed ways. They were never meant to mingle, never meant to speak of things that mattered, never meant to touch or kiss.

Never meant to love.

"Don't look now," said Warrick, his mouth close to her ear, "but he's there, by the wisteria arbor. With Mother."

"Who?" whispered Jessie, controlling with difficulty the impulse to swing around and stare behind her.

"Captain Boyd, scourge of absconders and wayward daughters, and seeker after rich widows."

Jessie pressed two gloved fingers to her lips to hold back an inappropriate smile. Schooling her face into blandness, she pivoted slowly as if idly surveying the crowded garden, her gaze skimming over the guests wandering the paths between the carefully tended roses and faultless parterres until she could see the wisteria arbor. A short, stocky man with gray-laced brown hair and thick whiskers was bending low over Beatrice's hand.

"I remember him," said Jessie, shifting slightly in a vain attempt to see her mother's face. "I noticed him on the beach. A very officious little man." She frowned as Beatrice began to walk with the captain toward the south lawn. "Are you quite certain Mother isn't seriously considering his suit?"

Warrick laughed loud enough to turn several heads in their direction. He leaned into her again, lowering his voice. "You must be joking. The man's fortune could only be described as paltry, and marriage is an economic institution, remember? At least as far as Mother is concerned."

Jessie brought her gaze back to her brother's handsome face. "Do you think she ever loved Papa? Even just a little?"

His smile turned sour. "Lord, no. Her parents arranged the match. She conformed to their wishes, of course, because conforming is what Mother does best, and she's continued to do her duty ever since, God help us all. Love never had anything to do with it."

The string quartet was playing Haydn now, the sweet, sad notes weaving a spell of melancholy over the low murmur of the crowd in the garden. Jessie watched her mother turn, her head coming up, the wide brim of her black satin bonnet lifting to show she was smiling. For one shining moment she looked unexpectedly young and happy, almost pretty, and Jessie felt her breath catch, for it was as if she had been given a glimpse of the young woman her mother had once been, the woman Jessie herself had never known. "Do you think she was ever in love?" she asked quietly.

Warrick widened his eyes and let out a huff of air between his teeth. "Mother? You must be joking."

Jessie found she couldn't look at her mother anymore, so she looked instead at the Blackhaven Bay String Quartet. She had known them since she was a child, these four aging colonists with their old-fashioned knee breeches and beautiful music and unselfish willing-ness to come along and add a gentle touch of England to any social gathering in this part of the island. Only there was something different about the quartet today. The man on the left was young, not old. He was turned away from her, but there was something painfully familiar about the length of his body, about the way he held his head, about the graceful way he moved . . .

"Warrick," she said, her hand tightening around her brother's wrist when he would have moved off. "Why is my groom playing the violin in the Blackhaven Bay String Quartet?"

27

WARRICK SWUNG HIS HEAD around and grinned. "You didn't hear? Jacob McCallister rode into the yard this morning sporting red spots all over his face."

"Red spots?"

"Measles. He had to go home. The remaining members of the quartet were saying they couldn't play without another violin, so Gallagher offered to take McCallister's place."

"No, I hadn't heard," said Jessie, her voice coming out oddly flat and hollow. She knew she shouldn't let herself stare at him, at Gallagher, but he drew her gaze with an inescapable, dangerous pull.

He looked magnificent, his body lean and powerful and humming with the potent, leashed strength of a feral wolf turned loose amidst a herd of sedate, contented sheep. She let her gaze rove over him, beguiled by the interplay of the familiar with the unfamiliar. She knew the delicate curve of the scarred wrist holding the violin to his shoulder, the graceful, fluid movement of arm and torso as he drew the bow across the strings with a reverence that was like a lover's caress. She knew him, but she did not know him side of him.

She had seen him swinging a pickax in a quarry and working horses in a paddock, his rough convict clothes soaked in sweat and layered with dust. She had seen him half naked, his wet chest gleaming in the golden glow of a setting sun or the brittle white flashes of lightning from a storm-cracked sky. But she had never seen him like this, dressed in the trappings of her own world. This might not be his world now, but there could be no doubt he had known a similar world once. The black long-tailed coat he wore was old and it didn't fit him well, yet he carried it with an insouciant grace few men in the garden could emulate. She stared at him, at the Celtic beauty of that half-averted face, at the lowered lashes that hid the rebellious green fire of his eyes, and she felt her breath catch painfully in her throat. For one stolen moment she allowed herself to imagine what it could have been like...

What it could have been like if he were just another colonist like the rest of them, here in her mother's garden by the civilized exchange of invitation and consent. A guest who could smile at her from across the mingling crowd with no fear of who might be watching, who could set aside his violin and walk toward her, the sun warm and free on his face. If she could simply rest her hand on the crook of his arm and walk with him beneath the alley of oaks, his head bending toward her as she looked up at him and smiled...

"It's a damnable nuisance, of course," Warrick was saying. "I could ill spare him from the stables on a day like this."

Guiltily aware of the flush rising to her cheeks, Jessie jerked her gaze away from the man with the violin. "Where did he get the tails?"

Warrick shrugged. "Presumably from the same place as the violin." He wandered away toward the smoking room then, his hands fumbling in the pockets of his waistcoat.

She told herself she wasn't going to look at him again, at Gallagher, but the lure was too potent to resist.

He was smiling, only not at her. He was smiling at the music he was making with his hands and his body and his soul. He looked relaxed, at peace, and there was a kind of contentment deep in his eyes such as she had never seen before. A contentment which in that moment she envied.

It felt like slow, painful death to look at him. To look at him and know he could never be hers. Then he glanced up. For one blazing moment their gazes met and the impact of it, the fiery shock of it, arced across the garden, leaving her shattered.

She swung away, her breath coming hot and thick in her throat, her chest pounding in reaction. She told herself she would be careful not to look at him again. But his music followed her, his music and the inescapable awareness of his presence.

She wondered if she'd ever be able to hear a violin again without thinking of this sun-filled garden and him.

"THERE YOU ARE, DARLING," said Harrison, coming up beside Jessie when she was helping one of her mother's more aged guests to maneuver into the shade of the eastern veranda. "Here, allow me."

With gentle solicitude, he took the elderly gentleman's arm and supported his weight while he carefully lowered himself onto the sturdy wooden bench. "My pleasure, sir," said Harrison, accepting the older man's thanks with a polite bow.

Standing beside them, Jessie looked at Harrison, at the straight line of his shoulders, at the ruddy color of his cheeks above the flare of his light brown side whiskers, and she felt a sudden rush of affection for him only partially fueled by guilt. He had always been like this, Harrison: mannerly and solicitous, kind and courteous. She would be happy married to him, she told herself; in time she would be able to find happiness with him.

He straightened, that smile she liked—the boyish, crooked one— quirking up the edges of his mouth as he turned toward her. "Warrick said you were looking for me."

"Yes." She tucked her hand through his arm and they strolled together along the veranda, the sad, lilting wail of Old Tom's pipes carrying to them on the breeze. The quartet must be taking a break, she thought, and she had to restrain herself from glancing around, although she couldn't have said whether she was hoping she would catch a stolen glimpse of Gallagher lounging at ease someplace in the garden or afraid she would. And then she felt disloyal for even thinking of such a thing, for thinking of Gallagher now when she was with Harrison. With her *betrothed*, she reminded herself. "I've been wishing to speak to you of something," she began in a rush, only to pause when she felt him stiffen beneath her touch. "What is it?" she asked, glancing up at him in surprise.

He stared straight ahead, his chin held high, his stiffly starched collar faultlessly white against the soft brown of his side whiskers. He was no longer smiling. "That man," he said sharply. "What is he doing here?"

She followed the direction of his gaze to where a young, dark-haired gentleman stood looking out over the formal gardens. "Ian Russell? He's a friend of Warrick's—they often hunt together. Why shouldn't he be here?"

Harrison's thin nostrils twitched. "You wouldn't have heard, I suppose."

"Heard what?"

"About his marriage. Can you believe it? The man actually took a common thief to wife."

"A thief?" Jessie's step faltered. "Oh. You mean, he married an emancipist." An ex-convict.

"Shocking, isn't it?" he said, utterly misreading her reaction. "As magistrate I had no choice but to take away all of his assigned servants, of course. He was excessively unpleasant about it."

"Oh, Harrison . . ." Jessie's hand slid from his arm as she turned to face him. "How could you? He could easily lose his land because of this."

Harrison pressed his lips together in a thin line. "He should have thought of that before he committed such an act of folly. I only enforce the rules, Jesmond; I don't make them."

It was true; a landowner could lose the right to be assigned servants for many reasons and marrying a former convict was only one of them. But Harrison didn't sound as if he regretted what he'd had to do. He had very firm views on the proper order of things,

Harrison did; an unshakable belief in the sanctity of birth and the importance of keeping ex-convicts out of both business and society.

"At least Russell had enough sense not to attempt to bring the woman here," he said, straightening the cuffs that protruded precisely the correct length below the sleeves of his coat. "Not that your mother would ever have countenanced such a thing, of course—however good a friend he may be of your brother's."

Listening to him and watching him, Jessie was struck by how very much alike they were, her mother and her betrothed. Beatrice might have bowed to Warrick's insistence that his friend be invited, but no ex-convict would ever be allowed to enter the Castle's grounds as anything other than a servant.

Jessie swung away, one hand coming up to rest against a nearby veranda column as she stared out at the crowded garden. "I understand that in New South Wales, former convicts used to be assigned servants themselves," she said with deceptive simplicity. "And they were allowed to marry—even before the expiration of their sentences."

"Yes, well, that was New South Wales. Fortunately we do things a bit better here in Tasmania." He came to stand beside her. "Now, what was it you wished to speak with me about?"

Turning her head, Jessie gazed up at her betrothed's familiar, well-bred face and knew she couldn't do it. She couldn't set a date for their wedding. Not yet. She sucked in a deep breath as if it might somehow ease the swell of panic within her, but the panic simply kept building and building until she felt an almost overwhelming, absurd urge to pick up her skirts and run. Run away from Harrison and the polite titters of her mother's garden party guests and the haunting strains of Gallagher's violin, floating toward her again on the flower-scented breeze.

"Jesmond?" said Harrison, looking at her queerly. "What is it?"

With effort, she summoned up one of the polite, artificial smiles she'd been trained to display since early childhood. "I was wondering if you'd like to play a game of croquet?"

IT WASN'T until much later in the afternoon, when the shadows were growing long in the valley and the throng of guests had begun to thin, that they managed to find the time for a game, she and Warrick playing as a team against Harrison and Philippa.

"The problem is, you're standing all wrong," said Warrick in that impatient way he had, stepping forward after Philippa had missed the hoop for the second time. "Now pay attention."

He went to stand behind her, his arms coming around her, his long-boned hands closing over hers as she grasped the wooden mallet. Jessie had been gazing off across the convict-scythed lawn toward the house where she could see Gallagher, no longer in tails, helping with the guests' horses. But something about the way Philippa went so very still, something about the sudden parting of her lips, the quick catch of her breath, drew Jessie's attention and held it.

She loves him, Jessie thought in wonder, watching Warrick continue to bark instructions, totally oblivious to the effect his nearness was having on the woman in his arms. *Dear God, she loves him.* And it occurred to Jessie, studying Philippa's flushed face and remembering the way a much younger Philippa had uncomplainingly hauled sails and cleated lines when Warrick took her sailing, or the way she had gamely carried fishing rods and dead ducks and whatever else Warrick imperiously ordered her to tote for him as she trudged in his wake, that Philippa must have always loved him. Only none of them had ever noticed it, for like all properly brought-up English gentle-women, Philippa was very good, so very good at hiding her feelings.

After that, Jessie watched them more closely, watched her brother's good-natured insouciance and Philippa's quiet grace and flawless manners. Only once more did Jessie catch a fleeting glimpse of Philippa's secret heartache, when Harrison said something amusing. Warrick's head fell back, the sun glinting on his ashen blond hair, his eyes sparkling with appreciation, his laughter ringing out rich and manly. For one unguarded moment, Philippa looked at him with such a deep and powerful longing shining in her eyes that Jessie had to turn away.

She stared off across the park, not really seeing the trees moving gently in the afternoon breeze. She wondered how she could have missed something so obvious until now. And then she thought that even if she had noticed that look on Philippa's face, before, she wouldn't have known it for what it was. Perhaps a woman had to experience that wild yearning, that burning need herself before she could recognize it in another.

THAT NIGHT, Jessie went looking for her brother and found him in the billiards room knocking balls around the table.

"Jess," he said, glancing up from where he leaned over the cloth-covered slate, studying his next shot. The light from the wall sconces glazed the high-bred bones of his face but left his eyes in shadows. "You still up?"

She paused in the doorway to watch him strike the plain with his cue stick, the white ball flying across the table to knock the red into the corner pocket with a sharp click. "Three points," she said, giving him a crooked smile.

"Want to play?"

She shook her head. "I wanted to ask you something." She pushed away from the door. "I've been thinking about organizing a picnic for next week with Philippa and Harrison." She hesitated. "Will you come?"

He straightened slowly, one hand reaching for the chalk, his gaze hard on her face. "Are you trying your turn at matchmaking or something?"

She gave a soft laugh. "Of course not."

"Huh." He set the chalk aside and turned back to the table. "Because it's a waste of time if you are. I have no intention of marrying Miss Philippa Tate. Not now—" he sent his ball cannoning into the other two balls "—not ever."

She went to stand with her hips leaning against the table, her arms crossed over the emerald-green bodice of her satin evening gown. "Have you ever thought of how Philippa feels about marrying you?"

He gave her a slow smile that didn't begin to warm his eyes. "What is there to think about? Philippa Tate is the epitome of the well-brought-up young Englishwoman. It would never occur to her to question what's expected of her."

"I think you underestimate how much she cares for you."

"Cares for me?" He bent over the table again. "Oh, I know she has a certain measure of affection for me. And don't get me wrong—I like her, too. I always have. But she's not at all the kind of woman I could ever love. She's too proper, too controlled, too *predictable.*"

"You think you know her, do you?"

He gave a typically arrogant male laugh. "Of course I know her. That's the problem. Where's the excitement in marrying a woman you've known your entire life? Who was betrothed to both your brothers before you, for God's sake. There needs to be at least some mystery, some element of the unknown in a relationship between a man and a woman." He struck his ball, missed the shot, and swore. "I know Philippa as well as I know my boots." He straightened. "And believe me, I don't fantasize about my boots."

Jessie watched him walk around the table. "Do you think that's what love is all about? Mystery and excitement?"

He swung his head to look at her over his shoulder and frowned. "What do you think it is?"

She braced her arms against the table at her sides, her head falling back as she stared up at the ornate plaster of the ceiling. "I think . . . I think perhaps love comes from finding someone you feel utterly comfortable with, someone who makes you comfortable with yourself. It's like . . . finding yourself, or maybe it's like finding the other part of yourself."

"Doesn't sound very passionate."

She tightened her fingers around the edge of the table, her gaze still on the ceiling, for she found she could not look at him and ask what she wanted to ask. "Have you ever made love to a woman?"

She heard the sharp intake of his breath beside her. "Jesus, Jess."

She turned to look into his pale, fallen angel face. "Have you?"

He stared back at her. "Yes."

"What's it like?"

He raked his hair back from his forehead in a distracted gesture she remembered from their childhood, then dropped his gaze to his feet, shifting uncomfortably. "Don't you think this is the sort of thing you should be asking Mother?"

"No. I already know Mother's opinion of the marital act. She sees it as something distasteful. Something women endure."

He fell quiet a moment, then gently set his cue stick down on the table. "They don't all," he said. He was staring down at the table, but she had the impression his thoughts were far, far away. "Simply endure it, I mean."

"You haven't told me what it's like," she said softly.

He glanced up. "It's like . . . well, it's a bit like eating, I suppose. It can be something you do simply because you're hungry and you need to satisfy a physical urge. Or . . ." He gave her his best wicked grin. "Or it can be a delightful feast."

She returned his smile. "What makes the difference?"

"The way you feel about the person you're with, I suppose."

"You mean, whether or not you love them?"

He shrugged. "Or at least whether or not you desire them. I've been told there's a difference between love and desire, but I'm not sure I understand what it is." He came around the table to stand in front of her, his gaze hard on her face. "And you've come to realize you neither love nor desire Harrison, haven't you?"

She nodded, not quite able to meet his eyes. She felt the touch of his hand against her cheek. "What are you going to do?" he asked quietly.

She leaned forward, her face pressed against the solid comfort of her brother's chest. He smelled of brandy and cigar smoke and the wildness that was consuming him. "I don't know. I wish I did."

He cupped his hand beneath her chin, lifting her head so that she was looking at him. "I'll come to your picnic," he said, and smiled when she gave a gurgling laugh.

~

THE NEXT DAY Lucas was on the south lawn, a hammer in his hand and the sun warm on his back as he worked banging apart the frames he'd built for the Corbetts' garden party, when a shadow fell across him.

He looked up, his eyes squinting against the morning sun as he turned. "Miss Corbett," he said, his voice coming out rough, double-edged. "You stand this close and you're liable to get hurt."

She didn't move. She was wearing a dark blue muslin dress with a tapering white collar and large sleeves gathered at her thin wrists by a matching white band. He let his gaze travel along the length of her, from the jaunty straw bonnet set at a rakish angle on her head to the tips of her expensive dark blue kid ankle boots, then back again to her face. "I want to go for a ride," she said, her chin coming up as she met his gaze steadily.

"You don't look dressed for riding."

"It won't take me long to change."

Deliberately, he turned his back on her, his hammer slamming against the rough lumber with a loud clatter. "I'm doing this," he said, not looking at her.

She came around to stand in front of him, her dark blue skirts swaying about her ankles with a gentle swish that filled the air with the sweet scent of lavender and starch and her. "I've already told Warrick to arrange to have someone else do this."

He looked up again, his throat swelling with an emotion he didn't want and couldn't afford. "And where would you be wanting to ride to, then?"

She tilted her head, the brim of her hat framing her face with a striking effect that took his breath. "There's something I want to show you."

He made his voice cold, curt. "And here I'd taken the impression you'd decided to heed my advice and stay away from me."

"I had. I've changed my mind."

He stared at her, at the silken curve of her cheek and the fullness of her lower lip and the gentle rise of her breasts as she breathed. He said, "It's dangerous, what you're about. You know that, don't you?"

He waited, knowing he was a fool yet still unable to stop the heavy beating of his heart as he watched a smile spread across her face, a saucy smile that was like a siren call, beckoning him on to destruction. "I know."

28

S EAGULLS DIPPED AND WHEELED, their white wings catching the brilliance of the sun, their harsh cries barely audible above the roar of the waterfall that shot over the stark face of the granite cliff to tumble white and frothy and quick to the sea three hundred feet or more below.

Lucas reined in his horse near the grassy edge of the bluff, his gaze narrowing against the sea- and sand-intensified glare as he stared down at the small inlet. The surf was gentle today, a lazy, light-sparkled turquoise swell that rolled onto the narrow crescent of shingled beach below with a softly rhythmic swish and drag.

Mounted on her dainty black mare beside him, Jesmond Corbett turned her face to the sea. "It's beautiful, isn't it?" she said, one leather-gauntleted hand coming up to grasp the brim of her jauntily masculine top hat as the breeze caught its long creamy gauze veil and floated it gracefully out behind her. She had a new riding habit of black worsted, with wide military-style cuffs and twin rows of brass buttons marching down the front and a lace jabot at her throat. She looked haughty and expensive and so vibrantly full of life it made his throat ache, just to look at her.

"Aye," he said, his voice rough, and swung out of his saddle to go help her dismount. "Is this what we've come to see, then?"

She twisted her head to look down at him, the brim of her hat tilting, her crooked elbow pointing to the sky as she tightened her grip against the wind. A wash of golden sunlight fell across her face to glaze the elegantly high bones of her cheeks as she shook her head. "Not yet. What I want to show you is at the base of the cliffs."

"So there's a way down, is there?" He held out his arm to her. Only, instead of taking it as was proper, she put her hands on his shoulders and smiled down at him with her eyes.

He went utterly still beneath her touch as he watched her smile turn teasing, naughty. "Think you can manage the climb, Mr. Gallagher?"

Reaching up, he grasped her slim waist, felt the strength of her young body so full of life and promise beneath his hands. "I think you're asking for trouble, lass."

She kicked her foot out of the stirrup. "Perhaps I am."

She slid from the saddle in a rush of fine cloth and feminine softness. For one stolen, dangerous moment, he let his arms close around her, held the warmth of her body close to his and breathed in the scent of her sun-kissed hair and skin. Her hands clutched at his shoulders, her head coming back, her mouth parting as she stared up at him. The wind gusted around them, rustling the long grass at their feet and bringing with it the briny scent of the sea and the quiet rush of the gentle surf. Her eyes were dark and wide, her body soft and yielding, and anyone, anyone could come along at any moment and see them.

He dropped his hands and stepped back, his entire body humming. It was madness, what she was doing, what she was allowing to happen between them. What he was doing. A madness that could lead only to destruction and despair. Yet he could no more stop it than he could stop the wind from blowing or the sea from surging deep and wide and endless.

∾

THEY FOLLOWED A HEARTSTOPPINGLY NARROW, steep path that ended in the jumble of dark rocks crowding the small pebbly beach. The roar of the waterfall was louder here by the sea. He stood on the shingle, his feet braced apart, his hands resting on his hips as he studied the soaring cliffs they'd just descended. This was a strange place, this rocky inlet she'd brought him to. The very air seemed to vibrate with an unearthly energy that left him feeling both intensely alive and oddly humbled.

"Is the path natural, do you think?" He glanced over to where she leaned against a sun-warmed boulder and found her watching him. The wind had loosed bits of her hair so that it blew around her face in soft silken wisps as she shook her head.

"Partially, perhaps. But not all of it. It's said this was once a special place to the local Aborigines, although most people don't know why."

"You do?"

She pushed away from the rock, her movements strong and assured in that way she had, the smile on her lips promising something that both lured him and scared the hell out of him. "Follow me," she said.

He followed her. There was a narrow ledge of sorts that curved toward the waterfall, along the base of the cliff just above the tumbled rocks at the water's edge. But it wasn't very wide and the wind was blowing stronger now, kicking up white crests on the waves and swirling the water into foam around the dark, jagged rocks beside them. "How in the name of all that's holy did you come to know about this?" he asked, watching her leap a small gap in the crude path, the trailing skirt of her riding habit thrown over one arm, the other hand braced against the cliff for balance. He wouldn't want to be trying to keep his feet on this path rigged out in the kind of getup she was wearing.

"My brother Reid and I found it one day when we were climbing about the rocks looking for starfish. I don't think anyone else knows about it."

One of his boots shot off the wet rocks and he swore. "About this bloody ledge?"

"About this."

They were close enough to the waterfall now that he could feel the mist cool against his face. Her cheeks were pink with exertion and fresh air, her chest rising and falling with her quickened breathing, the smile on her face so open and natural he had to look away. He tilted back his head to scan the rocks above. "You're trying to convince me there's something I'm missing, are you?"

She laughed again, a husky, breathy rush of air that was like a warm evening breeze skimming across exotic oceans. "Watch."

He watched, bemused, as she pivoted away from the cliff, her outstretched arms hugging the rocky wall. Slowly she inched her way forward, the roar of the falling water loud in their ears, the waves crashing into the rocks below to throw up a fine silver spray that caught the sunlight and dissolved it into a kaleidoscope of colors. He thought for a moment she meant to walk right through the tumbling white fall of water. Then he realized she must have gone *behind* it, because she disappeared.

"Faith and glory," he said opening his eyes wide, and went after her.

Flattening his back against the sheer stone wall, he squeezed between the cliff face and the tumbling sheet of water, the rock beneath his grasping hands and hobnailed boots growing dangerously slippery and wet. In high summer, he thought, swearing beneath his breath, the stream that fed the falls was probably thin and weak, but not now. Now it was raging and swollen with the spring runoff, narrowing the gap he had to pass through. He ducked his head as water splashed in his face, sluiced down his shirtfront, drenched the legs of his trousers.

And then he was through.

He lifted his head and blinked. It was neither deep nor grand, this cave, but hushed and intimate and filled with soft darkness lightened by the glow of the sun glimmering through the cascading water. The refracted light danced aquamarine and golden and pearlescent over black stone and cool white sand. The sounds of water filled the air, the roaring rush of the falls and the pounding of the waves against the rocks below. The sounds and the scent of water: the salt of the sea and the clean fresh tang of the falling stream that whispered of alpine meadows and shadowy rainforests and fern-filled gullies. Taking off his hat, he swiped a crooked elbow across his dripping face and heard her laughter ring out, warm and delicious.

"You're all wet."

He lowered his arm to find her watching him with sparkling eyes, her cheeks wet and shining. Water darkened the bodice of her riding habit and weighed down the sodden hem of her skirt. The fancy lace jabot hung limp and ill used against her wet throat. She looked bedraggled and adorable. He grinned. "So are you."

She shook her head, damp golden tendrils of loose hair plastered beguilingly against her gleaming white neck. "Not as wet as you."

"Huh." He sluiced his hand down one leg, then the other. "That's because I'm bigger than you."

Straightening, he grinned as she tugged off one of her gauntlets to wipe her face with her bare hand. "I'm afraid it's the waterfall that is a bit bigger than I expected it to be," she said, her words muffled by her hand.

He cocked an eyebrow at her. "A bit?"

She laughed at him with her eyes, her hand drifting back to her side. "A bit." Still smiling, she turned, her head tipping back as she scanned the light-sparkled walls. "It's magical, though. Isn't it?"

He watched her, mesmerized. He'd forgotten—no, he'd never known what it was like to take such pleasure in the world around him. She swung about in a slow circle, the unearthly beauty of the light dancing over her wet cheeks, her eyes shining with interest and pleasure, her lips parted in wonder.

He was conscious of a strange tightness in his chest as his determination to harden himself against her simply ebbed away. What he felt for this woman was all wrong, wrong and dangerous and doomed to heartache. Yet he couldn't seem to control it and he wasn't even sure he wanted to anymore. "Magic it is," he said softly.

Her head came about, her gaze fastening on his face. He saw the flush that rode high on her cheekbones, the downward sweep of her lashes, the rapid breathing that lifted her breasts against the wet cloth of her bodice, and he knew what it meant. Knew what she wanted.

She took a step toward him as he reached for her. His hand cupped the back of her neck, his fingers tangling in the loose hair that tumbled from beneath the curly brim of her hat. With an impatient gesture, she swept off the hat, the creamy veil fluttering about them as it drifted to the soft sand lining the cave floor. Then her hands were clutching his shoulders and her gaze was locked with his, her lips trembling into a smile that he caught with his kiss.

The kiss was sweet and good, a soft giving of unquestioning acceptance and joy that comforted and warmed his jagged soul. He thought for one deluded moment that he could control the kiss, control himself. But while there was much that was pure and spiritual in his feelings for this woman, he was still a man with a man's needs, and he ached for her.

He heard her whimper, felt her hands tugging at his shirt, freeing it from the waistband of his trousers so that she could run her soft lady's hands across the scarred flesh of his bare back. At her touch, his head came up, his breath hissing out between his teeth in startled delight. Their gazes met and caught as he began to flick open the brass buttons of her habit's bodice. His gaze never left hers. "Tell me," he said, his voice a ragged whisper as he pushed the heavy cloth apart. "Tell me if this is what you want."

"You know it is."

He drew a shaky breath, his forehead pressing against hers, his hands trembling as he opened the tucked and embroidered neck of her chemise, the filmy white batiste so fine he snagged it with the roughness of his fingertips. Her breasts were full and ripe and beautiful, the flesh translucent and delicate. Together they watched his hands, his fingers dark and hard as he curved them around her. At his touch, she gasped.

With swift urgency he pressed her back against the smooth stone of the cave wall, his mouth reclaiming hers in a hot, frantic kiss that went on and on. Then his hands sweeping down her thighs to catch at the fullness of her skirt and bunch it up. It was a movement without thought, driven by instinct and the insistent flame of desire.

"Lucas," she whispered, her head falling back, her voice a soft expulsion of air barely heard above the roar of the water.

He went utterly still, his cheek pressed to hers, his eyes squeezing shut, his hands fisted against her thighs. He lifted his head, his chest heaving, the cloth of her skirt slipping from his grasp as he brought up his arms to brace his hands against the rock on either side of her and look down at her.

She gazed up at him, her fingers caught in his shirtfront, holding him to her, her eyes wide, her head jerking. "No. Don't stop. I didn't mean for you to stop."

He shook his head, his breath coming so harsh in his throat he was shuddering with it. "You know where it will lead if we don't stop. You do know, don't you?" he asked and saw by the quick flaring of her eyes that she did. Oh, she knew.

He stared at her forever, his body trembling with want and the effort to control it. He wanted . . . Dear God, how he wanted to ease her down into the soft sand of the cave floor and lay bare all the wonders of her soft woman's body. He wanted to feel her legs wrapping around his hips and her hands clutching his bare shoulders as he drove into her and made her his. *His.* Except that he could never make her his, not in the way she deserved. He could only destroy her.

He brought up his hand to touch her cheek, a sad smile tugging at his heart as he rubbed his thumb across her swollen lips. Then he tipped his head to brush her mouth with his once, gently, and pushed off from the wall to swing away from her.

He went to stand at the entrance of the cave, his body hard and shaking with want. The mist from the falls felt cool against his hot face, the roaring rush loud in his ears. A taut silence stretched out between them, a silence filled with the sounds of water and their own strained breathing.

Then she said, "And if that's what I want?"

He looked at her over his shoulder. She stood slim and straight, one hand clutching together the cloth at her breast, her face pale and strained. He trembled with the need to go to her, to gather her up in his arms and comfort her. Only, how could he, when he was the problem?

"You know what I am," he said, the words tearing his throat. "You know what I am and you know what it means."

"I know. I've known from the moment I first saw you. It should have mattered, but it didn't." A queer smile trembled her lips. "You can't expect it to matter now."

He drew a breath deep into his lungs and then let it out again in a ragged sigh. "There can be no future for us. Ever."

She turned away from him, one hand coming up to cover her eyes. "You think I haven't told myself that, over and over? But it doesn't change the way I feel about you. Doesn't stop me from wanting you."

"Miss Corbett—"

"*Don't call me that.*" She spun to face him again, her hand falling away, her nostrils flaring with a swift intake of air. "What do you think? That I'm only using you as some sort of diversion? A thrilling pastime I'll eventually tire of and toss aside? That I might even make you pay in some hideous fashion for what we've done together?"

"No. I know you better than that." He reached out to brush his hand across the wetness that gleamed silver on her cheek. "But we will be made to pay, lass. Make no mistake about it."

She stared up at him, her beautiful eyes filled with such pain and yearning and confusion that it was terrible to see. "And if I don't care?"

"I care."

She looked away, her throat working as she swallowed. The silence between them filled with the roar of the waterfall and the surge of the restless sea. "I'm sorry. I didn't think—"

"No." He cupped her cheek, forcing her to look at him again. "That's not what I meant. You have your whole life ahead of you. What kind of man would I be if I let you ruin it by doing something now that you'll only live to regret?"

"And if it's not a life I want?"

He looked into her eyes to find them filled with an emotion so deep and rare and pure it stole his breath. For one, shining moment he lost himself in her eyes, in the warmth and goodness and gentle acceptance he saw there. But she didn't know . . . She didn't know what he was really like, didn't know the things that had been done to him, the things that he had done.

The things he planned to do.

"I'm a dead man," he told her, deliberately making his voice cold, his hands falling from her shoulders. "My life ended four years ago. You get too close to me, lass, you're only going to destroy yourself."

"It's too late," she said, her head tilting as she gazed up into his face. "Don't you understand? It's too late."

"No. No, it's not." Yet even as he said it, he knew he was wrong. It was too late.

For both of them.

THEY LEFT Cascade Cove soon after that, talking little as they climbed back up to the horses and turned to follow the track south along the coast. He didn't realize exactly where they were headed until they splashed across the estuary and he looked up to see the blackened walls of the Grimes House rising stark and broken before him.

"Why are we here?" he asked, reining in sharply.

She urged her mare across the overgrown garden. "I lost the gold locket I was wearing the day of the funeral. It isn't particularly valuable but I've had it since I was a child and I want to look for it."

He wheeled, the gelding cavorting beneath him, his gaze flashing quickly to where he had hidden the ketch's boat amongst the reeds and brush. Swearing, he kneed his horse forward in a rush. "You'll never find it."

"I can look," she said and slid out of the saddle without waiting for his arm.

He hesitated a moment longer, then went to help her.

"It's not here," he said after some fifteen nerve-racking minutes of combing through high grass and tangled shrubbery. Even with the sun shining warm out of a clear blue sky, the atmosphere around the tragedy-haunted homestead remained heavy and oppressive.

She raised her head, her gaze turning as he knew it inevitably would toward the estuary. "We went for a walk by those reeds. Perhaps I dropped it there."

He straightened with a jerk. "You could have lost it anywhere."

But she was already striding down the path, her laughter floating back to him with the breeze. "What's the matter? Are the ghosts bothering you today?"

He went after her. "The devil take the ghosts. You'll catch your death of cold, lass, wet as you are from that waterfall."

"Huh. You obviously underestimate the layers of wool, cotton, and whalebone protecting a gentlewoman from the dangers of the outside world. Although given—"

She broke off, her step faltering, one hand coming up to grasp the low branch of the stunted stringybark beside her. If she hadn't been looking so sharply she probably wouldn't have seen it, for he'd hidden it as best he could. He hadn't had time to finish repairing all the damage to the stern left by the rocks, but the work he'd done for Beatrice's garden party had given him access to both the tools and materials he needed and he'd made a good start, the new wood showing smooth and unpainted and damnably incriminating.

She stood quite still, half turned away from him, her hand gripping the branch until her fingers turned white. "This is why you didn't want me here, looking around," she said after a moment, her voice coming out low and breathy. "You're planning to escape." She swung her head to stare at him over her shoulder. "You are, aren't you?"

He looked into solemn, hurting eyes and felt her pain slam into him, felt his own pain yawning deep and undeniable. "Aye," he said. "That I am."

29

"WHEN?" JESSIE ASKED, not looking at him. They sat together in the sun at the end of the old dock. She had her arms wrapped around her drawn-up legs, her chin on her knees. "When will you be leaving?"

"The night of the next full moon."

She swung her head to stare at him. He had his back propped against one of the weathered gray pilings, one arm resting on his bent knee. "You're not the only one going, are you? It'll take at least six men to row that boat."

He thrust his legs out straight in front of him, his head tipping back as he returned her gaze steadily. "Aye. And will you be telling on us, then, Miss Jesmond Corbett of Castle Corbett?"

The tide was coming in, sending the water to lap against the sides of the dock. In the distant cove, seagulls cried, wheeling above the rumbling surf. She watched as the breeze stirred the ragged ends of his dark hair where it hung over the collar of his convict coat, and she felt a terrible fear seize her, so that it was all she could do not to reach out and hold him to her. Hold him safe. "If they catch you, you'll be killed. Or worse."

"I told you. I died four years ago."

She swallowed hard, wanting to say so much but unable to say any of it, the pain in her chest deepening until it was an agony. She sucked in a quick breath that was almost a sob and looked away again.

"It's for the best I'm going," he said softly. "After what almost happened today, you can't deny that."

Oh, it was for the best; she knew that. But what was best and what she wanted were two very different things.

She'd known he could never be hers, known the day was coming, this day when she would have to say good-bye to him. She'd known it, but now that it was almost here she wondered how she was going to bear it. How was she going to bear living a life that didn't include him? There was no going back to the life she'd lived before; no going back to the woman she'd been before she looked up at that rocky hill-side and saw him standing there.

"I could help you," she said, her gaze fixed on the gentle swell of the sea. The sea that would take him away from this life he hated, away from her. "I could get you clothes, food."

"No. If we're caught, anything you gave us would be traced back to you."

"I'm willing to take the risk."

"Well, I'm not."

She kept trying not to look at him, for fear of what he'd read in her face. Except how could she not look at him when she loved him so much and soon she would never see him again?

Turning her head, she let her heart drink in the sight of him: the straight, uncompromising line of his dark brows, the sun-dark-ened, hard angle of cheek and jaw, the sparkling fire of his Irish green eyes. She felt her love for him flare up hot and bright and eternal. And she knew that her love and the pain of losing him would both be there forever. Knew too that he'd seen it all—that he'd looked into her eyes and guessed the terrible secret of her soul.

"Lass," he whispered and reached out his hand to her.

She took his hand in hers, their fingers entwining tightly. They sat there for a long time, hand in hand. Then they arose and rode back to their separate lives.

THIS TIME, she did stay away from him. Far, far away. She read some more of *The Pickwick Papers* to Beatrice and went for long, solitary walks in the park. And early in the following week, Jessie went on her picnic with Harrison, Philippa, and Warrick.

It was Harrison who drove them to a high bluff overlooking the rocky coastline. There they spread a rug upon the grass and drank champagne from crystal glasses and ate pate de foie gras and cucumber sandwiches from white china plates with gold rims. Afterward, Harrison took Jessie's hand and they went for a walk along the flower-strewn hillside. A balmy, spring-scented breeze fluttered the blue ribbons of her hat and flattened the white jaconet muslin of her dress against her legs. They might have been two old friends out for a stroll, she thought. They *were* two old friends; only now they were also more, and that was the problem.

She felt wretchedly deceitful to be walking demurely arm in arm with the man she had promised to wed, while every call of a seagull, every crash of the waves against the distant rocks, the very softness of the breeze against her cheek, reminded her of another man. She could find no cause for shame in loving Lucas Gallagher. Yet she felt weighted down by guilt. And she realized that her guilt came not from what she felt for Gallagher nor for what she had done with him, but from the lack of honesty, the duplicity in what she was doing now.

Tilting her head, she looked up at the man beside her. The sun and the sea breeze had brought a healthy glow to his cheeks, a sparkle to his eyes that made him look younger and less serious, more like the boy he had been. There were times—times like this— when her affection for him welled up within her warm and good, and she believed that even though her heart would always belong to someone else, she could make Harrison happy. He expected so little of her, only that she behave with the decorum that their society demanded and furnish him with a comfortable home and well-reared children. He did not expect—perhaps he did not even want her to love him with the kind of wild excess of which she now knew she was capable. And the man she could love like that, the man she did love with all her heart, would soon be gone.

It was a thought that brought with it such a terrible ache, such a soul-gripping fear, that she wondered again how she would bear it. She knew only that she would bear it because she had no choice. By the next full moon, Lucas Gallagher would be gone or dead, and then her love for him would be just one more secret she kept hugged to her heart.

"Do you remember," Harrison was saying, his mustache lifting with a smile that brought a gleam of amusement to his eyes, "the time we came here for a picnic on Boxing Day? I was fourteen and you were ten, and some benighted person had given you an enormous kite for Christmas."

She laughed at the memory and looped her arm through his in a way that brought them closer together. "I remember. I thought it was so big that if I ran very fast down the hill, the kite would lift me up and I would fly. You tried to stop me."

"I tried. You pushed me down and ran anyway." He put his hand over hers, holding her close, and she saw the amusement in his eyes fade to be replaced by something else, something darker. "That was the day I knew I was in love with you and that I was the luckiest man in the world to be marrying you."

She tilted her head, her gaze searching his familiar, handsome face. "What if you hadn't fallen in love with me, Harrison? Would you still be marrying me?"

He huffed a small laugh, but she heard a hint of the irritation it was meant to conceal. "What kind of a question is that, Jesmond? I should think you'd know me well enough to know that I would always do my duty."

His duty. They had all been brought up to do their duty. Their duty to God and Queen and country, and to their family names. "But what if you had discovered you didn't even *like* me?" she persisted. "Then what would you have done?"

"Then I suppose I would have decided I was the most wretched man alive instead of the luckiest. Really, Jesmond; what is all this about?"

It was bad form, what she was doing, the way she was pressing him, but she didn't care. She wanted to know. "And if I had been a convict when you fell in love with me ail those years ago, Harrison? What would you have done then?"

"Good heavens." He sounded genuinely shocked. "As if I could fall in love with such a person."

She stopped and turned to face him, the sun bright in her eyes as she looked up at him. "Why not? I'd still be me."

He shook his head vigorously. "No. You would not."

"I could have been falsely accused. Or the victim of circumstances."

"It wouldn't matter. I could no more fall in love with a convict woman than you could fly off this cliff." He tried to make light of it, but his nose was quivering in that way he had and she knew he was becoming displeased with her.

She swallowed hard, conscious of a swelling at the back of her throat, a heaviness in her heart. He said he loved her and she knew he believed it. He certainly desired her. But she was beginning to wonder how he could love her when there was so much about her of which he seemed to disapprove. Now that she was to be his wife, she noticed that he voiced his disapproval of her more frequently and he seemed to expect her to change herself accordingly. To make herself into what he wanted her to be, the Jesmond of his imaginings. The Jesmond he loved but who didn't exist.

She thought sometimes that it was her fault, for he was one of the people from whom she hid parts of herself, so that she had never allowed him to really know her, to know all of her. Except that lately it had occurred to her to wonder how well she knew him. Theirs was not a world that encouraged openness or real honesty. Oh, actual mendacity and deceit were condemned, and loudly. But the very need for conformity and that cherished stiff upper lip seemed to foster dissemblance and insincerity and distance. It seemed strange to realize that she and Harrison had grown up together, yet she knew Gallagher better after less than a month than she would ever know Harrison after even a lifetime together. They would go through their lives together, she and Harrison, never really knowing what was in each other's hearts or in their minds.

"No, I don't suppose you could," she said quietly and would have turned away, only he caught both her hands in his, stopping her.

"Darling," he said, and she heard the thread of irritation in his tone again, despite the endearment. "There's something we must discuss." He pulled her closer to him, her hands held tightly. The breeze whipped at her skirts, flapping them out like sails. "I know you've been home only a short while and I haven't wanted to press you, but . . . " He grinned, a boyish, rueful smile that echoed again the Harrison of her childhood. "What I'm trying to say is, we need to set a date for the wedding. I go to Hobart soon but I should be back by the end of November. Shall we set the wedding for the first Saturday in December?"

He voiced it as a question, but she knew by his expression that he didn't expect her to do anything more than agree. She sucked in a quick breath, aware of a surge of panic as if she were caught in the deadly currents of Shipwreck Cove and they were pulling her down, down, sucking her into a life she no longer wanted. "I don't know if that will give me enough time," she said, floundering, helpless, torn. "I mean, there's so much that will need to be arranged—"

Harrison laughed softly. "I think you underestimate your mother. She's been planning this wedding for more than two years now, remember? She says she will have ample time."

Jessie dropped her gaze to her hands caught fast in his, hers gloved in blue, his in black. She thought of other hands browned by the sun and scarred by cruel labor, and she thought, *By December, he will be gone.*

Aloud, she said, "You have already discussed this with Mother?"

"Why yes. I thought I should."

It struck her as odd, for him to be discussing their wedding date with her mother before he broached the subject with Jessie herself. But then, he had probably been discussing the wedding with Beatrice for years.

"Jesmond?"

Something in his tone made her glance up. He was looking at her with that mingling of possessive tenderness and hunger that she was coming to know. His head dipped toward her and she held herself very still, willing herself to relax for his kiss.

He covered her mouth with his, his hands still holding hers captive between them. His lips were cool and dry and vaguely pleasant, moving against hers. But she felt no trembling onslaught of fierce and wonderful need, no soaring glimpse of the sublime, and she knew she never would.

If she had never glanced up on that windswept hill, she thought; if she had never seen an Irishman standing there dark and wild and beautiful; if his fierce eyes and untamed soul had never stirred her blood and stolen her heart, would she have been content with this life others had planned for her? Would she have known this welling of loneliness and despair?

She felt Harrison's grip on her hands tighten until it almost hurt, his breath quickening, his mouth pressing down on hers with a roughness that surprised and frightened her. But before she could react he ended the kiss abruptly and turned away, his hand shaking as he withdrew a white handkerchief from his pocket and patted his lips. The wind gusted, smelling of warm grass and the sea. From the copse of dark wattles near the top of the hill came the call of a thrush, low and sweet. But he said not a word and she thought he must have shocked himself with the intensity of his reaction to that kiss, here, in the middle of this sunny meadow, where the others might have seen them.

She watched him pulling himself together, hiding the improper bits of himself away, and she felt an ache of great sadness within her, for herself and for him. He had told her he loved her, but he didn't seem the least perplexed by the fact that she had never said the same to him. They had always been friends; he knew she held him in esteem and affection, and she supposed that for him that was enough. A man did not look for violent emotions in his gently bred wife; everyone was always telling her that. She suspected he would be shocked—horrified, in fact, if he ever guessed at the potential for physical passion she knew she possessed.

And it occurred to her as they turned to walk together back toward her brother and his sister, that this was simply one more aspect of herself that she would need to keep hidden from those who claimed to love her. Those whose love, she knew, was conditional upon her behaving—upon her *being* as society said she ought. And she wondered how many more parts of her life, of herself, she was going to have to hide. How much of herself could she ignore, pretend didn't exist, before, one day, she lost the essence of herself entirely?

30

WARRICK LAY ON HIS BACK in the warm grass, one foot propped up on his bent knee, his shirt open at the neck. He had his hat tipped forward, shading the upper part of his face, but his eyes were open, his gaze fixed on the sun-sparkled expanse of the sea and the billowing white sails of a ship just visible on the horizon.

"Why don't you sail anymore?" asked Miss Philippa Tate as calmly as if she were asking if he were hot or if he'd like another cup of tea.

He turned his head to look at her. She sat on the picnic rug, her lace-trimmed, rose-strewn skirts disposed modestly about her, one of her endless collection of parasols protecting her complexion from the ravages of the Australian sun. "That, Miss Tate, is an extremely prying, impertinent question. And prying, impertinent questions are very bad form."

She tipped the parasol back so that he could see her face, see the hidden smile in her eyes. "If you were anyone else, I wouldn't have asked. But since you're always telling me you have no patience with the dictates of polite society, I didn't think you'd mind."

"You know why I don't sail anymore, damn it," he growled.

His show of temper seemed to have no effect on her whatsoever. "I think you'd be happier if you did. I think you need it. I think your soul needs it."

"What the hell do you know about my soul?" he demanded, but she only smiled in that distant way she had and set her parasol to twirling.

He sat up and leaned toward her. "You know what it would do to Mother if I took up sailing again."

She met his gaze squarely, her big brown eyes dark with a quiet kind of understanding that always frightened him a bit. "You do any number of things that seem to be precisely calculated to upset your mother. Why not sail?"

He swung his head away to stare out over the heaving blue waters below. Sometimes it was like a sharp, slashing knife, his yearning for the sea, a pain so poignant and deep he used it to stab himself with, over and over and over.

"Have you considered hair shirts and self-flagellation?" she said in that same calm voice. "I understand they're very effective in purging the body of lingering illusions of guilt."

His gaze snapped back to her face. *"Illusions?"*

"That's right."

He looked at her, at the damask curve of her cheek, at the arc of her lips. "Why does everyone think you're so meek and proper?"

"Because I am."

"Huh. Not with me."

"No. Not with you." She stretched out her hand to touch his arm. "I'm worried about you, Warrick. You've always been as free and wild as the wind. But lately it's as if you have this fire burning inside of you. I'm afraid that if you don't do something to let it out, it's going to burn you up."

He should have been annoyed. If anyone else had said such a thing, he would have been annoyed. But they were old friends, he and Philippa. And she was also right.

He put his hand over hers, felt her fingers quiver and then lie still in his grip. "Do you know, I've always envied you," he said softly.

"Me? You've envied me?" She gave a startled laugh that brought a brush of color to her cheeks and made her look unexpectedly, almost breathtakingly attractive. "Whatever for?"

"You've always fit so effortlessly, so comfortably into your world. No, it's more than that; you're comfortable with who you are and it gives you such a sense of ... serenity."

"That's not serenity you see, Warrick. Only lack of imagination and courage."

He smiled. "What would you like to do that you're not doing?"

A strange light shone in her eyes, like a fierce hunger that was there and then gone. "Sail around the world with you."

He felt the smile die on his lips. "Ah, Philippa." Reaching out, he touched the soft, dusky fall of her hair where it lay against her slender white throat. "I'm the one who lacks the courage for that."

~

ABOVE THE DARK, indistinct shapes of the trees in the park, the moon hung fat and luminescent in a star-glittered, blue-black sky. It wasn't full yet, that moon, but it would be soon.

Jessie stood at the French doors of her room, her cheek pressed against the blue damask drapes, her gaze fixed not on the moon but on the dark hulk of the men's barracks across the distant yard. It hurt to look at that barracks and know he was there, locked in the darkness, although it hurt more to think of all the nights to come when he would no longer be there. But then, her love hurt. It was a forbidden thing, her love, forbidden and impossible. Even if he didn't try to run away, even if he stayed, he would never be hers, could never be hers. And she knew him well enough to know that this life he was living, this convict life of humiliation and degradation and abasement, was one he could not endure. He needed to go. It was right that he was going. But that didn't stop the thought of his going, the thought of the danger he faced, from cutting like a knife to her heart.

She had moved through these last weeks of her life weighted down by fear and sorrow. Fear and sorrow and guilt. In another few days, she would be driving into Blackhaven Bay with Philippa to deliver Harrison to the ketch that would take him down to Hobart Town. And when he came back, he would make Jessie his wife.

Sometimes . . . sometimes she thought it was wrong, what she was doing, marrying Harrison when her heart belonged to someone else. How much of a woman's heart, how many of her secrets, was she allowed to keep hidden from those close to her? Jessie wondered. Perhaps she would tell him when he came back from Hobart. Tell him not who she loved, perhaps not even how deeply, but tell him that she had loved another.

He deserved to know that, she decided, before he married her. But she wouldn't tell him before he left. She wouldn't tell him until long after this full moon.

THE TOWN of Blackhaven Bay stretched some half a mile long but only several streets deep along its pebbly, surf-battered shore. It was a pretty settlement, of neat, two-story houses and shops built in the Georgian style of sandstone and whitewashed timber, backed by green hills rising to the distant, rainforest-covered mountains. The town had grown both larger and more conservative with the settlement of the inland valleys, but it had begun its existence as a whaling port. When the whales were running, the tall masts of whalers still crowded the bay, and when the wind was in the wrong quarter the stench of death still hung in the air from the whaling station south of town. As picturesque as it was, the bay had always seemed to Jessie a place of poignant and terrible beauty, as if it were haunted by the souls of all the whales that had met such hideous fates here. She'd said as much to Harrison once, but he'd looked shocked and told her she was being both fanciful and blasphemous, so she'd never mentioned it again.

The wind was blowing from the northeast today, fresh and sweet with the clean scent of the open sea. But the ghosts were still there, Jessie thought, mournful and angry.

"At least you've nice weather for sailing," Philippa was saying as they strolled along the docks, waiting for the tide to turn. Beside them in the sun-glittered bay, the waves gently swelled, rocking the whalers that lay at anchor there beside Captain Boyd's royal frigate and the ketch Harrison would be taking to Hobart Town.

"Are you certain you won't change your mind and join me in Hobart?" Harrison said, smiling down at his sister. "You could take a ketch later in the week."

Philippa peered up at him from beneath her parasol, the twirling lace casting a revolving pattern of shadow and hatched light across her pretty face and the tucked, beribboned bodice of her yellow taffeta gown. "No, you heartless man. One of us needs to stay here and help Jessie prepare for this wedding."

Jessie laughed, but Harrison caught her hand and brought it to his lips in an unusually demonstrative gesture. "You don't think I'm abandoning you, do you?" he asked, his brows drawing together in concern.

"No, of course not," she said, her hand twisting to hold his, the familiar weight of guilt pressing heavily on her heart. For if truth were told, she was glad he was leaving, glad she would be having this time alone to prepare for her coming marriage . . . and to grieve for her coming loss.

"I've been meaning to tell you," Harrison said, drawing her hand through his arm as they walked along. "I was speaking to Captain Boyd this morning and he tells me they've received information that some of the men from the Castle are planning an escape. Seems they've a boat hidden away that they plan to use to join the sealers working the islands. He's sent word to Warrick of course, but there's not much else that can be done at the moment since they don't know where the boat is hidden and they've only the word of some convict blacksmith as to the identity of the men involved." His thin nose quivered. "Frankly, I think they ought to go back to gibbeting absconders, the way they used to do. That would soon put a stop to this nonsense. It's coddling these scoundrels that leads to—" He broke off as Jessie stumbled and caught at his arm with both hands to steady herself. "I say, Jesmond; are you all right?"

It was a curious sensation, as if the entire world had dipped and swayed beneath her. "I'm fine," she said hastily. "Did Captain Boyd mention when this escape is supposed to take place?"

"The night of the full moon, I believe he said. But you needn't concern yourself, my dear. The *Repulse* will be patrolling the coast from here north. If your men try anything, they'll be caught, never you fear."

Lucas was in the tack room cleaning a saddle when she burst in upon him.

"Miss Corbett," he said, his voice a lazy drawl, his hand continuing to rub the saddle soap in slow circles even as his heart twisted and leapt at the sight of her.

Since that day when she'd sat on the dock and he'd told her he was going away, he'd seen her only from a distance, for this time she really had kept away from him, riding seldom and always with her brother or Harrison Tate. But now she was here, the afternoon sun behind her shining warm and honey-rich on her hair, and the pain of it was almost more than he could bear.

"I've just come from Blackhaven Bay," she said, the rich burgundy satin of her full skirts swirling around her as she skidded to a halt at the threshold some five or six feet from him, her hands coming up to brace against the door frame, her chest heaving as if she'd been running. "Captain Boyd—the naval frigate—they know."

There was no mistaking her meaning. He set aside his cloth and stood to walk slowly to the dusty window overlooking the yard. But it was still a moment before he could speak through the crushing wrench of disappointment and anger and fear. "You're certain?"

She took a step into the small, low-ceilinged room, her voice dropping. "They don't know where the boat is hidden, but they know you have one. They know you plan to head north to join the sealers and they know when you're leaving."

He swung his head to look at her over his shoulder. "Do you have any idea who told on us?"

She shook her head. "Harrison said something about a blacksmith, but I'm not certain."

"John Pike," he said softly. He turned to lean his back against the room's whitewashed plaster wall, his arms crossed at his chest, his gaze fixed unseeingly on the basket-weave pattern of the brick floor at his feet. He said nothing more, but somehow she guessed the direction of his thoughts.

"Dear God," she whispered. "You can't mean to go anyway."

He glanced up. "It still might be possible. We could leave now instead of waiting for the full moon. Head south instead of north."

She stared at him, the blood draining from her face. "No. It's too dangerous."

He pushed away from the wall with a shrug. "It was always a risk."

"But . . . you can wait a few months. Let the suspicions die down."

"No. If they know we have a boat, they're going to start looking for it. It'll only be a matter of time until they find it. If we're going to go, it's got to be now."

"*Oh, God.*" She swung away from him, one hand splayed across her eyes. From the yard came the sound of a man's voice and the laughing call of a kookaburra. He was aware of the slow, painful passage of time, a silence scented with saddle soap and leather and damp brick. "I told myself it was best that you were leaving. Even though I was afraid for you, I still knew deep in my heart that it was best. Best for you and for me. But this . . . this is too dangerous. If . . . " She hesitated, her chest shuddering on a quick breath. "If you are going, don't tell me. I don't want to know."

He went to stand behind her, his hand hovering over her shoulder before dropping to his side again. "I hear your wedding date's been set for the beginning of December."

Her head came up, her eyes squeezing shut. "Yes."

"Don't do it."

She swung to face him, her eyes glittering, her face tight with the effort of controlling her emotions. He ached with the need to hold her, to touch her cheek and her hair and her mouth. "Don't do it," he said again, his hands curling into fists at his sides. "Tate won't make you happy. He'll only try to turn you into something you weren't meant to be and in the end, he'll destroy you."

He watched the cords in her slim throat work as she swallowed. "This is the life I was meant to live." She took a step back from him, and then another. Her lips parted and he thought she would say something more, but she only whirled in a swirl of burgundy satin and was gone.

"No," he said to the empty room. "No, it's not."

31

"HAVE YOU SPOKEN TO O'LEARY?" asked the Fox, his attention seemingly fixed on the task of filling a big zinc watering can at the ornamental fountain that stood in the center of the rose garden.

"Aye," said Lucas, one foot propped on the edge of the fountain, the afternoon sun warm on his back. "He says we go. Tonight."

"It rubs against the grain with me to have to admit it," said the Fox, grunting as he hefted the full watering can, "but I agree with him. What about the others?"

They turned to walk together between the curving rows of roses, stopping every few feet while the Fox carefully watered each bush. "If we do this," said Lucas, "we don't tell the others. Not until we're ready to walk. One of them must have spilt to Pike. We can't risk it happening again."

The Fox's lips curled away from his teeth in an ugly snarl. "The bugger. Before we leave, someone ought to—"

"No. If we do this it's going to be dangerous enough without adding any complications."

The Fox looked up, considering. "I take it you don't think we ought to go?"

"No. No, I don't."

"If we don't go now, they'll find the boat. You know they will."

Lucas shrugged, his hands on his hips as he looked off across the ornamental garden toward the park. "So we lose the boat. We can always get another one."

"They're not easy to come by, boats."

"Neither are lives."

The Fox jerked his head sideways and spat. "Some lives aren't worth living."

Once Lucas would have agreed with him. But now . . . now he thought about the simple joy of watching Jesmond Corbett's face light up with delight when she laughed, or the way her breath hitched when he touched her cheek, or the sweet, sun-warmed scent of her hair . . . . And he realized that at some point over the course of the past month his life had begun to have meaning again, to have value. To him and to her.

"The whole point of having the boat," he said, his hands coming up together as he swung around again, "was to join the sealers and get away from this hell mouth of an island. If we simply go south and lose ourselves in the unsettled areas down the coast . . ." He let his hands fall to his sides. "We might as well head for the mountains like every other fool who tries to bolt. Because we'll probably wind up dead."

The Fox upended his can with a violent splash of water that filled the air with the scent of damp earth. "If we bolted for the mountains, the dogs would track us down in a few days. You've always said it." They turned back toward the fountain. "With the boat, they won't know where we've gone."

"For a while."

The watering can hit the side of the fountain with a clatter. "Bloody hell. You're the one who came up with the idea of going tonight."

"I know." A flash of color drew his attention to the upper veranda of the house. "It was hard to think about giving up the whole thing after getting this close. But . . ."

The Fox followed his gaze to where Jesmond Corbett stood at the veranda railing. She must have been watching them, because she looked away quickly toward the mountains as if becoming aware of their scrutiny.

"Are you sure this new plan is such a daft one?" asked the Fox, nodding toward the veranda. "Or is it just that you're not as anxious to leave as you once were?"

"And what good would it be doing me, then, if I stay?"

"If you stay, at least you'll still be seeing her even if it's only from a distance. For some men that'd be enough."

Lucas sucked in a deep breath, the heavy perfume of Beatrice Corbett's roses filling his head. "It would be an unbearable agony."

JESSIE WAS HAVING tea with her mother in the drawing room when she heard men shouting. She jolted to her feet, her heart pounding, her tea spilling across the table, her chair crashing to the floor behind her as she leapt for the door.

"Really, Jesmond—" her mother began, but Jessie was already across the veranda. She pelted through the shadowed garden, the flounced skirts of her gown bunched up in her fists, the evening sun warm on her hatless head. She could see a group of men milling about the smithy and more men running, their boots scraping across the hard-packed earth and stone of the yard.

She noticed the stableboy, Charlie, hovering at the edge of the crowd and grabbed him by the shoulder, her hand tightening hard enough to make him wince as she swung him around to face her. "What has happened?" she demanded, her breath ragged with fear.

"'Tis the smithy," he said, his gray, nearly lashless eyes narrowed and gleaming in his freckled face. "Somebody done for the bloody bugger."

"What? Let me through here." She pushed her way forward, the knot of muttering workmen giving way before her.

It was Warrick who stopped her, snagging her arm with a quick,

"Don't look, Jess." He pulled her around, but not before she saw the man lying in an ungainly sprawl on the pile of horseshoes, one side of his head a sickening, bloody pulp of shattered flesh and bone.

"Oh, God . . ." She brought her hand to her face, her stomach giving an uncomfortable lurch. "It's John Pike, isn't it?"

Warrick nodded, his lips pressing into a thin, angry line, his angel's eyes hardening. "Some half a dozen of the men have bolted. Pike must have got in their way."

And then she heard it: the loud, heart-stopping peel of the estate's alarm bell beginning to ring.

LUCAS HITCHED his hip on one of the dock's old, broken pilings and crossed his arms at his chest, his gaze narrowing as he stared at the sun sinking in rapid splendor toward the hills in the west. It was getting late. Dangerously late. They'd be needing the darkness later to slip past Blackhaven Bay. But he sure as hell didn't want to try to negotiate the rocky mouth of this cove with inexperienced oarsmen after sundown and without a full moon.

The gray gelding shook itself against the flies, creaking its saddle leather and drawing Lucas's attention. He'd ridden here himself so that he could carry the few supplies they'd been able to gather together and get the boat in the water. The others were coming on foot over the hills, but they should have been here by now.

He went to slip the bridle from the gelding's head and loop it over the saddle. "You'll be right, mate," he said, stroking one hand down the gray's warm neck. "Go on now. They'll be along to find you soon enough." But the horse simply snorted and butted its head against Lucas's shoulder when he would have turned away.

The horse ambling behind him, Lucas climbed the small rise to the abandoned garden and stared at the path winding around from behind the ruined black walls of the Grimes House. The chill in the air seemed more noticeable than ever, the sense of warning and foreboding ominous enough to make him shudder. He thought about the woman who had once lived in this house and the young convict who had loved her—and died for it. Turning away, Lucas sucked in a deep breath scented with the dank air of the estuary tinged faintly with an old whisper of charred wood. And he felt the tragedy of this place cut through to his very soul to leave him bleeding and aching.

It was good he was going away, he told himself. He could imagine a future of nothing but pain and death here on this island. Yet he couldn't get away from the notion that he was making a mistake, that this escape attempt was hopelessly, fatally doomed. If it had been up to him, he'd have abandoned it completely. But the others were bent on going and they needed his strong arms at the oars and his knowledge of the sea. He couldn't back out on them now. Especially when he couldn't trust his own motives for wanting to stay.

He turned to walk back toward the estuary, but paused as a last finger of golden sunlight gleamed on something at his feet. Stooping, he parted the grass and found himself staring at a gold locket. Jessie's gold locket. With oddly shaking fingers, he picked it up and put it in his pocket.

He went down to the dock again, his sense of uneasiness increasing with each passing minute. He was about to climb the slope to the house and have another look when he heard the sound of running feet and men breathing hard and knew the others were coming. Stumbling with exhaustion, five men crested the rise, their faces gray and pinched and ... not quite right.

Lucas stepped forward to grab the Fox by the arm as he staggered to the end of the dock. "Where the hell is Daniel?"

The Fox hunched over, his hands braced on his thighs, his shoulders heaving as he sucked in air. "He's coming. He had something he needed to do."

"Do? What the hell could he have needed to do *now?*" Lucas jerked his head toward the man who stood still and watchful some distance apart from the three convicts the Fox had originally approached about the escape. "And what in the name of all that's holy is he doing here?"

"You'll not be leavin' without me," said the man, his jaw thrusting forward belligerently even as his gaze wavered nervously away. He was a big man in his early twenties, dark and raw-boned and Irish. Sheen, Lucas thought his name was. He'd arrived at the Castle only two days before and he'd kept pretty much to himself.

"He was with the others," the Fox said. "I couldn't get them alone to talk to them and it was getting late. I figured it was safer to bring him than to leave him. And he does want to come."

"We've room enough," said Lucas, eyeing the man. "Ever handle a boat?"

The man's face broke into a wide smile. "What you think? I'm from Achill Island."

Lucas grunted. "Get in the boat then. We leave as soon as Daniel arrives."

He was turning away toward the ruined homestead when the Fox caught his arm. "You know what this means, don't you, boyo?"

Lucas swung back around, his eyes narrowing as he searched the other man's thin face. "And what would that be?"

The Fox wiped his cuff across his sweat-sheened forehead, his chest still shuddering from the long run. "We've six men for the oars and a lad who knows the ways of the sea better even than yourself. You'll not be needing to come with us if you've a mind not to."

For one, terrible moment, temptation beckoned. "I'm coming with you," Lucas said and pulled away to go watch for Daniel.

JESSIE WALKED into the middle of the stables and stopped, her head tipping back, her hands hanging limply at her sides. She turned in a slow circle, the world a wet blur of shadowy rafters and whitewashed walls and bars of fading golden light streaming through high windows and wide doors.

She couldn't have said why she had come here except that Gallagher had, for a time, made this place his. She breathed in the familiar scents of hay and warm horseflesh and leather, and felt the loss of him like a rip in her being.

He had come into her life, a lean dark man with haunted eyes and an untamed spirit who captured her heart and stirred her soul and challenged her to be all that she'd ever dreamed of being. He had come and now he was gone, and she was left with loneliness and pain and a desperate, wild longing for the impossible. A longing for the impossible and a fear that churned her stomach and left her breathless and shaky.

Oh God, oh God, her mind screamed in a silent prayer. *Let him be all right. Let him get safely away. Please, please . . .*

They had ridden out almost immediately, Warrick and the overseer, the dogs barking and excited, the men grim-faced and determined. She had watched them go; yet she felt no sense of betrayal in wishing them failure. Warrick might be her brother but it was wrong what he was doing, hunting men down as if they were animals—men kept under threat of whip and chains and forced to work as slaves. Men whose crime was sometimes nothing more than a willingness to die for a noble cause.

She realized now that at some point the sun must have set. The chirping of the crickets had grown louder and the air cooler, the open doors showing only pale gray sky against the darkness of the stable's interior. In a nearby stall, a horse moved restlessly, crunching its oats and slurping water. It occurred to her that Gallagher must have seen to the horses before he left and for some reason, the thought undid her.

She sank to her knees on the cold, uneven brick floor, her rump settling back on her heels, the palms of her hands coming up to press against her stinging eyes. She was never going to get over loving him, she realized with an ache of awful certainty. Her love and the pain of losing him would forever be there, an eternal mingling of sweet joy and terrible, soul-wrenching sorrow.

The *clip-clop* of a horse's hooves hitting the hard-packed dirt of the yard brought her hands down, her chest jerking as she sought to catch her breath. She staggered to her feet, brushed stray wisps of hay and dirt from her skirt and fought desperately to bring herself under control. Her entire being was quivering with worry and heartache, but somehow she managed to draw on a lifetime of training in the suppression of emotion to pull herself up straight and hold her head high as she faced the open doors.

Unaccountably, she felt her heartbeat quicken and knew a rush of tingling awareness that she feared might be nothing more than wild, useless hope. She tried to damp it down, tried to tell herself it was impossible. But her feet were already moving toward the wide double doors. She heard the hoof beats pause, heard the creak of leather as someone swung from the saddle, his tread light upon the hard earth. A man's form appeared silhouetted against the moonlit sky.

"Oh, thank heavens," she whispered. "It is you." And she threw herself into Gallagher's arms.

32

"I THOUGHT YOU WERE GONE," she said hoarsely, her splayed hands running over the features of his face, his shoulders, his arms. She felt driven by an obsessive need to touch him everywhere, as if to be certain he was truly here and not simply a phantom conjured up from abject despair. She rubbed her cheek against his, felt his breath warm against her neck, and she had to squeeze her eyes shut against a threatening sting of tears. "I thought you were gone and it was as if I had lost a part of myself."

He caught her hands in his and kissed them, his features sharp and haunted in the moonlight. "I should have gone. For your sake as well as mine, I should have gone."

"No. Don't say that."

His arms encircled her shoulders, his hands tangling in her hair as he drew her in to him. "Some things are true even if we don't say them," he whispered. And then he was kissing her, kissing her as a drowning man might devour air, whole-mouth kisses of desperation and need and blind want.

She gave herself to him utterly, to his touch and his kiss and the warm rush of forbidden yet undeniable desire that thrummed through her. She could not get close enough to him. She strained against him, her tongue tangling with his, her breasts flattening against his chest. She lost all sense of where she was, of everything except the wild joy of having him again in her arms.

But he at least must have remembered they stood near the open doorway, for he tore his mouth from hers, whispered harshly, "This way," and pulled her with him into the dark, hay-sweet recesses of an empty stall, his mouth recapturing hers before they were halfway there.

Her back slammed against the smooth wooden partition of the stall, the panel rattling unheeded, her fingers digging into his shoulders as his hands closed over her breasts.

His touch was magic, his kiss a thing of splendor. It was like a whisper of heaven, to be this close to him again, to be able to hold him, to be held by him. And still she wanted more. She wanted to feel his man's weight bearing her down into the softly rustling hay. She wanted him in every way a woman can want a man and the realization brought her no shame, only a joyous kind of wonder.

His body arched to lift her up, then let her slide slowly, exquisitely down the hard length of him. She knew he wanted her with the same desperate passion as she wanted him, and it was a sweet exaltation even as the danger of this time and this place seemed to settle over them both.

"Lass," he said on a harsh expulsion of breath, his head tipping back, his eyes squeezing shut as he fought to bring his raging desires under control. "We're mad and no doubt about it. Anyone could come walking in. And I'm not sure we'd even hear them coming."

"Probably not," she said with a smile, her fingers digging into the muscles of his back, her lungs heaving as she gulped in steadying droughts of cool, hay-scented air. "It's just . . . it feels so good to hold you, I can't bear the thought of letting you go again."

He pressed his open mouth against her forehead, his arms slipping around her waist, his breath shuddering his chest as he held her tight against him. "I know."

She ducked her chin to lay her cheek against his chest and felt his heart beat strong against the side of her face. "Tell me," she whispered, her hands sliding up beneath his coat to splay against his back, the flesh strong and warm beneath his coarse shirt. "Can you tell me what happened?"

He cupped the side of her head in his hand, his fingers gentle as he stroked her hair. She looked up and saw his devil's grin flash quick and seductive in the shadows of the night. "Aye. But if I'm not to have you on your back in this hay, I'd best do my telling while I'm unsaddling the gray."

She breathed a soft laugh, caught his hand in hers and kissed his knuckles. "I'll light the lantern."

The light brought a warm golden glow to the center of the stables while leaving the two wings of stalls in vague shadow. Jessie hung the lantern from a hook in one of the supporting posts, the tin hitting the wood with a soft clang. She watched him strip the saddle from the gray's back and knew from the jerkiness of his motions that however great his joy in being with her again, the disappointment of his failed escape attempt ran deep. It was a thought that hurt, although she told herself it should not.

"You did mean to leave tonight, didn't you?" she said abruptly.

He looked up from unbuckling the bridle, his face set in hard lines. "Aye."

"And the other men? Warrick said some half a dozen are missing."

"They got off. Unfortunately one of them felt he had a score to settle with someone before he left the Castle."

Jessie reached out to run one hand down the white strip on the gray's nose. "I know."

He glanced at her, then went to work on the horse's near neck and shoulder with a brush. "Your brother's dogs picked up the man's scent right away. He'd barely made it to the cove when we heard the dogs barking up on the bluff."

"Did they catch him?"

Lucas shook his head. "No. But I knew they'd be on the beach before the boat made it out to sea, and it was still light enough that they'd be able to see which direction the boat turned. The *Repulse* would have picked us up before we got past Blackhaven Bay."

She continued to stroke the horse's face as he worked the brush over the animal's flank and around to the other side. "So what did you do?"

He paused for a moment, his head bent, his hands braced against the gray's withers. "I pushed the boat off and then rode back to meet your brother and the overseer, Dalton, at the top of the bluff."

"But . . ." She looked at him, her heart aching for what she saw flash ever so briefly in his eyes before he shielded it. "Why?"

He swung his back to her, his movements with the brush brisk, his voice deceptively light. "To delay them. I spun a wild yarn about being at the Grimes homestead when the escapees came up and launched their boat. It was a grand—and excruciatingly long-winded —tale I told, full of violence and heroism and ending with my ultimate escape from the clutches of the murderers. But not of course before I was able to discover their direction."

"You told my brother the boat went north?"

He met her gaze over the gray's broad back, his dark Irish eyes shadowed and mysterious. "*Och*, no; I told him they'd turned south. Dalton knows an Irishman would never prig on his mates. The *Repulse* will run north all right, looking to catch up with them. By the time that bloody captain realizes his mistake, the lads should have had enough time to lose themselves on one of the wilder peninsulas to the south of here."

She watched him lead the gray to its stall. "Didn't my brother wonder what you were doing at the cove so late?"

His voice came to her out of the dark recesses of the stables. "I told him you'd lost your locket there and I'd gone back to look for it."

"And he believed you?"

"Aye." He came at her, his ragged convict coat flaring open, his shadow leaping huge across the stable wall behind him. "Because I found it, you see."

She saw the gleam of warm gold in his palm as he reached up and pinned the round locket to her bodice, his fingers brushing gently against her breast. She watched his hands, then lifted her gaze to his face. "I'm sorry you weren't able to leave. I know how much you wanted it."

He shook his head. "I wanted to leave, yes. But I'd decided the entire scheme had become too damned dangerous. So now I keep asking myself if I stayed so that my mates would have a better chance of escaping or for another reason entirely."

"You would have gone if my brother hadn't ridden up when he did."

"Would I?" He turned away, his back held straight, his face cast in shadows. "Until I met you, I hated everything about my captivity on this island. I was willing to risk dying just to seize a chance to escape. But now . . . I feel as if I have something to lose." He paused. "And a part of me hates you for that."

She came up behind him, close enough that she could have touched him although she did not. She said, "Tomorrow, I want to go for a ride. Up to the rainforest."

He spun about, his eyes flaring dark and wide with comprehension. "Lass . . ."

She pressed the tips of her fingers against his soft, warm lips. "No. Don't say I shouldn't do this. Not this time."

He captured her hand in his, pressed a kiss to her palm. Over their joined hands, pale held fast by dark, his gaze met hers. "Some things are true even if we don't say them."

LATE THE NEXT morning they followed the track that wound through the foothills and up into the rainforest-clad mountains, the midday sun warm and bright as it filtered through the overhanging canopy of myrtles, wattles, and stringybarks. Lucas tilted back his head, his gaze on the antics of a colorful honeyeater, his thoughts a lifetime away. He would never get used to the pattern of the days here, to the cycle of the year in Tasmania.

Across the seas in Ireland, late October was a time of golden leaves scuttling before a cold wind, of pewter skies hanging low over dark, bare-limbed trees and waterlogged fields. But here in Tasmania, this was a time of vivid color and fresh life, of tulips and lilacs and bright green growth, of clear blue skies and balmy spring breezes. It disconcerted him, this reversal of the seasons, underscoring his exile and his alienation from all that was familiar in a way that was both subtle and profound.

He glanced at the woman who rode beside him, her back straight but relaxed, the fine black skirts of her expensive habit spread out around her, a faint flush high on her pale cheeks as she kept her gaze fixed on the path ahead. For Miss Jesmond Corbett, October meant spring. If she left here, he thought, if she went someplace like America, she would suffer there the same sense of dislocation he knew here. She would never feel quite at ease, never feel as if she entirely belonged. And then he wondered at himself for the thought, for she belonged to this place. She loved it; it was her home and she would live out the rest of her days here. When he did finally manage to escape from Tasmania, he would be leaving her behind. And the pain of it, the pain of his eventual leaving of her, was like a raw wound that bled every time he touched on it.

She had spoken little since they left the Castle. She was also having a hard time looking directly at him. Yet he knew from the tilt of her head that she was still determined on this thing she had decided to do. He thought for her sake that he shouldn't be letting this happen. But the need in him, the wanting, was deep and power-ful, an all-consuming drive that overrode common sense, self-preser-vation even. He might know on some esoteric level that they were making a potentially deadly mistake. But he didn't think he had the will to stop it.

In the weeks since they had visited the limestone caves, the stream had slowed, the boom of the low falls lessening to a melodic trickle. He watered the horses and tethered them where they could graze while she walked through the forest of thick, straight trunks and feathery ferns to a place where a windfall had let in the sun and grass grew thick and deep. He watched her sit on the grass, her skirts spread around her, her gloved hands clasped together in her lap, her head bowed. He had always yearned to touch her there where the delicate bones at the nape of her neck showed distinct and vulnerable against her smooth white skin. And so he allowed himself to do it now, a soft brushing of his fingers as he came up beside her.

He heard her draw a quick breath and then let it out slowly before she looked up at him, her eyes a dusky blue and solemn. She said, "I have decided that when Mr. Tate returns from Hobart, I shall tell him I cannot marry him."

He dropped to sit facing her, his legs crossed, his knees not quiet touching hers. He didn't say anything and made no further attempt to touch her.

She glanced down again at her hands laced so tightly together in her lap. "I do love Harrison, but it is as a friend only. I see that now. I honestly thought that would be enough. Perhaps if I'd never met you, it would have been enough. But I doubt it. I think I would always have been aware that there was something missing. Its absence would have made me miserable and in time I would have made him miserable, too."

"What will you do then?"

She looked up quickly. The smile spilling across her face was so natural and spontaneous that it took his breath. "What I've secretly always wanted to do: conduct a geological survey of the entire island. Most unladylike, don't you think? The majority of my inheritance is in land that is tied to my marriage. But I do have a small legacy that will be mine when I come of age next year. Perhaps I'll apply to the Governor for a land grant of my own. Some women have done it. Perhaps I could get you assigned to me."

"Lass . . ." Reaching out, he entwined his hand with one of hers. "I might not have escaped last night, but I will do it. I will be leaving one day. It's only a matter of time. I'll not be spending the next fifty years of my life as a convict in a British penal colony."

He watched the light fade from her face, her throat working as she swallowed and looked away toward the white froth of the falls. "I should have known that. It's just . . . so very hard. I feel as if I've been searching for you my entire life without even knowing it. Now that

I've found you, the thought of losing you is . . ." She wrapped her free hand around their entwined fingers, holding him tightly. "Beyond enduring."

"Yet you will have to endure it."

"I know. But not yet." She raised his hand still clasped between both of hers and laid it over her breast, her gaze hard on his face. "I want you to make love to me, Lucas."

"*Ah, muire* . . ." His hand trembled in her grip, his voice dry, scratchy. "You don't know what you're asking."

She lifted her head in that haughty way she had, although her smile was pure mischief. He thought he liked this smile of hers the best, for it hinted at all the parts of herself she normally worked so hard to keep hidden. "On the contrary, I know precisely what I am asking. I have received an excellent scientific education, and Genevieve has never believed that young girls should be sheltered from the realities of life and love." The smile faded, her eyes becoming wide and serious as she searched his face. "You think that because I am a virgin it would be wrong of you to lie with me."

He tried to smile but couldn't. His whole body was trembling now with the need to touch her face and her body, to take her in his arms and lay her down in this sweet, sun-warmed grass. "There are few who wouldn't see it that way."

Her nostrils flared with a quick intake of air. "Don't treat me as a child, as someone who doesn't know her own mind or isn't responsible for her own choices simply because she's a woman."

Reaching out, he brushed the back of his fingers against her soft cheek. "I have nothing but respect for you, lass. It's not that."

"Then what is it?"

He let his hand fall back to his lap. "You don't know me."

"I know you."

He shook his head. "You don't. There's too much I haven't told you."

"Don't you see? It doesn't matter. Not the whip scars on your back or the man you killed or any other dark terrible secret you can't bring yourself to tell me. None of it matters." She leaned forward, her features pinched with earnestness. "I love you, Lucas Gallagher." She put her splayed hand on his chest just above where his heart beat. "The man in here."

He felt his throat tighten with an upwelling of emotion he didn't want and couldn't afford. He'd known she desired him, but he'd never allowed himself to imagine that she actually cared for him, that what he saw shining in her eyes went beyond a deep wanting to love. It humbled him, this knowledge of her love, and troubled him. He took her hand in his and brought it to his lips, his eyes squeezing shut as he pressed his open mouth against her palm. "If I could have met you four years ago, in Dublin, when I was still a man with a future ahead of me and a heart to give . . ."

She eased her hand from his grasp to raise her arms and remove her hat, the movement lifting her breasts against the bodice of her riding habit in a way that made him ache. "What do you think?" she said, setting the hat aside. "That you would have been worthy of me then? That you're not worthy of me now?" She leaned forward to rest her hands on his knees, her beautiful eyes wide and earnest. "Don't you understand? *I love you.* You. The person you are now, today."

He made one last, half-hearted attempt to stave off what was about to happen. "There can never be anything between us. Nothing except danger and heartache; you know that."

"I know." She pulled off her gauntlet-style gloves and set them aside with her hat, like a lady come for tea. A shy smile curled her lips in a way that made him want to kiss them, to feel that smile. "Will you say my name?" she asked, her head tilting.

"Jessie," he said, and smiled at the delight that spread across her face.

"Now will you make love to me?"

He reached for her, his hands coming up to bracket her face. "I don't know how I could not."

33

JESSIE HELD HERSELF STILL, barely able to breathe as with exquisite gentleness he tilted his head and kissed her. She knew how badly he desired her, knew the fire within him burned hot and quick and wanting. Yet he was doing his best to control it, deliberately making this kiss sweet and tender, because for all her talk of knowledge and understanding she was still a virgin, with a virgin's uncertainty and fears. They had kissed and touched in the past, but she had only the vaguest idea of what lay beyond that, and he knew it.

His lips were so soft and warm, moving against hers. She let her hands curl up around his neck to hold him close, and he deepened the kiss, urging her mouth open beneath his as the kiss turned erotic. Carnal.

He tore his mouth from hers, his breath shuddering deep and fast in his chest. "I want to take off your clothes," he whispered, his gaze hard on her face.

She gave him a deliberately saucy smile that wobbled a bit around the edges. "Do I get to take off yours?"

"Yes." Smiling with his eyes, he reached to flick open the top button of her bodice, then the next. He kept his gaze on her face as he worked his way down the line of gleaming brass. Then they both watched as he spread open the edges of her bodice to reveal the delicate white confections of satin and lace and batiste that she wore beneath, and the swell of her upper breasts rising and falling with her rapid breathing.

"Ah, lass," he murmured, easing the stiff cloth off her shoulders and baring her arms to the warmth of the sun and the softness of his touch. "You're so beautiful."

She caught her breath as he ran his hands down her arms and up again, his thumbs sweeping beneath the fine batiste of her chemise to caress the flesh of her upper breasts. She let her head fall back, her fingers spreading in his sun-warmed hair. "You're only saying that because you want to get me out of my clothes. My mother warned me about men like you."

"Huh. I doubt your mother ever envisioned this." He moved to the fastening of her skirt. "Besides, I don't need to flatter you to get under your skirts; I already have permission, remember?"

"That's what comes of inexperience." Her elbows on his shoulders for balance, she lifted her hips so that he could draw away skirt and riding trousers in one sweep. "I see now that I should have made you flatter me first before I agreed to let you at my buttons."

"Buttons *and* ties *and* hooks," he said with a hoarse laugh. He rubbed his open mouth against her neck, kissed her ears, buried his face in her loosening mass of hair as he unhooked her corset and then went at the ties of her chemise. "All these layers. Most people think they're to give the English gentlewoman her rigid, properly molded silhouette. But the truth is they're here to discourage a man's wandering fingers. And other body parts."

She gave a soft laugh that ended on a caught breath as the last layer fell away. She felt shy and bold, frightened and excited, all at once. She was a wonder to herself, this shy-bold Jessie, reaching for the woman she was meant to be.

She traced the jutting line of his cheekbone with one finger. "I like it when you look at me like that."

"Like what?" he asked, easing off his coat and shirt so he could lay down beside her, one rough canvas-clad leg settling in close to hers.

"You look so fierce and frightening, and yet . . ."

"And yet?"

She turned into him, her hand coming to rest on his scarred forearm as she smiled up at him. "It makes me feel all warm and trembly inside."

He drew his hand in a feather-soft caress between her breasts, to her stomach. "Good. That's the way I want you—warm and trembling."

He kissed her then, kissed her nose, her eyelids, her neck, urging her onto her back. Then his head dipped lower. It occurred to her that she should have felt shy to have him looking at her like this, to have him touching her places she'd never even touched herself. But all she knew was a deep, aching need. She was losing her focus, her world narrowing down to sunlight and this man. She hadn't known . .
.

She hadn't know that her body could be so exquisitely sensitive, or that the simple touch of the man she loved could send her soaring. She hadn't thought that a man might kiss a woman, there. He knew things about her body she didn't know herself, knew how to set her aflame with a desperate need she barely understood. Yet he must have understood, for his hand was at the flap of his trousers and he was moving, sliding up to take her mouth in a rough kiss of hunger. The unfamiliar weight of him beguiled her as she felt him settle high up between her legs. She dug her fingers into his hips, clutching him to her and wanting, wanting. And he knew what she wanted, for he was pressing himself inside her, filling her. Joining himself to her. Giving himself to her.

But when the time came, he jerked away with a wrench that sent his seed spilling outside her quivering, empty belly.

~

SHE LAY in the curving shelter of his arm, the sun warm on her naked body, one hand resting on his chest.

"I never got to take off all your clothes," she said, her hand running in light circles over his bare skin. She wanted to touch him all over. Touch him and hold him forever and ever.

He smiled and brought his leg up to slide it down her stockinged calf to her riding boot. "I missed a few bits of yours."

She rolled forward, half onto his chest, so that she could look down into his sunlit face. She had never seen him looking so relaxed, so at ease, and she thought this must have been what he looked like before—before his life dissolved in pain and murder and the slowly grinding retribution of British justice. "We could do it again," she suggested naughtily, her fingers walking down to the open waistband of his convict trousers.

Laughing, he swept his hands to cup her buttocks and pull her completely on top of him. "Why, Miss Corbett, what an excellent suggestion."

She felt the length of him hard against her, her own laugh a breathy sigh of wonder and expectation as he cradled her face between his hands, his lips meeting hers in a kiss that ended all too quickly.

"What is it?" she asked, seeing the shadows that shifted deep in his eyes.

"'Tis dangerous, what we do. You know that, don't you?"

She sat back, straddling him, her knees on either side of his hips. "You're afraid we'll be caught."

"Aye. That too. I'm also sore afraid of giving you a babe." He spread his dark workman's hand against her naked belly. "Here."

Her head jerked once, in denial and swift consternation. "You pulled out."

"Aye. But it doesn't always work."

"So what does?"

The ease and contentment she'd seen earlier in his face was gone now. "There are things men can wear, but I've no way of getting any. Women know tricks—or rather, some women do. I don't."

She stared down at him, a heavy lock of her hair sliding forward over her shoulder. "Genevieve might."

He reached up to catch her hair and wrap it thoughtfully around his fist. "Would it be wise, you think, to ask her?"

"She wouldn't betray me, if that's what you mean."

"Not even if she thought it for your own good?"

Jessie shook her head. "She's always considered it a form of arrogance, for someone to think she knows what's better for another person than the person herself."

He opened his fist to release her hair. It fell against her breast, his hand following, her breath hitching as his palm closed around her. She brought her own hand up to cup his and hold it to her. "I'll ride over to the point tomorrow and talk to her."

"Ah, lass." He let his hands slide around her back to urge her down to him again, his lips moving against hers in a kiss as languidly purposeful as his touch. "I shouldn't be talking to you about preventing babies. I should be telling you we're mad, the both of us, to risk doing this again. We keep this up and we're bound to get caught."

She followed the beautiful hard line of his jaw, the curve of his cheek with her gaze. And it came to her that she could look at him forever. Only, they didn't have forever. "I can't stay away from you," she said with sudden fierceness. "Not anymore. I'm not that strong."

"Neither am I." His head came up, his lips finding hers again as he caught her to him and rolled her onto her back, trapping her beneath him.

She stared up into his shadowed face, saw the shadows lift, saw his mouth curl into a smile that made her feel weak and warm with expectation. "Now, about these clothes . . ."

~

THAT NIGHT after she finished dressing for dinner, Jessie dismissed her convict woman and went to stand in front of her dressing table mirror. A wind had come up outside, rustling the leaves and branches of the trees in the park and making the flames of the candles in their wall sconces leap and dance.

The flickering light showed her a golden-haired woman in a demure gown of old-rose peau de soie embroidered with blue flowers and trimmed with ecru lace. Her face seemed slightly more flushed than normal, her eyes wide and still, but otherwise she looked much the same as always. She thought it ought to reassure her, but it did not. She felt so very different inside of herself that she was afraid someone else would notice and *know*. Know that she had lain naked in a sunlit meadow and taken a man between her legs. A wild rogue of a lover whose rebellious soul called to the wildness within her. The secret woman within her.

If he had been anyone else, she would have proclaimed her love of him to the world, without hesitation and gladly. But he was an Irish convict, and the hopelessness of their love, the impossible tragedy of it, tore through her on a deadly wave of despair that battered her heart with fierce pain.

She tightened her face against the threatened weakness, one clenched fist coming up to press against her chest. She took a deep breath, then turned to extinguish her candles and cross the hall to speak to her mother. For while Jessie might need to hug the secret of her love to herself, she had also decided to end her betrothal to Harrison.

And that was something that Beatrice deserved to know.

34

B EATRICE'S ROOM LAY at the front of the house, across the wide
central hall from Jessie's.

It had always been Beatrice's room, even in the days
before Anselm Corbett's death. For as long as Jessie could remember,
her parents had kept separate rooms. When she grew old enough to
consider such things, Jessie had assumed they must both be private,
naturally unaffectionate people, or that their marriage had become a
source of disappointment to them both. Now she wondered if
Warrick was right, if they had never cared for each other at all.

Her knock on her mother's door elicited Beatrice's crisp, "Come
in." She was dressed for dinner in an austere gown of black watered
silk and seated on the burgundy satin covered stool facing her
dressing table. A convict woman was carefully placing pins in the
flawlessly upswept coil of Beatrice's graying hair. She did not look
around.

Jessie paused just inside the door, her hands laced together, her
heart pounding. She had been brought up to honor the wishes of her
parents, and it was the wish of both Beatrice and Anselm that Jessie
marry Harrison Tate. She felt as if a terrible weight had settled on her
chest, crushing her. She had disappointed her mother so many times

in the past and she was about to do it again. "Mother?" she said quietly. "I wonder if I might speak with you."

Beatrice met Jessie's gaze in the mirror, then dismissed her woman with a wave of her hand. "What is it, Jesmond?"

Jessie walked to the long front windows where the heavy burgundy velvet drapes stirred in a draft. This room had always vaguely surprised Jessie, with its dark tones and heavy mahogany furniture and sensuously rich fabrics. It hinted at a dramatic, almost masculine side to her mother that didn't seem to fit. Odd, Jessie thought, that it had never occurred to her that Beatrice might keep parts of herself hidden, as well.

"There is something I must tell you," Jessie said, turning to face the dressing table. She drew in a deep breath, as if gathering courage with it. "I have decided that I cannot marry Harrison."

If she had been expecting a dramatic reaction to her pronouncement, there was none. Opening her jewelry box, Beatrice calmly selected a large pearl ring and slipped it over her finger before saying, "I am sorry, Jesmond, but that is impossible. You are betrothed, and the wedding is scheduled for the beginning of December. The arrangements have all been made."

Jessie took a hasty step forward, then stopped. "Mother. This is not something you can simply dismiss. I cannot marry Harrison. I don't love him in the way a woman should love the man she marries."

Beatrice closed her jewel box with a snap, her eyes hard and narrowed as her gaze met Jessie's again in the mirror. In spite of herself, Jessie felt her stomach turn sickly. Inside, she might have been a disgraced six-year-old again, facing the prospect of endless, terrifying hours locked away in the haunted darkness of the tower room. "What nonsense is this?" Beatrice demanded, her diction painfully precise. "Your marriage to Harrison was decided upon years ago by your father. You never objected."

"I know," said Jessie, stricken with guilt. "But I do now."

"It's too late."

Jessie shook her head, her throat working as she swallowed. "It's not. It won't be too late until the marriage vows are said."

Beatrice arose with a stiff rustle of expensive silk, her movements controlled, dignified. She went to lock away her jewel box, then turned to face her daughter. In all her years of disappointing her mother, Jessie thought she had never seen Beatrice's face so severe, her eyes so icy with fury. But then, except in her desire to attend the Academy, Jessie had rarely set up her will deliberately against her mother's.

"We are not talking about legalities, Jesmond. We are talking about duty, honor, disgrace. A rigid code of acceptable behavior. A gentlewoman does not withdraw from such arrangements. If I were to allow you to end your betrothal now, you would be ruined. We would all be ruined, never able to appear in public again. Have you given even a thought to your brother? To the effect such a disgrace would have upon his position in society? And what of his friendship with Harrison? His marriage to Philippa?" *What about me?* Beatrice's entire tone suggested, although she didn't say it.

Jessie swung half away, one hand coming up to pinch the bridge of her nose. "Mother, Warrick doesn't want to marry Philippa. You know that. The marriage covenants that Papa and Malcolm Tate arranged between them might have seemed a good idea at the time, but they were wrong. You can't raise children together like brothers and sisters and expect them to grow up and marry."

Beatrice's thin nostrils flared in scorn. "You know nothing of such matters. We do what we must in this world, and you must marry Harrison Tate."

Her head held high, her body trembling badly, Jessie walked to the door. "I am sorry, Mother, but I plan to tell Harrison immediately upon his return from Hobart Town that I cannot be his wife."

She reached for the door handle, but her mother's voice stopped her, the voice that had cut Jessie so cruelly as a child and still had the power to make her bleed inside. "You have always been a selfish, self-serving child," hissed Beatrice, taking a quick step toward her. "You think only of yourself. Of yourself and your own ridiculous, petty wishes and interests. You have never tried to please me. Never made the least attempt to behave as you ought."

Shaking now with a confused mingling of hurt and raw anger, Jessie swung to face her mother. "You are wrong. I have tried. Ever since I was a little girl, I have tried and tried to be what you wanted me to be, but it has never been enough. I have never been good enough for you. All you have ever told me is how much I disappoint you and how ashamed of me you are."

Beatrice stared at her. "Is that why you're doing this? To punish me?"

"No. I'm doing this because I must."

"Because you must?" Her mother gave a brittle laugh. "You break your betrothal to Harrison, and everyone will believe that he is the one who called it off. They'll think he discovered that he was being tricked into accepting used goods. No one will ever marry you."

Jessie shook her head. She felt a stranger to the woman before her, this woman who had given her birth. "I am not going to live my life in fear of what other people might be thinking. What kind of morality is that?"

"Jesmond—" Beatrice took as step forward as Jessie wrenched open the door. "You do this, and I will never forgive you."

Jessie looked back over her shoulder, her throat so tight and sore it hurt to speak. "I'm sorry, Mother. But if I don't do this, I will never be able to forgive myself."

THEY SAT on the jumble of rocks at the base of the cliffs of Last Chance Point, Genevieve dangling her bare feet in the gentle surge of the receding sea, Jesmond Corbett with her legs drawn up close to her, her arms crossed upon her upraised, bent knees. The wind of the previous evening had died, leaving the day calm and balmy, the sky a glorious Tasmanian blue.

It had been weeks since they had met, but then, their friendship had always been like that, something snatched at in stolen moments, a vital connection that owed itself less to the frequency of contact than to a common way of looking at the world, a profound sense of mutual understanding. Over the years Genevieve had come to love this troubled girl like the daughter she'd never had. She had listened, today, while Jessie poured out the story of her confrontation with Beatrice and the decision about Harrison. But she couldn't help feeling there was something the girl was holding back.

"Where is the line, Genevieve?" Jessie asked now, her brows drawing together thoughtfully in that way she'd had since she was a child. "Where is the line between what a woman owes to others and what she owes herself?"

Genevieve blew out her breath in a long sigh, her gaze on the endless turquoise-blue swell of the sea. "I'm not sure there is only one line that's the same for all of us. Perhaps it comes down to the choices we each must make in our life. Each of us knows in our heart when a choice is wrong."

"But if a person is selfish—"

Genevieve reached out to touch Jessie's sleeve. "You're not."

Jessie bowed her head, the faint breeze stirring the small wisps of hair at the back of her neck. "My mother thinks I am."

"Perhaps your mother feels the need to justify to herself the choices she once made."

Jessie looked up, her gaze narrowing. "You mean her marriage to my father?"

"That's right."

Jessie stared down at a strand of seaweed caught on the rocks, thin brown streamers dancing gracefully with the action of the waves. "She never loved him, did she?"

Genevieve shook her head. "She had only met him once when her parents arranged the match. And under the circumstances, one could hardly expect affection to flourish between them." She saw the confusion in Jessie's eyes, and added: "Beatrice always considered Anselm a touch beneath her, you see. Her family was old gentry. Poor, but old."

"While the Corbetts were mushrooms," Jessie said wryly.

Genevieve smiled. "Something like that. Although I'm surprised she used that phrase to describe your father's family."

"No. But she uses it when speaking of people who have wealth yet are of inferior birth. Every time she'd say it around my father, she'd look at him in that way she has. It wasn't difficult to understand what she meant."

A goshawk arced overhead, screeching. Genevieve leaned back, watching the sun gleam bright and golden on the bird's outstretched wings. "She hasn't changed, has she?"

"I didn't realize you ever knew my mother," Jessie said, stretching out her legs to let them dangle over the edge of the rock.

"I knew her."

Jessie's head tilted, her gaze hard on Genevieve's face. "How?"

The soft eddy of the breeze brought with it the scents of brine and wet rock and eucalyptus from the trees at the top of the point behind them. Genevieve closed her eyes and drew the familiar smells deep into her being. "I promised your mother I'd never tell you that," she said, her heart heavy with new and old pain.

She was afraid the girl would press, but she didn't. A silence fell between them, a companionable silence filled with the quiet music of the waves and the raucous calls of the gulls. Then Jessie said, "Did my mother love someone else? When her parents arranged for her to marry my father?"

The girl's face was drawn, troubled. *Have you learned nothing from your life, Beatrice?* Genevieve thought with a spurt of anger. Aloud, she said, "Oh, yes. His name was Peter Fletcher. He was only a lieutenant in the army, but his family was old and proud . . . and even more poor than your mother's."

"Did he love her?"

"Profoundly. When her marriage to Anselm was first suggested, the lieutenant wanted her to run away with him."

"She never would."

"No. Never. Your mother's line has always been drawn very narrowly."

A ship had appeared some hundred yards or so off the mouth of the cove, the sun brilliant on its white sails as it plowed through the sea, running south. "All these years," Jessie said quietly, her gaze on the plunging prow of the ship, "and I never knew."

"She has probably forgotten herself. She would have made herself forget. She's like that."

Genevieve brought up a hand to shield her eyes from the glare of the sun. The ship was a frigate, the *Repulse*, running back into port. She glanced thoughtfully at the girl beside her. "She hasn't guessed how you feel about that Irishman, has she?"

Jessie shook her head. "I've never had a chance to ask how you knew."

"I saw your face," said Genevieve simply. "The night of the storm. When you looked at him, everything you felt for him was in your eyes."

"Perhaps I should take to wearing hats with veils." Jessie tried to laugh, but it came out twisted, frightened. "If my mother knew . . . " Her lips pressed into a thin, painful line and she shook her head. "I'm not sure what she would do. But she would make him suffer, I know that. She would blame him for my decision to break off my betrothal."

"When does his sentence expire?"

Jessie bowed her head, her clasped hands coming up to press against her nose and mouth. "Never. They're never going to let him go, Genevieve."

The frigate was so close they could hear the sails flapping in the breeze, hear the rush of the water against the sleek hull. Genevieve reached out and caught her friend's hand in hers. "Oh, Jessie."

"He says . . ." She looked up, her voice breaking so that she had to pause and swallow. "He says there are ways a woman can keep a child from growing inside her. Do you know them?"

Genevieve studied the girl's strained features. She had sensed that something powerful and life altering had happened to her young friend, something that went beyond her decision about Harrison and her confrontation with her mother. Now, Genevieve understood what it was. "Yes, I know. If you want, I can tell you."

Jessie nodded, her eyes glittering with unshed tears. She'd always been so fierce and strong, so demanding of herself, Genevieve thought. Even as a child, Jessie had rarely cried. "You want to tell me it's a dangerous thing we do," she said now.

Genevieve tightened her grip on the girl's hand. "Yes, it is dangerous. But you don't need me to tell you that." She knew a terrible fear, deep within her. A fear and a sadness, for she could see no way out for this pair of star-crossed lovers. Ahead lay nothing but heartache and disaster, and there was nothing Genevieve could do to stop it. "My dear," she said softly. "Simply remember that I am always here for you, whatever happens."

35

T HE BOY SAT WITH HIS BACK pressed against the rough stones of the hut, his legs sprawled out in front of him, his hands idle in his lap, and an old felt hat pulled low over his face. "She's in the meadow out the back, watching the sheep while they graze," said Dicken, not bothering to look up when Warrick reined in before him.

"Thank you," said Warrick. He started to turn his horse, then paused, his gaze, considering, on the youth before him. He was a strange boy, Dicken, almost disturbing in a half-wild, barely civilized way. In the weeks that Warrick had been coming here to this crude hut on the coast, he had seen the boy bring down everything from magpies to wallabies with his slingshot. Every time he killed, the boy smiled. And every time he smiled, Warrick wondered if it had been Dicken who left the gaping stab wound in Parker Jones's back.

"That black man, the convict I was looking for," Warrick said, asking the question that had been bothering him for so long, "Did you kill him?"

"Me?" One eye opened, the battered brim of the hat lifting as the boy peered up at Warrick. "Nah. I use a slingshot. Faine's the one likes knives."

Warrick's hand tightened on his reins hard enough to make his chestnut gelding throw up its head and snort in alarm. With soothing words, Warrick steadied the horse, then kneed it toward the sheep he could see grazing in the distance.

"WHY DIDN'T you tell me the truth?" he asked Faine later, as they lay sated and naked in each other's arms on the cloak he had spread for them beneath a blooming wattle tree. "Why didn't you tell me that you're the one who killed that black man I was looking for, that escaped convict?"

She lifted one slender shoulder in a careless shrug. "How was I to know the way you'd be reacting to such a truth?" She twisted her head so that she could see his face, her light brown eyes shadowy with thoughts he couldn't begin to grasp. "And you don't like it, do you? The fact that I killed him, for all he was a thief and a convict, and a black man besides."

"Don't be silly." He brushed her cheek with the back of his hand, his voice as gentle as his touch. "If he was threatening you violence, trying to force you, you had no choice."

"He weren't tryin' to do me nothing. It was the donkey, McBain, he was after."

Warrick's hand stilled against her face. "You killed him over a donkey? Stabbed him in the back?"

She rolled onto her side and raised herself up on one arm so that she could look down on him as he lay, flat on his back. "There, you see? You don't understand. You've no notion what it's like to be poor." She rested her hand on his naked chest, her caress slow and enigmatic. "You think it's all lyin' about in the grass and makin' love under the stars and bein' carefree and easy because we've nothing to lose. Well, that donkey's important to us, and I wasn't about to lose her."

Warrick stared up at her. He had always discounted the differences between them, between his life and hers. Now those differences seemed suddenly to open up between them, wide and unfathomable.

No, he didn't know what it was like to be poor. He wasn't sure he'd ever even considered what it would be like before now. Perhaps this was a part of it, he thought, this callous disregard for human life. Except...

He put his hand over hers, stilling it, his eyebrows drawing together in a frown as he searched her face. "Don't you feel anything? No remorse? No sadness, even? The man is dead."

She shook her head, her jaw hardening, her eyes flat. "He shouldna been trying to steal our donkey."

She stood up and walked, ethereally thin and beautiful, to where a small stream trickled over a stony course. By mid-summer the stream would be gone, but for now it still ran clear and sweet. He watched her kneel in the grass and stoop to scoop up a handful of water, the sun glinting golden and glorious along her bare back and lean hips. She was so natural, so relaxed, she enchanted him. Still.

He had been coming to see her for weeks, making love to her, holding her in his arms, telling her his dreams. Yet he knew that he'd never come close to making her his, never grasped the essence of her. What he wanted from her continued to elude him. And he was beginning to realize it always would.

"Why do you do it?" he asked. "Why do you lay with me? You say you don't love me."

She straightened and turned to face him, her lips lifting in a brilliant smile. "You're beautiful. Like an angel—you're like something from a different world. It's not often a body gets a chance to touch something from a different world."

He sat up, his forearms resting on his bare knees. "Don't you love me even a little?"

She cocked her head, studying him as if she were trying to understand him, trying to understand this need he had for her love. He knew she'd had other men, men to whom she'd given herself freely after that first rough taking in the hills of Scotland. Hadn't any of them wanted more from her, he wondered; more than what she'd been willing to give him? "I like you fine," she said slowly, as if reaching carefully for her words. "But how can I love you when I don't even know you?"

"Haven't you learned to know me some, these past weeks?"

"Some. But I could never really know you. We're too different."

He arose and walked toward her. He still felt awkward and a little shy, moving about naked the way she did, in the open. "I think," he began, then paused and smiled, reaching out to put his hands on her hips. "I *believe*, that two people can know and love each other instinctively—intuitively—the first time they meet."

She tilted back her head so she could look up at him. Her face was blank. "I don't even know what those words mean." She took his hand in hers and put it between her legs, where she was still warm and sticky from what they'd done together. "This is what I know. This is what we have. And this," she added, reaching out to close her other hand around his half erect penis.

To his shame, he felt himself swell again in her grasp. He didn't want this to be all there was between them. He wanted there to be something beautiful and glorious, something special, something profound. He'd never thought of himself as a romantic fool. But it occurred to him now that perhaps he was after all. He buried his face in the sweet fire of her hair and began to laugh.

After a moment, her laughter joined his. Then her mouth found his, and he wasn't laughing any more.

EARLY ONE EVENING, two days after her visit to Last Chance Point, Jessie was crossing the yard after paying a visit to Old Tom when she glanced up to find the stableboy, Charlie, pelting out of the stables toward her, one hand holding his hat planted on his head, his bony elbow pointing skyward. "Miss," he called, his eyes wide in his freckled face. "Miss Corbett. Oh, wait, do."

"What is it?" she asked, catching him by the shoulders as he skidded to a breathless halt. "What's wrong?"

"It's Gallagher, Miss." The boy's shoulders heaved, his mouth slack as he fought to catch his breath. "He's taken the gray and gone off, I don't know where to. But he was in a rare taking, he was."

"He has ridden out *now*?" Jessie narrowed her eyes against the glare of the setting sun, her gaze on the pink and gold touched clouds hovering over the mountains to the west. "But it's late," she whispered. "The barracks . . . " She swung back to the boy. "What happened?"

"Captain Boyd's been up at the house, Miss. They've found the six men who escaped, and Gallagher heard about it."

Jessie felt her heart begin to pound hard in her chest. *Thank God, thank God,* she thought; *thank God he wasn't with them.* Aloud, she said, "They've been caught? All of them?"

Charlie shook his head. "Only three, Miss. The other three are dead. And two of the ones in jail at Blackhaven Bay might not live long enough to hang."

Jessie knew a rush of nausea. She had seen men hanged, seen their faces turn black and distorted, their bodies stained with their dying release. "Were they good friends of Mr. Gallagher?" she asked softly. "The men who escaped, I mean?"

The boy nodded, his thin, bony head bobbing up and down. "One of them, the one they call the Fox, he was Gallagher's mess mate on the transport out. And another, Daniel O'Leary, was with him on the chain gang. Saved his life, Gallagher told me."

"Is he one of the men in jail, this Daniel?"

"No, Miss. Daniel's dead. The Fox killed him."

"Listen to me, Charlie." She glanced up at the house where Beatrice was doubtless already dressing for dinner. "I want you to saddle my mare while I quickly change into my riding habit. Tell the overseer Gallagher is with me and we're out late because I want to observe the Aurora Australis. And send someone to tell my mother, too."

"The what?"

"The southern lights. And Charlie," she added as he started to run off. He paused to throw her a questioning glance over his shoulder. "Thank you."

36

S HE FOUND THE GRAY tethered to the elm at the edge of the ruined garden, near the empty fountain. The man who had ridden it here was nowhere to be seen.

From the cove below came the familiar rushing sweep and drag of the tide, mingling with the grinding chirp of crickets as she nudged the reluctant mare across the abandoned garden toward the blackened house. The sun had all but disappeared behind the mountains, leaving the sky a pink-cast teal blue and reducing the colors of the landscape to muted tones of charcoal.

Shivering slightly, she drew up before the house, her head falling back as she stared up at the gaping, empty windows and cracked walls. She could not have said how she knew he was here, yet she did know. She found the old mounting block half-buried in the long grass and used it, then tied her horse to an iron ring set in the crumbling stone garden wall. "Easy, Cimmeria," she murmured, stroking the nervous mare's nose. "I don't think these ghosts hurt horses." She kept her voice light when she said it, but Cimmeria only snorted and threw up her head, the dainty, white-stockinged feet dancing sideways.

Since that long ago day when a much younger Jessie had stood in the polished, black and white marble hall and admired the Grimes' grand oak staircase, she had never entered this house. Now, her heart pounding in her chest, her throat dry, she passed through the open, blackened doorway into the shattered ruin of that same hall.

All the walls of the house, even those on the inside, had been built of convict-hewn stone, some fourteen or more inches thick. They still stood, reaching up to the darkening evening sky far above. But the oak staircase was gone, the tiles underfoot now cracked and littered with leaves and bits of charred wood too small to be carried off for fuel. Clasping her arms tightly against her chest, Jessie passed through a doorway on her right into what had once been the drawing room.

The shape of a man stood silhouetted against the darkening sky, his hands braced wide against the sides of what had once been an elegant set of French doors leading onto a flagged veranda over-looking the sea. A small mew of alarm escaped her lips before she could stop it.

"Tis it one of the resident ghosts you're expecting, then?" Gallagher said, his brogue broad and aggressive. "Tell me . . . " He dropped his arms to his sides and turned toward her. "Of the three, which do you think would be the most dangerous?"

She watched him come at her out of the night, as beautiful, dark and dangerous in his own way as anything spawned by hell. "You startled me," she said, her head tilting back so that she could look up into his beautiful, familiar features.

"I noticed. What are you doing here?"

"That's my question." She wanted to pound her fists in frightened anger against this broad chest. She wanted to cradle his face between her palms and kiss his hard man's mouth. She wanted him to hold her in his arms and tell her that he loved her as much as she loved him, and that he'd never do something like this again. Instead, she said, "Do you have any idea what they would do to you, for riding off like this?"

He shrugged, his mouth tightening into a bitter line. "A week's solitary confinement, maybe two, on bread and water. I've suffered it before—it and worse—and survived."

"So it's all right then, is it? How about if they decided to give you fifty lashes instead? Would that still be all right?"

He swung abruptly away from her, his back held painfully straight and rigid. "I'm not a man who likes rules, Jessie. I don't like being controlled or taking orders or conforming to other people's expectations. Sometimes . . . sometimes I just need to fly in the face of it all. Even if I have to pay for it."

A silence fell between them, a silence filled with the distant rumble of the surf and the whisper of the wind through the trees. She took a step toward him, then stopped herself. "I heard about your friends," she said, her voice falling awkwardly into the stillness of the night. "I'm sorry. But you shouldn't blame yourself. It's not your fault."

He spun to face her. There was an intense aura of recklessness about him tonight, of wildness that both frightened and excited her. "Isn't it? I'm the one who found the bloody boat. I repaired it, and I planned the whole stupid fiasco."

"It wasn't stupid. Someone told on you, and those men decided to go anyway. It was their decision. How does that make it your fault?"

"If I'd been with them—"

"If you'd insisted on going with them, then my brother would have seen the boat leave the cove and the *Repulse* would have picked up all of you in a few hours."

"Instead of a few days?"

She saw the chilling glitter in his eyes, and her heart shivered in fear. "You hate me right now, don't you?" she whispered. "For being English. For being a part of this whole brutal, dehumanizing system."

He walked up to her, the sea breeze blowing through the open doorway to ruffle his dark hair, the silver light of the moon glazing the intense, beloved features of his face. "I don't hate you," he said softly.

"Lucas . . . " She reached out to him, her hand shaking. "It won't make your friends' suffering any less just because you set things up so that you're suffering, too."

He took her hand in his strong, warm grip, his eyes narrowing as he stared down at her. "You think that's why I'm doing this? So I'll be punished?"

"Isn't it?"

She felt his hand tighten around hers, saw his chest lift as he drew in breath. "I don't know." Abruptly, he let her go and walked away to lean one shoulder against the old doorway, his gaze on the sea, the waves glimmering black and white-crested in the moonlight. "You shouldn't have come here."

"Why not?"

He pushed away from the doorway, his boots scraping over the rough, broken flagging as he moved to stand at the edge of the veranda, his hands on his hips. She followed him. They stood side by side watching the ceaseless march of the tide washing onto the beach below. After a moment, he said, "Do you realize you've never asked me why I killed that man, Nathan Fitzherbert?"

She turned her head to look at him. "I figured you'd tell me your reasons when you were ready."

"What makes you so sure I had a reason?"

"Because I know you."

He let out his breath in a harsh, guttural sound. "Is there such a thing as a good enough reason to kill another human being?"

"Probably not. But I can understand why a man might feel driven to it." She let her head fall back to stare up at the night sky, the stars oddly blurred in the purpling night. "You don't need to tell me."

"No. I should have told you before."

"If you think it will make me turn away from you," she said, the words strained by the tightness in her throat, "you're wrong."

"You haven't heard it yet."

She sank down to sit on the broken edge of the veranda, her legs hanging over the three foot drop to the ruined garden, her gaze on her hands folded in her lap. She wanted to know more about this man, to understand him better, to understand the darkness that haunted his wild soul. But she wasn't entirely certain she was ready to hear what he was about to say. "It happened when you were at university in Dublin, didn't it?" she said quietly.

She was aware of him hunkering down on his heels beside her, his forearms resting on his spread thighs, but she kept her gaze lowered. "I was visiting my sister Rose at the time," he said, his voice flat. "Rose's husband, Patrick Maguire, was a good friend of mine. He was a writer—a journalist. He had a printing press in his basement, a secret press that he used for the cause."

Jessie didn't need to ask which cause. In Ireland, there was only one real cause.

"That night, a troop of English soldiers came to the house. Someone must have told them about the press because they knew right where to look for it."

She glanced up. "Nathan Fitzherbert was one of them?"

He nodded, his face chillingly emptied of all emotion, his eyes as flat as his voice. "Fitzherbert was the officer in charge. He had six men with him. After they'd smashed the press, he let them take turns at Rose. All six of them."

Jessie sucked in a quick breath, trying to ease the sudden ache within her. *Oh, God,* she thought. *Oh, God, no.*

"Her husband, Patrick, and I tried to stop them. Fitzherbert blew Patrick's brains out. I thought he meant to do the same with me, but he had other plans for me. He made me stand there with his pistol to my head and watch."

Jessie realized her hands were clenched so tightly together, they hurt. She straightened them slowly and pressed them flat against her thighs. "Did she survive—your sister?"

"It didn't kill her, what those soldiers did to her. So the next day, Rose killed herself."

She drew up her feet to hook her heels on the edge of the veranda and wrap her arms around her bent legs, her face pressed into her knees. She had heard of such things happening, but always as something abstract, something distant. This had been done to the sister of the man Jessie loved—and by English soldiers. She felt sick and ashamed. "Did you try going to the authorities?"

"You mean to the English?" He let out a harsh sound that was not a laugh. "I tried. There is no justice for the Irish in Ireland. Not as long as the English are there."

His gaze met hers, his eyes black and shadowed. She realized she was holding her breath and let it out in a long sigh. "So you killed him yourself."

He picked up a broken bit of stone from the edge of the shattered veranda, turned it over and over again in his hand. "I followed him home from the pub one night. Caught him cutting across a park alone. I gave him a shillelagh and told him to fight for his life. But the shillelagh is an Irish weapon, not an English one." A fierce smile flashed across his face. "Since the English don't allow us to own guns, we've learned to fight with what we have, even if it's just sticks. He didn't have a chance."

She remembered an afternoon in early September in a death-haunted mountain clearing, and Gallagher swinging a branch with lethal skill at a bushranger's head. He was right; even armed with a cudgel, the Englishman wouldn't have stood a chance. But she said, "You gave him the opportunity to fight you, man to man. That's not murder."

"Isn't it?" His fist tightened around the rock. Smiling vaguely, he stared down at it, then hurled it explosively into the darkness of the night. "I set out to kill him and I did. Those weeks in between—between that night when the English broke into my sister's house and the night I killed Fitzherbert—they're a blur to me. I don't remember any of it. But I remember the killing."

"What did you do then?" she asked, her voice a broken whisper.

He rose in one swift movement and came to stand behind her, so close she could feel the heat of his legs against her back. "I left Dublin. Went into the Comeragh Mountains. But the soldiers, they found me eventually. I was all for confessing what I'd done, but my father, he said they'd no real evidence to convict me. He said my mother had already lost one child to the English and he wasn't sure she could bear losing another in such a way. So I held my tongue, for my mother's sake."

He paused, and the silence filled with the moan of the wind and the lonely cry of a curlew. "My father was right." His voice was wry, brittle. "They didn't have enough evidence to convict me of the killing. So they got me on treason charges instead, and my mother had to bear losing another child after all."

She tilted back her head to look up at his taut, dark features, one hand stealing up to rest against his hard thigh behind her. Beneath her touch, his convict trousers felt rough, coarse. "At least you were transported, not hanged."

He settled behind her, his arms coming soft and warm around her waist to bring her back against his chest. "What does it matter? She'll never see me again."

She gripped his arms, holding him close. "It matters."

He freed one hand to take off her hat and bury his face in the curve of her neck. She could feel his chest lift, pressing against her back when he breathed. He held her that way for a long moment, as the night breeze wafted up from the old garden, cool and sweet with the aroma of the sea and damp growing things.

"At first," he said, his voice rough, almost shaky. "I really thought I could do it, Jessie—be smart, beat the system, get my ticket of leave and survive. That was before I realized how well-connected Fitzherbert was. Before I realized that I was never going to be free again." He paused. "Unless I escape."

She drew in a deep gulp of air, her chest hurting. His arms felt splendidly right wrapped around her, enveloping her in his familiar warmth and strength. She loved him so much she ached with it, and now he was talking about leaving her again. "You were wrong," she said. "It doesn't change the way I see you."

He pulled her up onto her knees and drew her around to face him, his hands heavy on her shoulders, his features ghostly shadows in the night. "That's because you haven't heard the worst of it."

I don't want to hear, she thought, facing him, knees pressed to knees. *I've already heard more than I can bear.* But she didn't say it because she knew he would tell her anyway.

"You think I killed him for what he let his men do to my sister and for murdering Patrick Maguire. That played a part, it's true. But only a part." He brought up his hand to bracket her face with his thumb hooked under her chin and his fingers resting against her cheek. "Because what I was thinking about, what I was remembering when I killed Fitzherbert, was what he did to me."

"Don't tell me," she said, the words escaping before she could stop them, her head jerking as if to shake in denial.

"What he did to me, Jessie," he repeated, his voice as brutal and frightening as his words. "Because when the soldiers were finished with Rose, Fitzherbert had them hold me down. And then he used me the way his soldiers had used my sister."

"Oh, God," she said on a sob. "Oh, God. No." She was crying now, the hot tears spilling down her cheeks, over his hands, into her mouth, tasting salty, bitter.

"Yes." His hand moved on her face in a way that forced her mouth open. "So now you know. Now you know why it's an abomination that I even touch you, let alone do *this*."

He took her open mouth in a crushing kiss, a savage outpouring of passion and pain that was both profoundly arousing and punishing, although she could not have said whether he was punishing her or himself. She made a whimpering sound deep in her throat, her hands coming up. Only instead of pushing him away, she clenched her fingers in the coarse cloth of his coat and leaned into him, opening her mouth gladly to this rough onslaught. She tasted all the anger and self-loathing and need in his kiss, and gave him back nothing except surrender and acceptance and love.

He tore his mouth from hers. "Don't," he said, his breath coming in harsh gasps, his eyes haunted. "Don't do that."

"Don't do what? Don't kiss you? Or don't love you?"

He surged to his feet and backed away, his eyes wide and wild. "Don't do that especially," he said, and whirled away from her.

She stumbled up, the toe of one boot catching in the long hem of her habit, her knees weak with fear and the tremors aroused by his kiss. "Lucas . . . " She took a step toward him. His coat shone pale gray against the blackness of the house wall, his lean, strong back held taut with suppressed emotion and leashed violence. But she was not afraid of him; she was only afraid for him.

"You shouldn't have come," he said, his head falling back, the wind ruffling his dark hair where it fell over the collar of his rough convict coat. "Please, Jessie. Just go and leave me here. Don't you understand what I was trying to tell you?"

She took another step toward him. "I love you."

She heard him draw in a deep breath that shuddered his entire body. "Don't keep saying that."

"I love you."

He spun to face her, his eyes black in the night, his face contorted with the fierceness of the struggle he was waging with himself. "Jesmond. Stay away from me. Please. I'm not clean. I'm not worth . . . any of this. Not your love, not the risks you take to be near me, not the pain you're going to feel when I finally leave—or they kill me."

"I love you." She reached for him, but he caught her by the shoulders and held her at arms length, his fingers digging into her flesh. She thought for a moment that he meant to put her away from him. She could feel the fine tremors of want shimmying through him, see the anguish of his tortured soul burning in the depths of his eyes. Then his breath escaped in a soft keening moan and he hauled her up against him.

His kiss was desperate with hunger and need, a deep, frantic kiss of twining tongues and nipping teeth and breathless, gasping desire. His hands roamed her body, swept down her back to cup her bottom and pull her hard up against him. She held onto him, one hand splayed against the taut muscles of his back, the other tangling in his hair, holding him to her, her head falling back as he kissed her chin, her neck.

"I want you," he said, his lips moving over her throat, his voice a hushed murmur. "Here. Now."

"I want you more," she whispered, nipping his ear with her teeth, and heard his ragged laugh.

He pressed her up against the rough masonry wall, his hands tearing at the buttons of her habit, shoving down her corset, yanking open her chemise. He was rough, fierce with need, his breath easing out from between his teeth in a hiss of wonder as his fingers closed over her bare breasts.

She cried out, her head hitting the wall behind her as she found the flap of his trousers and tugged.

She gave herself to him with wild, joyous abandon, the fire-blackened walls of that tragedy-haunted house rough against her back, the sea-scented night air warm against her naked skin. She heard him say her name on a harsh expulsion of breath, felt his fingers dig into her hips hard enough to bruise. She watched his lips pull away from his teeth, his head falling back. Then he jerked down and away, an abrupt withdrawal that made her cry out in loss. He sank to one knee, a deep guttural groan tearing up from within him, his body hunching forward, his head bowed, his shoulders shuddering.

"Lucas." She went down on her knees beside him, cradled his head in her arms, her face buried in his hair. She could feel the pounding of his heart, the tremors still shivering though him. She felt her love flood through her deep and violent and bringing the sting of tears to her eyes. "Oh, Lucas."

His hands gripped her arms, his head coming up, his eyes narrowing as he searched her face. "I must be some kind of an animal, going at you like that," he said, his breath still so strained his voice was but a harsh tear. "You deserve better than to be taken up against a house wall in the open night."

She laid her palm against his cheek, rubbed her thumb across the fullness of his lips, felt her own mouth lift in a smile. "Actually, I rather liked it," she said and caught his soft laugh with her kiss.

∾

"AND PRECISELY HOW are you proposing to explain any of this to your family?" he asked dryly, bringing his horse in behind hers as they followed the narrow path up the hill away from the cove.

Jessie swung her head to look back at him, but thin bands of clouds had appeared on the eastern horizon, obscuring the moon and many of the stars, so that he was only a dark shadow following her through the silence of the night. She was slightly sore between her legs where he had been, and just the thought of it now was enough to send an echo of desire tripping through her again. It was a wondrous, powerful thing between them, she thought, this wanting. Powerful and perilous.

"I suppose my disheveled appearance and torn habit could be attributed to a tumble." Her voice shook slightly with the wanton direction of her thoughts. "Riding in the dark can be dangerous."

She heard him grunt behind her. "Very dangerous indeed," he said, exaggerating his brogue, "especially for wayward young lasses." Over her soft laughter, he added, "What were we supposed to be doing out here in the first place, then?"

"Ah, I've already thought of that. I left a message for my mother, telling her I wanted to observe the southern lights." She threw another glance at him over her shoulder. "Have you ever seen them?"

"Oh, aye. I've glimpsed them a time or two. Through small, barred windows."

It disturbed her as it always did, to think of him locked away night after night like some crazed beast. And it occurred to her now that this was probably the first night of relative freedom he'd known for a long time.

"Then look at them now," she said softly, reining in her mare as they crested the top of the bluff and the southern sky opened up before them in flickering gold-green splendor.

He rode up beside her, his head falling back, his body held breathlessly still as he gazed at the great, luminous arcs of colored light that flared across the sky in undulating folds of brilliance.

"It's beautiful," he whispered.

She watched him watching the magically lit sky. The wind flared the hem of his coat and ruffled the dark hair at his forehead. In the ghostly light, the beloved features of his face showed so strong and finely drawn, he stole her breath.

His horse moved restlessly beneath him, as if his hand had tightened suddenly on the reins. "I hear they're called the Merry Dancers, in Scotland. Now I know why." He swung his head to look at her. "Have you any idea what causes this?"

She shook her head. "It's some form of energy that seems to be attracted to the poles at this time of year, perhaps from the sun. But I don't think it's entirely understood yet."

They sat side by side for another long moment of companionable silence, sharing the majesty of the fiery flow of air moving rapidly across the heavens, rippling like wind-blown silk. Then he reached out to take her hand in his, his gaze on her face, his eyes glittering in the darkness. "Thank you. For this . . . " He drew his other arm out in an arc that took in the colored flares of the night sky. "And for the comfort and joy of your body." He brought her hand to his lips and kissed the palm of her glove, his eyes smiling at her. "And for rescuing me from the consequences of my own folly."

"I understand why you did it," she said, twisting her fingers to tighten on his hand. "I don't think I did before. But I do now."

He drew in a deep breath that lifted his chest. "I will try to escape again, Jessie. I can't stay. Not for you, not for the wonder of what's between us."

"I know," she said.

But knowing it and accepting it were two different things entirely.

THE OVERSEER'S eyes glittered in silent anger when she delivered Gallagher to the small, octagonal guard house. But Dalton's anger was directed at her, not at the man she had kept out past hours, and as an employee, the overseer could do nothing except mutter under his breath when she turned away.

She made her way through the still, dark garden to let herself in the side door of the house. As she passed the closed door to the music room, she heard the sweet strains of Beethoven's *Apassionata* being played with such heartbreaking emotion that she knew it had to be Warrick and not her mother at the piano. Beatrice might be technically flawless, but only Warrick possessed the ability to move a listener to tears with the power of his music. Dinner must be long over by now, she thought, and hurried up the servants' stairs to her room.

Once there, she quickly stripped off her riding habit and shrugged into her dressing gown. She was just reaching for the pitcher of water when the door behind her flew open with enough force to crash into the wall. She whirled about, one hand flying up to hold together the neckline of her gown, the other braced unconsciously against the washstand behind her.

Beatrice stood on the threshold, a band of angry color staining her cheeks, her body rigid with fury. "So you're home, are you?"

"Mother," said Jessie, her hand clenching in the fine silk of her gown. "You startled me."

"I know what you've been doing," said Beatrice and closed the door behind her with a snap.

37

"**H**AVE YOU LOST ALL SENSE OF WHAT you owe your family?" Beatrice demanded, the black silk skirts of her mourning gown swirling about her ankles as she stalked over to realign the candlesticks and vase on Jessie's mantelpiece with swift, jerky movements. "First this ridiculous nonsense concerning your betrothal, and now . . . this."

Jessie felt her heart begin to race sickeningly in her chest. "Mother—" she began.

"I want to know how long this has been going on," Beatrice interrupted, whirling to face her. "Since the afternoon of the storm? Or before?"

How long had it been going on? Jessie wondered, staring at her mother. When had it begun? That afternoon in the rainforest, when they'd shared that first, magical kiss? Or hadn't it really begun that first day, when she looked up and saw him standing in the quarry? For surely nothing in her life had been quite the same since.

"I can't believe you would do such a thing," Beatrice was saying, her hand coming up to press against her forehead in a distracted gesture. Jessie saw the glitter of unshed tears in her mother's eyes and knew a moment of profound shock. Beatrice never wept. "How could you do this? How could you do this to *me,* when you know how I feel about that woman?"

That woman. It took a moment for the sense of her mother's words to penetrate the numbing chill of Jessie's fear. *She doesn't know,* Jessie realized, sucking in a dizzying gasp of relief. *She doesn't know about Gallagher.* She pushed away from the washstand, her heart beating with unsteady lurches as if it had stopped and was only now starting up again. "Mother, what are you talking about?"

Beatrice's hand fell, her nostrils flaring with anger, and it occurred to Jessie that if there were tears in her mother's eyes, they were tears of rage. "Don't play the fool with me, Jesmond. I am talking about your visits to Last Chance Point."

Jessie stared at her mother. "Genevieve?"

Beatrice's entire body seemed to draw up in fury. "Don't you even think of lying to me."

Jessie walked over to sink down on the stool before her dressing table. "I have no intention of lying to you." She clenched her hands tightly in her lap, her gaze on her mother's flushed face. "Genevieve and I have been friends for eight years. I didn't tell you when I was younger because I knew you would have prevented me from seeing her. But I should have told you upon my return from England, and for that I am sorry."

"Eight years? You have been consorting with that shameless hussy for eight years?" They stared at each other, the lace of Beatrice's fichu rising and falling with her agitated breathing, her eyes wide, almost wild. "You are not to visit that woman again. Do you hear me?"

"She is my friend," Jessie said quietly.

"She is not at all a proper person for you to associate with. You know that. You have always known that."

"Why?" Jessie demanded, her head falling back as her mother stalked up to her. "Because she dared to snatch her own happiness from out of the living hell her parents envisioned for her? Is that why you hate her so much? Because she had the courage to do what you did not?"

Without warning, Beatrice drew back her hand and slapped her daughter across the face, the force of the blow strong enough to rock Jessie back on her seat. "You're just like her," Beatrice hissed, her jaw clenched so tightly that only her lips and throat moved with the words. "Always roaming about the countryside, doing odd things that might be precisely calculated to draw undue attention to yourself. You even look like her at times, when you're being willful and opinionated."

"Look like her? Why would I—" Jessie broke off, her thoughts whirling away. It all made sense, suddenly. The cottage that had once belonged to Jessie's grandmother but was now Genevieve's home. Genevieve's interest all through the years in the wellbeing of Jessie's mother and siblings. The easy camaraderie that had always existed between Jessie and the older woman—an affinity so unlike what Jessie had known with her own mother but which she believed could sometimes exist between mother and daughter. Or aunt and niece.

"Oh, God," Jessie whispered, staring at her mother. "Genevieve is your sister."

Beatrice took a step back, the pulse point in her neck throbbing wildly. "You didn't know?"

Jessie shook her head. "No. She never told me. She said she'd made you a promise, but I didn't know what about." She blew out her breath in a long sigh, one hand coming up to hold back a lock of hair knocked loose by her mother's hand. "Why? Why did you cut off all contact with her? How could you? Your own sister? You told me she died."

"She disgraced herself and her family. She brought disgrace on *me.* You have no idea of the humiliation I endured, the sly looks, the whispers. The pity." Beatrice stopped abruptly, drawing herself up, visibly putting her memories of the past behind her. "As far as I am concerned, I no longer have a sister. She died years ago."

Jessie searched her mother's face but found only coldness and anger. "Grandmama obviously forgave her. She left Genevieve the cottage."

Beatrice wheeled away. "My father never would have left my mother that property in the first place had he known she intended to do such a thing. I thought of disputing it, but our solicitors were not particularly encouraging and I finally dropped my objections in exchange for her promise. She said she would never seek out my children, never tell them of the relationship between us. I should have known better than to trust her."

"She didn't seek me out. We met by chance. I doubt she promised to turn me away." Jessie rose to her feet, one hand clutching the opening of her gown tight against her neck. "Who told you of my visits to Genevieve?"

Beatrice turned her head to look to look at Jessie again, her face composed, unrevealing, silent.

Then Jessie remembered sitting with Genevieve on the rocks and watching the wind fill the sun-struck white sails of the *Repulse* as it cut through the sea. "Captain Boyd," she said. "It was Captain Boyd, wasn't it? He came out here to tell Warrick they'd recaptured the men and he took the opportunity to carry tales about me to you."

Beatrice's hand fluttered up to touch her widow's brooch, then dropped, her chin lifting, her jaw tightening in a way that emphasized the puckered lines around her mouth. "You should have been here. I don't know what you were thinking, sending me a message by a stableboy, of all things. As if it weren't enough that you've been consorting with That Woman, now I have you riding out at night accompanied only by a groom simply to look at lights in the sky? This is not acceptable, Jesmond. What would Harrison say if he knew?"

"Mother," Jessie said wearily, "I am not marrying Harrison."

Beatrice turned toward the door, her movements and voice brisk, dismissive. "Such pre-wedding nerves are quite common. I've no doubt you'll come to your senses before Harrison returns. And then," she added tartly, opening the door, "your behavior will be his problem, not mine."

Jessie sank back onto the stool of her dressing table and watched the door close behind her mother. She stared at the panel a long moment, then hunched over, her arms wrapped around her waist, a fine trembling going on and on inside her.

~

WARRICK LET his fingers drift over the keys of the piano, his eyes closed, his soul lost in the melancholy of the music. It occurred to him that this was one of the things Faine didn't know about him— this intense and entirely uncharacteristic love of music. But then, there was much that Faine didn't know about him. Much that he didn't know about her.

They'd made love a second time that afternoon, after she'd told him about the black man, about Parker Jones. It had been intensely erotic and undeniably satisfying, an almost savage coming together. Yet he'd known—they'd both known that the magic had gone out of their lovemaking. And they'd known, too, that he would not lie with her again.

It was humbling to realize that she'd been right, that he hadn't loved her after all. He had only loved the idea of her. Or maybe what he'd loved had been the way she'd made him feel. When he was with her, he'd been drawn outside of himself, he'd been able to forget the raging fire that he sometimes thought would consume him from within. And then he thought about Philippa and the things she'd said to him the day of the picnic and the way the laughter had sparkled in her brown eyes. His fingers faltered.

"Perhaps you'd play more correctly if you actually looked at the keys, Warrick," said an acerbic voice behind him.

"Mother," he said, twirling around on the stool to find her standing in the doorway, the flickering light from the candlestick in her hand throwing somber shadows across her pale face. "Missing the point, as always."

"I need you to select one of the men," she said, her gaze fixed on some irrelevant feature to his left. She rarely looked at him if she could avoid it. And she'd been avoiding it since he was twelve. "Someone trustworthy—preferably one of the free workers. Send him to me first thing in the morning."

"Why?"

Beatrice swung her head to look directly at him, the features of her face pinching together in that way she had, as if she were mentally cataloguing all of his faults and inadequacies, and despising him for them. "If I need any interference from you, Warrick, I will ask for it. In the meantime, all I require is that you provide me with a suitable individual in the morning."

Warrick watched her disappear into the candlelit darkness, a tall, cold figure dressed in black. Then he turned back to the piano and brought his hands crashing down on the keys in a violent, discordant note.

Two days later Lucas drove Miss Jesmond Corbett to the dressmaker's in Blackhaven Bay.

She sat a proper distance from him on the plump leather seat of the shiny black shay, her shoulders back and chin up, her face turned slightly away from him as she stared out over sunlit fields growing lush and green in the warmth of late spring. No one seeing the two of them bowling down the road, side by side, would ever take them for anything more than a gentlewoman and her convict servant. But then, that's what they were, Lucas reminded himself, for all she'd taken his body deep into hers and tangled her fingers in his hair while she held his head to her naked breast.

Jerking his mind away from the image, Lucas spanked the reins against the mare's dappled rump, urging the horse into a faster trot that sent the shay swaying and lurching down the rutted road to the bay. He hadn't seen her since that night they'd shared beneath the brilliant splendor of the aurora, hadn't spoken to her. But he knew her now, and he knew that something was wrong.

"Is it because of what we did the other night?" he asked abruptly. "Are you regretting it?"

She swung her head to look at him, and one corner of her mouth lifted in a sad kind of half-smile. "No. Never. I love you." Her gaze held his for one brief, powerful instant, then veered away. The silence between them filled with the rattle of the harness chains and the rhythmic tattoo of the mare's hooves on the dirt road. He knew what she was waiting for, knew what she needed to hear from him, but he couldn't give it to her. Not now, not ever.

"It's my mother," she said after a moment, her voice tight, strained. "She found out about my visits to the cottage on Last Chance Point. I should have told her myself, of course. Long ago." She let out a huff of breath in a sound that was supposed to be a laugh but wasn't. "It's funny; I have never thought of myself as a coward. But lately I've realized that I am. I don't mean in the physical sense, but . . . emotionally. I have a very real fear of disappointing the people in my life, of making them angry or hurting them. I simply cannot bear the hideous, tense atmosphere that comes with disapproval and anger. With the result that somehow in the process of avoiding it, I seem to have lost touch with myself—who I am, what I want."

"I'd say most people prefer a calm life," he said, his attention on a turning in the road.

"Perhaps. But most people don't let their fear of disrupting that calm determine the choices they make in their lives."

"You're not a coward," he said quietly. "There's nothing wrong with trying to make the people in our lives happy. We just can't carry it too far."

She glanced up at him, the wide brim of her pale straw hat lifting to let the sun shine warm and golden on her face, the breeze of the carriage's movement fluttering the navy ribbons at her chin. He could see the confusion shining in her eyes along with a glimmer of newfound but painful self-awareness and understanding. He ached to take her in his arms and hold her, simply hold her in comfort. But there was a fish wagon rattling toward them up the hill from town, and she was a gentlewoman while he was her convict servant.

He kept his hands on the reins and his eyes on the road.

～

HE DROVE her to the dressmaker's, then left the horse and carriage at the livery stable and went for a walk along the pebbly shore. A warm spring breeze wafted around him, heavy with the briny scents of fish and hemp and the reek of melting blubber from the tryworks south of town. Narrowing his eyes against the reflected sun, he studied the ships riding at anchor in the bay. There was the usual assortment of coastal craft and what was probably an American whaleship, a storm-battered bark that must have just put into port and looked in sore need of a refit. Beyond that lay a two-masted schooner, ready to put out to sea, with white smoke billowing from her portholes and venti-lators and her decks swarming with constables.

There'd been a time when convicts had stowed away on ships leaving Tasmanian ports. They'd been known to hide themselves in barrels of cheese or wrap themselves up in spare jibs in the sail lockers—anything to escape their island prison. Now all ships leaving Tasmanian ports were required to undergo rigorous searches by the local constables. The American captains especially resented the British officials banging on the ships' casks and thrusting bayonets into bales and sacks, and setting off their stinking sulfur bombs. But there was no real choice; the captains either endured the humiliation or they went elsewhere for their supplies and repairs.

The constables were leaving now, climbing down the ladder to their waiting boat. Lucas turned to find a man walking toward him across the strand. The man was tall and thin, with a long-boned, New England face framed by straw-colored, swooping side whiskers. In spite of the sun, he wore a seaman's peacoat and black wool bell-bottom trousers stained with whale oil, and he walked with a familiar rollicking gait ruined in mid-stride by a slight limp.

"Lucas, me lad," he said, his craggy face breaking into a wide smile that revealed two gold eye teeth. "What in the name o' all that's holy are y' doing here at the bottom o' the world?"

JESSIE STRETCHED ONTO HER BACK, one arm bent up behind her head, her breath coming in long, deep gasps.

They lay together in the warm afterglow of their lovemaking, in the hidden sea cave behind the waterfall. The sand felt cool and sensuously soft beneath her naked flesh, the surge of the waves on the rocks below mingling with the thunderous rush of the waterfall to fill the cavern with a natural melody of vibrant life.

She rolled slowly onto her side and smiled softly as she gazed at the man beside her. He had his eyes closed, his lashes lying dark and impossibly long against the bronze thrust of his cheekbones. At rest he looked younger, she thought; more vulnerable. She let her gaze drift over the laugh lines beside his eyes, the gently sculpted curve of his lips, and felt her love for him swell in her chest, warm and aching and wondrous.

The beauty of his male body awed her, the hard strength of his muscles beneath the unexpected softness of his flesh, the perfect symmetry of torso and limb. She followed the long, powerful line of his naked legs down to the raw red scars on his ankles and knew a swift stab of the sick anger and fear she felt every time she thought of how much he had suffered.

How much he could still suffer.

She glanced back up at his face to find his eyes open, watching her. He smiled. "What are you doing?"

She raised herself on her bent elbow, chin propped on fist, and smiled back at him. "Looking at you."

He tangled his fist in the loose fall of her hair and tugged her off balance, so that she tumbled laughing onto his chest. "Do you like what you see?" he asked, his voice husky, his eyed gleaming with Irish mischief and a sensuous, exciting promise.

She gazed down at him. "I could look at you forever," she said, suddenly serious, "and still it wouldn't be enough."

He sucked in a quick breath, his lids drifting half-closed, hiding his eyes from her gaze. A swift rush of inexplicable fear seized her heart.

"Jessie . . . " He sat up, drawing her with him so that they sat facing each other. "There's something I must tell you." He laced the fingers of one hand with hers, squeezing so tightly it almost hurt. "I met an old friend of mine in Blackhaven Bay this afternoon. A whaling captain from Nantucket named Abraham Chase."

"An American?" she said in surprise. "How do you know him?"

A flash of wry amusement lit up his dark features, momentarily dispelling the unusual solemnity. "Never be asking a true Irishman how he knows an American sea captain."

"I'll try to remember that piece of worldly advice," she said lightly, although inside she was still afraid. Very afraid. "So, what is your Captain Chase doing here in Tasmania at this time of year?"

"His ship was hit by a bad storm a month or so ago when they were on their way home. They put into an uninhabited island to the west and managed to make enough repairs to limp back here." He paused for a moment, his gaze falling to their linked hands, a muscle bunching along his tight jaw as if he found it difficult to go on.

"Dear God," she whispered. "He's going to help you escape."

He looked up and met her gaze. He didn't say anything, but she saw the answer written in his eyes.

"How?" she demanded, small tremors beginning to course through her body. She wanted this so badly, for his sake. But just the thought of it actually happening brought her more pain than she was sure she could bear.

"He'll let me know when the *Agnes Anne's* been made ready to sail. The constables will search the ship before they leave the port, so he'll have to send in a lighter to pick me up at Shipwreck Cove."

She bowed her head, her hair falling forward to hide her face. She could hear the screech of gulls outside, a familiar sound that now seemed oddly out of place. She felt light-headed, adrift, removed from herself, as if this moment were happening to someone else. "How long?" she asked, her voice torn. "How long will it take before they're ready to leave?"

"A few weeks. He thinks the ship should be ready in early December." He reached out to her, his hands spearing into her hair to draw it back, his thumbs lifting her chin so that he could see her face. "You knew. You knew this day would come."

She swallowed, the pain in her chest building, building, until it seemed as if she were nothing but this screaming, impossible pain of denial and loss. "I knew. And I want you to be free." She tried to smile, but her lips were trembling too much. "More even than I want you here with me, I want you to be free. But that doesn't make it any easier."

She rose and went to stand at the entrance to the cave where the mist from the waterfall wafted cool against her skin. It should have seemed strange, walking about naked in front of him. But nothing had ever seemed more natural, more right. He knew her body better than she knew it herself.

"I can't go back to my old life," she said, her gaze fixed on the falling white torrent of frothy water. "Not now. Not after you."

She heard him rise to his feet, although she couldn't look at him, couldn't let him see her face. "Then make a new life for yourself."

She nodded, swallowing, swallowing, trying to swallow the threat of tears along with the pain. "The problem is, the life I want is with you."

"It can't be."

"I know." Her head fell back, her eyes painfully dry as she stared up at the smooth rock arching above. "Where will you go?"

"America, of course. Tis a grand nation they're trying to build—better by far than anything the world has ever seen. I want to be a part of it."

"I could come to America. I could find you."

He came up behind her, his arms slipping around her body to draw her back against the warmth of his naked body. "Your life is here," he said, laying his cheek against her hair, his breath warm against the side of her face. "Everything and everyone you love is on this island. It's your home. You wouldn't be happy anywhere else."

She turned in his arms to look up into his beloved face, luminous in the refracted light from the falls. "You think I can be happy without you?"

"In time, yes."

She shook her head. "You're wrong. Oh, I'll survive. And I know I'll find moments of happiness. But I'm never going to stop loving you, Lucas Gallagher. I'm never going to stop missing you, never going to stop wanting to be with you."

He cupped her cheek in his hand, his naked chest rising and falling with his breathing, his eyes deep and dark with his own pain. "You'll be with me, *mo chridhe*," he said, his voice breaking as he brushed his lips against hers in a kiss as soft as the mist. "For I'll be keeping you with me always, in my heart."

EARLY THE NEXT EVENING, Lucas was coming out of the last stall after feeding and watering the horses for the night when he walked straight into a fist.

Caught off guard, he stumbled back against the stall door, his arms flinging wide to catch his balance, the bucket he'd been carrying hitting the cobbles with a rattling clang that sent oats hissing across the smooth stones. He straightened slowly, backhanding a bloody trickle from his mouth as he eyed the man who stood before him.

The golden light of the setting sun streaming in the high arched windows gilded the man's angelically fair hair and aristocratic features, contorted now in an uncharacteristic snarl of cold fury. "Lock him up in the wool press for the night," Warrick Corbett told the two men with him as he turned abruptly away, one fist cradled in the other. "We'll send the bastard to Blackhaven Goal in the morning."

38

THAT NIGHT, A WIND BLEW UP from the Antarctic, a wild wind laced with freezing rain that pelted the windows and sent icy drafts whipping through the Castle halls. If it had been winter, a fire would have been kindled on every hearth, but it was late spring. At the Castle, all fires were allowed to burn themselves out on the first of October and out they stayed until the first of April, no matter how cold the weather.

When she dressed for dinner, Jessie put on a gown of finely woven mohair along with several extra petticoats and a cashmere shawl she clutched tightly about her shoulders as she hurried down the broad main stairs to the drawing room where it was the family custom to assemble for dinner. It seemed strange to her, to be going through all the normal motions of her daily life while inside . . . inside she was screaming with the pain of this coming, unbearable loss. But then, that was the way of her world: one hid away their true feelings, their true thoughts. One hid and hid and hid, until it was no wonder they were all lost, faint shadows of the people they might have been.

The cold had made her move quickly, so that she was early for dinner. Yet she found her mother and brother already in the drawing room, her mother enthroned on the settee with her embroidery, Warrick lounging beside the drinks table, the inevitable brandy in his hand.

Jessie felt the atmosphere of the room slam into her, making her falter on the threshold with a sense of deep foreboding. "What is it?" she asked, glancing from her brother to her mother and back again.

Warrick avoided her gaze with studied deliberateness. "I'm not staying for this," he said, and threw down what was left of his brandy with one quick flick of his wrist, the empty glass hitting the silver tray with an expensive click.

Jessie took a hesitant step into the room as he brushed past her, her gaze focusing on the woman beside the empty fireplace. "Mother?" she asked and heard Warrick go out, closing the door significantly behind him.

Beatrice remained seated, her body held with rigid composure, only her hands moving as her fingers worked the needle in and out, in and out. "I gave birth to three daughters," she said, not looking up, her icy voice low and even. "Three. And God leaves me with you."

Jessie drew in a quick, painful gasp of air. Beatrice might have hinted at such sentiments in the past, but only once before had she voiced them aloud so baldly, so hurtfully. "Am I supposed to apologize for being alive?"

Beatrice looked up, her needle poised in mid-air, her face tight with contained rage. "I had you followed, Jesmond. For the last three days, I have had you followed."

"Followed?" Jessie repeated, her voice rising with incredulity as she tried to understand the implications of her mother's words, tried to remember the movements of the last three days. The visit to the dressmaker at Blackhaven Bay. Those moments of sweet intimacy in the sea cave thankfully veiled by the falls. Yet the passage of so many hours hidden from sight must surely have been damning in itself. And then she remembered there had been a stolen kiss on the beach, a swift warm circling of arms and brushing of soft lips that anyone could have seen—if they'd been hidden and watching.

"All your life," Beatrice said in that same cold, flat voice, "you have been a trial to me. Always. But nothing—*nothing*—even begins to compare with this . . . this humiliation, this disgrace." The planes of her face flattened out, her nose quivering and her lips pressing down in repugnance. "A convict, Jesmond? An *Irish* convict? Have you gone mad? You could not have chosen a more scandalous, ruinous course of action had you set out deliberately to ruin us all. Did you actually imagine yourself in love with the scoundrel?"

"I do love him," Jessie said quietly, although inside she felt sick, sick.

"Good God. And you think that excuses your conduct?"

Jessie tightened her grip on her shawl, her head coming up. "I am ashamed of nothing I have done."

Beatrice stared at her, gray eyes glittering with an old, old resentment. "No. I can see that. You're as shameless as Genevieve."

Jessie walked to stand at the French doors and look out at the darkening garden, toward the yard. "Where is Lucas?" she asked, her gaze on that huddle of brick and stone buildings. She felt so cold, so very cold inside, her fear like a thick layer of ice on her heart. "What have you done with him?"

"If you are referring to that vile Irishman, your brother has had him locked in the wool press. He'll be taken to Blackhaven goal at first light."

Jessie spun to face her mother. "To goal? But . . . he's done nothing."

"Nothing?" Beatrice set aside her embroidery and rose with awful malice, the black satin of her mourning gown rustling stiffly about her. "Is that what you call this reprehensible misconduct? Nothing?" Her eyes narrowed. "Tell me truthfully: are you with child?"

"No."

"Are you certain?"

Jessie shook her head, her throat working hard as she sought to swallow the upsurge of emotions that threatened to swamp her. "What are you going to do to him?"

"That depends largely upon you."

"Me?"

"Come December, you will marry Harrison Tate, as planned."

Jessie felt the room begin to spin dizzily around her as she realized where her mother was going with all of this. "No."

"You will marry Harrison Tate," Beatrice said again, "or that piece of Irish scum you took as your lover will hang for murder."

"Murder?" The wind whistled through the cracks around the French doors, rattled the glass in their frames, flared the candles in the wall sconces. "What murder?"

"Two of the men involved in last month's escape attempt are willing to testify that Lucas Gallagher murdered John Pike."

"They're lying. The man responsible for the blacksmith's death is dead himself."

"Of course they're lying. It doesn't matter. The Irishman will still hang."

In the sudden silence that followed those words, Jessie could hear the ticking of the mantel clock and the howling of the wind outside. She felt a rage begin to build inside of her, a rage so deep and hot and shaky it left no room at the moment for cold or fear. "And if I agree? If I marry Harrison, what happens to Gallagher?"

"Until the wedding, he stays in goal in Blackhaven Bay. After that, he will be returned to Hobart for reassignment."

"You would do such a thing? See an innocent man hang?"

"I'd hardly describe him as innocent."

The two women stared at each other across a space filled with anger and dancing candlelight and the freezing air of tradition. "You force me to do this," said Jessie, her voice low and oddly calm, "And once Lucas is safe from you, I will never, ever look upon your face again."

"Yes, you will. Because in time you will come to see that I was right." Beatrice squared her satin-covered shoulders, her head lifting with the fierce determination and pride that had always been hers. "I will do whatever I must to protect this family's reputation, Jesmond. Anything. Don't make the mistake of forgetting that again."

∾

THE NEXT MORNING, Jessie rose from her bed in the cold, flat light of dawn and went to pull back the curtains and open the shutters at the French doors overlooking the yard. The wind had lessened during the night, although the clouds still hung thick and low over the valley.

She sighed, her breath frosting the glass as she rested her forehead against one of the small panes. The cold glass sent an icy shock through her, but she almost welcomed it. For so many hours she had felt dead inside.

She hadn't told her mother she would marry Harrison, but she was beginning to realize there was no way out. It was wrong, she knew, to marry a man for such a reason. It did no good to argue to her conscience that the fault was Beatrice's for forcing such an impossible choice. It was still Jessie who was making that choice, who was putting Lucas Gallagher's life above Harrison's future happiness, above her own honesty and honor.

Once she would have told herself that Harrison loved her, that she would hurt him badly if she called off their marriage as she had originally decided to do. But the new Jessie had learned to be more honest with both herself and others. And she knew that by marrying Harrison, by making him think she went to the altar with him willingly, she would be living a lie every day for the rest of her life. Oh, she would try to be a good wife to him. She really would try. But she knew she would never be able to give him what he really wanted from her. Her heart and soul belonged to another man and always would.

"Lucas," she whispered, her eyes closing against the threatening sting of tears as a terrible sense of loss squeezed her heart. He could never have been hers, she knew that. But it didn't make the ache any easier to bear.

Opening her eyes, she rubbed her fist against the misted glass to clear it. They would be moving him to Blackhaven Bay soon. She had thought about trying to see him before they took him away, but she knew Warrick had given his men orders to keep her away from the woolshed. The constables at the goal would be easier to corrupt. If

Beatrice could bribe men to engineer Gallagher's destruction, then Jesmond could surely buy her way in to see him.

And contrive at his escape.

~

THEY PUT him in solitary confinement at first, in one of a row of cells only three by six feet. The size of a coffin.

There was no window and no heat, although at least they left him his clothes. Usually they took away a man's clothes, too. Fed once a day on bread and water and deprived of light, sound, human company, dignity, and warmth, men often went mad in those cells. If he closed his eyes, Lucas could hear their screams echoing on and on, trapped forever within the cold stone walls.

He tried not to close his eyes.

The problem with solitary confinement was it gave a man a lot of time to think. Too much time, when a man's thoughts were all of pain and regret and useless rage. For the first time in all the long years of his imprisonment, Lucas willed his mind to go blank.

It seldom worked.

After a few days, they took him, blinking, out into the light, and put him in another cell. A larger cell some ten to twelve feet square with a small barred window high up near the ceiling and five other prisoners.

"You just can't get away from some people, now can you?" said a familiar voice.

Turning, Lucas looked into the eerie yellow eyes of the Fox and felt himself smile.

~

"IT PAINS me to have to admit it, but you were right, Lucas me lad," said the Fox as they walked around the goal's small exercise yard, later that day. He was still weak from the bullet he'd caught in his side and he leaned some on Lucas's arm, but other than that he was little changed. "We shouldn't have gone."

Lucas shrugged. "It might have worked."

The prison was built in a square, its kitchen and cells ranged around three sides of an inner court, with the goaler's house forming the fourth side and the exercise yard fit into the complex's southeast corner. The walls were built of thick sandstone, but they weren't high, probably no more than ten feet, Lucas thought, looking at them.

"Why'd he do it?" Lucas asked, averting his gaze as they all did when he passed the blood-stained triangle, for the exercise yard was also the flogging yard. "Why did Daniel kill Pike?"

The Fox shrugged. "He squealed on us. One of the lads admitted he'd let it slip. It wasn't like Daniel to allow a man to get away with something like that."

"So what happened to him?"

"Daniel? Bullet hit his jaw. He asked me to kill him, and so I did. He wouldn't have lived and he was in terrible pain, but I'd have done it anyway. We'd made up our minds to it beforehand."

Lucas nodded. It was an old, old story in Tasmania: two mates drawing straws to see who got to be murdered and who got to hang for it. Dying was the one sure way to escape the British penal system, except that despite all they'd been through, most of the men here were still afraid of what a vengeful God might do to a suicide.

"And the other men?"

"Two of them died in the fight. Bailey didn't get a scratch, although that new lad, Sheen, he lost an arm. They're in another cell. I don't see them much."

They said nothing for a time, walking together in silence. Then Lucas said, "When do they send you down to Hobart?" All capital cases were tried in Hobart.

The Fox squinted up at the sun. "Next month. They seem to be taking their own sweet time about it."

"In a hurry, are you?"

The Fox laughed. "Not so much, any more."

~

ON A MILD but overcast morning two days later, Warrick was strolling back from checking the breeding stock in the cow barn when he saw Miss Philippa Tate coming across the yard toward him.

She was wearing a cherry red pelisse with a matching broad-brimmed bonnet that formed a beguiling frame for her dusky ringlets and pretty, full-cheeked face. But her color was unusually high, her soft brown eyes narrowed in a rare display of anger. "Why did you do it?" she demanded without preamble, stopping in front of him. "How could you do such a thing?"

He stared at her in surprise. "Do what?"

"Arrest the Irishman—Jessie's groom."

"Gallagher? He was implicated in the murder of my blacksmith." He studied her flushed cheeks and knew a frisson of suspicion and what felt startlingly like a rush of possessive jealousy. If that bloody Irishman . . . Warrick took a quick step toward her. "What is he to you?"

"He's nothing to me. But Jessie is my friend, and I know you didn't arrest him because of what happened to your blacksmith."

He went very still. "What did Jess tell you?"

She let out her breath in a small huff. "Do you think she'd say anything to me? Harrison's sister? Of course she didn't. She didn't need to. It was there in her face every time she looked at him."

"I never saw anything," said Warrick, his voice rough with his own anger.

He watched her stare off across the yard, toward the stables, her chin lifting, the breeze fluttering the round brim of her bonnet. She looked surprisingly mature and enviously at peace with herself, despite her anger with him. He knew a ripple of admiration and something else, something he thought might be regret. They'd always been so close, but lately he'd felt as if she were slipping away from him in some way. Some way he didn't want.

"You wouldn't," she said with a tight smile.

He put his hands on his hips and tipped back his head, his legs spraddled wide in a deliberately arrogant pose. "Oh? Why is that?"

She swung to face him again, her eyes full of something he wasn't used to seeing there when she looked at him, something he thought might be scorn. "Because the only person you have ever loved is yourself."

"Bloody hell." He straightened with a jerk. "And who have you ever really loved?"

"You."

He gave a harsh laugh. "You don't expect me to believe that, do you?"

Her face was bleached of all color now, her eyes wide and dark and hurting. "No. If I did, I wouldn't have told you."

She made as if to brush past him, but he snagged her arm and hauled her back around again. "I should think you'd be the first to thank me for getting rid of that bloody groom. After all, it's your brother Jess is marrying."

She looked at him, at his face, then dropped her gaze to where his fingers curled around the braided cuff of her dress. He imagined he could feel her pulse beating there, thrumming through her, shuddering them both. But all she said was, "I don't think Jessie should marry Harrison."

He leaned into her. "Oh you don't, do you? Why ever not?"

She sucked in a quick breath that lifted her full, high breasts. "Because he'll never be what she needs, and she doesn't know how to handle him. He'll destroy her—they'll destroy each other."

He laughed again, although even to his own ears, his laugh sounded forced, jeering; a show of bravado thrown in the face of truth. "I never knew you had such a taste for melodrama."

"You never knew me at all," she said. And this time when she jerked away from him, he let her go.

39

I T WAS HARD ON OLD TOM, taking over the stables again. He had other men to help him, and the boy, Charlie, of course. But without Gallagher it was too much for an old, sick man.

Jessie found him grooming Finnegan's Luck in the stables on a rainy afternoon. She watched him send Charlie off to the south paddock to bring in a chestnut mare, then she walked through the wide double doors and stood near the cobbled entrance where she'd be able to see anyone approaching before they came close enough to overhear what she was saying.

"Lass," said Tom, glancing up from cleaning the stallion's near front hoof. "Sure then, but 'tis a wet day for a ride."

She shook her head. "I don't want to ride. I need to talk to you."

He must have seen something in her face, because he let the stallion's hoof down and straightened, wiping his hands on his leather apron. "All right."

Finding it difficult to begin, she wandered the upper aisle, fidgeting with his grooming tools and running her hand over the smooth, polished seat of a saddle. The scents of saddle soap and leather and hay enveloped her, hitting her with a flood of bittersweet memories that seemed to twist all the hurting places inside of her, making her ache with sadness.

Dropping her hand, she swung about again, her gaze hard on the old man's weathered, gray-whiskered face. "I need help, Tom. It's wrong of me to ask it of you, I know. But I've thought this over for endless hours and I just don't see how I can do it on my own."

It was raining harder now, big drops that pounded the packed dirt of the yard and filled the air with the smell of wet earth. He glanced at the rain-drenched yard, then back at her. "What is it you're wanting to do, lass?"

"Break Gallagher out of Blackhaven Goal and get him on board a whaleship headed for Nantucket."

To her amazement, a gleam of amusement lit his watery brown eyes. "Oh, is that all?"

She felt an answering smile tug at her lips, although a moment ago she'd have sworn she'd never smile again. "That's all."

He picked up a brush and began to work it over the bay's withers. "When would this be happening, then?"

"When the *Agnes Anne* is ready to sail. Lucas said it would be sometime after the first of the month, but I'll need to talk to the captain to make certain."

"I want to help, too," said Charlie, scooting in through the door.

Jessie whirled, her heart jamming up into her throat. The boy must have only pretended to run off to the paddocks, then doubled back behind the stables to creep around the side and listen. He stood now in the entrance, his hands fisted at his sides, his freckled face white with fierce determination.

She reached out a shaky hand to touch his shoulder. "I am genuinely grateful for the offer, Charlie, but I can't allow you to put yourself at risk of punishment."

"They won't be able to do me nothin' if I go to America, too," he said, staring up at her with old, hard eyes. Eyes like that didn't belong on a boy his age.

She shook her head. "No. It's too dangerous. You might be recaptured. Even killed."

Behind her, Old Tom let out a derisive snort. "And 'tis a fine future he'll be having, then, if he stays here in Tasmania, is it? The way I see it, if the boy's willing to take the risk, it's no' your place to stop him. It's his life."

Jessie met the old man's gaze and smiled sadly. "You're right, of course." To Charlie, she said, "I would like your help. I think we're going to need it."

It was later, when she was leaving the stables, that she turned to put her hand on Old Tom's arm and ask him suddenly, "What does *mo chridhe* mean?"

He looked at her with sad, knowing eyes. "*Mo chridhe*? It means 'my heart,' lass. My love."

~

"YOU NEED to find someone competent to help Old Tom in the stables," Jessie told her brother the next day as he sent the shay rattling down the hill to Blackhaven Bay. The morning was cool but fine, the sun reflecting off the blue waters of the bay in bright dazzling glints. But all Jessie could see was the fortress-like sandstone walls of the goal standing dark and somber at the edge of town.

Warrick looked up from handling the ribbons, a boyish scowl settling over the perfect features of his face. "I *had* someone—the best bloody groom I've ever seen. Until you decided to use him for something else entirely." He spanked the reins against the mare's rump, urging the dapple gray on even faster. "I tell you, Jess, I never expected you to serve Harrison such a backhanded turn."

She swung her face away, one hand coming up to grasp the brim of her bonnet to keep it from flying off as the shay lurched and rattled along at a dangerous speed. Warrick always drove too fast. "I wasn't using Lucas Gallagher for anything, Warrick. I love him."

"A convict, Jess? A bloody Irish convict?"

Her gaze jerked back to him. "My God. You sound like Mother. I'd no notion you were such a snob."

An unexpected band of color stained his perfect cheekbones. "I'm not a snob," he said in a peculiar, strained voice.

"You certainly sound like one. Oh, Warrick . . . " She reached out to touch his sleeve in a sudden rush of emotion and need. "I would have expected you of all people to understand the confusion of my feelings about Harrison."

The color on his cheeks darkened, but he only pressed his lips into a tight line and said nothing.

They had reached the outskirts of town now and were turning to run along the strand. She could see some three or four ships riding at anchor, along with the smaller coastal craft. She studied the rocking hulls and waving masts and found the *Agnes Anne.*

"Sometimes, friendship can deepen, Jess," Warrick said suddenly. "Even when you don't expect it to."

She looked at him, surprised by his words. "This one won't."

"Then why are you getting married next month?" he asked, looking at her hard as he reined in before the livery stable. But she only shook her head. "I'll not be letting you near the goal," he added, "if that's what you're thinking, coming here with me today."

"No, of course not," she said with forced lightness, stepping down without his help. "I only want to visit my dressmaker and then perhaps go for a walk along the bay. Shall I meet you here in, say, two hours?"

JESSIE SAT on a low stone wall facing the beach on the edge of town and watched a tall seaman with sandy-colored side whiskers and the forthright, direct gaze of an American walk toward her. He had a hitch in his stride that seemed to emphasize the rollicking nature of his gait and made him look faintly rakish, like someone Lucas would know. The thought made her smile sadly.

He didn't come right up to her, but paused nearby, his gaze fixed on the faint line of the horizon where blue sky met blue, blue water. "I hear y' been lookin' for me."

Like him, she stared out to sea. "You are Captain Chase?"

"Aye."

"I understand you are a good friend of Lucas Gallagher."

He glanced down at her, quickly, then away. "Aye. That I am."

"Did you know he's been put in goal?"

"I'd heard."

"Well, I'm going to get him out."

SHE DIDN'T WEAR A NIGHTCAP.

Warrick hadn't known that about Miss Philippa Tate, and it surprised him as he looked at her asleep in the shadows of her big four-poster bed, her hair spread across the pillow in a dark satin wave. She'd been right, what she said to him that day. He didn't know her, not any more. She'd always known him, always accepted him for what he was—his wildness, his pain, his dreams and fears. Warrick thought he must have known her once, when they were children. He wondered when they'd lost that.

The grating of the safety match sounded abnormally loud in the stillness of the night. He held the flame to the wick of the candle of her chamber stick, watched it flare up golden and surprisingly bright in the darkness of the night. Around them, the big house shuddered, as if wakened by the wind blundering against its walls. Then all was still again.

She must have sensed the light in her sleep, for she stirred. He watched her eyes flutter open, close, then widen. She moved quickly, reaching for the dressing gown laid across the seat of a chair near the bed.

His hand got there first.

"My congratulations," he said, giving her a smile that showed his teeth. "Most women would have screamed."

She sat back, her hands fisting in the covers, although to do her credit, she didn't yank them up to her chin in an ostentatious display of maidenly modesty. "You've been drinking," she said, that infallible calm of hers firmly in place. Most people thought her a model of conformity, of compliance. But she wasn't. She was just one of the lucky ones, for she was naturally much the way her society expected her to be. She didn't need to pretend, didn't need to hide—or at least, not as much as some of them.

"I have been drinking, yes," he said, giving her a low bow. "Only, not as much as you might think."

"Why are you here?"

Straightening, he raised his eyebrows and gave her his best leer. "In your bedroom? At one in the morning? Wouldn't you naturally assume I'm here to ravish you?"

She stared up at him, the candlelight gleaming over her pale face and throat, her eyes dark and unfathomable. "Some might. I wouldn't."

"No?" He wrapped one arm around the bedpost and leaned into it. "Perhaps you don't know me as well as you think you do." He paused for effect, but when he didn't get one, he spun away. "As a matter of fact, we need to talk."

"Why here, now?"

"I found it appropriate."

He turned to find a soft smile curving her mouth. "You mean, because it is entirely inappropriate?"

"Yes, I suppose."

To his surprise, she threw back the covers and swung her legs out of bed. "Why do we need to talk?" she asked, standing up. She didn't try for her dressing gown again, but then, she didn't really need it, swathed as she was from neck to ankle in yards and yards of tucked and trimmed linen.

He stared at her across the six or seven feet of candlelit night that separated them. He was suddenly, utterly serious. "You told me the other day that you love me."

She crossed her arms in a movement that pulled the cloth of her gown tight against the full, naked breasts beneath. "Did I?"

Apart from her face, he could see nothing but her slim white neck, bare feet, and that shrouded swelling of her breasts. And still,

still he felt a curl of desire awaken deep within him. It disconcerted him, for he hadn't expected it, wouldn't have come here now if he had. "Don't play your parlor games with me, Miss Philippa Always-Oh-So-Correct Tate." He pointed an accusing finger at her. "You know you did."

"I was angry."

He'd expected her to deny it, so he had a hard time bringing himself to ask the next question. He hadn't realized until now how vitally important her answer was to him. He'd always taken her so very much for granted he'd somehow missed noticing how terribly much he needed her in his life. "Did you mean it?"

Her chin came up, and he held his breath, waiting for her answer. "Yes."

His breath eased out on a slow, aching sigh. "How long? How long have you loved me?"

She made a low sound that might have been a laugh. "I can't remember a time when I did not."

"It's a child's love, then," he said, walking toward her.

"It was, when I was a child. I'm not a child any more."

"No. No, you're not." He reached out to touch the dark hair that curled against her breast. To his surprise, his fingers were shaking visibly, and he let his hand fall to his side again. "Are you telling me that when you were betrothed to Ethan and then to Reid, you loved me?"

"Yes."

He gazed down into her still, upturned face. "If Ethan hadn't died, would you have married him, even though you loved me?"

"I told you I'm a coward.' She brushed past him and went to the closed windows, her back to him. "Besides, you were promised to the sea then, remember?"

"You say that as if you were jealous."

"Of the sea?" She put her hands on the drapes, opening them so that she could stare down at the moonlit gardens below. A pale blue glow shone over the finely etched features of her face. "I was."

"You told me the other day I should start sailing again."

She turned abruptly to face him. "Will you?"

"Perhaps." He went to stand in front of her, close enough that his body threw its shadow across her and he could see the rapid beat of her pulse at the base of her throat. "How much do you love me?"

She tilted back her head to stare up at him, her hair sliding dark, long and seductive down her back. "Enough to let you take me," she said hoarsely, "here and now, if that's what you want."

"I suppose it's easy enough to offer," he said, somehow managing to keep his voice light and his hands hanging awkwardly at his sides, "when you know I would never take you up on it."

Her gaze locked with his, she reached down to clutch at fistfuls of the voluminous linen that fell about her. In one fluid motion, she drew the night rail up and off, then let the fine cloth drift in a white cloud to the rug at her feet. The light from the window limed her naked body, soft and so beautiful it made him ache just to look at her. She was made smaller and rounder than Faine, and pale, so pale, for she had never lain naked in the sun-warmed grass. As he watched, her bare breasts rose and fell with her rapid breathing.

He reached out, slowly, to brush the backs of his fingers against her cheek, then let his hand trail down her slim throat, across her upper chest. He cupped his palm and let it hover for a moment over her breast. Then he touched her there, boldly, deliberately, his hand closing over her. He thought she might shrink from him in revulsion or fear. He expected her to shrink from him. Instead, her lips parted, her breath keening out in an exhalation of surprise and delight. And then he knew. He knew that she'd meant what she said, and that she not only loved him but she desired him as well.

It was the hardest thing he'd ever done, to stop touching her, to take a step back and stoop quickly to snatch up her nightdress from where it lay, a pool of chaste white against the darkness of the floor. He held it out to her, and after a moment she took it, clutching it to her. "You don't want me," she whispered, her eyes dark bruises, her voice like a painful tear.

He touched his fingertips to her full lips, felt them tremble. "I want you. Believe me, Philippa, I want you. But not like this. And not here, and not now."

He gave her a slow smile, and after a moment, she returned it. Then he let his fingers slip through her hair to grip the back of her head and draw her to him for his kiss.

40

HARRISON URGED HIS CHESTNUT gelding down the drive to the Castle at a fast trot—a faster trot than perhaps was quite the thing, for he was finding it difficult to control his impatience. He'd been away from Jesmond for a month now, after having already waited for her for more than two years, and he was feeling anxious and slightly ill-used. Soon, he reminded himself; soon she would be his. It was a thought that quickened his breath and sent the blood thrumming through his veins in anticipation and a raw surge of lust that he found both repugnant and vaguely frightening.

And then he saw her, a tall, slim woman cutting through the trees of the park, her long legs reaching out in that rather mannish, assured stride of hers that he'd never liked. She must have been for a walk, but she was headed back toward the house now and had reached the drive. The day was cool, a gloomy late spring day of low gray clouds and mist that swirled in phantom wisps through the reaching branches and heavy leaves of the oaks, birch, and elms. She wore a navy mantle with gold braiding against the chill, and a navy bonnet with a wide brim that lifted as she turned. Her face was pale and thinner than he remembered it, and so beautiful it made him ache just to look at her.

"Jesmond," he said, reining in the chestnut beside her and swinging out of the saddle. He didn't sweep her into his arms, for that sort of exuberant, demonstrative behavior wasn't proper, and even when in the grip of strong passion Harrison was always unfailingly proper. But he did take both her hands in his and press them tightly as he brought them to his lips, her fine kid gloves smooth and cool beneath his touch, his gaze meeting hers.

"Harrison," she said, her hands caught fast in his. "Welcome home."

Her smile trembled slightly, and he thought he caught a glimpse of a faint sheen of tears in her eyes which surprised him, for Jesmond seldom cried, even as a child. But when they turned toward the house together, her arm captured by his, he looked at her again and decided he must have been mistaken. She hadn't seen him for a month, and yet she seemed remote, as if her thoughts were far, far away. She never really seemed to miss him when he was away—at least not any more than she missed, say, Philippa or Warrick. And it came to him as he looked into her pale face that she had never needed him, either, not in the way he wanted her to need him. Sometimes it seemed to him that she needed her inappropriate and highly unfeminine pursuit of knowledge, her walks beside the ocean, her wild rides through the countryside, more than she needed him.

But it was a disturbing thought, and so he pushed it away.

THAT NIGHT, alone in her room, Jessie went to her clothespress and took out the elegant satin dress embroidered with white rosebuds that was to be her wedding gown. She'd had it made up before she left London, as per her mother's instructions, in what seemed like a different lifetime.

She spread the dress across her bed, her hand skimming over the icy blue satin and lace trim. Once she had taken a childlike pleasure in the selection and fitting of this, the dress she would wear for her wedding. That joy was gone now, its place filled by a deep, abiding sorrow sharply edged with guilt. It was wrong, what Beatrice was doing—what Jessie herself was doing—to Harrison.

He hadn't changed, Harrison. He was still honorable and funny and slightly stuffy, all at the same time. He hadn't changed, but Jessie had. Or perhaps she'd simply learned to know herself a little bit better.

Sweeping the dress up into her arms, she pressed her face into the silken folds. But when she wept, it wasn't for Harrison, but for a fierce-eyed Irish convict locked fast behind the thick limestone walls of Blackhaven Bay goal.

"I WISH you could have told me," Jessie said as she walked beside Genevieve along the wave-battered beach of Shipwreck Cove. The crash of the surf was loud in their ears, the wet sand hard beneath their feet. Overhead, gulls wheeled screeching against a gray sky. The rain had stopped, but the air was still cool, the waves swollen and white-flecked. The weather and the sea matched her mood, Jessie thought; dark and somber and angry.

"I made your mother a promise," Genevieve said, one hand coming up to catch the wisps of white hair blowing about her face. "Do you blame me for it?"

Jessie smiled. "No. I understand. But I'm glad I know now."

It was the first time she had visited the cove in the weeks since she'd learned the truth about Genevieve from Beatrice. So much had happened since then, so much she wished she could talk to Genevieve about but couldn't. It was bad enough that she'd involved Old Tom and Charlie in what she was doing; she couldn't drag Genevieve into it, too.

"I hear Harrison is home," Genevieve said suddenly.

"Yes."

"People in town seem to think you're still marrying him."

"I am."

Genevieve stopped and put out her hand to touch Jessie's arm, turning her. "Why, Jessie? I thought you had decided against going through with it."

Jessie sucked in a deep breath that shuddered in her chest, her head falling back as she stared up at the restless gulls. "Lucas is being sent back to the Government."

"Oh, Jessie . . . Have you been found out?"

Jessie shook her head and swung away to hide her lying face. "Do you think mother would let him live, if she knew?" She stared out at the surging, foam-flecked waves, the endless ache in her chest burning and burning. "Genevieve," she said, her gaze still on the thundering surf. "I want you with me at the vicarage before the wedding. I want you to help me into my dress."

"Gladly. You know that. But surely your mother—"

"Mother won't be there. Not with the wedding being held at St. Anthony's."

"I thought arrangements had been made for the ceremony to be held inland."

"They had. I changed them."

"I'm surprised Beatrice allowed it."

Jessie looked around, her lips twisting into a fierce smile. "I insisted." Beatrice hadn't liked it, of course, but in the end she had given way. The important thing to her was that Jessie marry Harrison. Quickly.

"And Harrison?" Genevieve asked quietly. "Does he know what you're asking me to do?"

"Not yet. But even if he refuses to have you at the actual wedding, I want you there with me, before."

Genevieve's eyes were narrowed, intent, as she studied Jessie's face. "There's something you're not telling me."

Jessie reached out to grasp her friend's hand—her *aunt's* hand—and held it tightly. "Oh, Genevieve. Don't ask. Please, don't ask. Just help me get through this."

Genevieve stood very still, her features drawn and troubled. "All right. I will. If that's what you want."

"It's what I want."

TWO DAYS LATER, Jessie drove into Blackhaven Bay with Old Tom and Charlie. While Charlie roamed the outside of the jail in a deceptively idle study of the sandstone walls and surrounding area, Jesmond bullied and bluffed her way into having her brother's former servant, Lucas Gallagher, brought to her in the turnkey's room.

The room was cold and low ceilinged, with a sandstone flagged floor and a single, small window crisscrossed with iron slats. Despite the open window and the room's position just off the narrow, arched stone entrance passageway, the air here was foul with the smells of prison—the heavy odors of effluvia and unwashed human bodies mingling with an overwhelming, soul-chilling crush of hopelessness and despair.

She stood in the center of the room, her hands clutched together, her breath coming short and fast as she listened to the opening of the heavy door from the courtyard, the scrape of rough boots over flagstones. She hadn't come to see him before this for fear that her mother might learn of her visit and take steps to prevent Jessie from seeing him again. But the *Agnes Anne* was almost ready to sail, and all was in place for Gallagher's escape. She had come to tell him of their plan.

And to say goodbye.

She stared at the open door to the passageway, her heart desperate for her first glimpse of him in so many weeks, her throat tight with the unbearable knowledge that this would be the last time she would ever see him. Did he blame her, she wondered, for his being here? Did he regret that long chain of events that had brought him here? That had brought her here?

Having been raised in Tasmania, Jessie knew only too well what weeks in a colonial prison could do to a man. She'd been expecting his appearance to have altered. But it was still a shock when his lean, familiar form filled the doorway. He was so thin and pale, with several week's growth of beard shadowing his cheeks, his clothes unwashed and ragged, his beautiful green eyes hidden by carefully lowered lids.

"That will be all, thank you," she said, her voice cracking treacherously as she nodded to the constable. "My groom will call you when I have finished."

Gallagher's head snapped up, his body arrested as he stared at her.

"But ma'am—" The constable's eyes bulged out, his Adam's apple bobbing up and down as he swallowed. "I can't leave—"

Jessie looked down her nose at him "Don't be ridiculous. This man is not in here for an offense; he is simply being returned to the Government. There are certain details concerning the management of my brother's stables that require clarification, and I don't care to do discuss them before an audience. You are dismissed."

The man's dirty cheeks suffused with color. "Yes, ma'am," he mumbled and shuffled out past where Old Tom waited in the entrance passage, his back discreetly turned.

Jessie swung to Gallagher, her horrified gaze taking in the hollows that lay beneath his fine cheekbones, the gauntness of his frame. "My God," she whispered as the door to the courtyard clanged shut behind the constable. "What have they done to you?"

He caught her by the shoulders, holding her at arm's length when she would have thrown herself against him. "Easy lass. You'll not be wanting to touch me. I reek of prison."

She twisted out of his hold and pressed her body against his anyway, her hands clenching in the coarse cloth of his coat. "How could I not touch you?" She stood on tiptoe to rub her cheek against his over and over again, her eyes squeezing shut, her heart breaking in her chest. "How could I not, when I have ached to touch you every moment of every day these many weeks?"

"Ah, Jessie," he whispered, burying his face in her hair, his hands sweeping roughly down her back. "I never thought I'd be seeing you again, let alone touching you." And then he was kissing her, his mouth taking hers in a kiss of savage despair. Of hello and goodbye.

Reluctantly she drew away from him. "The *Agnes Anne* will be ready to sail by Monday," she said quietly, her gaze flashing to the open door to the passage where Old Tom waited. "We have a plan to get you out of here."

"Monday?" He stared at her, his gaze intent. "I hear you're marrying Harrison Tate come Saturday."

She nodded, unable to speak.

He reached out to brush his knuckles against her cheek, his touch as soft as his voice. "Why, lass? Why did you decide to go ahead with the wedding?"

"I have my reasons."

She saw his jaw harden. "Tell me it's got nothing to do with me." He caught her chin between his thumb and fingers when she would have turned away, and lifted her face toward the light from the open window. "Look me in the eye and tell me it's got nothing to do with me. If you're carrying a babe—"

She jerked away from him, terrified he might see in her face the awful truth of what she was doing. "I'm not with child. Although God help me, I wish I were. At least then I'd have a part of you to keep with me always."

"Mother of God," he said on a harsh expulsion of breath, coming up behind her. One hand brushed the nape of her neck in a light caress that was there and then gone. "I hope you'll be happy with your Harrison, Jessie. More than anything, it's what I want—for you to be happy."

She swung to face him, the pain of losing him stabbing her chest so fiercely her voice broke with anguish. "*Oh, God.* I don't know how I'm going to bear this, when just the thought of never seeing you again is more agony than I could ever have imagined." She reached out to capture one of his fine, scarred hands in hers and bring it to her cheek, her gaze roving his beloved face with the desperate need to memorize every line, every subtle nuance of shadow and light. A sad smile trembled her lips. "Did you ever love me? Even just a little?"

He let his fingertips skim over her cheeks, her lips. "I have always loved you, *mo chridhe*. Even before there were stars in the sky, I was loving you. And long after every star in the heavens has faded to dust, I'll still be loving you. Beyond forever."

THE NEXT MORNING Jessie was in the cutting garden, filling a basket with bridal wreath and ranunculus, when she looked up to see Harrison coming through the rose-covered wrought iron archway that marked the entrance through the hedge.

"There you are, Jesmond." He came down the narrow brick path toward her, his fingers worrying the fobs that hung from the gold watch chain against his silk waistcoat, his aristocratic features tight with that look of concern and disapproval that was beginning to make Jessie's stomach twist with nerves every time she saw it. "I've just learned your mother will not be attending Saturday's ceremony."

She bent to cut another ranunculus. "St. Anthony's overlooks the bay," she said with deliberate calm. "My mother never goes within sight of the sea."

"Yes, I know. But Jesmond—" He broke off to lift the basket of flowers from her as if it were an overwhelming burden. "Here, let me take that." Looping the basket over his own arm, he fell into step beside her. "How can the mother of the bride not attend the wedding? What will people think? I thought you'd arranged for the wedding to be held in one of the inland towns."

"No." The word came out stronger than she'd meant it to so that he looked over at her in mild surprise. "I mean . . . " She forced herself to smile and reached out to rest one hand on his sleeve. "St Anthony's is our church, Harrison. It's where we will be attending worship every Sunday, where our children will be christened, and . . . " Her voice trailed off as she saw the warm glow that leapt into Harrison's pale gray eyes at her words. She felt a traitor to him and to herself; she felt diminished by her own lack of honesty. But how could she tell the truth? How could she say to a man like Harrison, *I don't care what people will think; I don't want my life to be ruled always by fear of other people's opinions.* How could she say to him, *I don't want my mother at my wedding because what she is doing to me—what she is doing to us both—is unforgivable.*

Of course she could say none of that. So she swallowed the treacherous surge of feelings that rose within her and said quietly, "I think we ought to be married here at Blackhaven Bay, where we will live out our lives."

"If it's what you want." He put his hand over hers, capturing it when she would have turned away. "Only, surely you want to have your mother with you at such a time, to help you dress, to share the moment with you?"

She looked up into his handsome, familiar face, and drew in a deep breath. "Harrison, there's something I've been meaning to discuss with you," she said in a rush before her courage failed. "I would like Genevieve Strzlecki to attend our wedding."

"Genevieve Strzlecki!" He dropped his hand from hers, his brows drawing together as he stared at her in a moment of stunned silence. "This is some sort of a jest, isn't it?"

"No." She slipped the flower basket from his loose grasp and turned away, her hands shaking slightly as she reached to cut a spray of baby's breath. "No, I am most serious. Not only has Genevieve been my dearest friend for years, but she is also my aunt. I want her at our wedding."

"Your *aunt*?" He took a quick step up the path, away from her, his fine coat flaring open as he planted one hand on his hip, the other hand coming up to rub his forehead in a distracted gesture. "Good God, how can this be? She is not at all a proper person for you to know."

In that moment, he sounded so much like Beatrice that Jessie could only stare at him. *I am marrying my mother,* she thought in a wave of despair. But aloud, she said, "Genevieve is my mother's sister, Harrison. I have only just discovered the relationship, but it would mean a great deal to me to have her at my wedding." She paused, then added shamelessly, "Especially since my own mother won't be there." Setting aside the secateurs and basket, she closed the distance between them, her arm slipping around his silk-covered waist as she reached up to brush his smooth cheek with a soft kiss. "Please?"

It was the first time she had ever touched him in such a familiar way, spontaneously, and he looked both surprised and gratified. "All right." He smiled down at her. "If it makes you happy."

She found to her shame that she could not meet his glowing gaze. She felt like the vilest sort of harlot, to have sunk so low as to win what she wanted from him with smiles and manipulation and suggestive caresses—the full panoply of feminine wiles she had always scorned and disdained. Never had she done such a thing before. But she knew in that moment that this could easily become the pattern for their marriage.

He was not the type of man who would ever willingly treat her as an equal partner, as someone with intelligence and opinions and wishes of her own that he needed to take into consideration as he ordered their lives together. If she tried to discuss things with him honestly, if she tried to meet him head on or argue with him as another man might do, he would never compromise with her, would only grow angry and end up scorning her, perhaps even hating her. There was a reason, she thought, why women under their husbands' power had learned to use subterfuge and flattery and the lure of their bodies to get what they wanted. Women's ways were the ways of the weak because in their society, women were weak.

But she wondered how long a woman could use the methods she had always despised before she came to despise herself.

GENEVIEVE PERCHED ON A LOW, three legged stool at the base of her garden, a drawing pad balanced on her knees, her eyes narrowed against the wind, a stick of charcoal hovering in her fingers as she studied the battered rocks far below. Humming lightly to herself, she brought the charcoal down in a series of bold black strokes across the paper. When the sun shone brightly out of a clear blue sky and the sea swelled with gentle serenity, she liked to use watercolors. But on days like this, when the fine promise of spring seemed to have disappeared beneath the onslaught of a series of storms sweeping up from the Antarctic, she found charcoal a more appropriate medium.

She glanced up again, this time turning her head toward the overgrown drive. Someone was coming. Someone on a high-stepping chestnut that fidgeted and jibed at the bit as if sensing its rider's hesitation.

Genevieve rose, her gaze on the man nearing her doorstep. Leaving her paper and charcoal on the stool, she walked toward the cottage, her long skirts brushing the scraggly wet leaves of the roses and daisies of her sea wind battered garden. She watched, her heart thumping with suppressed hope, as he swung gracefully out of the saddle, a tall young man with fair curls and the face of a somber angel. He was staring at the door of her cottage. He hadn't seen her yet.

"May I help you?" she called.

He swung about, one hand coming up to remove his smart beaver hat. "Mrs. Strzlecki?"

"That's what I call myself, yes." She smiled. "Although I'm sure your mother has told you I've no right to either the name or the title."

She saw an answering gleam of mischief light up his fine gray eyes. "I am Warrick Corbett," he said, as if she hadn't watched him grow to manhood, even if from a distance.

"I know."

He gave her a charmingly shy smile. "I understand you're my aunt."

"Yes."

He held out his hand. "I'd like to know you."

She drew his hand through her crooked arm and held it tightly, more tightly than she perhaps should have, for although she was his aunt he didn't know her, had only just met her. "Come into my kitchen and I'll fix you a nice . . . " She'd been about to say *a nice cup of tea*, but she looked up at him and laughed, surprised by the tears in her eyes. "Brandy, I think."

41

T HAT SATURDAY, JESSIE AROSE at dawn to a wedding day filled with low gray clouds and a raw, blustering spring wind heavy with the scent of coming rain.

Throwing a cloak over her dress, she let herself out the side door of the house and went for a walk through the misty garden. But the neatly edged paths and formal plantings proved too controlled for her troubled soul, and so she left the garden and cut across the park to the pond. The grass beneath the soles of her kid boots felt slippery with early morning dew, the wind bracing against her cheeks. She went as far as the new stone wall surrounding the family burial ground, then stopped to look back at the Castle, its double rows of sandstone arches and flat-topped tower rising somber and dark in the flat light.

It still hurt, to think that after today this would no longer be her home. But the anger and alienation of the past few weeks had done much to lessen the pain of her leaving. Once she had expected marriage to Harrison to change her life. But she knew now that her life would never change, not unless she found the courage to change it, to change herself. She had always thought of courage in terms of physical courage—the daring required to set a horse at a high wall or climb a steep cliff or sail across the seas to an unfamiliar land. But she knew now that there was another kind of courage, the courage she needed to be herself in a world that demanded conformity even at the expense of honesty; the courage to stand firm against other people's attempts to control her, to make her into what they wanted her to be; the courage to suffer through the pain and unpleasantness of their disappointment and anger when she could not—should not —do what they wanted her to do.

All her life she had tried so hard to be the daughter her parents wanted her to be, to make them happy, to make them proud. She hadn't thought that a woman could be too loyal, too self-sacrificing, too noble and giving. She hadn't realized that in the effort not to betray those she loved, she could betray herself. Somewhere, somehow, she had lost sight of that line, that line between what she owed those she loved and what she owed herself. She wasn't going to lose it again. She had promised herself she would try to be a good wife to Harrison, try to make him happy, and she would. Only not at the expense of being true to herself. That was a promise she was making to herself, today.

With a sigh, she turned to walk along the pond, its gray surface ruffled by the morning wind. When she reached the old apple tree she paused, her head tilting back as she stared up at the leafy branches shifting with a shivering rustle against the low pewter sky. The air smelled of wet earth and new green fruit, but if she breathed deeply she could almost—almost catch the scent of apple blossoms.

In marrying Harrison, she might be marrying a man she did not love in order to save the life of the man she did love, but she was still being true to herself; she knew that. This decision might have been forced upon her by her mother, but it was still her choice, a sacrifice she made freely and for all the right reasons. She hadn't lost herself in her love for Lucas, she had found herself. It was the tragedy of their lives that they hadn't been able to keep from losing each other.

Now standing here beneath a cold, uncaring sky on this, her wedding day, Jessie felt the ache of that loss bite painfully deep, all the way to her bones. It was never going to go away, this grief of losing him. In time she knew it might lessen. But now it was an agony so sharp and profound she could feel a howl of unbearable loss building inside of her, building and building until she was clutching her crossed arms to her stomach, her body hunching over as a silent scream welled up from within her. A soundless shriek of mourning that twisted her insides and kept coming and coming and coming. The wind blew around her, cool and damp with mist. She heard a scattering of raindrops and the sound of footsteps hurrying toward her.

She straightened with effort, one fisted hand pressing against her open mouth in an effort to choke down that silently welling howl of loss. Then pain turned into something like panic as she recognized the small, wizened figure of Old Tom coming fast across the park, his gait awkward, his features drawn with worry.

She flung herself forward, her cloak streaming out behind her in the wind as she ran across the park. "What is it?" she cried, reaching the old man just as he stumbled, her hands flying out to catch his shoulders before he fell. "What's happened?"

Tom braced his hands on his thighs, his breath coming in quick pants. "I've had a message from the *Agnes Anne*, brought by one of the seamen. He says Captain Chase reckons there's a bad storm coming through and he wants his ship gone from Blackhaven Bay and well out to sea before it hits."

Jessie's hands dug into the old man's shoulders so hard she practically shook him. "But they can't leave now! Chase said he'd take Gallagher with him. He said—"

"Listen, lass. They'll still send a lighter to the cove to pick up Gallagher. But it's got to be this morning."

"This morning?" Jessie let go of the old man's shoulders to swing around in a wide, frantic circle of gray sky and blurring treetops. "Oh, God. Can we do it?"

"Aye. Aye, we can—if we can get a message to Gallagher and to the lad in the gaol's kitchen. To be honest, tis better today than Monday, for you'll be getting married at just the time the prisoners take their morning exercise. Which means that Captain Boyle and his lieutenants will all be at the church when Gallagher and the Fox go over the wall."

LUCAS TILTED BACK HIS HEAD, his eyes narrowing as he studied the jumbling clouds hanging low over the prison's exercise yard. The day was cool and dark and damp, with a wind that battered his face and had a bite that warned of a coming storm. In prison the days often blurred, one into the other. But he knew what today was. Today was Jesmond Corbett's wedding day.

Now, it was also the day of his escape.

He circled the yard with the other prisoners, his body tense and alert as he waited for the sound of the diversion that had been planned to draw away the guard. But his gaze kept drifting back to the cross atop that distant church spire just visible above the high stone walls surrounding him.

He couldn't understand why she was doing this, why she was marrying Harrison Tate. Sometimes . . . sometimes in the lonely, desperate hours of the night, when Gallagher lay on his thin pallet and stared into the foul darkness, treacherous doubts would seize him. Sometimes he would think that perhaps she had come to regret her feelings for him, the things they had done together. He'd tell himself he was a fool to think that a woman such as Jesmond Corbett could still love this man he'd become, this stinking, degraded convict lying on a prison floor. Sometimes he could almost believe she had turned in relief from him to the companion of her childhood, the man she had always expected to marry.

Except that Lucas knew her, knew that he was the one she loved, the one she would always love; knew that her love for him was as strong and deep and eternal as his love for her. And then his soul would ache for her, because he'd think that maybe she was marrying Harrison Tate in despair, in the hope that she might find some sort of peace and happiness with a man who loved her even if she didn't love him.

Except that she was wrong. Harrison Tate might love her, but it was a killing kind of love, a love that was more about possessiveness than about joy and tenderness; an inwardly focused love that was about taking, not giving; a love that would try to change her into Tate's image of what Jesmond Corbett should be. A love that would destroy the wonderful woman she was meant to be.

An authentic-sounding howl cut through Lucas's thoughts to yank his attention toward the central courtyard where thick black smoke could be seen billowing up above the inner wall. There were shouts of alarm and the sounds of running feet. From his position near the door in the wall that separated the exercise yard from the inner court, the constable straightened with a jerk, his fleshy, unshaven face going slack as he turned to see the smoke.

"Bloody hell." Lunging forward, he threw open the stout wooden door, then reeled back at the sight of flames leaping from the kitchen. "You," he said, grabbing the arm of the nearest prisoner and thrusting him through the doorway toward the central well. "Get in there and grab a bucket. All of you. Quick."

The constable might be old and fat and slovenly, but he was conscientious enough to make certain he herded all of his prisoners out of the exercise yard and into the court. But he didn't bother to shut the door behind him, let alone lock it, and he was so busy helping to organize a line from the well to the fire that he didn't notice Lucas hanging back and grabbing the Fox's arm to whisper, "Quick. Through the door again."

The Fox's yellow eyes widened in surprise, but he followed Lucas without question, stepping back into the exercise yard just as first one rope, than another came hissing over the wall.

The wall was only ten feet high and rough enough that it was easy to climb with a rope, even for men debilitated by weeks in prison. "Where are the horses?" Lucas asked as he dropped lightly to his feet beside Charlie on the far side of the wall.

The boy threw a nervous glance across a hundred and fifty feet or so of open ground. "There, in that stand of gums," he said as the Fox came down in an awkward rush, one hand clutching his side, his breath hitching in an attempt to hold back a groan.

Lucas slipped an arm under the other man's shoulder. "Can you run?"

"I'll run," said the Fox.

But he was leaning heavily on Lucas by the time they reached the trees. Old Tom had sent three horses, including the familiar gray, but one look at the Fox's face told Lucas they might as well leave the third horse behind.

"If we get separated," he said, throwing the Fox up onto a strong, fleet-footed bay, "just head for Shipwreck Cove."

The Fox fumbled for the reins, his eyes wide and staring. "I can't steer this thing."

"You just hang on," Lucas said as the boy scrambled up behind the older man with a barely concealed sneer. "Let Charlie worry about the steering. Now get out of here."

Slapping the bay's rump, he reached for the gray's reins and then paused, his gaze caught by the small sandstone church built high on the hill overlooking the bay. The ceremony must be starting soon, he thought with a swift ache in his heart. The church steps were crowded with gentlemen in top hats and tails, their dark, thin silhouettes moving in somber contrast to the flamboyant colors and flaring skirts of the women's gowns.

For one, unguarded moment, he stared at that distant hill, his gaze searching the elegant, well-dressed throng in the hope of catching one last glimpse of the woman he loved. He wondered what he would do if he did see her. He imagined sending the gray soaring over the stone wall into the churchyard, turf flying up from the gelding's big hooves, the colorful crowd scattering like rose petals before a whirlwind as he swooped down to snatch up the bride and carry her off across his saddlebow like some dark marauder of old. Except . . .

Except that he couldn't expose her to the dangers of this wild escape any more than he could ask her to share the inevitable hardship that he would face alone and impoverished in a strange land if he did manage to reach America. And he reminded himself that she was at that church right now, marrying Harrison Tate, by choice. She had not chosen to be here, waiting with the horses, when he escaped from prison. It was only now that he realized some part of him had been secretly hoping to find her here, ready to join her fate to his forever.

He swung into the saddle, his gaze straying one last time to the distant church—just as the alarm bell began to ring out over the prison. "Bloody hell," he swore and drove his heels into the gray's sides.

THE WIFE of the vicar of St. Anthony's kept a bedroom at the front of her house for the use of the brides who came in from the surrounding estates to be married by her husband in the church that lay just across the graveyard from her side door. The vicarage itself was a large, convict-built house of sandstone that overlooked the sullen gray bay with its white flecked waves and rocking ships now battened down against the coming storm.

Clad in layers of petticoats, a fine lawn chemise, and satin corset, her hair carefully dressed with rosebuds and white satin ribbons, and satin slippers on her feet, Jesmond Corbett stood at the bedroom's front window and stared out at the town below. From here she could see the square, somber outline of Blackhaven goal lying dark and quiet under a dull, heavy sky.

"It's time to put on your dress, child," said Genevieve.

Jessie turned from the window to study her aunt's serene face. "Genevieve," she asked as the satin dress slipped over her head and shoulders, "whatever happened to Count Strzlecki? You never told me."

Genevieve tugged at the full skirt, her head bowed as she smoothed the embroidered satin over Jessie's voluminous petticoats. "He died. Two years after we fled Tasmania."

Jessie stared down at her aunt's white hair and thin shoulders. "Did you regret it then? Running away with him, I mean?"

Genevieve straightened, her soft blue eyes meeting Jessie's. "No, never. Even if we'd had but two days together, I would never have regretted it." She gave Jessie a sad smile. "Now turn around so I can do up the back."

Jessie swung about obediently. "So what did you do--all those years between when he died and when you came back here?"

Genevieve's strong fingers went to work at the row of hooks up Jessie's back. "That's when I traveled. Russia. Italy. Bavaria." Her gaze met Jessie's in the dressing table mirror, a ghost of a smile lightening her eyes. "And I took lovers. Society had already decided I was a very naughty woman, so I had nothing to lose. And I do think men can be deliciously entertaining creatures—apart from their other uses."

The two women laughed. Then Genevieve's smile faded, her eyes growing distant, pensive. "I even came to love one or two of them, you know . . . although never in the way I loved Stanislaw. I think it was when I came to realize that I would never again love any man the way I loved him that I decided to come home. It seemed the right thing to do. And it was."

Her hands tightened on Jessie's shoulders, drawing her around until they stood face to face. "Jessie . . . " She hesitated, the pale flat light from the window washing over her pinched, troubled face. "Just because I never found that kind of love again doesn't mean that you won't. It seems that way, now, but you never know."

"I know," Jessie said, smoothing her hands down over her embroidered skirt. "But I do think I will find some measure of happiness in this marriage, Genevieve. Harrison has always been my friend. If I can't have love, at least I'll have friendship."

"Jessie," Genevieve began, then broke off as an alarm bell began to ring out over the town below.

Jessie whirled to the window, her fingers curling around the edge of the wooden sill as she stared at the thick black smoke billowing up from the goal block.

"It's your Irishman, isn't it?" said Genevieve, coming to stand beside her. "He's escaped."

"Yes." Jessie pressed her forehead against the cold glass. She could see the constables pouring out the entrance gate of the goal. And two horses, their tails streaming out behind them as they lunged up the hill.

"He's the reason you're doing this," said Genevieve slowly. "Why you're marrying Harrison. Beatrice is responsible."

Jessie swung her head, the side of her face still resting against the pane, her heart beginning to thump wildly. "She said she'd have him hanged for murder, Genevieve. You know she could. It's been done before."

Genevieve nodded, her lips pressing into a thin, hard line. "Does he have a way off the island?"

"A whaleship, waiting up the coast to take him to America." Jessie's voice came out cracked, broken. A heavy sadness pressed her chest, stealing her breath and killing her slowly, deep inside where it mattered. She felt her throat thickening up, her eyes stinging with the threat of tears she didn't dare let escape, for once they began she was afraid they'd never end and how could she walk down the aisle drowning in tears?

"My dear." She felt Genevieve's hand touch her cheek. "You want to go with him, don't you?"

"More than I want to take my next breath," Jessie said with a gasp, the pain in her chest becoming unbearable now.

"It would be dangerous, I know," said Genevieve. "Running from the authorities, only to find yourself in a strange country, with no money, and with a man about whom you know so little."

Jessie scrubbed the heel of one hand across her eyes and felt the hot wetness of tears slick on her palm. "It's not that. You know it's not that."

"Then what is it?"

She turned to stare wildly out the window at the churchyard. Only a few stragglers could still be seen; everyone else was in the church waiting for her. "It wasn't even possible at first," she said softly. "The ship wasn't supposed to be ready to leave until next week, after the wedding. Only now that they've sailed early—" She paused as a great yearning welled up inside her, stealing her breath, turning her voice into a painful whisper. "How can I leave now with Harrison waiting for me at the altar? He's done nothing to deserve that kind of humiliation and pain—nothing except love me and want me. How could I even think of doing something like that to him?"

Yet she was thinking of it, scanning the lane beyond the lychgate for a horse or an unattended carriage. If she left now--

"Jessie, guilt and a sense of obligation are no reasons for marrying a man."

"Aren't they?" She turned wide, pleading eyes on her friend. "I was willing to marry him to save the life of the man I loved. Shouldn't I be willing to do this, for Harrison?"

"You would marry him simply to keep from hurting him? Out of pity? Jessie—" Genevieve seized her hands and gripped them tightly. "You think Harrison would want that if he knew? What about your Irishman—what of the hurt you're doing him? And more importantly, what about yourself? I know you think you can marry Harrison and still hold onto the person you are, but it won't work. This marriage will make you both miserable."

Jessie jerked away, shuddering, her gaze going to the wind-whipped waters of the bay. She wondered, her heart thudding wildly, if he'd reached the cove yet. If she left now would she reach there in time? *Could* she leave?

"It's a terrible choice to have to make," Genevieve said into the heavy silence that lay between them.

A brisk knock startled them both. They whirled to face the opening door where the iron gray hair and broad, pleasant face of the vicar's wife appeared around the panel. "It's time," she said with a smile just as the church bells began to ring.

42

JESSIE WALKED DOWN the flagged pathway toward the open church door, her rosebud-strewn skirts clenched in her lace-gloved hands, a hollow, aching pain in her chest. She couldn't see the altar or the groom and vicar who awaited her in the candlelit depths of the church, but she could smell the musty air scented with beeswax and cold damp stone, hear the murmur of voices mingling with the sweet strains of the familiar music. The deafening peal of the church bells went on and on, ringing out over the somber gray bay and the stone, convict-built town now beginning to stir into a frenzy of activity and determined pursuit.

All her life, Jessie thought, she had been moving toward this moment, this marriage to Harrison and the future that had been planned for her since birth. Yet as she neared the door, her steps faltered, her chest heaving with her agitated breathing. The cool, storm-driven wind buffeted her with the scents of the sea and faraway places and the wondrous, secret promise of all unknown tomorrows. She stared at the shadowy interior of the church looming before her and knew suddenly and irrevocably that she was about to make a dreadful mistake, that this wasn't the future she was meant to have. The future she was meant to have lay elsewhere with another man. And she knew that even if she and Lucas both died today reaching for that future, it was still meant to be. She felt a weight of pain and guilt, deep within her, for it would hurt Harrison terribly, she knew, if she left him like this. But not to leave him would be worse. For both of them.

An incoherent cry escaped her lips as she whirled to Genevieve walking beside her. "I can't do this, Genevieve. I thought I could, but I can't and I shouldn't."

Genevieve caught Jessie by the shoulders, the older woman's eyes glowing with the warmth of affection and a glint of pain. "Then go, child. Sometimes . . . sometimes, running away is the right thing to do."

Jessie clutched Genevieve to her in a fierce hug. "Will you tell him —tell them all—that I'm sorry? Try to explain to Harrison—to Warrick and Philippa—why I had to do this?"

"I think Warrick and Philippa will understand," said Genevieve, drawing back to hold Jessie at arm's length. "Hopefully in time Harrison will too." Another name, unspoken, hung in the air between them. But they both knew that Beatrice would never understand and never forgive. Smiling through her tears, Genevieve kissed Jessie's cheek, then pushed her away. "Now *run*."

Hands fisting in her skirts, Jessie ran. She heard the vicar's wife stuttering, "But, but, but . . . What is she doing? She can't run away now!" and a man's sharp-voiced shout, but she didn't turn, didn't hesitate. Her slippered feet flew down the path to the lane, past the solemn rows of moss-covered headstones and out through the lych-gate, then veered to the left where the familiar figure of an old man stood holding the reins of two horses, one a big, fast chestnut, the other a blood red Irish hunter.

"*Tom*," she said with a gasp, taking the leather reins of Finnegan's Luck in her lace-gloved hand. "What are you doing here?"

"I thought you might be needing a fast horse," he said, tossing her up into the saddle in a flurry of petticoats and satin skirts. "Although if you don't mind my saying so, lass," he added, scrambling up onto his own mount, "you left it a wee bit late."

"But Tom—" She wrenched Finnegan's Luck around toward the top of the bluff and brought the rein ends down across the stallion's rump with a crack that sent it leaping forward. "They'll know you helped me—that you helped Lucas escape."

"Aye." He sent the chestnut plunging up the hill beside her. "Which is why I'm thinking maybe I'll do my dying in America."

Lucas checked his horse at the top of the bluff, his gaze raking the angry waters of the cove below. The wind was blowing harder now, snatching at his coat and knocking spume off the tops of the white-capped waves. He half expected to find the cove empty of anything except the wave-smashed, spray-darkened rocks, but the whaleboat was there, its bow pulled up on the sand, its stern rocking back and forth in the noisy rush of the surf. "Faith and glory," he said. "They're here." Throwing a fierce smile at Charlie and the Fox, he sent the gelding sliding down the hill to the beach.

One of the *Agnes Anne's* officers, a small, wiry Portuguese with dark hair and eyes and mahogany skin, was standing on the foam-swirled sand. He turned as they came up, the wind snatching at his words. "We were about to give up on you, mate."

"I'm glad you didn't," said Lucas, his boots sinking into the wet sand when he swung down from his horse.

"Personally," said the Fox, his breath coming hard and fast, his face white as he stared down at Lucas. "I think I'd rather you left me to hang."

Laughing softly, Lucas reached to take the other man's weight when he slid out of the saddle. "Did the ride open your wound again?"

"No." His legs wobbling, the Fox splashed through the surf to the wave-kicked boat. "But I think I wet myself when that demonic child you put up behind me decided to try to make our horrid beast fly down the hill."

"Horses don't fly," said Charlie, his voice rich with scorn, and scrambled over the gunwale into the whaleboat.

"I don't like the way those rocks are disappearing under the waves," said the Portuguese, shouting to be heard over the roar of the sea and the buffeting of the wind.

Lucas put his shoulder to the bow to help run the boat out into the oncoming line of thundering breakers. "I know this cove. You need to keep well to the right on your way out."

A wave broke against the wooden side of the hull, soaking Lucas up to his chest with a freezing cold spray. Clenching his teeth, he hauled himself over the rail into the pitching boat. The tide was against them, the tide and the wind, blowing out of the southeast. The prow of the boat lunged up with the swell of an incoming wave, then crashed down again with a bone-rattling smack as the six men on the benches set their oars.

Turning his back to the shrieking gale, Lucas scanned the scrub covered bluff above the cove, his breathing slowing as the heady rush of exultation brought on by their escape began to fade beneath the onslaught of a fierce, choking grief at the thought of what he was leaving behind. He had lost her, lost her forever, and for one aching moment, he almost—almost—regretted the leaving of this place, her home.

A movement at the top of the path drew his attention. Someone was coming. He watched, his heart beginning to thump wildly, as a familiar bloodred Irish hunter hurtled down the hillside toward them, trailed by a chestnut he also recognized. He could see the slim, straight figure of the woman who moved in easy synergy with the stallion, a woman wearing rosebuds in her flowing gilt hair and ice blue satin skirts that billowed behind her as her horse hit the sand and stretched out into a headlong run.

"*Wait*," Lucas cried, the boat rocking crazily as he lunged to his feet. He whipped around to the officer. "Put back in. Quick."

"What the hell are you doing?" shouted the Portuguese. "And what the hell is she doing?"

"She's coming with us," said Lucas and laughed out loud.

She didn't wait for the whaleboat to reach the beach but sent the hunter charging straight into the surf, the powerful, dark red legs sending fans of spray high into the air, the stallion's head flinging up as it felt the sand begin to give way beneath its hooves. Watching her, his heart jumping up into his throat, Lucas thought she meant to drive Finnegan's Luck into even deeper water. But she was already kicking her foot from the stirrup, the white satin of her wedding gown eddying around her as the horse shied back from the looming boat and she threw herself into the swirling foam.

"*Jesmond,*" he shouted, his voice a hoarse rasp of stark terror. The swell of a great wave lifted the boat up toward the roiling sky, and she was lost from his sight. "Jessie," he cried again, hanging over the side. Timbers creaking, they crested the wave and rode it down into the trough, and she was there in a froth of satin, her head up, her feet kicking out behind her. "Mother of God," he swore, reaching to snag her arms and drag her wet and gasping over the gunwales of the boat. "And is it drowning yourself you're after, Miss Corbett?" he demanded, his fingers digging into her arms as he dragged her up onto her knees to face him.

Her head fell back, clumps of wet golden hair framing her dripping face as her lips curled up into a smile that stole his heart all over again. "I can swim," she said, or started to say, when he hauled her hard up against his chest, his mouth crushing hers in a fierce kiss of joy.

Beside them something hit the water, kicking up a spout of spray. A boom reverberated around the cove.

"Bloody hell," yelped the Fox, looking up from helping Old Tom scramble into the boat. "They're shooting at us."

"Get down," Lucas shouted. Shoving Jessie behind him, he whirled to face the shore. The wind blew strong against his back, the waves breaking against the boat to throw up a cold white spray. The crashing roar of the surf drowned out the sound of horses' hooves as the new riders sent their mounts plunging down the slope to the beach. There were two of them. Constables from the prison, Lucas thought, from the looks of them. As he watched, one of the men checked, then wheeled his horse to send it scrambling back up the hill.

"What's he doing?" asked Charlie, his freckles standing out stark on a white, pinched face.

The whaleboat shuddered, the bow rising up on the crest of a great wave as the seamen struggled to pull away from the shore again. The Fox wrapped his hands around the rail and held on tight, his strange yellow eyes glowing with a fierce light as he stared at the shore. "Going to warn the *Repulse*, I'd say."

The other constable, the one with the gun, had reached the beach by now. Reining in hard, the horse fidgeting beneath him, he began slowly but methodically to reload.

Lucas felt the touch of a soft hand on his shoulder. "Do you think he could hit us at this range?" Jessie asked, staring at the man on the beach.

"If he's good, yes. We're not making a lot of headway against this wind." He wrapped his arm around her. She was shaking and cold, and he drew her close, putting his body between her and the man on the beach. "Try to keep behind me."

"Look," she said, her fingers tightening around his arm, but he had already seen them. Two more men, the tails of their dark dress coats streaming in the wind as they sent their horses flying down the slope in a murderous charge. One of them, a tall, slim young man, his hat gone, his angel-fair curls raked by the wind, reached the beach just as the constable was bringing his gun up to his shoulder to fire. With a furious shout audible even to those in the boat, the younger man whipped his horse into a frantic, headlong rush across the sand. The constable's head came up; he half turned, but he didn't lower his gun. Without reining in his horse, the younger man threw himself through the air, his lean young body slamming into the constable to knock him from the saddle and topple them both into the sand, the musket discharging harmlessly into the storm-darkened clouds roiling overhead.

"Who the hell is that?" demanded one of the oarsman, never missing a stroke.

"My brother," said Jessie. Her gaze shifted to the other rider. "And Harrison Tate."

JESSIE WATCHED as Harrison rode forward, not checking until the waves swirled into foam around his horse's nervously prancing legs. Back straight, head high, he stared at her across the choppy expanse of swelling, gray-green waves that separated them. He was too far away for her to see his features well, but she knew him, could read the pain and hurt in every line of his body. *I'm sorry,* she thought, a terrible ache in her heart. *Oh Harrison, my old friend, I am so sorry.*

But hurt was one of those emotions Harrison never allowed himself to express or even feel. As she watched, his body grew rigid, his hurt twisting, turning itself into the one emotion Harrison did allow himself: anger.

A deep and dangerous anger.

43

"ARE YOU MAD!" the constable screamed, his rough boots flailing in the spent wash of the waves as he struggled up onto his elbows.

"No, but you must be," said Warrick, reaching for the musket and shaking it in the other man's full, fleshy face. "You stupid bastard, my sister is in that boat. You could have hit her." He stood up, his head bent as he used his free hand to brush the wet, clinging grains of golden sand from his clothes. "Bloody hell, Jess; this was a new coat."

"Your coat!" screamed the constable. "Your coat? I think you busted my leg."

But Warrick wasn't paying him any attention. Slowly, he walked to the man who still sat, reins slack in his hands, his gaze fixed on the small whaleboat lurching up, beam to the wind, as it cut through the swelling waves.

"Who is he?" Harrison asked, not turning his head. "Who is that man, that *convict?*"

Warrick looked up at his friend, the familiar profile showing taut and fiercely cold against a wind-tossed, storm-darkened sky. "He's an Irishman. You've seen him. He was my groom."

His body still held rigid, Harrison swung his head to look down at

Warrick through granite hard eyes. "A groom. Are you telling me *my wife* has run away with an Irish convict groom?"

"I'm sorry, Harrison," Warrick began, although it struck him as a damnably inadequate thing to say to a man who'd just been left at the altar.

Harrison wasn't listening anyway. His hands tightening on the reins, he wrenched his horse's head toward the path that led to the top of the bluff and urged the storm-spooked gelding forward.

"Where are you going?" Warrick shouted after him.

For a moment he didn't think the other man would answer. Then Harrison checked, his horse sidling with its rider's impatience as he swung about. "To get Captain Boyd and the *Repulse*. That whaleboat's not going to get far in this sea. Even if they have a ship waiting off shore for them, there's a good chance we'll be able to catch them. And then I'm going to hang that bloody Irish bastard," he added before he wheeled again and kneed his mount into a furious gallop that sent sand flying up to be caught and blown away by the wind.

THE SEAMEN from the *Agnes Anne* were strong, practiced oarsmen who settled easily into a rhythm that sent the whaleboat striking through the heaving waves. Once clear of the dangerous rip tides and submerged rocks at the mouth of the cove, the boat's small triangular sails were run up and they swung toward the northeast, heading out to the open sea where the Yankee whaler lay at anchor waiting for them.

Jessie sat with her back against Lucas's chest, his arms holding her tight against the warmth of his body. Together they watched the jagged outline of the coast recede behind a gray-green expanse of choppy water. It hurt, looking at those familiar green hills and knowing she'd never see them again, knowing that her chances of ever seeing any of her loved ones again were slim. It hurt. But she could never regret what she'd just done.

She felt him stir behind her, his breath fluttering the wet strands of hair at her neck. "Why did you come?" he asked quietly.

She picked up one of his hands—his beloved, work hardened, scarred hand—and laced her fingers with his. "Don't you want me?"

His arms tightened around her. "Always," he whispered, his chest moving against her back as he let his breath out in a long sigh. "But as I remember it, you were getting married today. To someone else."

"After my mother found out about us," she said, her head falling back against his shoulder as she stared up at the looming, storm-darkened sky above, "she told me that if I didn't go through with the wedding to Harrison, she'd have you hanged for the murder of John Pike."

She felt him go utterly still behind her. "And you agreed to it? You were marrying him for *me*?"

She turned in the circle of his arms to stare up into his dark, narrowed eyes. "You think I should have let you hang?"

He brought up a shaky hand to brush the wind-whipped hair from her face. "I think marriage to Harrison Tate would have been a slow death for you."

"I would die for you," she said simply.

His hand tightened in her hair. "You might very well die with me."

"We're not going to die." She nodded toward the Yankee whaler riding at anchor before them, her sails struck, her decks tilting in the rough sea. "There's the *Agnes Anne*."

"Aye," he said in a strangely flat voice, and she realized that his gaze had fastened on something else, something behind them. "Only unless I miss my guess, that's the *Repulse*. And she's coming fast."

Jessie swung about, and her heart stopped.

Its great sails white against a boiling gray sky, the *Repulse* slid out from behind Last Chance Point, its prow rising up to shoulder the waves aside in twin cascades of spray.

"Bloody hell," swore a lanky, thin-faced man who looked amazingly like Beatrice's favorite gardener. One hand clutched to his side, he lurched to the stern, his strange yellow eyes squinting against the wind. "It's the bloody British navy."

"They wouldn't run us down, would they?" asked Charlie, his eyes wide, his teeth clenched tightly as if to stop them from chattering.

Old Tom let out a harsh snort. "Of course they would."

Jessie tore her gaze away from the oncoming frigate to look up at Lucas. "Would they?"

"They might." He gave her a wry smile. "Although probably not with you on board."

She threw a quick glance at the black-hulled bark, its deck swarming with shouting seamen, its tackle squealing as they prepared to haul up the whaleboat when it came alongside. Except that the small boat was still some distance away from the Yankee whaleship, while the frigate was gaining on them fast, tacking hard to starboard. Watching the ship's prow cut through the water, Jessie knew suddenly what Captain Boyd was doing.

"The *Repulse* doesn't need to run us down, does it?" she said, her voice barely audible above the noise of the wind and the spray and the booming canvas. "It only needs to come between us and the *Agnes Anne.*"

Lucas met her gaze squarely and nodded.

The Portuguese officer must have realized what the *Repulse* was doing, too. Hand on the tiller, he began barking orders to his men. They close-hauled on the starboard track, the boom swinging, the near rail slicing through the waves as the boat canted sharply, the snapping sails billowing white against an angry gray sky. They were still nearer to the *Agnes Anne* than the *Repulse* was to them, but the frigate was closing quickly.

Out here, in the open away from the shore, they were beginning to feel the fury of the coming storm. The small whaleboat lifted and plunged through heavy seas white with foam, the wind blowing in savage gusts that thundered the canvas overhead. The Portuguese officer was shouting again, the men leaping to trim the sails. Struck by a high wave, the whaleboat lurched and shuddered, losing momentum.

Jessie tightened her grip on the rail, the flying spray wet against her face as she stared at the frigate crowding all sail as it bore down upon them.

"If they don't turn now, they won't be able to," said Lucas, his arm coming around her shoulders to pull her in tight against him, his gaze fixed on the approaching ship.

Jessie swung her head to look at the waiting bark and understood what he meant. The expanse of heaving, foam-flecked waves between the boat and the whaleship had become too narrow to allow the frigate to slice safely between them. And still the frigate plunged down on them, jibs booming, its bowsprit and elaborate martingale thrusting forward like a mighty braced lance. She thought for one wild, terrifying moment that the frigate meant to ram them after all. She turned in Lucas's arms, and he held her so hard against him she didn't know if it was his heart she could feel beating or her own. The wind shrieked around them, deluging them with cold spray as a wave broke against the whaleboat's side. There was no sky, only the darkness of the frigate's great prow looming over them. Then the ship shuddered as if answering sluggishly to its helm and veered away to port.

"Heavens above," said Lucas, his arms warm and strong around her as she clung to him, the boat rocking crazily in the frigate's wake. "That was close."

"I THOUGHT for a minute there I was going to be fishing pieces of y' out o' the sea," said Captain Chase, his legs braced wide, his long yellow teeth biting down hard on his pipe.

They stood beside him on the rolling deck of the American bark. Someone had thrown a blanket over Jessie's shoulders and she clutched it to her, shivering, her legs feeling so weak and shaky she was grateful for Lucas's strong arm around her waist. She could smell the paint and freshly sawn wood of the newly repaired ship mingling with the familiar sharp tang of the sea and something else: the underlying, pyre-like stench that clung to all whalers.

All around her the ship reverberated with sound—the shouts of men, the slap of bare feet on the deck, the squeal of tackles as the whaleboat was fixed high and dripping and the anchor chain pulled in with a wet, weedy rattle. A whistle bleated; hemp uncoiled, and the mainsail rose up, the wind catching the canvas and bellying it out with a booming snap. The ship gave a great heave, and Jessie staggered, her gaze flying to Gallagher. He smiled back at her with his eyes.

Then his arm tightened hard about her. "*Christ,*" he said. Turning to stare at the frigate, she saw what he had seen.

The momentum of the chase had carried the British vessel well beyond the Yankee bark, for a ship under full sail at sea takes time to turn and even longer to stop. But the frigate could now be seen to roll almost lazily in the whirling eddy of its own wake, its pace slackening as the sails were reset. Then the wind spread the frigate's canvas and the mainsail adapted. Slowly at first, then more rapidly, the frigate swung to starboard, spray flying up from the curl of its bow wave as it cut through the water toward them.

"Oh my Lord," Jessie whispered. "They're coming after us."

The whistle blew again, and the bark's mizzen sail rattled as it ran up overhead. The bark heeled beneath their feet, the port flank lifting as the prow turned toward the wide oceans beyond. But the whaler was sluggish, its sails few, its hull weighted down with the booty of four years spent hunting the oceans of the world.

"Will they be able to catch us?" she asked.

"Aye," said the Captain, his pale eyes narrowed against the salt and spray thrown up by the wind. "If she's a mind to. Look at the sail on her. She's designed t' be able t' run down merchantmen—and a merchant ship carries a lot more sail than a whaler."

The bark was picking up speed now, its deck pitching and rolling as it ran northeast. They could smell the promise of rain as the gale swung to come at them out of the south, fiercer now, bellying out the canvas and shrieking through the rigging, the timbers of the ship squealing with the thud and crash of the mounting waves against the black hull. Staggering with the roll of the ship, Jessie went to wrap her hands around the rail and watch the cascade of angry water rushing past. The frigate was almost upon them now. She saw the blue ensign of the water police snapping in the wind and knew real fear.

Lucas was standing near the helm, talking to the Captain, but something he saw in her face brought him to her. He came up behind her, his arms warm as he drew her back into the lee of his strong man's body. Together they watched the frigate crowding sail to come abreast of them.

"They're going to catch us," she said, leaning her head back against his shoulder, one hand resting on his at her waist.

"Aye." He nuzzled her neck, his breath warm against her ear. "You don't need to worry. I don't think any real harm will come to you."

"It's not myself I'm worried about." She turned her head to look at him over her shoulder. His eyes were the color of the sea, a dark and stormy green. Love for him flooded her chest, filled her heart until it ached. "I don't regret it, you know. No matter what happens, I'll never regret running away with you."

For a moment, he squeezed his eyes shut, his mouth held tightly as if he were in pain. Then he buried his face in her hair, his voice rough as he said, "God, how I love you."

She tilted her head up to rest her cheek against his and smiled. "I know."

The frigate was some twenty yards away now, running parallel to and slightly ahead of the bark. As Jessie watched, a puff of smoke bloomed from the other vessel's flank, followed by a flash of fire and a boom that drifted to them over the water as the frigate fired a shot over the American bark's bow.

"Son of a bitch," swore Chase, lunging forward, shouting sharp orders to his crew.

The frigate was near enough that the men working its decks were clearly visible. Jessie half expected to see her brother or perhaps Harrison, but it was Captain Boyd, still in his dress uniform from the wedding, his sword buckled to his side, who came to the rail with a speaking trumpet.

"Ahoy there, bark," he shouted, his nasal voice high pitched, his accent clipped. "Heave to."

The American captain came to stand at the side, his own voice deep and powerful enough to carry the required distance without a horn despite the noise of the wind and the high-running sea. "That's the Stars and Stripes you just fired on, you bastards."

Captain Boyd drew back his shoulders and puffed out his chest. "You are in a British colony, and therefore amenable to British law."

"Like hell," yelled Chase. "We're outside the three mile limit. Or didn't you notice?"

Boyd half lowered the horn, his head turning as if he were listening to someone behind him. He nodded, and the horn came up again. "Members of your crew were observed picking up three of Her Majesty's prisoners from shore. That makes you liable to be pursued and stopped on the high seas."

"Not in my book."

There was another pause; then Boyd gripped his megaphone with both hands. "I must insist that you heave to."

The Yankee braced his outstretched arms against the rail and leaned into it. "This is an American ship. In case you don't remember, we fought a revolution against you imperious bastards and won. And then we whipped your asses again not that many years ago over just this sort of nonsense."

The captain of the *Repulse* went rigid. "Will you heave to?" he snapped through his trumpet.

Jesse watched in amazement as a wide grin spread across the Yankee captain's face. "I will not."

"Very well. You have five minutes to reconsider. Then if you do not heave to, we shall have no choice but to open fire."

44

"WHERE ARE YOU GOING?" Jessie demanded, catching Lucas's arm when he would have swung away.

He turned toward her, his face expressionless, his eyes flat and hard. "To find the Fox and Charlie, and tell them we're giving ourselves up."

"Like hell you will," growled the Yankee captain, taking a step forward and biting down hard on his pipe.

The wind ruffled Lucas's dark hair as he stood tense, the bones of his face standing out sharply beneath the taut skin as he stared at his friend. "I'll not have you putting your ship—and your lives—on the line for me."

Chase planted his hands on his hips, his wide spread legs easily absorbing the roll of the ship's deck. "Since I'm the captain here, I don't see how you have much to say about it. This is an American ship, and I'll be damned if I'll heave to for that strutting little cock. His lot might think the seas of the world are theirs to rule as they please, but I for one don't intend to encourage them in their arrogance—even if it means getting my ass shot out of the water." He paused to throw an apologetic glance at Jessie. "If you'll pardon my saying so, ma'am."

Gallagher's eyes glittered with a hard, cold light. "And Miss Corbett?"

"I don't think they'll fire at us with a lady on board, if that's what you mean."

"And if you're wrong?"

Jessie thrust herself between the two men, her hands coming up to grasp the lapels of Lucas's rough coat. "I will not have you turn yourself in because of me."

He caught her hands in his. "Jessie—"

"No." She looked up into his fierce, proud, beautiful face. "Do you think I could live with myself, knowing I'd been responsible for your recapture?"

She saw his jaw tighten, his chest lifting on a slow, even breath. His grip on her hands tightened, then let go. "When the five minutes are over, I'm giving myself up."

Chase turned to shout to his first mate. "Mr. Vieira? Take Mr. Gallagher here below decks. Clap him in arms if you must, but I want him kept there until further notice."

The mate came up to them, an impassive look on his swarthy face, his hand on the pistol shoved in his belt. "Aye, cap't."

Chase's thick, pale brows drew together as he threw Lucas a hard look. "Gallagher?"

The two men stared at each other for a long, tense moment. Then Lucas brought up one hand in the gesture of a fencer acknowledging a hit. "If I'm going to die, I'd rather do it with the wind in my face."

WARRICK STOOD WELL BACK from the frigate's port side in the shadow of the rigging. He held himself quite still despite the heaving of the deck beneath his feet, for he had always felt as at home on water as he did on land, and even the ending of his boyhood dreams hadn't changed that. The canvas overhead buckled and snapped in the wind, but he kept his gaze on the bark that dipped and rose with the violent swelling of the sea.

He could see his sister at the rail of the Yankee whaleship, although he didn't think she could see him. She still wore her satin gown, the skirts hanging limp and sodden, one sleeve torn. The rosebuds she'd woven in her hair for her wedding to Harrison Tate were gone.

He'd always thought they were close, he and Jess, and he felt slightly aggrieved that something so profoundly important had been going on in her life and she hadn't confided in him about it. But then, perhaps she'd known what she was doing, keeping her secret, because when he'd learned the truth, all he'd thought about was the effect her indiscretion might have on his future ability to secure assigned convicts to work his estate. He hadn't considered how important this convict might be to her, hadn't considered the effect of his actions on her, on her life. It occurred to him now that he might have more of his mother in him than he'd ever realized, and it was a thought he didn't like.

Beside him, Harrison gripped his pocket watch in one hand, the gold case gleaming in the dull light. Only he wasn't looking at the time. He too was staring at the Yankee ship, at the woman who was to have been his wife and the man who now held her.

"What the devil were you about," said Harrison, his jaw so tight he was practically spitting the words out. "What could you have been thinking to assign a man such as that to act as your sister's groom?"

Warrick crossed his arms at his chest and studied his lifelong friend dispassionately. "Such as what, precisely? Such as an excellent horseman? Or such as a well-educated man, whose only real crime was that he loved his country and fought against oppression?"

Harrison looked at Warrick as if he'd just shouted *Hurrah for the green.* "Have you run mad?"

"Why? Because I have a faint glimmering of understanding as to why the Irish hate us? Or because it didn't occur to me that Jess might perceive the man behind the rough convict clothes and fall in love with him?" He rocked back on his heels. "Well it didn't occur to me. But then do you honestly believe you know everything there is to know about your own sister?"

"Of course I do," said Harrison, his fist tightening around his watch. But Warrick saw the shadow of doubt in the other man's eyes and smiled. "Oh, no you don't, my friend. And neither do I. I've known Philippa my entire life, yet I never really knew her, never understood the complexity and beauty of the woman she is."

Harrison gave a harsh laugh. "What are you trying to tell me? That you've suddenly decided you're in love with her?"

"Yes," said Warrick, more serious than he'd ever been in his life. "Yes, I am."

Harrison leaned forward, his chin jutting out belligerently. "Well that's too bloody bad, my friend, because there'll be no marriage between your house and mine. Not after this."

Allowances must be made, Warrick reminded himself, for a man who has just been jilted at the altar. "If you think Philippa will let you prevent our marriage," Warrick said evenly, "then you know her even less than I thought you did."

Harrison closed his watch with a snap and thrust it into his pocket. "It's time," he said, starting forward but staggering with the roll of the ship so that he had to make an undignified grab for the rail. "Captain?"

From where he stood, Warrick could see the expression on Jess's face as she stared at Harrison and he knew he'd been right, that she hadn't realized they'd come aboard the *Repulse*. He watched her say something to the man beside her, watched him tighten his arm about her as if in comfort. And for one unexpected moment, Warrick found himself wishing that the frigate had never caught up with them, that this doomed pair of lovers had somehow managed to escape—even if it did mean he'd probably have to sail to America some day himself if he ever wanted to see his sister again.

"Ahoy, bark," shouted Captain Boyd through that absurd speaking tube of his. "Your five minutes are up. Will you heave to?"

The canon on the *Repulse's* port rail were manned and ready, the seamen's slow matches glowing in the gloom of the day. It was just a bluff, of course, but the whalers had no way of knowing that. The Yankee captain might have been willing to help Gallagher escape the island but he wouldn't risk losing his ship. It looked as if Harrison was going to get his chance to hang Lucas Gallagher, after all.

"I say," shouted Boyd into the wind-filled silence that had greeted his words. "Will you heave to?"

A wide, malevolent grin split the American captain's sun darkened face. "Go bugger yourself, you bloody popinjay. Fire on us if you will, but you try to board us, and I promise you, you'll lose more men than I will."

Hot color suffused the English captain's face. "You are refusing to heave to?"

"You got it, your lordship."

Boyd threw an uncertain glance at Harrison, who nodded and said, "You have no choice but to open fire, captain."

Warrick started forward with a jerk. "*Bloody hell.*"

Captain Boyd turned from the rail, the speaking trumpet still gripped in one hand at his side, his voice raised. "Aim at her sails and rigging, men. Ready—"

Warrick hit the captain between the shoulder blades with the flat of both hands hard enough to make him stagger. "What the devil do you think you're about here? This was supposed to be a bluff."

"I say—" began Boyd, swinging about.

"No, I say." Warrick thumped the little man's chest with one pointed finger. "My *sister* is on that ship."

Harrison caught Warrick by the arm and tried to pull him back. "She's there by choice, Corbett. If she—"

Warrick whipped around, his balled up fist smashing into Harrison's jaw to send him staggering back, his tailbone hitting the deck with a jarring thump that had the breath huffing out of him. "You shut up," hissed Warrick, standing over the fallen man with both fists raised.

"I say, I say, I say," bleated the captain. "I shall have you clapped in irons, sir. Charges will be pressed."

Warrick straightened and turned slowly, his fists still clenched, his breath coming hard and fast. "You fire on that whaler, and I promise you, by the time I'm through with your career, you won't be able to find a position as cabin boy in this navy."

Hot color suffused Boyd's cheeks. "You can't threaten me on my own ship."

Warrick gave the captain a wide, cold smile. "It's not a threat."

"That man is an escaped prisoner of Her Majesty the Queen," said Harrison, backhanding a trickle of blood from the corner of his mouth as he got awkwardly to his feet. "And the Americans harboring him are guilty of conspiracy."

"And Jess?" Warrick turned to stare at his old friend, an ache of sadness and loss building in his chest. After this, nothing in their lives would ever be the same again, he thought. But then, not much of their lives had been real before. He let out his pent-up breath in a long, wistful sigh. "And to think I always believed that you loved her."

Harrison gave a harsh, incredulous laugh. "Why do you think I'm here? Oh course I love her."

"No." Warrick shook his head. "Not really. If you did, you wouldn't be doing this." In one explosive movement, he seized the speaking trumpet from the English captain's slack grip and hurled it with a violence that split the shoulder seam of his coat and sent the instrument tumbling end over end through the air. "This isn't about love," said Warrick, watching the trumpet hit the water with a splash. "It's about possession. Control. Jess knew what she was about when she ran from you."

Shaking the hair from his face, he stared across the narrow expanse of choppy water to where his sister still stood at the rail, her eyes wide with a tumult of emotions, a sad smile of love and farewell on her lips as the bark began to pull away.

"Hey, Jess," he called, somehow managing to smile back at her. "You owe me a new coat."

∽

JESSIE STOOD at the ship's side and watched her brother until he was no more than a dark speck on the deck of the frigate receding into the distance. Then she turned in Lucas's arms and wept.

LUCAS WATCHED his wife as she stood at the prow of the ship, the wind feathering her beautiful golden hair away from her face, her gaze on the fiery path of light spilled across the swelling sea by the rising sun. She'd been his wife for almost two days now, and it was still a wonder to him.

They'd been married by Captain Chase in a hurried ceremony held even before the green shores of Tasmania had faded from their sight. But then the storm had hit, and for two nights and a day, the ship had reeled beneath the onslaught of a furious gale as rain slashed the decks and the sea transformed itself into great mountains and valleys of water that lifted the small ship up, up, only to send it swooping down again to a shuddering crash. It wasn't until the dawn of the second day that the skies cleared and the wind dropped, and the sea calmed to a lazy swell.

After so many hours of violence, the comparative quiet and gentle movement of the ship had awakened them. Hand in hand they had climbed the companionway to the storm-wrecked deck to stand here at the bow and watch the dawning of the new day.

"We survived," she said, her gaze still fixed on the sun breaking over the eastern horizon in a glory of gold and orange shading to red and pink. A gentle smile curved her lips. "There was a point there when I was beginning to think we might simply sink into a cross sea, never to be seen again."

"And are you regretting it, then, this rash step you've taken, Mrs. Lucas Gallagher?" he asked, slipping his arms around her waist and drawing her back against his chest.

She swung her head to look at him over her shoulder, her eyes wide and still. He traced the features of her face with his gaze, the curve of her cheek, the fullness of her lips, the strong line of her jaw.

Awe filled him at the thought that he was finally free and she was here beside him. Awe and fear.

A fear that he'd been unpardonably selfish, to let her come away with him, to let her give up so much for him, because he might never be able to provide her with the kind of life she'd been born to, because he might not be the man she could truly love forever with all her heart. He thought he had been that man once, but somewhere in all the horror and pain and endurance of the last years, he'd lost a part of himself, a part of who he used to be, and he wasn't sure he was ever going to find all of himself again.

Her hand came up to touch his cheek, and he saw that she was no longer smiling. "You were my destiny, Lucas. Whatever happens, I'll never regret running to what was meant to be. I told you that."

And he understood then that they'd both lost parts of themselves over the years, to life and to the struggle to survive. But they had control of the rest of their lives now, and they had each other and a brave, vital new country waiting for them across the sea. "I love you," he said, rubbing his open mouth against her hair. "I'll always love you."

A cat's paw of wind ruffled the sunlit surface of the sea and danced the studding sail above their heads. His arms still clasped tightly around the woman he loved, Lucas lifted his face to the breeze and drew the taste of joy and freedom deep into his being.

AUTHOR'S NOTE

LYING IN THE SOUTH PACIFIC OCEAN off the southern coast of the Australian continent, the island of Tasmania is, today, a peaceful land of picturesque stone villages nestled amidst gently rolling green countryside; of pristine waterfalls and enchanted temperate rainforests; of rugged, nearly impenetrable wilderness areas of awe-inspiring grandeur.

Yet behind this quiet beauty lies a dark and violent past. Tasmania witnessed both the most shudderingly brutal excesses of the British convict system and the complete genocide of the island's warlike Aboriginal inhabitants, who were hunted to extinction as thoroughly as the now-vanished Tasmanian tiger. The stone ruins of such infamous penal institutions as Port Arthur and Macquarie Harbor still seem to echo with the tormented screams of the thousands of men who suffered and died there. It is perhaps not surprising that Tasmania is said to be one of the most "ghost haunted" places in the world.

Originally named Van Diemen's Land, the island changed its name to Tasmania in the 1850s when it became a separate colony. But the island was popularly known as Tasmania for decades before its

official name change, so for the sake of familiarity I have used that
name here.

A startlingly rich collection of early nineteenth-century towns, home-
steads, and penal institutions are still preserved on the island and
make fascinating visiting for those interested in the past. I would
especially like to thank the friendly staff of Entelly House, Clarendon
House, Stanley House, and Richmond Gaol, for patiently answering a
multitude of questions. My heartfelt thanks as well to the owners of
the Fox Hunters Retreat, a convict-built coaching inn in the quaint
village of Campbell Town, who provided me with an unforgettable
experience. The tale of Finnegan's Luck owes much to an amusing
collection of reminiscences by Tom Roberts, who once handled trou-
blesome horses for the British cavalry. The tragic stories of the
fictional Grimes House and the children stranded aboard the
wrecked ketch were inspired by familiar Tasmanian ghost stories,
while Lucas Gallagher's escape from a fictional Blackhaven Bay
echoes similar feats accomplished by more than one Irish convict
with the aid of the American whalers who once plied the southern
oceans.

ABOUT THE AUTHOR

CANDICE PROCTOR is the author of more than two dozen novels, including the best-selling Sebastian St. Cyr historical mystery series and other historical fiction written under the name C. S. Harris.

A former academic with a PhD in history, Candice loves to travel and has spent much of her life abroad, living in Spain, Greece, England, France, Jordan, and Australia. She now makes her home in New Orleans, Louisiana, with her husband, retired Army officer Steven Harris.

https://www.facebook.com/CSHarrisAuthor
http://csharris.blogspot.com
www.csharris.net

Contemporary Romantic Suspense, writing as Candice Proctor:

Confessions of a Dead Romance Writer (coming in 2017)

Contemporary thrillers, writing as C. S. Graham:

The Archangel Project

The Solomon Effect

The Babylonian Codex

CPSIA information can be obtained
at www.ICGtesting.com
Printed in the USA
LVHW041138230723
753225LV00027B/249